The critics ado

The Very Daring Duchess

"A vibrant, passionate story."

—Jo Beverley

Starlight
A *Romantic Times* "Top Pick"

"The quick pace, touch of magic, and absolutely endearing characters bring readers that warm glow and wonderful feeling so special about a romance. Miranda Jarrett continues to reign as a queen of historical romance."

—*Romantic Times*

"Delightful.... The story line is fun and filled with non-stop action, as expected from a Miranda Jarrett novel."

—Harriet Klausner, *Klausner's Bookshelf*

"Beautiful and mysterious ... *Starlight* is bursting with excitement ... very romantic and fast-paced."

—*Rendezvous*

Star Bright
A *Romantic Times* "Top Pick"

"Another winner . . . an entertaining Georgian romance ... filled with twisting intrigue and loaded with engaging characters."

—Harriet Klausner, *Klausner's Bookshelf*

"As the companion to *Starlight, Star Bright* twinkles just as brightly with shining humor, poignancy, and magical charm that enchants. Ms. Jarrett's ability to always draw the reader into a fast-paced tale peopled with likable and realistic characters and a thrilling plot is a crowning achievement, and *Star Bright* delivers what readers expect from this romance luminary."

—*Romantic Times*

Sunrise

"Enchanting.... Loved this, Miranda!"

—*The Philadelphia Inquirer*

"Poignant, endearing, tender, and charming."

—Patricia Gaffney, *New York Times*
best-selling author of *The Saving Graces*

"Jarrett...draws her protagonists vividly and with charm."

—*Publishers Weekly*

Moonlight

"Five stars! ... Fast-paced and delightful!"

—Amazon.com

"What a touching, heartfelt story! ... Every detail will keep you wanting more. Beautifully written."

—*Rendezvous*

Wishing
A *Romantic Times* "Top Pick" and a "Pick of the Month" for January 1999 by Barnesandnoble.com

"Sheer pleasure...."

—*Rendezvous*

"Readers are sure to find themselves swept off their feet by this utterly enchanting and imaginative romance by the mistress of the seafaring love story. Delightfully charming and fun, yet poignant, exciting, and romantic, this is Miranda Jarrett at her finest!"

—*Romantic Times*

Cranberry Point
Named Amazon.com's #1 Best New Romance Paperback and a "Pick of the Month" by Barnesandnoble.com

"A vivid and exciting portrait of colonial America. A memorable tale of trust and love, of healing and passion, and most of all the magic of romance."

—*Romantic Times*

"[A] passionate love story rich in history and characterization. . . . This is an award-winning saga from a sensational author." —*Rendezvous*

"Everything Jarrett does is magic."

—*Affaire de Coeur*

"A delightful book, well-crafted and vividly written. I'm enchanted."

—Linda Lael Miller, *New York Times*
best-selling author of *My Lady Beloved*

The Captain's Bride

"Fabulous . . . loaded with action and high-seas adventure."
—*Affaire de Coeur*

"Deliciously entertaining . . . a swift, rollicking romance . . . with a richly textured understanding of the seafaring life."

—Mary Jo Putney, *New York Times*
best-selling author of *The China Bride*

Books by Miranda Jarrett

The Captain's Bride
Cranberry Point
Wishing
Moonlight
Sunrise
Starlight
Star Bright
The Very Daring Duchess
The Very Comely Countess

Published by Pocket Books

Miranda Jarrett

The Very Comely Countess

SONNET BOOKS
New York London Toronto Sydney Singapore

This book is a work of fiction. Names, characters, places and incidents are products of the author's imagination or are used fictiously. Any resemblance to actual events or locales or persons, living or dead, is entirely coincidental.

An *Original* Publication of POCKET BOOKS

A Sonnet Book published by
POCKET BOOKS, a division of Simon & Schuster, Inc.
1230 Avenue of the Americas, New York, NY 10020

ISBN: 0-7434-1793-3

First Sonnet Books printing October 2001

10 9 8 7 6 5 4 3 2 1

SONNET BOOKS and colophon are trademarks of
Simon & Schuster, Inc.

For information regarding special discounts for bulk purchases,
please contact Simon & Schuster Special Sales at 1-800-456-6798
or business@simonandschuster.com

Front cover illustration by Alan Ayers

Printed in the U.S.A.

For Ms. Nizz and all her friends, big and small:
Sidni & Gloria-Beyoncé Manks,
Regina Valentine Place,
Sharon Canasta,
Ciera Harper-Hills,
Lane, Mandy, Bella, & Marlon Lallen,
Doreen LiPinto,
Margie, Marrietta, Oceana, & Frank Worrié,
and, of course, the fabulous Harriet.

A good imagination is a most glorious thing!

1

London
May, 1799

The Duke of Harborough's carriage lurched to a rumbling start, or at least as much of a start as any vehicle could make for itself so close to Whitehall in the middle of the day. The iron-bound wheels scraped over the cobblestones and the springs sawed back and forth with a queasy rhythm as the driver tried to make his way through the carts and chaises and wagons, porters and sailors and apprentices and idlers that always crowded the streets near the Thames. The sun was too bright and the river too rank, and, with a groan, William, the present Earl of Bonnington, sank back against the leather squabs and pulled his hat lower over his eyes, trying to keep out every last ray of the infernal sunshine that was making his head ache even more.

"Will you tell me now what ails you, Will?" asked Edward, the seventh Duke of Harborough, Earl of Heythrop, Baron Tyne, and a gentleman who, unlike William, never shied from the midday sun. "Aside from your usual depravities, that is."

"I would not dream of keeping anything a secret from you, you insufferably cheerful bastard," said William, without raising his hat from his eyes. "What ails me is simple, and not in the least depraved. I am in great need of a new woman."

Edward chuckled, more amused than a true friend had any right to be. "Having finally wearied of Emily, you are in the market for her replacement?"

"I did not 'weary' of Emily," said William. Emily had been his last mistress, a luscious little dancer he'd set up in keeping for nearly two years, until her avarice had finally counterbalanced her uninhibited imagination and abilities, and with a parting gift of rubies, William sent her on to an older marquis. "One was wearied *by* Emily, but never *of* her. It is Jenny I must replace."

"Ah." Instantly Edward sobered. "Jenny."

"Yes, Jenny." William pushed his hat back from his face; there'd be no hiding in any discussion of Jenny Colton. "Have you any notion of how close she came to getting us both captured?"

Uneasily Edward nodded. Jenny had been his idea, and now she'd be his fault as well. "I'd some idea of the problems, aye. Your report made it clear enough that the arrangements had not gone, ah, exactly as planned."

" 'Exactly,' hell," said William with disgust. He hadn't wanted to mention this in the Admiralty Office, not knowing who might be listening even there, but here now in Edward's carriage he had no such qualms. "She decided she was far too *intelligent* to follow orders, and began plotting and playing games she'd no notion how to finish. Thanks to her, we weren't alone on that beach, and we left at least three French soldiers dead on the sand to prove it. If the fog hadn't been thick when we cleared the harbor, then the coasters would have swept us up for certain."

There wasn't much cheerfulness to be found in Edward's face now. "Where is Jenny at present?"

"Back in the theater at Brighton," said William, "where I fervently hope she remains for the rest of her mortal days, or at least for mine. I've no great desire to be shot dead on a foreign beach, or to explore French republicanism through the wonders of the guillotine on account of some third-rate actress."

He could make light of it now, but the *Fancy* had barely slipped beneath the French guns to the open sea. It had been close, damned close. No wonder his head ached just from remembering.

Edward frowned, restlessly tapping his fingers on his knee. When he'd given up active duty to assume his title, he'd also given up wearing his gold-laced captain's uniform except for dress, but the years he'd spent in the Navy still showed as much in the formal, straight-backed way he carried himself as it did in his sun-browned, weatherbeaten face. He didn't look like any of his fellow peers in the House of Lords, and his experience was beyond theirs, too, having served with honor at the Battle of the Nile with Admiral Lord Nelson.

"I am sorry, William," said his friend now. "I thought you'd find Jenny amusing. I thought she'd be to your, ah, taste."

William allowed himself a small, exasperated grumble. It was bad enough that the scandal sheets breathlessly painted him as a sinfully charming rake-hell, a carefree despoiler of maidens and defiler of wives. It simply wasn't true. Not entirely, anyway. He was very fond of women, and women in turn were very fond of him, and he'd never seen the wickedness in obliging their fondness, or letting them oblige his. But to have Edward believing these exaggerations and treating him as if he were no better than a stallion in perpetual rut—well, enough was enough.

"I am not insatiable, Edward," he said testily. "And I do not regard these runs across the Channel as pleasure jaunts filled with drinking and whoring. I know that is precisely what we wish the French to believe, but if I begin to believe it, too, then I'm as good as dead. Hell, if you chose Jenny only to warm my—"

"She came highly recommended," said Edward defensively. "For her reticence, that is. Not her other, ah, talents."

"Oh, no, of course not," said William with a certain resignation as he settled back against the cushions, arms folded over his chest. "Spoken like the old married man you are. You're so blessed content with your new little wife that you can't bear to think of us wicked old bachelors behaving decently at all."

"My contentment has nothing to do with this." Irritably Edward tugged at one white linen cuff. "You know damned well I'd never willingly put you at risk, not after you've already done so much for the Admiralty and the country as well."

"I know, Ned. But do recall that you're the great hero, not I." William sighed. No one who knew them both would ever make such a mistake, which was exactly why he had been so successful with his missions.

Who would believe anything so patriotic, so *selfless,* of the Earl of Bonnington? "I am simply tired and cross, and I want nothing more than a drink to settle my temper. But I do believe I shall choose the next hussy myself."

"I wouldn't wish it otherwise," said Edward, grumbling but still clearly relieved that William wasn't going to raise more of a row about Jenny than he had. Not that William would. He and Edward had known one another since they were boys running wild together through the Sussex countryside, nearly twenty-five years ago now. While their lives since then had taken very different turns, that bond would always be there between them, and was certainly not worth straining for the sake of a self-centered chit like Jenny Colton.

"And no more actresses, Ned," warned William. "They're too damned caught up in preening over their own beauty to be trusted. You cannot imagine the strain of being penned up in the *Fancy's* cabin with Jenny Colton for a fortnight of dirty weather."

Edward nodded. "But a woman won't be much use to you as a distraction if she's not beautiful."

"A different kind of beauty, then. More subtle. More like a true lady." William sighed again, rubbing the back of his neck. He'd shaved and washed and changed his clothes before he'd called upon Edward, but he still felt gritty and edgy from lack of sleep. "A lady who'll understand that there are perhaps times when she would do well to be quiet and listen."

Edward snorted. "The woman will be posing as your mistress, Will, not your wife. Though to hear you, perhaps that's what you're finally searching for, eh? A lovely demise to your overrated bachelor-hood?"

"Oh, hardly." William grimaced. Ever since Edward had fallen in love and married last year, he'd become the most earnest of matchmakers. It wasn't that William had any real argument against marrying—his own parents had been happy enough models for him—but he simply couldn't see any reason *for* it, either, not just yet. Eventually, when the time was right to sire an heir, he'd have to find himself some well-bred young lady to carry the family name, but not in the immediate future.

"All I wish for now is a replacement for Jenny," he declared, "a sweet-tempered little hussy with a strong enough stomach for the sea, one who will take orders like a soldier and be willing to risk her pretty neck for the sake of her king and country. I'll know the woman when I find her, Ned. Perhaps she'll even find me first."

Edward groaned, reaching for his hat from the seat behind him. "Oh, aye, most likely she will. They always do with you, don't they? But at least she'll have two months or so to chase you down."

"Two months?" repeated William with surprise. "I thought I'd head out again Monday, to finish—"

"Two months," said Edward firmly. "Maybe longer. After this last adventure, I think it best to let the French forget about you for a bit. Ah, here we are, home at last."

Harborough House had been built by Edward's grandfather, in a time when all the grandest houses were made to rival, and sometimes outdo, the royal palaces themselves. Though its location overlooking the long sweep of Green Park was no longer quite as fashionable as it had been in the old king's time, the house itself remained one of the most imposing in London. Outwardly it was also one of the most grim, built of gray stone made gloomier still by the city's constant rain of soot. A row of tall columns ran along the façade above a rusticated ground floor, and a pediment along the roof was meant to suggest a classical temple, complete with life-size statues of goddesses aloofly surveying whichever lowly mortals were arriving in the courtyard below.

But while the exterior of the house remained stark and severe, the inside had blossomed under the fresh touch of Edward's wife, a lady famous for her great artistic gifts. Remembering the warm, sunny houses of her native Naples, Her Grace had replaced the dark, heavy furniture with light woods and airy designs, ordered the walls painted shockingly new colors of rosy pink, golden yellow, and cerulean blue, and made sure that, whatever the season, the rooms were filled with flowers brought fresh from the country.

She'd transformed the house into a place that fashionable London loved to visit, and William was no exception. The hall was cool and inviting after the noisy, dusty streets, the mingled scents of the lilacs, snapdragons, and honeysuckle arranged in two tall marble urns a fragrant welcome. While Edward quickly sifted through the small pile of letters and cards presented by a footman, William's gaze rose to the painting hung in a place of honor and attention between the twin staircases.

It was, of course, painted by the duchess herself,

for she always placed her newest work there for her guests' amusement, admiration, and criticism. The paintings changed often, for Her Grace was prolific as well as talented, but in all his visits to Harborough House, William had never been struck so instantly, or so intensely, by a picture as he was by this one.

The subject was simple enough, a beautiful young woman painted as the pagan goddess Venus, seated on a bench with her hands resting loosely in her lap. Her round cheeks were deliciously rosy, almost flushed, and wisps of her auburn hair had escaped from the ribbon around her head to curl around her face and neck. Her gaze wasn't directed at the viewer, but at something beyond, the unguarded expression in her wide, gray-blue eyes so rapt and joyful that William nearly turned to look behind him.

"So you like my new picture, Bonnington?" asked the duchess, suddenly there at his side. At once William turned to bow and kiss the back of her offered hand, a hand still daubed with some most unducal paint smears. "It pleases you?"

If Edward was an unusual duke, then his wife was a thoroughly unusual duchess, not the least because she'd hurried to greet her husband here in the hall instead of waiting to receive him in her own rooms. She'd obviously come directly from her painting studio, too, for she wore a paint-stained striped half-gown over a full-sleeved white chemise, her dark hair tied back in a kerchief and gold hoops swinging from her ears, more like a gypsy than a peeress.

"This new picture does please me, Francesca," said William, his gaze already wandering back to the painting, "so much so that I'm neglecting you entirely."

"William is feeling churlish, my dear," said Edward, looping his arm fondly around his wife's waist as he bent to kiss her. "He even admits it. He is tired, and ill-tempered, and thirsty, and therefore cannot be responsible for his behavior."

But William was too engrossed in the picture to rise to Edward's challenge, too lost in the image of the rosy-cheeked young woman.

"She's the one, Edward," he said softly. "Mind how I told you before I'd know the next girl when I saw her. This is the one, in this painting. This is the girl."

"What girl?" asked Francesca, her dark eyes lighting with curiosity. "Whatever are you saying? Ah, my dear friend! You sound at last like a gentleman ready to fall in love and marry!"

"Perhaps I am, if I could only find this fair goddess of yours," said William, trying to make a jest from his inadvertent confession while Edward glared at him over Francesca's shoulder. The duke and duchess were closer than most married couples, but there was still a good deal about Edward's more dangerous activities in the Admiralty that he would rather his wife didn't know, and William's secret ventures across the Channel were among them. "A lady as lovely as this one, a perfect English Venus—how could I not fall in love outright?"

"Fah, what do you know of beauty?" Francesca wrinkled her nose with contempt. "When you look at this picture, you're seeing the girl as I painted her, not as you'd see her for yourself."

"You're saying I'm no judge of a pretty face?" asked William, bemused. Certainly all his worldly ex-

perience among the fair sex should account for
something. "That I've no eye for telling a sow's ear
from a silk purse?"

But the duchess was serious. "No, Bonnington, listen to me. Real beauty is more than a pretty face, and
deeper, too. Women see more in our sisters than men
ever will, and discover the beauty that comes from
grace, or intelligence, or cleverness, beauty that you
men so willfully overlook. You could come within
three paces of this girl as she really is, and not recognize her."

"I would know this lady anywhere," said William
confidently. She was so fresh and different from any
other woman of his acquaintance that perhaps she
truly *was* the girl—no, the goddess—he was meant to
marry, and for perhaps an entire two seconds, he
amused himself with the notion. He'd certainly do
worse than to find her divine little face smiling up at
him from the pillow each morning, at least for a
while. "How could I miss such beauty, such breeding,
such elegance?"

"And how perfectly you prove my point, Bonnington!" said Francesca with a merry laugh. "Granting
her all manner of gifts and talents, simply because I
dressed her as a goddess!"

"You can't claim all the credit, Francesca," insisted William. "Not for that face. To have her gaze at
me like that, all sweetness and devotion—what man
could want for more?"

" 'Devotion,' hah," said Francesca, shaking her
head and lifting her gaze toward the ceiling with dismay. "When I drew this girl, Bonnington, she wasn't
gazing at you. She was watching the antics of the

ducks on the pond in St. James Park. She didn't even realize I was sketching her. I never spoke to her, or learned her name, nor will I likely ever see her again. A great pity, that, for I'd love to draw her again."

"But surely the lady's sweetness, her gentility—"

"She was *not* a lady, Bonnington," said Francesca, the hoops in her ears swinging emphatically against her cheeks, "at least not how you mean it. She was an orange-seller in the park with her empty basket on the bench beside her, and her look of happiness likely came from having sold all her wares so early in the afternoon. *That* was what made her as beautiful as any goddess to me, and that was what I wished to capture: her satisfaction and her rare joy in the afternoon."

An orange-seller. William smiled wryly as his sentimental ideal disintegrated. The girl would never be his countess, then, nor anyone else's, either. All the beauty in the world wouldn't compensate for her parading through the park selling fruit and likely herself as well. A pity, a royal pity, and William sighed with genuine regret as he looked at the painting again.

Not that he was ready to forget her completely. She still might do as his companion on board the *Fancy*. An orange-seller wouldn't be shy, but she'd know her place, and wouldn't cause mischief by putting on airs above her station the way Jenny had. No one of any consequence would miss her if things went amiss and she disappeared, either, for London swallowed up common girls like this each day. She'd be malleable, agreeable, and obedient, and she'd still be beautiful, no matter how Francesca had tried to deny it. If he let the chit keep the clothes, she'd likely agree to whatever he wished. She'd do, then; she'd do.

And once he found her, perhaps he could steal a bit of that glowing, enchanting joy of hers for himself.

"Thank'ee, lad, thank'ee," said Harriet Treene, smiling as she handed the little boy his orange. He took the fruit solemnly, staring at it in his hand like a golden prize as he trotted back with it to his hovering nursemaid. The poor overbred little gentleman was so trussed up in white linen and leather slippers, his blond hair long and curled like a girl's, that it was a wonder to Harriet how the sorry mite could even manage to move that much. If he were *her* son, he'd be running barefoot and free like a regular boy, getting into dirt and mischief. But then if he were hers, he'd be selling oranges, too, instead of buying them from her, and with a wry shake of her head, she shifted the remaining fruit to the front of her basket, smoothed the checkered cloth around them, and turned down the next path.

"Sweet Indian oranges, oh, so sweet!" she called, her voice lilting up and down. Every girl had her own cry, as distinctive as a bird's call, and in the four years since Harriet had begun she'd never stopped perfecting hers. It had to be loud enough to be heard over a summer crowd, yet clear and never shrill, as sweet upon a buyer's ears as the orange would be upon his tongue, and as easy to call with a tired voice at sunset as it was early on a fresh new morning.

But Harriet's workdays rarely lasted so long. To her considerable pride, she nearly always sold every last one of her share of the oranges from Shelby's wagon before the Westminster bells chimed three. Not only would her penny-laden pocket swing against her leg with a comforting heft, but she'd earn a precious hour of time for herself in the park, an hour worth more to her than all the coins together.

She'd only eight more oranges left for today. On an afternoon this fair, she could sell them all to a single party, if luck were with her. Resolutely she lifted her head and smiled sweetly, eagerly, as if her shoulders didn't ache from her basket's straps and the sweat wasn't prickling her forehead beneath her wide straw hat or trickling down her back inside her shift. No, instead she must look as if selling these eight oranges were her greatest single pleasure in the world, and sound as if she meant it.

"Sweet Indian oranges, oh, so sweet! Buy me sweet Indian oranges, oh, *so* sweet!"

"Here, darling, here," called a man's voice behind her. "I'll try your sweet oranges."

"Ah, good day, sir, good day!" Harriet turned gracefully with the basket before her, on her toes the way she'd seen the fine ladies do so their skirts would twirl and flutter around their ankles. Gentlemen liked such niceties; she'd learned that here in the park, too. "Fine Indian oranges, sir, direct from the ship what brought them! How many shall you try, sir? How many shall you take?"

The gentleman was astride his horse, a tall bay with black-stockinged legs that seemed to echo the man's own dark polished boots and buff-colored pantaloons. With her view shaded by the broad straw brim of her hat, those well-muscled legs were all Harriet could see of the man, but they were enough to judge that he rode often and in more challenging places than this park.

He was wealthy, too. Only rich men could afford to wear clothes that were so perfectly tailored and so flawlessly spotless. Faith, even the *soles* of his boots were blacked and polished! Clearly it took as many servants to ready him for his day as it must take grooms to curry and comb his horse. A fine gentleman like this could afford the rest of her basket without thinking twice, and before Harriet lifted her gaze she lightly bit her lower lip to make it redder, then smiled.

And gasped.

He was, quite simply, the most beautiful gentleman she'd ever seen. She couldn't describe him any better than that. He had black hair cropped fashionably short, a straight nose and a firm jaw and chin with a disarming cleft, and beneath the black slash of his brows his blue eyes seemed to glint and dance with some wicked secret, just between the two of them. He was tall and lean, with broad shoulders, his clothes tailored to display his natural elegance without being foppish or overdone.

And when he returned her smile, she felt herself turn soft and melt inside like butter left in the sun.

"Here you are at last," he said, easily swinging himself down from the horse to stand before her. "I knew I'd find you, sweetheart, though it's taken me nigh on a week of searching through this infernal park."

Instantly Harriet's smile took on a wary edge. Was she such an addlepated ninny as that, to forget everything she'd learned here on these paths? She was eighteen, no green lass; she knew something of the world. She'd seen what became of girls who disappeared into the bushes with gentlemen, eager to lift their petticoats for an extra shilling or two. Men were men, no matter how fine they dressed or how blue their eyes, and always believing that because she sold oranges, the rest of her could be bought as well. "Searching for her," hah: did he truly judge her simple enough to believe such trumpery as that?

She plucked one of her oranges from the basket, not only holding it out for him to admire, but also to remind him exactly what was for sale, and what wasn't.

"Mine be the sweetest oranges in the park, sir," she said, tossing the orange lightly in her palm. "You'll find none better, sir, not for all the silver and gold in a great Pharisee's purse."

"Pharisees? Here?" he asked, cocking one bemused black brow as he gently stroked his horse's nose. "In St. James Park?"

"Aye, sir," she answered promptly, though no one else had ever questioned her about Pharisees and their habits before. "And I ask you, sir, where else would a Pharisee o' fashion go a-walking in London, eh?"

"You amaze me, lass," he said, leaning forward and lowering his voice as if to share a fresh confidence with her. "Here I'd thought they'd be carried about in a sedan chair like any other gray-bearded worthy!"

"Oh, no, sir, they be walking for their constitutions, and in this very park." She grinned; she couldn't help it. Who'd have guessed such a handsome gentleman could banter like this? "Where else would you have them Pharisees go, sir? Tripping through Covent Garden to pick through yesterday's turnips and greens?"

"To the Tower?" he asked, sweeping his arm through the air with a dramatic flourish. "To London Bridge? To White's to parse the rules of the faro table?"

She laughed, delighted both by the foolishness of the images and with the playful wittiness of his words. "Nay, sir, they must stay here in the park, to buy me sweet oranges!"

He chuckled in return, a warm, rich, conspiratorial sound. "Then I must be sure to look for these worthies, to pay my respects. Considering this park is home to a true goddess like you, why not Pharisees, and pharaohs, and even a sibyl or two?"

"No goddess, sir," said Harriet. "Only an honest lass what wishes to make an honest bit o' coin."

"Ah, but you *are* a goddess, and I've the proof." He reached into the front of his dark blue frock coat, and drew out a folded sheet of cream-colored paper. Carefully he unfolded it, and held it up for her to see. "There you are, proof enough. Can you deny now that you're Venus herself?"

Once again Harriet gasped, but this time not with admiration. The page was covered with red-chalk drawings of *her,* sitting beside the duck pond. The likenesses were unmistakable, her face and form as expertly captured as the portrait-prints of the queen and king pinned over the bar in every taproom and tavern in the country.

But that was exactly what unsettled Harriet, and

angered her, too. Her face was, well, *hers*, one of the few things that truly belonged to her alone, and to see it set down there for every passerby to study and criticize—the too-round cheeks and the wide-set eyes and the nose with the little bump on the bridge like a sheep's, even the way her hair was curling into untidy wisps around her forehead, every line drawn while she'd been completely unaware—how could she not feel as if something had been stolen from her?

"Here now, sir, how did you come by those?" she demanded, her cheeks flushed. "I never gave no artist leave to do such a thing, and it—it be wrong, it do, like stealing!"

"Hardly," said the gentleman, surpised by her reaction. "Consider it an honor, my dear, and a flattering one at that. What woman wouldn't want her beauty captured so splendidly?"

"*I* wouldn't," declared Harriet, dropping the orange back into the basket and reaching for the sheet of drawings. "Those be mine, sir, mine! That thieving, conniving artist robbed me of me face, sir, sure as if he'd clipped me pocket, and I've a mind to call the watchman on him, if you don't give them pictures to me."

But the man held the sheet up in the air, out of her reach. "Ah, ah, sweetheart, pray contain your fervor! These pictures aren't mine to give away, nor would the artist who drew them be pleased to hear you call her thieving and conniving."

Harriet scowled, lowering her hand. "A woman drew them pictures?"

"A lady, you ungrateful creature," he said lightly,

somehow making that sound like an endearment instead of an insult. "Her Grace, the Duchess of Harborough. And despite how you're threatening her, she would gladly draw you again if you'd but present yourself at Harborough House. Likely she'd even pay you for your time, more than you'd make in a day here with your oranges."

"She would not!" scoffed Harriet with a disdainful sniff. "A duchess drawing pictures, paying to make pictures of *me*—that's stuff and nonsense, sir, nonsense and stuff!"

"Perhaps it is," he agreed, his smile curving wryly to one side, "and perhaps, sweetheart, it isn't at all. You've spirit and beauty enough for ten goddesses, but even the most clever deity must learn to discern true opportunity from empty promises."

"But you've made me no offers, nor promises, neither!"

He shrugged with disarming carelessness. "So I haven't, have I? You *are* clever, lass. I'd have to say I've judged you right."

She sniffed again, keeping her chin high. "Then mayhap *you* be the Pharisee, trying to judge me this way or t'other."

This time he laughed outright, his eyes crinkling with pleasure. Slowly he lowered his arm, refolded the sheet with the drawings, and tucked it into her basket behind the oranges.

"There," he said. "The pictures are yours, to do with what you will, even burn them, if that's what pleases you most."

Swiftly Harriet covered the folded paper with her hand, half expecting him to change his mind and try to take it back. Surely pictures like these must be worth a pretty sum, even to a rich man like him. But instead of taking the paper, he reached for her hand, bowing forward slightly as he raised her fingers to his lips, his *lips,* oh, dear God in Heaven, and now he was kissing the back of her hand the way she'd seen gentlemen do with fine ladies, his mouth brushing lightly over her skin, grazing it, teasing it, warming it, making her flush and stammer like a worthless, befuddled idiot.

And he felt it, too. She could tell from the way he looked at her when he freed her hand, the odd half-smile that could—should—have been smug but, curiously, wasn't. Instead he seemed almost thoughtful, as if considering her in an entirely new way.

"If you ever change your mind, sweetheart," he said softly, "bring that paper to Harborough House, and you'll be welcomed like the goddess you are, with nectar and ambrosia. Now good day to you, my Venus, and sweet dreams for your night."

Still she stood there like a dumbstruck ninny, watching while he lifted his hat to her—to *her!*—before he climbed back upon his horse and gathered its reins to head down the path and forever, forever from her life.

And at once Harriet came back to life.

"Wait, sir, wait!" she called breathlessly, hurrying after him. "Your orange, sir! You forgot your orange!"

He turned in the saddle, and she held the orange up to him.

"Ah, so I did," he said, winking as he leaned down to take the orange from her. "I'd leave behind my head, too, if my hat weren't there to keep it in place upon my neck. I've forgotten my orange, and to pay you as well."

"You *are* a clever gentleman, aren't you?" she said, tipping her head to one side to wink back as she echoed his own words back to him. Oh, what she was doing was a dangerous game, bold as new-polished brass. She'd never behaved like this with any other man she'd met in the park, and if her brother-in-law ever learned of it, he'd thrash her royally for being so forward and wanton.

But this gentleman wasn't like any of the others, and he certainly wasn't like any man she'd met among the costardmongers and butchers who lived in her street. He was young and rich and wickedly handsome, but what made him different was less tangible, something that hovered in the air between them like a conjurer's trick, something she couldn't find the words to explain. Most likely she would never see him again, for London was a grand, sprawling place, and his station in it was far, far above hers. But for this moment she could fancy, she could dream. That much in life came for free, even for girls from Threadneedle Court.

"You owe me nothing, sir," she said now, squinting a bit as she looked up at him and the sun behind him. The shadow of his hat's brim shielded his eyes from her, his expression unfathomable, and she gave a nervous little laugh at her own daring. "You gave me the pictures, sir, and now I'm giving you the orange. For remembering me by."

"But I won't forget you, lass," he said, his voice low and so unexpectedly earnest that she almost could believe him. "Indeed, I doubt I ever shall."

"Oh, nay, sir, of course you won't," she said. "Leastwise you won't until after you eat the orange."

Harriet turned away quickly then, so he would not see the regret in her face, and turned back to her life as it was, as it must be, and the ripe, golden fruit in the basket before her.

Sweet, oh, so sweet . . .

Abbeville, Finisterre

Republic of France

Alone at the last table at the Coq d'or, Jean-Luc Robitaille ignored his wine and plotted revenge.

The inn was nearly empty at this time of the night, and Robitaille was grateful for the quiet. Translating the English newspapers took all his concentration, laboriously sifting through the narrow gray columns word by word. With a groan, he rubbed his thumbs into his eyes, and willed them to make sense of the tiny letters in the wavering candlelight. His eyes were growing as old as the rest of him, and faster, too, in the service of the country, long hours each night toiling against the enemies of the Republic. With the port at Brest squeezed shut by the British blockade, Abbeville's smaller harbor had grown in importance, and Robitaille's influence as overseer of the port's safety had flourished with it.

But there, at last, when he felt sure his sight would fail him, he discovered the one name he sought, the one he hated most in this life and would into the next. Now the confusing English words seemed to fly beneath his eyes as he read, devouring everything he could find and learn of this man, his weaknesses and his strengths and his habits. But most of all Robitaille hunted for the one special key to his fate, the one person that the Englishman loved and treasured most in the world.

In spite of his pain and bitterness, Robitaille smiled. His chance would come soon, and he wouldn't fail to seize it for his own. His network of contacts spread clear across the Channel to England, but this, this, he would save for himself. Almost lovingly his gnarled fingers lingered over the page, tracing the printed name of the Englishman who must be made to suffer.

The English Lord Bonnington who had murdered his son.

2

"*O*h, Bett, you should see the shawls them ladies are carrying now on their arms against the chill!" said Harriet to her sister as she plunged her arms deep into the soapy wash-bucket. "Every color you can think printed bold, and some as big as a coverlet, but so fine and dainty-made they say they'll slide through a gold ring, easy as that."

Bett nodded eagerly, drying each dripping pewter plate as Harriet handed it to her. "Lud, Harriet, who'd think wool would spin so fine?"

"But I heard 'tis not true wool from sheep," said Harriet, lowering her voice in confidential triumph. "I heard 'tis combed from the bellies of goats."

"Goats! Go *on!*" exclaimed Bett, scandalized. "Them great ladies wearing goat-hair!"

Harriet nodded, confident in her knowledge, for she'd heard it direct from a Bond Street milliner this very afternoon in the park. Although Bett was five years older, she seldom left Threadneedle Court, for her husband, Tom, didn't like her straying too far from their pie-shop downstairs. Besides, with Tom's old mam to look after, plus the little one underfoot and a second already swelling the front of Bett's worn apron, Bett didn't have much time for herself, let alone for considering what the grand ladies were wearing to walk in St. James Park. Though Bett swore that her life was what she'd always wanted, it made Harriet sad to see how worn and weary her sister had become, and more determined, too, that she'd do better for herself.

"But they be proper rare goats, Bett," explained Harriet solemnly. "Goats that belong to the King o' India himself. Goats that do nothing but lie about on new, green straw so's their hair grows special soft and long. Kaz-me-yeers, that's what them goats is called, and so's the shawls."

"Kaz-me-yeers," repeated Bett, with a sniff of contempt. "More French wickedness, Harriet, that's what *that* be, and them goats, too, and if'n I ever—"

"If you ever what, Bett?" demanded Tom as he thumped up the stairs and into the room, puffing furiously at the white clay pipe he held clenched in his teeth. Because of the heat, he worked with his shirtsleeves rolled high, and the dark hair on his arms was dusted with the flour from the pastry for tomorrow's pies, just as his apron was blotched with layers of greasy spots and bloody stains from the pork fat and rabbit meat he'd bake inside. "What rubbish are you swearin' to do now?"

"I'm not swearing anything, Tom," said Bett anxiously, wiping her wet hands on her apron. "Harriet and me are tidying up after supper, that's all."

"She's fillin' your head with wrongful thoughts,

that's what she's doing," said Tom as he glared at Harriet. "She's givin' you notions above your station."

"I am not!" said Harriet indignantly, her head high and her hands on her hips, ignoring the soap suds she'd scattered on her skirts. This was not a new argument between her and Tom, and not one she shied from, either. "There be no sin in speaking of the fine world outside of this house, Tom Fidd!"

"Oh, aye, no sin beyond making you two unhappy with the lot God gave you," answered Tom, his voice rising with righteousness. "Lustin' after fancy shawls that come from heathen goats—"

"Hey-ho, and *you* listening on the stairs for our tittle-tattle!" said Harriet with gleeful triumph. "What right do you have t'go spying on poor Bett and me like that, Tom?"

"Don't, Harriet, don't," pleaded Bett, wringing her hands as she hovered between them. "Tom don't mean it!"

But Tom was too intent on Harriet to hear anything else. "It's my right as master o' this house to know what's said an' done under my roof," he thundered, his face flushed an angry red. "It's my right to know what my wife an' her shrew o' a sister are contrivin' behind my back!"

From the cradle across the room came a shrill, sleepy wail of protest.

"There now, Tom, you've woken the babe!" cried Bett, hurrying to gather the fretful child into her arms before she ran from the room, leaving Tom to fume at Harriet.

"Do you be happy now?" he demanded. "Upsettin' both my wife an' little Nan with your yammerin'?"

Unhappily Harriet looked after her sister. She hadn't intended to make things worse for Bett—she'd never wish that—but it wasn't in her nature to back down to Tom's bullying, either. "Bett was my sister before she was your wife, and still is!"

"D'you think you'd have a place in this house if you weren't?" said Tom, jabbing the air with the stem of his pipe for emphasis. "D'you think you'd have a place anywheres without me?"

"Oh, aye, and where else would you find another willing to rise before dawn to toil for naught?" Even Tom would have to admit this was true. Harriet worked as hard for him as she had for her own father, when he'd been alive to run the same shop. Each morning when the stars were still out and the moon yet to set, Harriet would be standing at the old oak table below, chopping the cockscombs and rabbit livers extra fine for the Shropshire pies before she'd leave for the park.

"Don't I give you half me orange-money?" she continued. "Don't I help Bett with the washing and tidying and looking after your daughter and mother?"

"I've give it all up in a blink if I could be rid o' you an' your clackin' tongue, Harriet Treene," said Tom, thrusting the pipe back into his mouth and puffing furiously. "Why aren't you wed an' looking after brats o' your own, instead of bedevilin' me and Bett? Somewheres in London there must be some poor deaf sot willin' to take you to wife, sharp-tongued bitch though you be."

"Maybe I want more than some poor sot," said

Harriet fiercely. "Maybe I want better for myself than the sorry men in this street!"

Tom snorted, and pitched his voice high and reedy as he made her a purposefully ludicrous bow. "Oh, aye, if you please, m'lady Harriet, what needs have her fine gentleman an' her goat-hair shawl!"

She wouldn't answer, not that, and instead grabbed the bucket of washing-water and fled down the stairs, sending the soapy water sloshing angrily over her shoes with each step. By the time she reached the street, her stockings were soaked as well, but she was still too furious to notice or care, and with both hands on the handle of the bucket she dumped it into the street. The dirty water swirled and eddied across the paving stones, iridescent bubbles glistening among the filth from dozens of slop-buckets and chamberpots.

Why was it so wrong to want more? No one she knew understood what she wanted from her life; sometimes she wasn't sure that she did herself. It wasn't just the goat-hair shawls or the other finery that she craved, either. What she longed for was far, far more complicated than that.

She wanted her basket of oranges to be but a beginning, not an end. When she tucked away her earnings beneath the loose floorboard that only she had discovered, she did it against the day when she could be the one with the wagon of oranges and apples, selling them to other girls.

From the wagon, she'd progress to an elegant little shop like a coffeehouse, but for ladies only, tucked in among the mantua-makers and milliners. She'd serve the ladies tea and dainty sweets and pastries to restore them between their visits to the other shops, and offer them a place where they could meet their friends, just as the gentlemen did in taverns and clubs. She'd even picked a name—The Orange Tree—to remind her of where she'd begun, and she could already see the signboard in her mind, a tree with a curly-tailed monkey perched among the fruit.

But even that dream wasn't enough, not without someone to share it. She refused to trade Tom Fidd for another bully, simply for the sake of being a wife instead of a spinster, and she wouldn't marry an apprentice, the way Bett had, just to keep her father's shop in the family. She longed for a lover who'd actually *love* her instead of trapping her up against the wall in an alley to grope about under her petticoats. She wished for a man who would listen to what she said instead of expecting to be obeyed, a husband who would be her friend and companion instead of her tyrant, a partner who'd make her laugh and work beside her. That was how she'd remembered her parents being together, their love and happiness filling the warm pie-shop when she'd been a tiny girl.

That was what she wanted, and what she never seemed fated to have, and hot tears of longing and frustration stung her eyes as she stared down at the puddles of dishwater at her feet.

And thought, yet again, of the gentleman she'd met in the park yesterday.

He'd flirted shamelessly with her, tossing bright, clever words to her to catch as if they'd been flowers, and he'd grinned when she'd tossed them back to him. He'd called her as beautiful as a goddess to make her smile, and he'd called her clever, which had pleased her infinitely more. He'd sworn he'd never forget her, which, while being patently untrue, was a compliment she'd let herself savor anyway, just for the sake of dreaming in her narrow little bedstead at night.

And the drawings: he'd given those to her, too. She gave a reassuring pat to her pocket where she'd put the folded sheet, even though she knew it could have gone nowhere else. Beneath the layers of her skirts, they'd be safe from both dirty washwater and Tom's prying eyes, her own secret companion wherever she went.

It wasn't because the drawings were of her that made them so precious, but because *he* had given them to her, along with that quick offer of such dizzying hope as to seem untrustworthy even while asleep. To present herself to the Duchess of Harborough, to venture inside a house as grand as a palace, to sit while Her Grace drew more pictures of her, *her,* Harriet Treene—faith, was there ever such a fairy-dream as that?

She touched her pocket again, feeling the stiff, folded paper tucked inside. No dream, then, nor wishful imaginings. The gentleman and all he'd said had been real enough one day ago, and he'd had no reason to invent the duchess nor her offer, not with the pictures as proof.

One day away from selling oranges, same as if it were a rainy day, that would be all, and she needn't tell anyone else where she'd gone or what she'd done. The gentleman had assured her the duchess would pay her well for her time: another handful of coins to squirrel away, another step closer to making her dreams real and being done forever with Tom Fidd and skinned rabbits and emptied chamberpots on the cobbles of Threadneedle Court.

She looked down at those same wet cobblestones now, and gave a quick, determined nod. She was no low quivering coward, was she? She was always saying she wanted more from her life. Well, then, here was all the *more* she could want, waiting for her to claim as her own, pretty as you please, if only she'd be brave enough to seize it.

She would. She *would*. And when she smiled up at the patch of dark sky framed by the rooftops overhead, it did seem as if tonight the moon shined a little more brightly just for her.

"So His Grace tells me you've much experience in such matters, miss," said William, trying to be agreeable to the determinably unpleasant woman standing before him. He always did try to be agreeable to women—his mother had insisted upon it when he was a boy, and he remained naturally inclined to do so, anyway—but this one was making it deuced difficult. "You enjoy this kind of work, Miss—ah?"

Blast, he'd forgotten her name already, and though he coughed to cover his mistake, she knew, and let him know she knew, too, with a pitying smile.

"Miss Jonson, My Lord," she supplied, all withering resignation. "Miss Lucretia Jonson, as is spelled out plain on my letter of introduction."

"Ah, yes," he said uncomfortably, glancing over to the letter that was already in the hands of his manservant, Strode. He'd given the letter only the most cursory glance, instantly realizing that Miss Jonson would not suit him any better than the four other woman who'd preceded her through his parlor this morning.

Blast Edward for sending them to him here at his own house, forcing him to interview each one as if he were hunting for a new housekeeper. No, an "assistant," for that was the peculiar way that Edward had explained the position to the applicants. As if William bloody well needed *assisting,* like some ancient in his dotage. Hadn't he made it clear enough that this time he'd find Jenny Colton's replacement himself?

He cleared his throat, barely keeping the grumble of impatience to himself. "Miss Jonson. Yes. Quite."

Quite, indeed. Edward couldn't have picked a more extreme opposite from gaudy Jenny. This Miss Jonson was round in a lumpy, uncompromising fashion that hinted darkly at far too much hidden corsetry, her tight-lipped mouth sour and disapproving, perhaps from that surfeit of whalebone and lacing beneath her high-necked gown, and the only words he could think to call the color of her hair— snuff? dun? drab?—were more suited to describing prickly, coarse wool for shooting-breeches than a lady's crowning glory. No one would believe for a moment that such a creature was his mistress, and especially not the French.

But that girl from the park, the orange-seller, Francesca's Venus—she'd be perfection itself. It wasn't only that she was the loveliest young creature he'd met in months, but that she was bright and quick-witted as well, in a way that would wear most admirably in the *Fancy*'s close quarters. Oh, an empty-headed woman was well enough in a crowded ballroom or bedchamber, especially if that empty head was beautiful, but for solitary companionship and longer amusement he'd always take a clever woman, hands down.

Of course, the girl *spoke* those clever words like the braying costardmonger she was. Her clothes and hair were appalling, her political loyalties unknown, and he doubted she ever did more by way of bathing than to splash at her face and hands from a washbowl. Yet still she'd taken firm possession of William's imagination, haunting him, teasing him, and generally driving away every other thought of every other woman.

Including the dreadful example standing before him in the middle of his parlor. How Edward's heart must have leapt in his medal-spangled bosom at all her unimpeachable references and talents! But then Edward wouldn't be the one drifting about in the Channel with a whalebone virago named Lucretia, exactly like that bloodthirsty old Borgia hussy. "You seem, ah, most accomplished, Miss Jonson."

"Thank you, My Lord," she said with a nod of smug acknowledgment. "I do not believe the duke would have sent me here if I were less than qualified for the position of your assistant."

Qualified for many things, yes, but as for posing as his mistress—not until they'd begun cutting blocks of ice from the depths of hell, and likely not even then. William nodded and frowned solemnly, hoping he looked as if he were weighing all of Miss Jonson's merits in the most considered and reasoned way.

What he was actually considering, however, was if Francesca had heard from his orange-selling Venus.

He'd been so sure she'd appear at Harborough House after he'd given her the pictures, but three days had come and gone, and still she hadn't, at least not that Francesca had told him. Perhaps he should call on the duchess himself, just to inquire. After all, the girl might have shown herself today. She might be there now, sitting on the bench in Francesca's studio with the sunlight turning her glorious hair to strawberry-gold and her lips to—

"His Grace said you would not sail again until the end of next month, My Lord," said Miss Jonson, her voice jarring him back to his own parlor. "But I can be ready to travel with a day's notice, My Lord."

"Then you are a far more accomplished traveler than I, Miss Jonson." William rose, his expression purposefully impassive. "I regret to disappoint you, Miss, but I do believe that His Grace was a bit, ah, premature to arrange our meeting. I have no immediate plans for returning to France, and in fact, His Grace himself was the one that suggested I linger here a bit longer in London."

Miss Jonson's brows arched indignantly. "You would dawdle here in London, My Lord?"

"Linger," he corrected. "Not dawdle, Miss Jonson. Linger."

"Only another expression, My Lord, for shirking your duty!" She turned to snatch the letter of introduction from the startled Strode's hands. "When our country is at war, My Lord, certain sacrifices must be made!"

"But I do make sacrifices, Miss Jonson," he protested mildly, thinking of how close he and the *Fancy* had come to being captured not a fortnight before. "Rather great sacrifices at that."

Pointedly Miss Jonson glanced around his parlor, from the overstuffed chairs to the silver tray with his morning chocolate and biscuits to the clipped wool carpet on the floor beneath their feet. "I can well imagine your sacrifices, My Lord."

William's smile now held a healthy measure of relief, a distinction he doubted Miss Jonson noticed. "I have dashed your hopes for any great show of heroism from me, then?"

"Irrevocably, My Lord," she said as she stalked to the door, brushing aside Strode's hurried attempt to open the door for her. "Good *day.*"

"And good day to you, Miss Jonson," said William with a bow, though she'd already gone. The best he could say was that now his day would improve.

"Miss Jonson has gone, My Lord," announced Strode, stating the obvious by way of proclaiming his own return. A short, stocky man with a faceful of freckles, Strode had been with him since William's sixteenth birthday, and in return for listening to William's thoughts, fears, and general observations for so many years, he now felt entitled to certain small freedoms. "There are no others waiting."

"And a damned good thing, too," said William as he plucked the last triangle of toast from the rack and slathered it with marmalade. "In another minute, Strode, I vow that last one would have called me out as a coward."

"Yes, My Lord," said Strode, deftly intercepting a golden blob of marmalade before it dripped onto the carpet. "But perhaps, My Lord, His Grace was merely taking you at your word when he proposed these other candidates. You didn't care for Miss

Colton because she wanted to seduce you, and now you don't like this Miss Jonson because she doesn't. To be sure, My Lord, you must be a proper confusion to the duke."

"I am not a confusion, Strode," said William as he briskly dusted the toast crumbs from his fingers. "I merely wish to choose my companions for myself. Now please send to the stable to have Caesar saddled and brought around."

"For the park, My Lord?" asked Strode, more of a statement, really, for William often rode early in the day, to clear away the musty cobwebs of the previous night's drink.

But this morning William had more than mere brandy-induced cobwebs occupying his thoughts. "Not the park, no. I mean to go to Harborough House."

He reached into his pocket for the orange that the girl had given him, idly turning the bright round fruit in his fingers. She'd said it was to remember her by, and it certainly was doing its job.

"You can't keep doing that, My Lord," scolded Strode crossly. "Stuffing old fruit into the pockets of your coats like you were some street-organ monkey! You'll ruin that blue superfine, My Lord, stretching the wool out like that, and then it will be my lot to try to steam them back to shape."

William grinned. "Then you believe I should eat the orange, and be done with it?"

"What I believe, My Lord, is that you should forget the chit that gave you that wicked fruit," insisted Strode, his jaw thrust stubbornly toward William. "Wanting to trust a common girl like that with your life—it's not proper, My Lord, nor right."

"And I believe it may be both," said William, slipping the orange back into his pocket, "though the devil help me if I'm wrong, eh, Strode?"

It was easy enough to find Harborough House. Harriet had often seen it across the park, so large and decorated with so many windows and carvings that it scarcely seemed right to call it a mere house instead of a palace.

It had loomed larger still as she'd come closer, gray and forbidding and not at all welcoming to a girl from Threadneedle Court, and Harriet's courage nearly failed her as she started up the white marble steps to the door. There was dust and muck from the street on her shoes after her long walk, and she couldn't help peeking back over her shoulder to see if she'd left footprints on all that snowy marble.

But then, hadn't she come here at the invitation of the Duchess of Harborough her own self? Didn't she have the pictures folded safe in her pocket now, ready to show anyone who'd question her right to be here, now, thumping the brass knocker, polished so bright she could see her own distorted reflection peering back at her?

Not that she'd long to study it. She'd barely rapped the knocker when the door behind it opened, just widely enough for the long face of a footman to stare balefully out at her.

"Shove off, hussy," he ordered, pointedly looking from her shoes to the tip of her hat. "You've no place on His Grace's front steps. Go 'round to the back if you've business with the housekeeper."

"My business 'tis not with the housekeeper, but

with Her Grace the duchess!" exclaimed Harriet indignantly. She'd left home early so that neither Bett nor Tom would see that she was wearing her best striped petticoat with the yellow jacket to match, new thread stockings and a fresh yellow ribbon on her wide-brimmed straw hat. She might only be an orange-seller, but she did know how to dress herself for calling on a great lady. She knew she looked fine, and stylish, too, and no nasty-faced footman should be pretending otherwise.

"I've been invited here particular, Master High-and-Mighty," she said, "so's you go and tell Her Grace I've come, and now I'm here."

The footman snorted, and began to close the door, but not before Harriet shoved her way into the opening, wedging her body halfway inside. She was strong for a woman, and she wasn't afraid to let this rascally footman know it, either.

"I told you I was here to see Her Grace," she said, purposefully raising her voice to make a row, "and I'm not about to shove off until's I do. Get on now, be quick an' fetch her!"

"Impudent baggage," growled the footman, trying to push her back through the doorway. "I'll not take orders from the likes of—"

"*Santo cièlo,* Peters!" called a lilting female voice from inside the house. "Whatever are you doing tussling with that woman in the doorway?"

The footman muttered a final, single syllable for Harriet's benefit before he turned toward his mistress's voice. "Forgive me, Your Grace, but this low hussy is just leaving."

"I am not!" Deftly Harriet wriggled past him and

into the hall, straightening her hat where he'd knocked it askew. She guessed the woman standing halfway down the curving stairway must be the duchess, though she certainly didn't look like any of Harriet's notions of how a proper English duchess should look.

To begin with, she wasn't much older than Harriet herself, and with her black hair and dark eyes, she was foreign-looking, not English at all. She didn't dress like an English lady, either, leastwise not the ones Harriet saw in the park: this duchess wore no jewels nor plumes nor Kashmir shawls, but a rough linen smock covered with streaks and blotches of paint tied over her gown, a gaudy scarf wrapped around her head, the fringes trailing over her shoulder, and gold hoops in her ears like some thieving Gypsy-woman.

Aye, a Gypsy, not a duchess, and peculiar enough to make Harriet wonder if the handsome gentleman in the park had played some wicked trick upon her.

"This do be Harborough House?" she asked, raising her chin with cautious determination. "And you be the duchess herself?"

The woman nodded vigorously, her gold hoops swinging against her cheeks as she rushed down the steps to Harriet.

"And you, *you*, are my Venus, come at last!" she exclaimed as she seized both of Harriet's hands in her own. "Oh, how glad I am to see you, and how delighted Bonnington shall be, too!"

Belatedly Harriet curtseyed, or at least attempted to while the duchess still held tight to her hands. But then if Her Grace were an artist, like the gentleman had told her in the park, then Harriet supposed she would behave as differently as she dressed. And, of course, being a peeress, she was entitled to do whatever she pleased, anyway.

"Peters, Peters, however did you not recognize this dear, dear lady?" continued the duchess as she tugged Harriet back up to her feet. "However could you be so blind?"

Peters's face was stony as he bowed. "I am sorry, Your Grace."

The duchess sighed with exasperation. "You still do not see it, do you, Peters? Look at her—*look!* She's the girl in the new painting, the girl I thought sure was lost to me forever!"

Harriet looked to where the duchess was pointing, and felt her face grow hot. There between the twin staircases hung a painting—a painting of *her* that had clearly been done from the drawings the gentleman had given her.

"Oh, Lud, look'ee," she whispered, forgetting the duchess as she took a step forward to stare at the picture. Who would have thought her own face could look so fine, grand as the queen herself in a heavy gilded frame?

"That's twice now this picture's left a viewer speechless," said the duchess, chuckling. "Either a most rare mark of my genius, or a very low one, I cannot decide which."

Harriet flushed again, for she couldn't recall the last time someone had faulted her for being silent. "It be a handsome fine picture, Your Grace, and I don't be saying so just because it's me own face in it."

"Thank you," said the duchess, her smile genuinely pleased, and not the least bit haughty. "And I must thank you, too, for the pleasure I had in painting it. That's your doing, you know. There's a special quality to your face and person—*bellissima*—that makes it a joy to draw, Miss—Miss—"

"Treene, Your Grace," supplied Harriet promptly, ducking another quick curtsey. "Harriet Treene, of Threadneedle Court."

"And how delighted I am to make your acquaintance, Miss Harriet Treene," said the duchess cheerfully. "While you made a splendid Venus, it's much better to be able to call you by your Christian name."

"Aye, Your Grace. But it's about that Venus-part that I come calling this morning." Her heart thumping, Harriet drew the folded sheet of drawings from her pocket. The gentleman had assured her that the duchess would be willing to pay her well for the privilege of drawing her again, but now that it came to asking her outright, Harriet felt as bold as that polished brass knocker on the door, and she fully expected that smug cove of a footman to toss her down the steps for speaking so forward. "The gentleman what found me in the park said you'd be wanting to draw me again, like this."

"You mean Bonnington?" The duchess's smile faded as she took the sheet of pictures. "He told you that?"

"Aye, Your Grace." She'd said the wrong thing, she could tell that from the unhappy look on the duchess's face, but still she plunged onward. "Mr. Bonnington, he told me—"

"He's a lord, not a commoner," interrupted the duchess with another sigh. "He's the Earl of Bonnington, and the very devil with women, you know. He'd no right telling you any of his sweet tales."

"He didn't tell me any I'd not heard before, Your Grace." But a pox on that handsome gentleman for not telling her he was a lord his own self! "Being in the park, I've likely heard them all by now."

"Oh, I'm sure Bonnington could surprise you with a few new ones." The duchess smiled ruefully. "And if you've any sense of self-preservation, you'll not listen to a single honeyed word of his."

"No, Your Grace," answered Harriet promptly, as if she hadn't already listened, and lapped up those sweet words as greedily as any bee. "Not one."

"I should hope not." The duchess gave her shoulders a small shrug of resignation. "But Bonnington is a charming rogue, isn't he? They say he has the gifts to seduce any women he pleases, and make them thank him afterward, too. I do know that when he winks one of those bright blue eyes of his toward me, *me*, a most contented wife, I can well believe it."

"Aye, Your Grace," answered Harriet softly. A rakish earl must never have a place in her heart, or her dreams, either. But didn't she feel like the greatest fool in London now, wasting her fancies on such a man, letting herself believe that his smile had been specially meant for her! "I'll be taking me leave, then, Your Grace, and not be troubling you no more."

"What, because of him?" The duchess looked up with surprise. "I still do wish to draw you, Miss Treene. That was no tale, not even from Bonnington. If you can spare me the time, I should like to have you sit for me in my studio, so I might draw and paint you to my heart's content. And you may be sure that I shall pay you for your time: yes, yes, I shall insist. Does a guinea for the afternoon sound agreeable?"

Harriet gulped. A guinea was more than she could earn in a week of sunny days selling oranges, but there was still more to be settled than mere price alone.

"That be agreeable, aye, Your Grace," she said, trying to sound as if people offered her such enormous sums every day. "But there's something I must say first. I've seen them prints of fancy pictures in taverns, and I've seen what them ladies wear, which be exactly nothing. Posing for you be all well and good, but I'll not be pulling off my shift, not for a guinea, nay, not for a hundred! I'm an honest woman, Your Grace, and I mean to stay honest, and I'll not take anyone's coin to be otherwise."

The duchess nodded, her expression turning unexpectedly thoughtful. "An honest woman in London: *che miràcolo!*"

"I don't want to be an orange-seller for always, Your Grace," said Harriet firmly. "I want to be bettering myself, and not by lifting me petticoats, neither. I mean to do it fair, using my wits and talents."

"Ah, an honest woman with good sense!" marveled the duchess. "Surely we must be the only two such in this entire fool's paradise of a city, aren't we, Miss Treene?"

"Harriet, Your Grace," said Harriet impulsively. "Miss Treene sounds like something I'm not. Harriet suits me better."

"Harriet it shall be, then, if you prefer." The duchess smiled warmly, smoothing her palms along the front of her paint-stained apron. "But no matter.

I promise that you shall always keep your shift, and your honesty with it."

Harriet nodded, too, her own smile coming more slowly. This duchess might not be what she'd expected, not with her strange clothes and the foreign words that peppered her speech, yet still Harriet trusted her, and liked her, too. Despite having married a duke, this lady must be as much at odds with her world as Harriet was with her own. The only two honest women in London: ha, how that would make Bett laugh when she heard it, her sister Harriet paired with the Duchess of Harborough!

"There now, we've settled that," said the duchess briskly, frowning a bit as she glanced behind Harriet to gauge the sunbeams that streamed through the tall windows framing the door. "Not a moment too soon, either, if we are to make use of this daylight. Come, this way, back to my studio, and we shall begin."

"Good day, Peters," said William. "Pray tell Her Grace I've come to divert and amuse her."

"Her Grace is not at home at present, My Lord," said Peters solemnly.

William frowned. "She's always here at this time of day, Peters. Unless by not at home you mean she's simply not receiving?"

"She is in her studio, My Lord," said Peters. "She requested that she not be disturbed for any reason."

"Ah, but you see, Peters, I am not a mere *reason,*" said William confidently, sidestepping the footman to begin up the stairs to Francesca's studio. "She'll see me, I'm sure of it. No need to dog my heels, Peters, I know the way to her rookery."

But still Peters hurried after him. "Her Grace's orders were most specific, My Lord. She has engaged a new model for posing, and—"

Instantly William wheeled to face the servant on the step, hope soaring. "A new model? The girl from the park that she painted as Venus, the one with the hair like sunshine and a mouth like crushed strawberries?"

"It is the same coarse, common-bred girl as is in the painting, My Lord," said Peters with pained resignation, "though I would not venture an opinion regarding the crushed strawberries."

"Then you must trust me, Peters," said William, now bounding up the stairs two at a time. "I wouldn't forget a mouth like that on any woman."

The duchess's studio was to the back of the house, up under the roof in an attic that had formerly been used for storage and servants' quarters. Only the closest of the Harboroughs' friends were invited to see how Francesca had transformed the space into a sanctuary for herself and her art. Extra dormers had been cut into the slanting roof to flood the room with light, and to offer for inspiration one of the finest views of London's most fashionable rooftops as well as Westminster's square towers. In addition to Francesca's easel, paints, portfolios, and other artists' necessities, the room was crowded with all manner of antiques and curios, for the duchess was a terrible magpie, much to the despair of her orderly nautical husband.

Much of the clutter had come with her from Naples—exotic shells and cameos and mosaics, marble busts and architectural fragments, a length of crimson velvet and scraps of Venetian lace, a Roman bench with striped cushions and a gilt chair with sphinx heads for arms—and while some of it was reputed to be of great value and antiquity, a great deal more was simply interesting rubbish.

To William, who always appreciated good theater, the studio had seemed less a workplace than a stage for displaying both Francesca and her talents, a constant, vivid demonstration of her most un-English gift for high drama. How straitlaced Edward had come to wed such a rare bird remained a mystery. Even William found that each time he climbed the back stairs to Francesca's studio, he had the unsettling sense of being an actor stumbling into the middle of a play where he'd forgotten his lines.

But not this morning. As soon as he reached the studio's doorway and saw his orange-girl standing very still with a wreath of flowers in her hair, posing there in the square of sunshine while Francesca drew her, he found he knew exactly what to say.

"You're here, lass," he said softly, reaching into his pocket to pull out the orange and hold it out before him. "You came, and I remembered, just as you wished me to."

She gasped as soon as she heard his voice, forgetting her pose to turn toward him. Swiftly her gaze flicked from his face to the orange in his hand and back once again to his face, her blue eyes wide with wonder.

Then the surprise faded, and the wonder with it, and that luscious mouth turned firm and resolute and not at all welcoming: strawberries now devoid of any sweetness whatsoever, and perilously close to tart.

"You followed me," she said. "That don't be right."

"Yes, I did, and yes it is," he answered, taking a step closer. "Right, that is. You see, sweetheart, I've something to ask of you, an invitation, if you will, for I've—"

"Nay, stop," she ordered. "Not one word more."

"But if you'd only hear what—"

"Nay, I shall not," she said again, firm and final. "Whatever it be from you, I'll have none of it."

3

"*Perdizione,* Bonnington," said Francesca crossly as she tossed her charcoal stick aside. "Why are you here? Didn't Peters tell you I was not at home?"

"I'm sorry, Francesca," he said, a blanket apology that he hoped his friend's wife would accept. He *had* behaved badly, interrupting her like this and without a decent greeting, either, but he'd been so intent on seeing the orange-girl again that he'd forgotten everything else. "Pray forgive me, if you can."

"Oh, hush," she said with a sigh as she sat back in her chair, a sigh that also proved she wasn't half as cross as she pretended. "Contrition does not become you. I should have known you'd appear here soon, anyway. You may not be contrite, Bonnington, but you are exceptionally predictable."

"True enough." William understood that this predictability was not entirely meant as a compliment, but he was willing to overlook it for the sake of peacemaking. "You knew I'd come, and I did. Especially when you have chosen this fair lady as your model."

He glanced back at the girl and smiled, a smile that she determinedly did not return.

Which, of course, Francesca noticed. "You will leave *her* alone," she ordered urgently, lowering her voice for William's ears only. "She is showing wonderful good sense in keeping away from you, and I can only hope that you will respect her wishes."

William frowned. At least he now knew that Edward hadn't confided his true intentions toward the girl. "Ah, Francesca, I'd never guessed you'd so foul an opinion of me as that!"

"It is not an opinion," she answered, briskly brushing the black charcoal dust from her fingers, "but a conclusion, drawn from considerable evidence. Edward has told me so many tales of your conquests that I know there must be twice as many that he hasn't, and I have noted how often your name appears in the scandal sheets, linked with this woman or that. But most of all I've the proof of my own eyes and ears. You, my dear friend, are the very devil with women, and I won't let you ruin this poor girl beneath my own roof."

Damnation, this was what came of being agreeable to ladies. "That's hardly fair, Francesca."

"Isn't it?" she countered. "I know perfectly well how charming you can be, Bonnington—it's the reason I adore having you about as Edward's friend, particularly at my table—but you have already meddled with this girl quite enough."

"That's not what I meant," he said, his dark brows drawing into a deeper frown. "I don't care a fig for whether you're being fair to me or not. I meant *her*. Just because she sells oranges in the park doesn't mean she's a half-wit out of Bedlam that needs you protecting her. She's not at all stupid or dull. Far from it, in fact."

"He be right, M'Lady," said the girl herself, pulling the flowers from her hair as she joined them. "I can look after my own self, same as always. If his lordship here behaves bad with me, I can set him to rights sharp enough that he won't do it again."

"You'd box my ears for me, wouldn't you?" asked William with unabashed delight. "The moment I behaved the least bit dishonorably toward you, you'd let me know, wouldn't you?"

" 'Course I would," said the girl with a fierce gleam in her gray-blue eyes, her hands curled in fists at her waist and the wreath of flowers looped incongruously around her wrist. "Go on and try me."

"I'd rather not, thank you," said William. "But if Her Grace here will permit it, I would like ten minutes of your time to chat. Ten minutes alone with her, Francesca, if you please."

The girl cocked her head to one side. "Hey-ho, *ten* minutes? I'll wager I'll be done me listening in five, see if I'm not."

"You can see already how little your precious ten minutes will accomplish, Bonnington." Unappeased, Francesca twisted her mouth to one side, twirling the fringes of her scarf in her fingers against her shoulder. "Better for us all that I should have Peters show you to the street."

"Please," he said, his voice automatically sliding into the lowest, most confidential register, the tiger's purr that women liked so much. "Please, Francesca. Peters can do with me what he will, and Edward, too, if I bring any harm or shame to this young woman in the ten minutes we are alone together."

"Not even you could seduce her in that time." Francesca tossed up her hands and rose with an indignant *shush* of her skirts. "*Bène!* Ten minutes, Bonnington, no more. She is the most perfect model I have discovered since I left Naples, and I will *not* let you ruin her for your own entertainment."

She swept from the room and didn't look back, the red heels of her slippers clicking on the stairs. Tossing the orange lightly in his palm, William smiled as he watched her go; he truly was very fond of Francesca, and happy, too, that she and Edward had found one another.

"You didn't tell me you were an earl," said the girl behind him, more of an accusation than a statement. "Not once, you didn't. You let me think you was an ord'nary gentleman."

Slowly he turned, the orange still in his hand. "You didn't tell me your name, either, which makes you every bit as guilty as I."

She blushed, which amused him, considering how neither of them was particularly guilty of any blush-worthy sin.

Not yet, anyway. He still had his ten minutes.

"Perhaps we should begin again, sweetheart," he continued with a slight bow, "and introduce ourselves more properly. I am William Manderville, Earl of Bonnington. Your servant, ma'am."

"You don't be anyone's servant, not you," she scoffed, then remembered herself enough to drop him a curtsey. She moved with natural, confident grace, the lush curves of her body clear through the rough linen of her clothes. She hadn't given up wearing stays, the way all the fashionable ladies had done, but he liked how the tight lacing held her waist in small and pushed her breasts upward beneath the modest kerchief tucked into the front of her bodice. "I be Harriet Treene—Miss Harriet Treene—and I sell oranges and I make pies."

"Pies?" he asked, mildly mystified.

"For the pie-shop," she explained proudly, "the best Shropshire pies you ever tasted, made after me father's own receipt. 'Course, it be Tom Fidd's shop now, on account of him marrying my sister Bett after Da died, but Tom couldn't make them pies proper without me, no matter what he claims."

She leaned closer, more confidential. "Soak the rabbit pieces in buttermilk before you chop them fine," she said. "That's the secret, and what makes the meat special tender."

"So that's it, is it?" How had they traveled so quickly from charming blushes to butchered rabbit? He had never much cared for savory pies, suspecting that shrewd piemen could chop and hide all manner of unsavory leavings and scraps beneath their crusts. He'd much rather think of her in connection with sweet oranges, but at least it proved she wouldn't turn squeamish if a mission went wrong, and she was confronted with the sort of butchery that men contrived for one another.

"Aye," she said with solemn satisfaction. "That's the secret. Though I don't mean to always be baking pies or selling oranges. I mean to raise myself higher than that. One day I'll have a shop of me own that sells tea and chocolate and sweets, a neat, tidy little shop for ladies only. I'll do it, no mistake. You'll see, and everyone else will, too."

He found her confidence oddly touching. When was the last time anyone had told him their dreams, or the last time any of his friends had even admitted to having any? He'd never seen a woman look so determined, enough that he didn't doubt that she would someday get her tea-shop, and make it prosper as well.

But by telling him her dreams, she'd also unwittingly handed him the golden key to persuading her to join him.

"You will have to sell a great many oranges to begin a fine place like that," he said, holding the one in his hand up for emphasis. "The lease on a shop in a fashionable neighborhood would be very dear indeed, and then there would be the furnishings and linens and such, even before you brew your first pot of tea."

Her chin rose, more resolute. "I'm saving me coins, M'Lord. I may not have me shop tomorrow, but I *will* have it, even if it takes me years and years."

"What if I said you could have it, oh, by the end of this year? Would you be willing to listen to my proposition if that were the prize?"

The resolute chin remained, but that guilty blush returned, too. "I won't be your whore, M'Lord. Not even for me shop."

The speed of her denial made him smile. In his experience, the more vehement the first refusal, the sooner the lady would ultimately give in. Not, of course, that that would matter in this case.

"I'm not asking you to be become my mistress,

Miss Treene," he said lightly. "Only to pretend that you are."

"Hah, nonsense and stuff." She scowled, and wrinkled her nose. "What kind of rubbishy talk is that?"

"It's not rubbishy in the least," he said. "It's the God's own truth. There are certain, ah, services that I perform for His Majesty, certain activities that take me to France and that I trust will help end this infernal war a bit sooner. I need a young woman to travel with me who can appear to be my mistress, and if you agree, I will reward you every bit as handsomely as if you'd actually been in my keeping."

"Go *on*," she said scornfully, her disbelief obvious. "Why would the king ask a great gentleman like you to do his spying upon the French?"

William smiled. "For precisely that reason, sweetheart. No one expects it of me. And I would not call what I do 'spying.' More properly being a messenger."

"But you just told me," she argued. "That means it don't be a secret no more."

Damnation, but she was quick. "Oh, it's still a secret, but simply a secret between us, rather like your father's regarding the pies." He plucked one of Francesca's drawings from her easel, purposefully studying it instead of the girl herself. "Besides, if you should choose to betray me to the French, or even to that sister of yours, I could always have you locked away in the Tower for treason."

"You would not," she said, but there was enough uncertainty in her voice to prove she did in fact believe him. "No one would care if you did, anyways."

She tried to laugh, but failed so wretchedly that he wondered if anyone *would* care—not even that sister of hers. It was exactly as William had predicted, exactly as he'd wished. Yet there was something so miserably hollow and forlorn about her laugh that he could take no satisfaction from her loneliness, even if it served his needs.

"Someone would care, lass," he said, instantly wishing the words unspoken. Someone would care, yes, but it must never be him. He couldn't, or risk losing everything.

But all she did was shake her head, sniffing back tears that she resolutely did not let fall. "Besides, Her Grace said you was a famous rake and a charmer, and that you could have any lady you wished. Of all them, why would you ask *me,* even for pretending?"

"Because you are the most beautiful young woman I have met in ages," he said honestly, holding up the drawing as if it were all the evidence either of them needed. "Because you are clever, strong, and brave, and because I doubt very much you'd let any Frenchman beguile you, no matter how beautiful he says you are."

"Nay, he would not," she said firmly. "But I warrant that is why the king asked you to do this."

He couldn't resist teasing her. "Because I won't let any Frenchmen beguile me?"

"Nay," she said, not laughing the way he'd expected. "Because you're strong and brave and clever. I wouldn't trust you with me life if you weren't, not for all the shops in the world."

His grin faded. She'd certainly gotten to the heart of his proposal fast enough, hadn't she? He had wanted a woman he could trust before he went to France again; how could he object if she wanted the same?

"I suppose those are the same reasons I'm willing to trust you, too," he said softly. "I'm not so eager to meet Monsieur Guillotine that I wish to rely upon some scatterbrained female."

She nodded earnestly. "I don't be scatterbrained, M'Lord. I don't dither, not a bit, and I don't fear easy, neither, 'specially not if you pay me toward me shop. You can trust me, no mistake. But answer me this, if'n you please: why are you risking your life for such?"

"Why, lass?" Oh, he hadn't expected her to ask that. His reasons were complicated, so tangled that he'd never really sorted them out for himself, let alone to tell another.

Perhaps he'd begun just because Lord Spencer had asked him, or because he'd wanted to prove to himself that he wasn't nearly as selfish and shallow as the rest of the world indulgently judged him to be. Perhaps he'd needed to test himself, to choose the harder path, to show he could be as daring and ruthless as Edward, even if he'd never be the famous hero that his friend had become. Perhaps he'd wanted to do the right thing for his king and his country, for once to be noble instead of simply being a nobleman.

And, moodily, he'd no intention of telling her any of it.

"I was bored," he said instead, taking care to smile with the proper world-weary air as he tossed aside Francesca's drawing. "This amuses me."

Instantly the disappointment showed in her eyes. She didn't believe him, not at all, but she didn't question him further, which, in an odd way, seemed worse to William than if she had.

"What would you have me do, M'Lord?" she asked. "If I agree, what be my work?"

"No work at all, not really," he said, plunging in with a heartiness that still didn't dispel the awkwardness of that unanswered question. "Especially not to begin with. Let the duchess draw you and paint you, as she's already begun to do."

"Her Grace—she knows nothing of this?"

"Nothing," he said firmly. "Nor would the duke want her to, not with the danger involved. The *ton* is already clamoring to know who you are from that single painting below in her hall."

"They are not!" she exclaimed, more shocked than flattered.

"They are indeed," he said. That was a masterpiece of understatement. He'd have to fight off a veritable army of other admirers when he appeared with her on his arm. "Beauty is always admired, and yours is most rare indeed. Let the gossips froth and frenzy, and then, once you are properly dressed, I shall show you about. The theater, the pleasure gardens, a gathering here or there, enough that the French will pronounce me thoroughly besotted with you."

"Might we go to Vauxhall?" she begged, her eyes round. "I've never been there."

"If it pleases you," he said, taken aback by his own sudden anticipation at sharing something so banal with her. He shouldn't care; he should be beyond that. How long had it been since he'd first marveled at the fireworks in the summer night sky over Vauxhall—could it really be fifteen years? "Then we shall sail to France in my sloop, conduct our, ah, business, and return. None of it will be difficult, though there is risk, and there is danger. I won't lie to you about that."

"I don't be afraid of them Frenchmen," she declared. "You can be sure of me, M'Lord. But how long would you be wishing me to do this?"

"As long as it pleases us," he said, meaning, of course, as long as it pleased *him*. "With me, you will become known. Obviously I won't be able to take you with me to court, but you shall certainly meet the prince, for he always has an eye for a pretty new face. You'll become famous, an original. When I finally set you up in your shop—our parting gift—you will have the ladies flock to you. It's as much a surety as life ever offers."

At first she didn't answer, looking down at the wreath in her hands. Restlessly she plucked at the flowers, tearing the bright petals apart, her movements betraying the uneasiness she was trying to keep from him.

"How do I know you won't be expecting more?" she said finally. "You're an earl, aye, but first you be a man. You want everyone believing I'm your whore. Why should I be thinking you won't believe it, too, and demand your way with me?"

"Because of this." Before she could realize what was happening, he caught one arm around her waist and pulled her close and kissed her. It was a well-practiced kiss, his mouth hot and sure upon hers, an experienced kiss that was sensual and forceful and as determined to give pleasure as well as to take it. It wasn't much of a challenge, for he'd been attracted to her from the beginning, and the feel of her body against his, warm and soft and intensely alive, combined with the sweetness of her lips, surpassed even his expectations.

To his surprise, she didn't fight him, instead going very still in his arms. Also to his surprise, she didn't seem to know how to kiss in return, most rare in a low-bred wench. But he was more than willing to teach her, of course, coaxing her, teasing her, leading her untutored eagerness into a deliciously full-flowered, responsive kiss that inspired happy small whimpers of startled delight from her, whimpers he'd dearly love to fan into moans and cries and out-and-out shrieks of earth-shattering bliss.

As educational demonstrations went, he'd have to admit it was an astounding success.

Gently, reluctantly, he released her. Her lips were wet and full and red, her cheeks flushed, and when she opened her eyes she seemed almost dazed.

Almost, but not quite, or else she wouldn't have been able to hurl the wreath of flowers so hard at his face.

"Why'd you do that?" she demanded furiously, backing away from him. "You lying bastard! You *promised!*"

Deftly he caught the wreath with one hand, pink petals scattering across the front of his dark blue coat. Passion, passion: was there ever anything as dangerous—and as fascinating—when mingled with true innocence?

"I didn't promise anything, Miss Treene," he said as evenly as he could, considering how much he wished he could kiss her again. "But I did answer your question. Or rather, you answered it for yourself."

"You did not, you great lunking rogue!" she cried

indignantly, her hands knotted at her sides in tight, frustrated fists that he suspected he'd be wise to avoid. "*I* did not!"

"But you did," he said, brushing away the broken petals and smoothing the linen on the front of his shirt where she'd mussed it. He tried to remember if he'd ever been called "lunking" before; there was, he supposed, a first time for everything. "I kissed you, and you responded with exceptional fervor. That was more than mere sparks between us, Miss Treene. I can assure you, with a smattering of tinder, we'd have had a full-blown conflagration. But that's not what either of us wish, is it?"

"Not me," she said vehemently, and rubbed the back of her hand across her mouth with emphatic disgust.

"Nor I," he said, though he knew perfectly well she hadn't been repulsed by their kiss, no more than he'd been himself. "For if I did succumb to your temptations and seduce you—if I were to make you my mistress in fact as well as in our little fancy—then I could never trust you to behave objectively or rationally toward me again. You simply could not do it. It is a female weakness, I know, but my sense of adventure is not so great that I'd risk my life for passing pleasure."

Adventure and passing pleasure. Harriet sputtered, unable to find the words to express what she felt. Was that really all that kiss had meant to him, adventure and pleasure? Despite the duchess's warning, she hadn't expected him to kiss her, and when he'd neatly tipped her back over his arm like that, she'd been so surprised she hadn't even struggled.

More fool she, she thought grimly. If she'd boxed his ears like he'd deserved at the first, then he wouldn't have been able to work his wickedness upon her, kissing her until she'd turned slack as an old doll of rags and her head seemed to spin in delicious, giddy circles. Being kissed by Lord Bonnington was beyond anything she'd ever experienced, and as different as night and day from the pawing, slobbering boys and men who'd attempted the same sort of liberties with her before—no, kissing the earl had been more like a night sky full of falling stars, shimmering as they'd dropped around her.

But to him it had been only idle, passing pleasure, not worth risking again.

"*Your* bloody-awful pleasure!" she cried furiously. She couldn't tell which was more gravely wounded, her pride or her heart, but either way she wasn't going to let him escape without suffering his share, too. "Is that all you be thinking of, you sap-headed cull?"

"There now, you're proving my argument again," he said with maddening evenness. "Whether you loved me or hated me, as a woman you would become incapable of letting your head overrule your heart, not even for the greater welfare of your country. And so, Miss Treene, you are entirely—*entirely*—safe from me."

"What kind of green girl do you think I be?" she demanded incredulously. He might kiss like a dream, but he certainly didn't know the first thing about fighting, or about women, either. "One kiss from you, and you be thinking I lose me wits, easy as that? *You* be the daft one if—ah, ah, Y'Grace, you've come back!"

She dropped into a rapid curtsey, her head bowed, as much to hide her discomfiture as from respect. She'd hate for the duchess to see how blatantly she'd ignored her warnings about Lord Bonnington, or how her resolve had disintegrated as easily as the flowers in her wreath. Her face felt hot, her lips tingling and oversensitive: surely Her Grace would guess what had happened, one more reason for Harriet to wish Lord Bonnington to the bottom of the deepest, coldest sea.

"Well, yes, I have returned," said the duchess archly, her arms crossed over her chest as she stood in the doorway to the studio. "Your ten minutes are done, my dear Bonnington. I trust they were as enjoyable as you'd hoped?"

The earl sighed, and shook his head. "They were hardly the most felicitous ten minutes of my life, Francesca," he said. "Although I was my most persuasive, Miss Treene has rejected my offer, and accepted yours instead."

Harriet's head jerked up. What game was he playing *now*? She hadn't accepted or rejected anything. Or was this his way of taking back his tantalizing offer, and the tea-shop with it? Had it been only part of his plan to prove her "female weakness"? Did he think that by kissing her silly, he'd make her forget the rare chance he'd dangled before her? Well, *she* had not—hadn't he said his own self that she was clever?—nor was she going to let him forget, either. Ooh, he'd be sorry he'd tangled with her, wouldn't he!

"Aye, Y'Grace, I have," she said firmly. This wasn't going to be easy as coaxing someone to buy two or-

anges instead of one, contriving matters like this between fine, grand folk like these. She was sorry, too,
not to be entirely honest with the duchess, but her
pride—and her tea-shop—were at stake. "If you still
wish me to come here and pose for you."

"I most certainly do." The duchess's smile was
bright with triumph, enough to make Harriet wonder
if she, too, needed to best her friend the earl. "You
have made the right choice, Miss Treene, and the
honorable one that you wished."

"Aye, Y'Grace," said Harriet, then added a regret-
ful sigh. If the earl wanted to make this seem more
difficult, then she could add a few hindrances her
own self. "Though I will only be coming here when
I'm done selling me oranges for the day, and when
they spare me at the shop at home. Maybe once a
fortnight, maybe less. I know you will pay me, but
what with coming and going here, I cannot do it that
regular."

"Then let me make up the difference!" exclaimed
the duchess impulsively. "No, I'll do better than that.
Not only shall I compensate you for your time and
wages, but you will stay here, in this house, as my personal guest."

"Oh, Y'Grace!" gasped Harriet. She'd been an-
gling, true enough, but she hadn't expected to gain so
much so fast. "Oh, Y'Grace, that is too generous, too
generous by half!"

But the other woman had already seized the idea
as her own. "Of course it isn't, my dear, not at all.
This way, with you here, I can draw and paint you as
long as I've daylight, or even by candles, if I'm inspired."

"Meaning I have to stay here the whole long day and night?" asked Harriet uneasily. There'd be no private meetings with the earl and no tea-shop if she had to wait constantly upon the duchess. "Meaning I can never go out walking in the park beneath the sky?"

"Yes, yes, of course," said the duchess impatiently. "You're going to be my model, Miss Treene, not my prisoner. I wish to make a series of pictures to capture all your moods and expressions, and in diverse situations and costumes. Lah, it makes the most perfect sense—*bellissima!*"

It did to Harriet, too, though her palms were damp and her heart racing at the step she was taking. She'd never slept anywhere other than in her father's house in Threadneedle Court, and even though Tom wished her gone, she'd never seriously believed it would happen. And to abandon not only her home but her orange-selling as well on the impulsive whim of a duchess—oh, what would she do if the earl didn't keep his promise now?

Which, from the way his dark brows were now constricted over his elegant nose, he seemed most disinclined to do.

"My dearest Francesca," he began earnestly, ignoring Harriet as he rocked back slightly on the heels of his well-polished boots. "Whatever will Edward say to such a bold plan, having a common girl like this living as a guest under his own roof?"

Harriet gasped indignantly. "And what be wrong with that, M'Lord, I ask you? What be wrong with *me?* Common don't mean thieving, you know. Her Grace won't have to be counting her tablespoons when I leave."

"Nor shall I, Miss Treene," said the duchess, scowling darkly at the earl. "Lord Bonnington is simply behaving like any good English nobleman, mistrusting anything or anyone different from himself and his good roast beef."

In defense the earl screwed up his mouth and puffed out his cheeks, making Harriet wonder how a man so stuffy and unyielding could have made the proposal to her that he had, let alone have kissed her so emphatically.

"I was only looking after your welfare, Francesca," he said, managing to sound simultaneously wounded and aloof, "and advising you to consider what Edward will say."

"He will say that this is the most marvelous idea I have had in months," declared the duchess, briskly gathering up her drawings from where the earl had scattered them. "Edward knows I have been quite starved for inspiration here in London, and he will be vastly pleased to learn that I have found it at last. And as for inviting Miss Treene to be my guest in our house—ah, Bonnington, fortunately my darling husband is not nearly as concerned with the proprieties as are you. Otherwise, you know, he never would have married *me*."

While Bonnington grumbled, the duchess laughed, turning back toward Harriet as she reached again for her charcoal stick. Still not quite sure exactly what posing for the duchess entailed, Harriet froze in place as soon as the other woman began to draw her, sweeping broad strokes across her paper.

"I suppose it will be best that you hide yourself

away here, Miss Treene," continued the duchess, frowning a bit as she concentrated, "for as soon as I show these pictures to my friends, all of London will wish to know you. You'll be as celebrated as Emma Hart was after George Romney painted her, and *she* became Lady Hamilton."

Harriet didn't dare move, but she still couldn't keep herself from darting her gaze toward Lord Bonnington, standing just behind the duchess's shoulder.

This was exactly what he'd predicted would happen, wasn't it? And wasn't it also exactly what she'd wanted, the proposal she'd been determined that he wouldn't forget for the sake of her tea-shop, and in spite of that wicked kiss?

And he hadn't forgotten, not at all. She realized that the moment he caught her eye. With the duchess occupied with her drawing, he'd somehow shrugged away that pompous, aristocratic bearing like a coat that didn't fit, and he'd stopped being disdainful and earnest, too. Instead he'd become out-and-out gleeful, his handsome face alive with amusement at what had just happened, and when, slowly, he winked at her, it was with that familiar conspirator's understanding she'd remembered from the first day in the park.

The cunning rogue: he'd planned this all from the beginning, toying with her when she thought she'd been the clever one, making him do what she wished, instead of the other way 'round! Wink at her, would he, acting as if she were already a part of his mischief! Ah, what she could say to a low trick like this, and who could blame her?

But as much as Harriet wanted to explain to him precisely what she thought, there was no possible way that she could now, not and ruin everything before the duchess. He was trapping her into compliance, knowing she'd have to listen in helpless silence while the duchess's charcoal scratched over the paper.

Yet she wasn't really trapped, was she? If she truly wished to, she could stand up and leave and be done with them all, and return home without another word. No, she must be honest: she was staying here because she wished to, because she wasn't a coward, because she desperately wanted to see what would happen next, because whatever did was bound to be infinitely more exciting than her other life could ever be.

Because in her other life, there was no wickedly handsome blue-eyed earl asking her to become his partner, no other man in her entire experience who was, in an unsettling way, so much like herself.

"How do you mean to dress her, Francesca?" he was now asking, sliding back into being the properly indolent English lord. He was posing exactly as she was, thought Harriet, and clearly he'd had considerably more experience at it, too.

"Dress her?" repeated the duchess, clearly more interested in her drawing than in his question. "Oh, how I always dress anyone posing here, I suppose. You know I've chests and chests of fancy-dress, costumes, and headpieces and such. I'll put her in whatever suits her character."

"I meant for day," he continued, as if Harriet had become some mute, deaf, unfeeling object in need of correcting, or at the very least as if she'd left the room. "For undress. You cannot intend to leave the girl as she is, with such an abysmal disregard for fashion."

The duchess sighed impatiently, pausing to glare over her shoulder at the earl. "Miss Treene is perfectly agreeable as she is, Bonnington. She's not a princess royal, you know. She's an orange-seller."

That pricked at Harriet's pride—she had, after all, chosen her very best clothes to come call at Harborough House—and it might have hurt more if she weren't so sure that the earl was plotting something more.

And he didn't fail her. "But for now, Francesca, through your doing, she is also the guest of the Duchess of Harborough," he said, so severely he was almost scolding. "Unless you mean to hide her away up under the eaves with the servants, she must look the part, out of respect to you and Edward, and your position."

"Respect! *O, santo cièlo!*" exclaimed the duchess. "Bonnington, this is more of your English worrying and foolishness, nothing more!"

"Then let me set my own penance for being so foolish, my dear," he said indulgently. "Permit me to take the girl to a mantua-maker and have her turned out properly, so that you will not be shamed by her presence."

"No penance will make you behave less a fool, Bonnington," warned the duchess, "and now you are growing tedious, too. I understood that Miss Treene had wisely rejected your advances, yet now you wish to bedeck her—"

"No clothes, Y'Grace," interrupted Harriet firmly. "I'll be earning whatever I take from you, but from His Lordship—ah, I'll not be accepting gowns and such from him, not for nothing."

The earl attempted to look grieved at being so misunderstood; Harriet was impressed. "I don't offer them to win you, my dear. It is more for the sake of the duchess, to help preserve her dignity by making you a more presentable visitor in her house."

"*Perdizione,* Bonnington!" The duchess raised her hands and looked up toward the ceiling in exasperated supplication. "How Edward can spend so much time in your company is quite beyond me."

"Edward is my oldest friend," explained the earl with disarming simplicity. "He trusts me."

"Trust, ha." Again the duchess looked toward the heavens and sighed, a resigned sigh to show that while she was fond, quite fond, of her husband's oldest friend, she didn't believe that simplicity for a moment. "No woman outside of Bedlam should trust you."

Now it was the earl who sighed. "Very well, then. No mantua-maker. She must make her way on her beauty alone, without any embroidered muslin or lace to ease her way."

"And she shall do perfectly well," said the duchess. "You know I have warned Miss Treene of all—*all*—your weaknesses, my dear Bonnington, and she will be far more likely to box your ears than give you a kiss in return for your trouble."

Oh, Lud, not another kiss, thought Harriet with dismay, but to her surprise now when she'd a perfectly guilty reason for blushing, she didn't. The earl came to stand before her, his hand gracefully out-stretched with the palm open and up, and as he bowed, a lock of his dark hair flopped over his forehead in the most distracting way imaginable.

"Ah, Miss Treene, you won't box my ears, will you?" he said softly, his smile warm, his eyes teasing. "You would trust me, wouldn't you?"

Guilty, guilty, and dangerous, too . . .

He wasn't just asking for her trust out of playful flirtation, and they both knew it even if the duchess didn't. If Harriet said yes, she'd be accepting far, far more. She'd be saying yes to a daring game without any rules, to risking her life to go with him to France, to the chance of being captured as a spy, to being shot or hung or guillotined, but also yes to the one chance she had to earn the future she'd always longed for, and the excitement she'd always wanted.

She stared down at his hand, her heart pounding. *No* to *yes* in an hour's time: oh, might Heaven help her, what was she doing?

Yes was such a tiny word, but once she'd said it, she'd also be saying farewell to selling oranges in St. James Park, to Bett and Tom Fidd and her lonely spinster bed under the eaves in her father's house, and to Threadneedle Court where she would always be a willful, headstrong chit who wanted too much from life.

Farewell forever, and no going back.

All she'd have to do is say yes, and put her life in the offered hand of the gentleman before her.

"Come, lass," he said softly, and he winked again. "If the Duke of Harborough trusts me, can't you, too?"

"Aye, I'll trust you," she breathed, the words scarcely audible as she lay her fingers lightly across his palm. *"Aye."*

She would trust him, aye. But as he lifted her hand to his lips to seal that trust, Harriet knew the real test would lie in trusting herself.

4

"$\mathcal{I}$ told you, Bett," repeated Harriet. "I've given up me oranges, and I've taken a place in the house of the Duchess of Harborough that will pay me four times as much in an hour than I'd make in a fortnight."

Her sister paused with the knife over the uncut pie, her mouth open with disbelief. "Go *on*, Harriet! You won't be going nowhere, not when Tom hears of it, and 'specially not to no duchess's house!"

"Oh, aye, I am," said Harriet eagerly, "and I mean to go this very day, soon as I gather up me things."

Bett plunged the knife deep into the pie, freeing the fragrant steam to hiss out as the crust collapsed inward. "You'll be doing nothing o' the sort, Harriet Treene. A place with a duchess! Doing exactly what? Emptying her royal chamberpots?"

"Nay." Harriet tipped her chin to one side, the way her ladyship had asked her to do to let the light shine more fully on her face. "I be posing for her, sitting still as a stone while she draws and paints me picture."

"You?" exclaimed Bett incredulously. "A duchess making pictures of you? What kind of nonsense be that talk, eh? Why would any lady give *you* good money for sitting idle?"

"Because she likes me face," answered Harriet, blushing even as she spoke. It sounded so vain and boastful, a claim like that, even if she were only repeating what the duchess had said. Strange how she'd never been considered much of a beauty here on her own street—as a girl, when her hair had been a brighter shade, she'd been teased unmercifully and called Red Harry—yet all the gentry now seemed determined to treat her like the Queen of the May. "She said I inspired her."

"Oh, you be powerfully inspiring, true enough," countered Bett, concentrating on cutting the pie into wedges. "Who'll be *inspired* to do the morning tasks for Tom if you go, I ask you? Who'll help me, looking after the customers in the shop, and with the children and the house and such? You, that be who, the way Da always wanted it to be."

"And what of my wishes, Bett?" Harriet held two battered tin plates out for the sliced pie, ready to carry them to the men waiting expectantly at the table in the front of the shop: quite possibly the last two slices of Shropshire pie she'd ever carry. "The shop belongs to you and Tom now, and Da's long past caring what become of it. I've got me own plans now, and me own life."

"You ungrateful hussy!" Shocked, Bett shoved the pie toward her. "You owe us to stay!"

"This time the only one I be owing is me," said Harriet urgently, ignoring the plates. "Oh, Bett, listen to what I'm saying! At last I've a chance to better me own self, to follow me dreams!"

" 'Better yourself?' " Bett snorted derisively. "More like puttin' on airs, as fancy and foolish as a heathen ape in silk petticoats! You do be every bit as bad as Tom says, Harriet, always wishin' and wantin' after things you've no business to have."

"And where's the sin in dreams, Bett?" pleaded Harriet. "You're always saying you've everything you could ever wish here with Tom and your babies. Can't I have me own dreams, too?"

Bett's mouth grew tight with righteous disapproval, years of resentment finally bubbling over. "There be good, honest dreams, and then there be ones that come from greedy longings, and not being content with the lot the good Lord has given you."

Harriet's chin jerked up in quick defense. "What the good Lord gave me was wits and grace, and I'll not be squandering either by sitting here on my bum in the middle of rabbit-guts and lard for the rest of me mortal days!"

Bett gasped, outraged, and thumped the plates down on the table. "Then clear off, Harriet Treene, clear off now for your fancy duchess-friend! Never say you're me ungrateful excuse for a sister again— go *on*—and mind you only take what's fair yours when you go!"

"Oh, aye, as if I'd be wanting anything that wasn't!" Furiously Harriet ripped the apron strings from around her waist and threw the apron at her sister before she ran up the backstairs to her room to pack her things, fighting back her tears with every step.

She'd been eager to tell Bett all about the duchess and everything she'd seen and heard at Harborough House, the same way as she'd always told stories of the park. She'd wanted her sister to share her excitement, and while she couldn't exactly tell her about the earl and his plans for her, she had wanted to share the good fortune that seemed to be coming along with him.

But before Harriet had been able to begin, Bett had accused her of being unfaithful and ungrateful, hateful words that had been as sharp as the knife in her sister's hand. Knowing that most likely Bett was only echoing Tom's beliefs didn't make what she said any better, or any less painful, either.

Nay, in a way such truth made things worse. Ever since Bett had married her father's apprentice, Harriet had tried to pretend that she and Bett were still the closest of sisters, but in truth Bett had long ago shifted her allegiance to her husband. It didn't matter that Tom Fidd was scarce worth Bett's pinkie finger; *she* believed he was her lord and master, and all the times that Harriet had tried to convince her sister otherwise were now, at last, being tossed back in her face.

But there was more to it than that. Because Harriet had dared to dream beyond Threadneedle Court, she'd now become the disloyal sister, the ungrateful daughter, the unnatural one who'd neither husband nor children, the wickedly ambitious one who no longer had a place in the house where she'd been born.

It hurt to have Bett say such things, it *hurt,* but at the same time, Harriet knew her sister was right: the sooner she left Bett and Tom and the shop, the happier for them all.

But oh, how Harriet prayed that she'd been just as right to trust Lord Bonnington!

William rested his arms on the *Fancy*'s taffrail, watching the white gulls against the blue summer sky, their wings motionless as they hovered lazily on the breeze. The sun was luxuriously warm upon his back through the linen of his shirt, the deck smooth beneath his bare feet, for here on board his sloop he forgot London formality along with the gray London fog, and dressed with the same comfortable freedom as his crew. That would change by nightfall, of course, when he was to meet a party of old friends ashore for a supper of turtle and venison at an inn at Isleworth, but for now the Thames and the summer afternoon were his to enjoy as he pleased.

It had, all in all, been a most tolerable fortnight. He had left London and gone south to the coast to rejoin the *Fancy*. After a few impromptu races in the bay against other gentlemen with yachts and sloops, races he'd handily won, he had sailed her up the river to moorings here near Twickenham.

A barge filled with day-revelers passed close by the *Fancy*, the tinny sounds of the small band on board nearly drowned out by the passengers' laughter, the men drunkenly bowing and the women waving their handkerchiefs and gloves in his direction. Idly he waved in return, trying not to imagine Harriet Treene's face among the giddy, rosy-cheeked women.

It wasn't easy, nor had it been ever since he'd left

her at Harborough House. She was also the main reason for his leaving town, for he'd wanted Francesca to have sufficient time to scatter her pictures about among her friends and build the speculation and interest about Harriet's identity. He couldn't notice her until that had happened; gentlemen in his position simply did not pluck orange-sellers straight from the park for any lasting favor, no matter how lovely the girls themselves might be. There were, after all, certain proprieties to be maintained, even in improper behavior.

But no matter how hard he'd tried to keep himself occupied this week, Harriet had remained in his mind, awake and asleep and especially in that mazy time in between. It wasn't always the same, of course. Sometimes it was the changeable gray-blue of her eyes that he recalled, or the unexpected grace of her movements, or even the way she'd laughed when they'd jested back and forth about the Pharisees in the park. He couldn't recall the last time he'd been so taken by a woman, especially one he couldn't have.

Absently he drummed his fingers along the polished rail, forgetting the pleasure barge and the gulls as he pictured the way the sunlight had filtered through Harriet's hair when she'd been posing for Francesca, washing over her face and along the seductive line of her throat. He had always been very fond of women's throats, particularly the small, fascinating, sensitive hollow that seemed made for a man to kiss. True, he'd only kissed Harriet once, and only then to prove a point, but still he thought a great deal about kissing her again, and in a great many other interesting places upon her person besides her lips.

What he did not like contemplating, however, was how he, not Harriet, seemed to be the one who'd entirely missed the point he'd been trying to make about emotions and their effect upon reason. Hell, he couldn't even form a coherent sentence to explain his dilemma, let alone find an answer to it, and with a resigned grumble he returned to the less complicated and more enjoyable consideration of her person.

"Ever vigilant, aren't you, Will?" asked Edward dryly as he joined him at the rail. "I trust you set a better watch when you're in French waters, else I'll never let you leave this river again."

"And if I cannot trust the saintly Captain His Grace the Duke of Harborough to board my sloop, then I've no right to be the *Fancy*'s master," answered William, neatly sidestepping Edward's question. He had in fact been so preoccupied with Harriet Treene that he hadn't heard Edward's boat come alongside, or his friend climb on board, either, but he wasn't about to confess such a humiliating lapse, especially not to Edward. "My men all believe you not only command the seas, but walk upon water as well."

Edward grinned. "Then why the devil did I have to bother with that wherry from the shore?"

"Because you're a perverse bastard by nature, and always have been," said William. "You've come deuced early for supper, haven't you?"

"I could not wait for the venison, Will, nor that excellent punch you have promised." But Edward's smile was short-lived, the way it was all too often these days. "Besides, I wished to speak with you first alone, without the others. Your people here on the *Fancy* are unchanged?"

"The same faces as always," said William, understanding that this was Edward's discreet way of asking if the *Fancy*'s small crew was not only the same men, but of the same unquestionable loyalty as well. Given the riskiness of William's activities, he couldn't afford for them to be otherwise. All six members of his crew were Sussex men raised up as smugglers, with families living close to the Bonnington lands at Charlesfield, and the Admiralty exemption passes that each man carried excusing them from serving in the Navy were more than enough to guarantee their silence. "You would recognize most all of them."

Edward nodded with approval, turning to squint up at the *Fancy*'s masts and rigging. "You've a trim little vessel here, Will, and a fast one, too. I heard you shamed both Dysart and Walters—packed them off with their tails hanging between their legs. The betting-books in all the clubs were filled with their losses after the races."

"The winds smiled upon me," said William with a modesty that neither of them particularly believed. "I trust you placed your wager on the winning side, Ned, and not against me?"

Edward gave his shoulder a quick shove. "I'd sooner throw my money into the ocean. I'm not a complete idiot, Will. I remember how you'll lay on every last scrap of canvas if it means you'll win, with nary a thought for your own worthless neck."

William bowed grandly over his bare shin, taking the remark for the compliment it was. As boys, he and Edward had spent far more time mucking about in boats along the coast and in the marshes than in their schoolrooms, with the result that they were considerably more familiar with tacking close to the wind than with Cicero and Aristotle. As men, neither now would wish it otherwise.

"But the races were a clever idea, Will," admitted Edward. "No one can ever say the *Fancy's* just for show, like another pony in the stable. I'm sure the races have already found their way into the Paris papers, one more example of the decadent English nobility at play. And the practice will do you all well. You'll be needing that speed to outdance the French, and sooner than I thought, too."

"Another run?" William strived for Edward's offhanded manner, and to keep the excitement and anticipation from his voice.

"Aye," said Edward. "More likely two weeks than the two months at home I'd promised you. Come to me tomorrow, and I'll explain more."

He sighed heavily, his feelings clearly opposite from the wild exhilaration William himself was now feeling. "I am sorry, Will. There's no help for it. Which brings me to the other reason why I have come calling early, and that is the outspoken young woman who is currently living in my house."

"Harriet Treene," said William fondly, and if he'd been unable to suppress his excitement before, now he was simply grinning like a sot. "My dear little orange-seller. Is she well, then?"

"Thriving," said Edward with rare understatement. "Most likely because she remains in London while you are here and safely distant from her. Damnation, Will, you don't really intend to take that girl to France with you, do you?"

William's grin widened. "And why the devil not?

She's perfect, Ned. Absolute perfection. She's beautiful without realizing it, she's sturdy as a yeoman's country wife, and not squeamish in the least. Nothing will frighten her, including Robitaille. She told me so herself."

Edward's scowl deepened, and not from the brightness of the sun, either. "Did she now?"

"Oh, yes, in so many words." William tapped his thumbs restlessly along the railing, wondering why Edward was so blatantly mistrusting him. "That's another thing I like about her. She speaks what she feels, without any missish reservations whatsoever. She's as direct as any of the *Fancy*'s men. It's thoroughly refreshing, really, the same as the rest of her."

"But the *Fancy*'s men know the danger of what you're doing, Will, and this girl doesn't."

"And I say she does," said William firmly. When it came to women, William most definitely had the advantage in experience over his friend. "You must trust me about this, Will. Common women are different. They don't expect much from life. Do you know what this lass wishes as a parting gift? Not diamonds, or pearls, or other greedy rewards, but a tea-shop, so she can serve tea and cakes to grand ladies. Can you imagine that? A *tea*-shop, for all love!"

But Edward, ever proper, failed to share his amusement. "I do not see the sin in her wishing to provide honorably for herself. Given her station and dubious family, she likely has few other prospects or connections."

"I know that, Edward," said William impatiently, wishing his friend would not insist on viewing him as such an insensitive boor. "She's told me as much, too, the poor dear creature. No family at all to speak of, or to care what becomes of her, whether it's here or in France."

At first Edward didn't answer, staring out over the river instead as he clasped and unclasped his hands behind his back. "But she does, Will," he said finally. "She has Francesca and me."

Now William was the one who paused, unsure what to say next. What in blazes was Edward plotting, anyway?

"I know Francesca's taken with the girl, Ned," he began uncertainly, "and that she's painting and drawing her over and over, the same as Romney did with Emma Hart. But that's not the same as her being party to what you and I and little Harriet herself are doing."

Edward smiled, and William knew then that they were passing into more hazardous waters. "Francesca knows everything, Will. I told her myself."

"You *told* her?" repeated William, too stunned for much else of a reply. Edward had always insisted that his wife not know too many details of his current activities so she wouldn't worry overmuch. At least he had until now. "Oh, hell, Ned. You told her *everything?*"

"Aye," said Edward, brushing aside a stray lock of blond hair that the breeze had blown over his forehead. "She knows, and she's leapt into the breach to help you as well. You recall how in Naples she delighted in selling antique rubbish to wandering dilettantes. She was damned good at it, too. Now she has tossed all that dubious experience into making sure that everyone from the prince on down is speaking of nothing and no one else but your dear orange-seller."

"Then I am in her debt," said William. "She has made my little ruse vastly more simple."

"Perhaps she has," said Edward, "and perhaps she hasn't. Francesca is taken with Miss Treene, Will, quite, quite taken. So much so that she thinks your little plan doesn't go far enough. She believes that while the world might envy you having Miss Treene for your mistress, for her—and for you and Miss Treene—that sort of pretense isn't enough. Francesca would rather you simply married the girl outright."

"*Marry* her?" repeated William, aghast. He was repeating everything that Edward said like some infernal poll-parrot, but he couldn't help it. "Marry Harriet Treene?"

"Why not?" asked Edward, his eyes glinting in the sunlight with a certain predatory glee. "You know Francesca is half Italian, which makes her an incurable matchmaker. She cannot help herself."

"She hasn't said anything to the girl yet, has she?" demanded William hoarsely. "She'll ruin everything!"

"No, she won't," said Edward, "and she hasn't. My wife is far too clever to be so direct. Besides, she soundly believes that you have finally met your match in Miss Treene, regardless of her antecedents."

"My match in an *orange-seller*?"

"Perhaps. You considered the notion yourself the moment you saw Francesca's first painting in my hall. Besides, the girl *is* perfection, isn't she?"

"But not like that, not to take into the family!"

William envisioned the long row of life-size portraits that hung in the great hall at Charlesfield, one grim ancestor in foolish clothing after another, and imagined, too, the collective horror simmering on the wrong side of the grave if he were to introduce a low-bred costardmonger as the mother of the next Earl of Bonnington. "Can you fathom what my sisters would say to a common-born lass like that taking my mother's place at the head of the table?"

"Good morning and good night, please and thank you, the same as they would to any other lady."

"For God's sake, Edward, be reasonable!"

"I rather thought I was." His friend wasn't smiling any longer, and William suspected that this must be the expression on his face just before he gave the command to blast an enemy's ship to eternity. "You will recall that my own wife is common-born, and it has never been a hindrance to the love and regard I have for her."

"Francesca is different!"

"She is indeed," said Edward, his grim expression showing that, for what felt like the hundredth time in this conversation, William had blundered and said the wrong thing. "But since Miss Treene is as determined on this course as you are, I shall let the pair of you decide your destinies together. If you choose Abbeville, and the next little journey being planned for you, then you shall have the gratitude of your king and your country, and mine as well."

"How deuced kind of you," answered William sourly. He never liked it when Edward shifted from being his old friend Edward to being the voice of the Admiralty instead, especially now when it seemed so damned unnecessary. "Do remember me to His Majesty, won't you?"

But Edward ignored his sarcasm. "Mark what I say, Will," he warned. "Miss Treene may prove to be the best companion you have ever had. I hope for your sake she is. But she will be your responsibility, yours entirely, and it will be your duty to see that she returns safe to England to open that tea-shop. For if any harm comes to her, you shall answer to me."

William looked down at the deck and shook his head, his half-smile bitter. He had never expected Edward to lecture him like this, or over such a matter, either. Of course he knew how to take care of a woman, tending to her little wants and needs; that was part of being a gentleman, wasn't it?

Yet when he thought of Harriet Treene, of how she'd listened so seriously when he'd explained his proposal, he realized the responsibility would be far more than fetching ratafia for a lady in the ballroom. She was trusting him with her life, with a completeness that Jenny Colton and the others before her never had offered. For that matter, he wasn't sure any woman had, not to him.

But Edward was right about one thing: Harriet Treene *was* an innocent—clever, brash, and common, but an innocent still—and when he remembered the wistful regret she'd let him glimpse when she'd said no one would miss her, well, that alone was enough to make him want to protect her long enough to open that tea-shop. He wanted her to trust him, and what was rarer still, he wanted to be worthy of that trust. It was, for him, a most novel sensation.

Damnation, he should never have kissed her, not even the once.

Harriet sat on the long bench in the duchess's studio, her body turned precisely as she'd been placed, one hand beneath her chin. She wore an odd sort of loose gown that depended upon thin cords wrapped around the waist to give it shaping and gold clasps along the shoulders to keep the sleeves closed, and as a special favor to the duchess she'd left off her shift and stays beneath it. A small crown balanced precariously on the top of Harriet's unbound hair, and on her bare feet were red leather sandals that tied at her ankles. It was precisely the kind of costume that the duchess adored, and that Harriet secretly thought was silly, and not even the tiniest bit pretty.

But just as she would have described the gown's color as dirty yellow while the duchess called it golden saffron, Harriet had learned in these last two weeks that the nobility often thought and acted differently from everyday folk. The duchess had been nothing but precious kind to her, true enough, but in addition to choosing these peculiar clothes for posing, she'd also insisted upon constant *washing*.

To Harriet's shock, she'd first made her remove every last stitch of her clothing and sit naked as a new babe—*naked!*—in a great pot of soapy water while a servant scrubbed her so hard her skin had turned red as a boiled prawn. Her hair had received the same unhealthy attention and then had been rubbed dry with a scrap of silk to make it shine more, the servant fussing so long with the brush that Harriet had longed to seize it from her and finish the job herself. When her clothes were finally returned, they, too, had been so laundered and mangled and ironed that they scarce smelled or felt like her own.

There'd been other, more difficult lessons to learn as well. As carefully as Harriet dared, she'd studied everything that the duchess and her friends did— from how they used a fork for eating, and not just a knife and spoon, to the way they addressed their servants, to how they swept their skirts to one side when they sat—and tried to adapt them all for herself, however daft they might seem. She was clever enough to realize that these were the little ways that separated women like her from ladies like Her Grace, and as difficult as it was to change, she'd need such manners when she mingled with the gentry in her tea-shop—and to play her part with Lord Bonnington, when he returned for her.

If he returned.

And that waiting, for Harriet, had been the hardest part of all.

Now she gazed across the studio, through the window to the rooftops beyond, and tried to keep the boredom from showing on her face. There had been days selling oranges when she had been cold, or wet, or exhausted, but she had never once been bored, or stiff from sitting so long in one position. It wasn't in her nature to be still, or to be shut away indoors, either. When she'd agreed to Lord Bonnington's proposition, she'd expected her life to blossom with excitement and adventure, if not exactly with romance, but at this snail's pace, she'd have done better to remain with Bett and Tom.

Another sunny day, rare for London: where, she

wondered crossly, was the earl spending it? She'd wager all her savings that *he* wasn't sitting on a hard bench, wearing odd and uncomfortable clothing, while three grand ladies spoke of him as if he were no more than another chair or table.

"This girl is quite divine, Francesca," drawled Lady Cavendish, an older woman with long, stiffened ringlets hanging from beneath her bonnet and a little black dog curled asleep in her lap. "When I first viewed your picture, I was convinced that you'd created an unreachable ideal, but here I see that Nature has surpassed herself."

"She is the finest inspiration an artist could wish," declared the duchess, dabbing at the canvas before her. She only pretended to work when there were visitors in the studio, just as she put aside her paint-covered old apron and didn't crumple failed drawings to hurl them across the room or mutter darkly to herself in Italian. "Her profile alone is a gift."

Before Harriet had come to Harborough House, she'd never known what a profile was, let alone been praised for hers. The way the duchess had explained it, a profile was the way your nose connected your forehead and chin, but since you could never see it for your own self—Harriet knew, for she'd tried to do it in the looking-glass—it scarce seemed worth the fuss.

"Very fine, very fine," said Lady Snellgrove, echoing her friend's opinion. Both she and Lady Cavendish were determined ladies of fashion, the kind who decided who and what should be embraced by the *ton* each season, and, according to the duchess, Harriet and her profile had instantly won their favor.

"What an irony that such a visage was not matched by birth to a spirit of equal nobility."

"An irony, and a pity, too, when one thinks of how rarely true beauty is coupled with breeding," agreed Lady Cavendish sadly. "Nature can be most barbarously cruel. Consider how the loveliest spring flowers can rise from the foulest dung-heap, and marvel all the more at this girl's grace."

Harriet sniffed, all the emotion she was permitted to show. *A dung-heap, hah: the Cavendish daughters must be wicked plain for their mother to be so uncharitable.*

"But how fortunate, Your Grace," chirped Lady Snellgrove, "that you found this girl before some gentleman did!"

The duchess sighed dramatically. "*Santo cièlo,* but they already have! Once I showed my paintings, they all clamored to know her. I shall keep her here as my inspiration as long as I can, but la, la, who can say how long that will be?"

She lowered her voice in tantalizing confidence, and the other two women eagerly leaned closer so as not to miss a single word. "There is one gentleman who has been most persistent in his attentions, and because he is a dear friend of my husband—ah, ladies, she is young, and she is beautiful, and I can hardly expect to compete with a rich and handsome lover. All I can say is that I must paint her while she still is mine."

Harriet barely suppressed a gasp of surprise and indignation, too. While the duchess had made a few tentative inquiries about her relationship with Lord Bonnington, she'd never hinted that the man himself had appeared. Gentlemen asking after her? Handsome lovers vying for her attention? Faith, she'd not heard a word of it! After each long day in the studio, Harriet had taken supper in her room and gone to sleep soon after nightfall, with nary a lover of any sort hiding beneath the bed.

Unless she meant Lord Bonnington. He was the duke's friend, wasn't he? What if *he* had come asking after her, and that proud footman at the front door had sent him away at the duchess's order? What if he never came back, and that was the end of their adventure together, done before it had fairly begun?

"I heard the prince himself was asking after her," said Lady Snellgrove in an excited whisper. "I heard he wished to put her in keeping in Brighton, out of the jealous paths of the Princess Caroline and Mrs. Fitzherbert."

"Nonsense, Maryanne," scoffed Lady Cavendish with world-weary omniscience. "This girl is far too young and fresh to appeal to His Majesty's tastes. I should hazard a different sort of lover entirely. There are gentlemen who delight in capturing the belles of the season as their brides, and then there are other gentlemen who would rather be known for carrying off prizes of another kind, ones that they wish to gild and bejewel and display to the envy of their friends. *That* is the sort of gentleman who will finally sweep this girl to her inevitable disgrace."

"How wise you are, my dear. It is, of course, the way of the world," intoned Lady Snellgrove as she solemnly smoothed the back of her pea-green glove, as if such breathless gossip was not the very meat of her existence, and to Harriet not one whit different from the tell-tattle of the butcher's wife in Thread-needle Court. "We can only pray that this girl makes that wicked, indulgent gentleman pay dearly for the privilege of her ruin."

Oh, aye, and that is all I am to you, thought Harriet resentfully: another low strumpet born only to be used and cast off by another high-bred gentleman, less a woman than a Sunday sermon to be heard and forgotten. Hadn't she seen it in the eyes of every grand lady she'd sold an orange to in the park? How she'd love to make them all see different about her, see the *truth,* how she was clever and quick and more noble at heart than they'd ever think of being!

"Indeed," said Lady Cavendish, her own bejeweled hand idly stroking the silky ears of the little dog in her lap. "But surely Your Grace will grant us the merest hint as to the gentleman's identity? A word or two, so we might know the rogue's name?"

Aye, tell his name, implored Harriet in silence. *Tell us all the rogue's name that I might know it, too!*

But the duchess didn't have to. Her butler, Peters, did it instead.

"Your Grace," he said, bowing at the doorway to the studio. "Lord Bonnington is here to see you."

All four women turned in unison, and all four were smiling as the earl sauntered into the studio. He had that effect upon women, and the warm, winning smile on his face as he greeted them did nothing to diminish it.

Yet while the three ladies cooed and preened and teased him as he bowed over each one's hand in turn, even pausing to praise Lady Cavendish's sleepy dog, Harriet knew no such pleasure. To finally see him again, to have him so close, his very male presence filling the studio with its warmth and confidence, was almost beyond bearing.

He wore a flawlessly tailored superfine frock coat in a dark, rich blue that she now associated exclusively with him, a color that brought out the same sunny color in his eyes, and beneath that a pale yellow waistcoat with the gold chain of his watch draped across the front. His trousers, too, fit to perfection, in that slightly indecent light tan that no mortal man would ever manage to keep clean, and at his cuffs and collar showed the perfectly precise amount of white Holland.

But as perfect as all this was, he didn't have the Bond Street dandy's self-conscious bearing to go with it. There was more of the country than London in him, an effortless and barely contained energy that would always keep him from being another handsome, overbred courtier. He didn't have the coloring for it, either: beneath his slightly tousled hair, his face had more of the ruddy brown of the sun than Harriet remembered from the last time she'd seen him, as if while she'd been hidden away indoors, he'd been somewhere frolicking happily beneath the summer sky.

Another time she might have been angry, or at least jealous, and with good reason, too. But as soon as he left the other women and came toward her, his smile now for only her, she forgot everything else but how very glad she was to see him. Somehow she managed to keep to her pose, but her face flamed hot and her stomach roiled and churned with nervous excitement.

"And what fair goddess do I have the honor to address this day?" he asked, bemused, as his gaze flicked over her costume and the gilded lyre on the bench beside her. She wondered if he could tell that beneath the yellow drapery, she was as naked as a new babe; she certainly prayed he couldn't. "I'll freely admit, my dear, that my memory of you fine folk on Mount Olympus is a shaky one at best, so you must help me. Are you Clio? Terpsichore?"

"Calliope, M'Lord," said Harriet happily, her own smile finally released from her pose. "That be who I be. Calliope, the muse o' epic poetry."

As soon as she spoke, she heard the smug, mocking titter from Lady Snellgrove, made all the more humiliating by the obvious way the lady tried to turn the sound into a cough. The earl's expression abruptly darkened in wordless sympathy.

Harriet flushed again, but no longer with pleasure. "Calliope, *My* Lord," she repeated carefully, striving to copy the diction and grammar that she'd been hearing in the duchess's voice this last fortnight. "That be who I *am*."

It wasn't perfect, not by half, and she couldn't help wincing with frustration.

But to her surprise, the earl didn't seem to care. Instead he reached out for her hand, lifting it to his lips the same way he'd done that first afternoon in the park.

"You *be* whomever you please, Calliope," he said gently, yet loud enough so the others would be sure to hear. "I may forget my mythology, but I do know that no goddess-muse worth her salt worries over what us lowly humans say or do. You *be* who you are, and to Hades with anyone who thinks otherwise."

"Aye, M'Lord," she said, not bothering to keep the triumph from her voice, nor the wonder, either. How could she not, when he'd so openly taken *her* side? "I shall do that, M'Lord."

"Do not make idle promises to me, my fair Calliope," he said with mock severity, giving her fingers a last squeeze before he released her hand. "Show me. You're immortal, aren't you?"

"Aye," she said, her grin now worthy of the crown on her head. "I be a true immortal goddess, which beats any sap-headed Pharisee, don't it? Like the queen o' hearts beats any knave, red or black?"

He laughed outright, his eyes crinkling with shared merriment as he, too, remembered that first time they'd bantered over the orange in the park.

"She most certainly does," he agreed, "and so should you. So there, my goddess-muse. Be worthy of your powers. Decide what would please you most to do in this world, this moment, and then do it."

"Most, M'Lord?" This was like being in the park again, too, with him challenging her with tantalizing words that had more than one meaning. She tipped her head to one side, considering how best to answer him, and as she did the open shoulder of her sleeve began to slither down her bare arm. Quickly she grabbed at it, and realized what her immortal's wish would be.

"If Her Grace be finished with me sitting for today, I'd wish I could be done with this trumpery gown, M'Lord," she announced grandly, "and I'd have me another stitched that be more pretty and fitting for a muse."

The earl narrowed his eyes like a shopkeeper appraising her tastes. "Indian muslin and French silk and a dollop of silver-thread embroidery, with plumes high as a steeple for your hair? Would that suffice for a deity?"

"Aye, and right finely, too," she said, giggling at her own audacity. She'd refused such an offer from him before, but somehow now it didn't seem so much an obligating gift as the first step they'd take together. "That be proper raiment for any goddess."

"Raiment" was a word whose meaning the duchess had explained to her only this morning, and proudly Harriet glanced past the earl to see if Her Grace had noticed. But what the duchess—and the two other ladies—was noticing was considerably more than an improved vocabulary. Their knowing expressions told an entire story: that the easy, teasing banter between Harriet and Lord Bonnington was all the proof they needed that an acquaintance, an understanding, already existed between them. Here Harriet had been worrying over taking that first tentative step of going with the earl to the mantua-maker, while Calliope and the Pharisee had been busily sealing her fate, and their plan with it.

"Then come with me now, my dear Calliope," said the earl, taking her hand to raise her from the bench. His fingers were warm around her hand, silently encouraging her to trust the decision she'd already made, to trust *him*. "I would not dream of keeping a goddess waiting."

"But I must change me clothes first!" exclaimed Harriet as she stood, tugging self-consciously at the loose-fitting costume as it slid over her naked body. "I cannot go into the streets like this!"

"*Naturalmente,* of course you can," said the duchess, smiling with a certain triumph of her own, and one that Harriet would never have expected. "We are done here, and I should never dream of standing in your way. Ah, Miss Treene! You *are* a goddess, exactly as Bonnington says, and all you must do now is never to let him forget it."

5

*H*arriet sat on the seat across from William, taking care to keep squarely in the center of the leather-covered cushion with her back straight, her knees and ankles primly together, and her hands clutching the edge for, it seemed, dear life itself.

"Do you find my driver reckless, sweetheart?" he asked lightly. "If you wish, I can ask him to go more slowly."

"Oh, nay, M'Lord!" she exclaimed, though her eyes remained wide with trepidation. "It be most easy and fine, I'm sure. 'Tis only—'tis only that I've never ridden in a carriage me own self, and I'd never thought it would be so jigged and jumbly."

William smiled, wishing his wicked imagination wouldn't be so damned quick to picture her in another form of jigging and jumbling. He was trying to behave honorably with her. He truly was, which was why he was taking such care to sit here on the other seat rather than beside her, nobly absorbing some of that distressing jumbliness.

But the costume that Francesca had chosen for Harriet this morning—a thin yellow antique gown that kept slipping and sliding over her obviously un-corseted body, her surprisingly lovely toes displayed in the red sandals, her hair loose and tumbling over her shoulders—would have made a holy saint have sinful fits, and William had never been much of a saint.

"It's the cobbles beneath us, lass, that make for such a ride," he explained, sternly trying to order his thoughts as well to less perilous roads. "On an open road, you'd find it much more agreeable."

"Aye, M'Lord," she agreed halfheartedly, leaning forward to look from the window, the sun glinting on the pinchbeck crown. "But leastways here you be—*are*—cleared up high from the dust and muck."

"What's up too high seems to be my title," he said, "and given how closely we shall be working together, lass, I'd rather we settled on more equal footing. No more 'M'Lord' between us."

Her eyes widened, scandalized. "But you do be a proper lord, and 'tis only right that I call you such!"

"Not even an improper lord needs constant reminding," he said wryly. "I'd rather hoped you could call me Bonnington, as my friends do. If, that is, I might call you by your given name in return."

"Oh, aye, who does not call me Harriet?" But still she gave her head a small, skeptical shake, unconvinced. "Bonnington seems such a mouthful, worse'n 'M'Lord.' Is that truly what your mam and da called you from the cradle? Did they say that whole blustering Bonnington business when they held you over the basin for christening, or shout it from the kitchen step when you be wanted in for supper?"

He could not even faintly imagine his mother, the dignified dowager countess, standing on the kitchen step at Charlesfield, let alone shouting across the courtyard and down the drive for him to come to supper. Besides, Mother still insisted from habit on calling him Carew, his old title before Father had died.

"Bonnington's what everyone calls me now," he said lightly, avoiding explanation, "but my first given name is William, like every other male in my family back to the days of the Conquerer himself."

She grinned, and he should have realized what would come next. "William, is it? Then Will I shall call you, lovey and familiar-like, on account of us pretending to be sweethearts."

"As you please, my dear Harriet." He leaned back comfortably against the squabs and grinned in return, not entirely sure either why he was permitting such a liberty or why he was enjoying it so much. No one save Edward called him Will—certainly no other woman in his life had dared—but it sounded wonderfully different and fresh in Harriet's voice. He liked it, liked it so vastly much that he'd no choice but to say what he did next.

"Pretending, yes," he said as lightly as he could. "That's what's at the bottom of this pretty charade, isn't it?"

Her grin remained, but subtly changed, more determined, more resolute, and unexpectedly more beguiling as well.

"Aye. Especially that part about being sweethearts. I don't be such a green fool as to believe that, Will, nor to have me head turned by you. I'll not risk me heart or me tea-shop for the sake of five minutes' amusement and nine months of regret."

"Exactly so, dear Harriet." It was, too. At least that was what he *had* been thinking. But for her to speak of her heart like that: none of his friends or their women would dare be so sentimental. For them, passion had nothing to do with love, and was kept quite separate from love and other embarrassing attachments. But for Harriet, lovely, enticing, plain-speaking Harriet, hearts and love and sex and bastards were all mercilessly connected, and she wanted none of any of it, at least not with him.

Did she really think he'd only be good for five *minutes* of amusement?

"Exactly, *exactly* so, me dear Will." The carriage turned, shifting just enough to send the fabric slithering once again off her shoulder: a lovely, round, rosy shoulder, as sweetly tempting as a ripe peach. It could have been an accident, but William wasn't sure, not when she left the shoulder bare, adding an impatient little shrug that he could hardly ignore.

Blast, but the sun was making the carriage deuced warm today, as warm and close as a bake-oven, and surreptitiously he ran his finger along the inside of his collar, trying to ease the damp linen away from his neck.

"Pretending, that's all it be," she continued, tipping her head toward her bare shoulder. "And no trouble will come of it unless we start forgetting what be real or otherwise, and believing what we shouldn't."

Her smile seemed to soften as she looked at him, her blue-gray eyes almost apologetic. He'd thought the current fashions for unstructured gowns would have made him more immune to the sight of her in the loose costume, yet again and again his gaze returned to the full curves of her breasts, how they gently swayed and tormented him each time she moved her arms. Now she slowly smoothed her sleeve back over her shoulder, her fingers lingering where the golden fabric slid over her skin.

What was it Francesca had said, that he'd finally met his match in Harriet Treene?

Gruffly he cleared his throat. "Now then. We have much to plan, lass, and not much time to do it."

Instantly she turned serious as a deacon, her hands now clasped in her lap. "The first part of your plan be already done, Will. You coming to Her Grace's studio like you did, like we was the oldest of friends—why, Lady Snellgrove and Lady Cavendish will have every last one of their lady friends whispering that tale all over the West End."

"Only the beginning," said William firmly. This was better, with him in control again and all business, the way things should rightly be. "I intend to spoil you so outrageously this afternoon that those whispers will become fully fledged shouts, loud enough to be heard clear across the Channel to France."

"You don't have to do that," she said quickly. "There will be plenty of tattle anyways."

"Ah, but I shall enjoy spoiling you," he said, which was true, as any of his past mistresses could attest. "Besides, as charmingly costumed as you are at present, I should rather prefer you dressed more conventionally before we visit Vauxhall."

"Vauxhall!"

She said it with such wonder that he immediately thought again of the pleasure he'd have in showing the gardens to her, the fireworks and the paintings and the dancing, and the countless cozy dark nooks among the trees and shrubbery where lovers met.

"You didn't forget, Will!"

"I promised, didn't I?" He must move on quickly, before he let himself be distracted again. "The theater one night, too, I think, though that, alas, will most likely be all the diversion we'll have time for before we sail. But that should be sufficient to establish my interest in you, without having to shift you from Harborough House to a place of your own."

Her expression was curious, interested without being greedy. "What kind of place would that be?"

"A small house or cottage, or apartments on one of the squares," he explained. "Such arrangements for mistresses vary, depending on convenience and the depth of both a gentleman's pocketbook and his infatuation. We'll save those questions until after our little journey to France."

"You have a house of your own, don't you?"

"As a rule, a mistress doesn't see her gentleman's home," he said, adroitly sidestepping her question. Of course he had a house—actually he had four, scattered about—yet for some reason he shied from telling her. Suddenly, with her, four houses, plus the lands and stables and tenants and servants that went with them, seemed like a precious lot for one person to possess.

"On a lark, perhaps," he continued, "when a gentleman's wife and family are in the country, he might have his mistress spend a night, but not as a regular guest. As wicked as we men can be, there still remain some rules."

She nodded, willing to accept what would be, in most other worlds except his, a patently immoral arrangement. "Do you have a wife, Will?"

Now where in blazes had *that* come from? Surely Francesca, with her matchmaking aspirations, must have mentioned his being a bachelor. Did she really believe he'd behave like this if he were in fact married?

Had he given her any reason to believe that he wouldn't?

"No, my dear Harriet," he said, "I do not. There is no Countess Bonnington beyond my mother. I am as completely unfettered and unattached as a man can be."

She sighed, settling back against the squabs herself. "I am grateful for that, Will. This may be naught but pretending, and for a fine reason, too, but I'd not wish to pretend if it would wound or dishonor your lady-wife, even if it meant losing me tea-shop. Now, how long before we sail?"

So his humble orange-seller had a conscience to match her beauty, and morals that she would not sacrifice, not even in exchange for her treasured tea-shop. He couldn't recall looking for such qualities in women he knew, nor had he expected to find them in her. That they were made her superior to most of the grand ladies at court as well as all the others who had passed through his bed, and superior to himself as well.

"Only eight days, Harriet," he said softly, "eight days before we must clear England for—for another place. Ah, here is Madame Deauville's shop now."

The carriage rolled to a stop before the ladies' shop, home to one of the most fashionable mantua-makers in the city. Within the curving bow window was displayed a single exquisite chemise of imported muslin, styled in the giddiest heights of fashion, with a Kashmir shawl, kid slippers, a bonnet, and gloves arranged around it by way of suggestion. Through the window, inside the shop, several customers could just be glimpsed, ladies dressed every bit as extravagantly as the display itself.

"Ooh, what a shop!" marveled Harriet, holding onto her crown as she peered through the window. "Fancy such a grand spot just for ladies' fripperies and kickshaws!"

The driver opened the door and flipped down the step. William climbed out, turning back to help Harriet join him.

But instead of taking his hand, she shrank back into the shadows of the carriage, shaking her head as she stared balefully past him to the shop's window.

"I cannot do this, Will," she said in a tiny voice. "I thought I'd be brave enough, but that store and them ladies—I've no place among them, Will, and so they'll tell me, the instant they see me gotten up like this."

"Oh, Harriet." Gently he took her hand, though he didn't try to pull her forward or force her against her will. He was sure he hadn't misjudged her, but this, in a way, would be her first genuine test. Better to find out now in London than in France if she wouldn't be up to the challenge. She had to be able to think quickly and cleverly, or this whole arrangement would collapse.

And he wanted her very much to succeed.

"Those ladies are the ones who don't belong in your divine company, lass," he said, hoping to distract her from her shyness. "Recall that you are the goddess, my dear Calliope, and they the lowly mortals."

Her smile was wobbly at best. "They be righteous noble mortals, Will."

"But *you* are the goddess, and if you believe it, then so will they. Remember, we wish them to talk about us when we have left, or else this endeavor will be for nothing."

"They should know me face already from the duchess's pictures. That's what Her Grace said, anyways." She took a deep breath, visibly gathering her courage. "All them ladies that came to the studio— they knew me."

"Then most likely these will as well," he said. "Francesca can be most remarkably thorough when she sets her mind to a task."

She nodded briskly, though the uncertainty still showed in her face as she looked past him to the elegant shop-front.

"You're better than them all, Harriet," he said. "Don't let them think otherwise, not of you. It's no different from selling oranges in the park. Now remember what we must do together, as partners, and remember your tea-shop. Hell, remember *me.*"

She laughed then, the uneasiness finally washing from her face like soot before a spring shower.

"You be such a blooming gentleman, Will," she said, taking his hand and lifting her skirts free with the other as she climbed down. "Now mind you watch after me bum. If this trumpery gown tears, I've not a stitch beneath to keep me from shaming me own self something wicked, and you too, on account of being with me. You'll just have to cover me nakedness from behind with your coat, and save us both."

Gentleman or not, William nearly choked and no wonder he followed as close as he could, her hand linked through his arm as they swept past the doorman into the shop. Harriet was holding her head high with all the assurance of the crown that she still wore, her bearing graceful and regal. Even if he hadn't been charged with guarding her decency, William wouldn't for the world have missed her first meeting with Madame Deauville.

He hadn't long to wait. Madame herself came gliding toward them, her expression managing the balance between welcome and reserve. Unlike many of the other drapers and mantua-makers in London, Madame Deauville truly was French, an émigré who'd escaped from the same guillotine that had claimed so many of her best customers among the aristocracy. Her seamstresses and assistants, even the boys who carried packages to the customers' carriages—all were French as well. She had Parisian hauteur and elegance to match the keen business acumen that had made her Bond Street shop a lasting success.

"*Bonjour,* My Lord Bonnington," she said with a graceful curtsey that was the precisely calculated depth and length appropriate for an earl. Of course Madame recognized William, and doubtless remembered his generosity, too, but she was not nearly as certain about the costumed young woman beside him. "How honored we are to see you once again!"

"And *bonjour* to you, Madame," said William. "I cannot fathom how you do it, Madame, but I vow each time I see you that you grow younger and more beautiful."

Madame smiled serenely. "You are too kind, My Lord," she murmured, but her expert gaze was already appraising Harriet, noting everything from her bare toes in the red sandals to the crooked crown. "You have brought me a new young ... lady to dress, yes?"

Harriet heard that slight, doubting pause, exactly as the older woman intended. The Frenchwoman could see the difference between an earl's wife or sister and his mistress a mile away, and measure her respect accordingly. The other customers in the shop had also stopped their conversations and had shamelessly turned to stare and eavesdrop, and Madame's assistants, too, had frozen into place with lengths of ribbons and lace in their outstretched hands.

But Harriet refused to be intimidated. William was expecting more from her, wasn't he? He was unashamedly spending who knows how much to dress her in a shop like this, having brought her here in his carriage, on his arm, linking his name with hers. But what mattered even more was that he *believed* she could do this, bless him, and she was determined to do her best to reward his faith in her.

"Not a lady, M'dame, nay," she said cheerfully, "but a goddess, come down t' mingle with the mortals."

"*Vraiment.*" The only surprise Madame registered was to arch one blue-veined hand elegantly over her breast. "Dare I inquire as to which, ah, goddess is honoring my shop?"

"Calliope," said William with such endearing promptness that Harriet knew without looking at him that she'd said precisely the right thing. "Goddess of—of—oh, sweetheart, what was it again?"

"Epic poetry," supplied Harriet helpfully. "That be the special long poems, Will. Her Grace told me so."

"And Francesca being Francesca, and most wise in such affairs, it must definitely be so." William patted her hand, and smiled at Madame. "Her Grace the Duchess of Harborough is quite a scholar in the antique, you know."

"I have understood that, yes," said Madame, obviously taking note of how familiar Harriet seemed to be with both the earl and the Duchess of Harborough.

"Which be why she's so fond of me," said Harriet, nodding with one hand on her crown to keep it from falling. "She's made me Calliope, and Aphrodite, and Hera, and Pandora, and oh, so many others."

"In her pictures," said William proudly, running his fingers up and down her forearm. It was wrong, she knew, but she did like how he touched her in these small ways, reassuring and yet intimate at the same time. "Surely you have seen Her Grace's latest paintings, Madame, inspired by this lady's rare beauty? Already the pictures have been copied in the windows of the print shops in Westminster and along the Strand. Everyone in town speaks of nothing, and no one, else."

"*Mais oui*, My Lord," said Madame quickly, regarding Harriet with new—or at least newly feigned—appreciation. "Now I do believe I recognize the lady's face."

"How could you not?" He beamed at Harriet, his approval so warm that she could not help blushing. She'd never known a man who could put so much into a smile, more than most folk could say in a hundred words of chatter.

Steady, steady, Harriet, me girl, she told herself sternly. *'Tis all a game to him, same as when you smile to sell another orange, the same as what you did to him in the carriage with that slippery sleeve. A game, and naught else that will last.*

"And surely, Madame," he continued, "you can understand why she has quite made me her slave, and why, too, I have brought her to you. If my darling goddess is to dwell in this mortal world, then she must be dressed with the highest style and grace."

This Madame could understand: indulgent, infatuated gentleman were always good for trade. "Very well, My Lord," she said, motioning for an assistant to join her. "If you can but tell me what the lady requires—"

"Everything," declared William with an airy wave of unconcern. "A half-dozen chemises to begin with, the underpinnings to match, bonnets, stockings, slippers, a shawl or two. You know better than I. Whatever she pleases, and all of it at once. As you can see, Madame, her need is somewhat dire."

Harriet gasped. A half-dozen chemises! She'd never had so many new gowns, whether stitched by herself or cut down from Bett's castoffs. And bonnets and stockings and slippers and a shawl, the same shawls that she'd told Bett about: faith, she'd never had so much, nor did she want it now, not even from William.

No, *especially* not from William.

"Please, Will," she whispered urgently, leaning into him so Madame wouldn't hear. "That be far too much."

His brows arched with surprise, his smile turning endearingly crooked as he kissed her in the center of her forehead.

"It's far too little, sweetheart," he said fondly, tracing his thumb along her jaw. "Consider it only the beginning of the good things to come between us, yes?"

She began to protest again, then stopped. She must not forget that all this was being done for show, with a careful purpose in mind. Of course Will would be fond, and of course he would want to lavish her with gifts. That was how gentlemen rewarded their mistresses, wasn't it?

And how mistresses earned such rewards—oh, how much of this was pretend, how much real?

"*Très bien*, My Lord," said Madame briskly, unwilling to let such a plum escape on account of another's scruples. She nodded in Harriet's direction, and motioned for her to follow. "If you please, Calliope."

"*Miss* Calliope," corrected Harriet, her chin rising so sharply that this time the crown toppled clear from the back of her head. "I may be a goddess, aye, but here in London I be *Miss* Calliope."

But whether she was called Harriet Treene or Calliope or Her Majesty the Queen herself, she still could not have been more amazed by all that happened to her that afternoon in Madame Deauville's shop. While William waited, she was taken to a small chamber with tall looking-glasses and a silver tray with tea, lemonade, and sweet biscuits. Oversize books of bound fashion engravings, hand-tinted to show colors as well as style, were stacked on a table between two chairs, and a small display case, lined with white satin, held fanciful jewelry made of dark-red coral and creamy cameos set in gold.

But Madame was determined not to squander time on nibbling tea-cakes or perusing pictures. Instead she swiftly replaced Harriet's goddess-gown with a narrow shift with sleeves hanging off her shoulders, of linen so sheer as to be nearly transparent, and pale pink stockings that looked no different from her bare legs. Yet when Harriet asked hesitantly after stays and petticoats, Madame disdainfully replied that only common women and farmers' wives wore such prudishly outmoded undergarments. Prudish and common she must be, decided Harriet in silence, for she'd never worn so little before any woman other than her sister.

Dutifully she stood before the looking-glass with her arms outstretched like a doll's while Madame and her assistants draped first a length of palest pink muslin across her shoulder and around her waist, then shook their collective heads and tried another swath of fabric, over and over until Harriet could scarcely recall which had been chosen and which cast aside.

In a way it was exactly the same as being costumed for a pose by Her Grace, dressed to impersonate some other woman. Her own opinions were disregarded with indulgent, faintly pitying smiles from Madame and her assistants, as one would dismiss a child's requests—or those of a *common* female—and when at last Madame had finally exhausted her ideas, Harriet learned why.

"Ask Lord Bonnington please to join us, Mariette," said the Frenchwoman, critically plucking at the final length of Indian muslin pinned around Harriet's upper arm to suggest a tiny gathered sleeve. "I believe he shall be most satisfied with our results."

"Lord Bonnington here?" asked Harriet with a startled gulp as her hands fluttered to cover her breasts. The unfinished chemise was cut much lower than anything she'd ever worn before, leaving so much of the swelling curves of her breasts bare that the pink crest of her nipple showed. "With me bubbies tumbling out like this?"

"*Mais oui,*" said Madame, her expression curious. "It is the fashion, Miss Calliope, and not so low as last season. You may tuck in a scarf for modesty, *vrai,* but I do not believe that will be to His Lordship's tastes. He is the one who must be pleased by what he sees, and gentlemen like ... display. Surely you would not deny him this small pleasure? Surely you must agree?"

Surely Harriet must, indeed, for what true mistress would object? If she were a lady, then she might choose something less fashionable and more modest, but not while she was supposed to be in William's keeping. With grim resignation she dropped her hands to her sides. Madame nodded with approval, and eased the neckline back to where it had been.

Harriet swallowed hard, and tried to convince herself that it was only a style, a fashion, something she'd seen on elegant women dozens of times in the park. She tried, and failed. It had been bad enough that William had been able to ogle her in that slip-sliding costume, but in this—ah, she'd be more decent if she stood in the street with only a foggy morn for cover. Nay, gotten up in such a fashion she looked as if she *walked* the street, and sold herself common there, too.

"I believe you shall be most pleased with our choices, My Lord," Madame was saying as she ushered William to a chair. "But then, with a beauty like your goddess's it would be most difficult to choose wrongly, yes?"

The delicate, feminine air of the little room seemed to accentuate William's masculinity, reflecting him over and over in the looking-glasses. He dropped into the offered chair, the little gilt seat squeaking in protest beneath him, and stretched his legs out comfortably before him. His eyes seemed heavy-lidded, almost bored, as his gaze wandered over Harriet's body in the revealing shift, playing his part as perfectly as any Drury Lane actor.

But, oh, what Harriet would give to be able to show that same sort of nonchalance! The worst curse of her ginger-red hair was that she blushed faster and shamefully deeper than anyone, as if the color of her hair would somehow flood beneath her skin. Standing here before him, she could feel the familiar heat begin to spread, from her cheeks to her throat to clear over her chest.

Mind, 'tis only a game, Harriet, only a game to him as it should be to you, too!

"The waist remains high for day, My Lord, to give a line *à la sylphide*," said Madame, plucking at the snow-white muslin that drifted over Harriet's shoulder. "The better to show your goddess's fair charms, yes? You can see for yourself that that the muslin is the finest available, imported exclusively for this house from India itself, and the trimming shall be this pale blue silk."

One of the assistants hurried forward to offer an embroidered ribbon that Madame then artfully wrapped below Harriet's breasts, at once both lifting them up and accentuating their ripeness as she tied the ribbon into a trailing bow at the small of Harriet's back.

"There is nothing, My Lord, like the purity of a fine white muslin to set off the milkiness of the *décolletage,*" said Madame, coyly weaving a shawl of soft bluish red wool around Harriet's arms to draw even more attention to her breasts. "You see how this shawl's color—amaranth, it is called—is the most perfect foil for Miss Calliope's eyes and coloring, and all most flattering. Nothing heavy, nothing dark, all lightness and—"

"Do *you* like it, Calliope?" drawled William, stranding Madame with her hands in midair. "Is this what you fancy for yourself, sweetheart?"

She knew immediately that this was not the proper time for the truth. To admit that she felt shamefully exposed, that she was at heart every bit as dowdy and common as Madame Deauville expected—none of that mattered now.

She forced herself to forget the revealing chemise and how his gaze had settled upon her breasts, even to forget that telltale blush, and instead remembered how much he was trusting her, how much was at stake.

"M'dame says this be the newest fashion, Will," she said, wheedling shamelessly as she smoothed the dangling fringe on the shawl. "You'd not want less for your own goddess, would you?"

"*Très bien!*" Madame clapped her hands softly with her first show of genuine approval. "How wise you are to see that a goddess must always present herself at the pinnacle of taste! In this chemise, with this shawl, you might walk among the most fashionable Parisians at the Palais-Royale, and be remarked by all for your grace and style!"

Harriet nodded eagerly. "Aye, Will, that be true! You did say you wished me to look me best when you take me to France next week, didn't you? Mind, you said you'd wish to show me off to all the other gentlemen."

Abruptly his gaze lifted from her breasts to her eyes. Only for a second, for an instant, but more than long enough for her to see the lust and boredom replaced by unabashed amusement, and admiration, too.

"What a deuced clever girl you are, my dear," he said, the world-weary mask sliding neatly back into place. "I've never met another like you."

"Thank'ee, Will," said Harriet with a grin, for she understood what the others would not: that he really *had* intended that as a compliment. In two sentences, she'd managed to let slip the news of their voyage to France, and also an explanation for it that no one would doubt. In a shop like this, such news would doubtless be repeated and embellished, and by week's end, be reported as gospel in the scandal sheets.

But then this was what she and William did best, wasn't it, tossing words back and forth like jugglers at a market-fair, the way that no other man had ever done with her? Only Will had never called her a shrew or a sharp-tongued bitch. To him she was "deuced clever," and that, to her, meant more than all the muslin gowns and Kashmir shawls in London.

"Thank'ee, me darling Will," she said again, remembering to draw back her shoulders and preen a bit, the way a happy mistress should. "You be precious clever your own self."

He chuckled, and winked broadly. "We'll have our merry jaunt to France. I keep my promises, sweetheart. You know I do. And just as I've promised to take you to that little inn on the hillside in Abbeville for the best oysters on the Continent, so I wish you to have the proper fripperies to make you happy."

"Abbeville! *Mon Dieu,* My Lord, the risk, the dangers!" gasped Madame, her customary reserve slipping. "With England and France at war, they say the Channel is filled with warships!"

William shrugged carelessly, his smile unconcerned. "The greater the risks, Madame, the greater the sport. I shall stand my *Fancy* and her crew against any mere navy tub, French or English. Besides, there is nothing quite like dodging beneath enemy guns in a shifting fog to add piquancy to one's appetites."

He leered pointedly at Harriet. "Especially for oysters with my cunning little goddess. We'll have two more of those shawls, Madame. I want my goddess kept snug and warm at all times."

"Very well, My Lord," said Madame, obviously struggling to hold her tongue. An earl was a treas-

ured customer, no matter how foolishly he might behave. "*Très bien*. I shall have everything sent—what
is it, Mariette?"

The young assistant dipped uncertainly in the
doorway with a basket in her hands, her round face
ashen. "Madame, there has been ah, an unfortunate
misadventure."

"Misadventure?" echoed Madame, her voice
frosty. "Misadventure, fah! Mariette, you know I am
not to be interrupted like this when I am with a lady."

"*Oui, Madame.*" Still the girl lingered, her hand
reaching into the basket. "This lady, Madame. This
misadventure concerns her, and so I thought—"

"Oh, Lud, whatever has my Harriet done now?"
asked William indulgently. "What's the nature of this
misadventure, *mademoiselle?*"

"I—I cannot say, My Lord." Swiftly she looked
down into the basket, and before Madame could tell
her not to, she pulled out golden, tattered scraps of
shiny fabric, scraps of what had been Harriet's Calliope costume. "I took the costume to the back room
for the new boy to wrap, but when I returned, he was
gone and this was—like this, all cut apart to pieces,
with the knife stabbed into the table beside it, and
I—"

"Enough, Mariette!" ordered Madame sharply,
snatching the basket with the tattered costume from
the girl. "Go back to the workroom, and say nothing
more to anyone until I have spoken to you first!"

"It don't be of any account, M'dame," said Harriet, swiftly rising to the girl's defense. "I be here for
new things anyways."

But as Mariette hurried away, Madame Deauville

turned back, her face composed again as if she hadn't heard Harriet at all. "You cannot know how I regret this, My Lord," she said contritely. "Though there is no excuse for what this boy has done, there is an explanation. François is new arrived from France, and he has suffered much and seen more in these horrible wars."

"I have already forgotten it, Madame," said William, a soothing model of understanding. "And so, I am sure, will Her Grace. As Miss Calliope has said, the costume was not of any value, and is easily replaced."

But later, in the carriage alone with Harriet, he did not seem nearly as forgiving.

"I'm a mind still to call the constable on that French boy," he said. "Considering the violence of his actions, I would feel a great deal more at ease knowing he was in the care of a gaoler instead of the forgiving Madame Deauville."

"But that be wicked cruel, Will!" exclaimed Harriet indignantly. "Think on what that poor lad must have seen, living in a country with people acting like heathens, lopping off the heads of their own king like he be no more than an old stewing-hen! That be enough to make anyone act a mite queer."

William shook his head. "I'm sorry to appear cruel, pet, but I'm not as convinced that this boy wasn't acting from specific and planned malice. I fear he wasn't thinking of old King Louis so much as of us."

"Because Madame and her people all be French?" asked Harriet curiously. She knew plenty of people who refused to give their custom to anyone who'd come from France, on account of the war. "Because you don't trust them Frogs, no matter how nice they seem?"

"Because of many things," he said vaguely, looking away from her and out the window, an unwelcome and evasive sign that she'd already come to recognize, and to dread. "Harriet, if you do not wish to continue with me in this endeavor, I shall understand completely."

Harriet sighed unhappily, pleating the muslin of her new chemise between her restless fingers, her pleasure in the afternoon rapidly disappearing. She'd been sure earlier that he'd felt the same magic that she had, that same simmering connection that seemed to link them together without words.

"It's because I spoke too soon, isn't it?" she asked. "Because I told Madame we were going to France before you did, and spilled it all outright?"

"Oh, hardly." He smiled, though he continued to avoid meeting her gaze by looking from the window. "I'd guessed from the beginning that you'd the wit for this kind of clever deceit, and you've only proved me right. Rather it's that I do not want you to feel, ah, obligated to continue in such a hazardous situation after what has happened today."

Harriet stared at him, and blinked. "That be all? That I might be scared off by some violent little Frog who cut up a costume I hated anyways? *That* be all?"

He turned back to face her. "Well, that's a good beginning," he said with maddeningly feigned nonchalance, "if not exactly all."

"Then I shall *tell* you, me fine Lord buffle-headed Bonnington!" she cried. "You have asked me to be your partner in this, and you asked me to be brave and clever, and I be doing it best as I can, and I won't turn coward and quit now when things just be turning interesting!"

"You are all those things, Harriet," he said softly, "everything except a coward. And as for things turning interesting—ah, pet, I pray that neither of us may feel a moment's regret."

But to her sorrow, from his voice she realized he already did.

6

"*You* are being skittish as an old mare, Will," said Edward as he leaned over the charts of the French coast that were spread across his study table. "Madame Deauville could be Marie-Antoinette herself, she's that much a royalist. She's not about to harbor spies for either Buonaparte or those ninnies in the Directory, nor is she going to put her entire trade at risk for the sake of one destructive boy."

Still unconvinced, William only shook his head. On this warm summer morning, in the well-insulated elegance of Harborough House, the possibility of French spies chasing him and Harriet Treene to the dressing room of a mantua-maker's shop seemed far-fetched at best. Intellectually, he knew that Edward was right: there were many reasons against Madame Deauville's knowledge of the boy's destruction, and none to support it. Yet for the past two days, the suspicion had only grown in his thoughts, ceaselessly if irrationally.

"The boy has vanished, Will," continued Edward

firmly. "He has not been seen by Madame Deauville or any of her staff since that afternoon. Odds are he shocked himself so badly that he's run off for good, never to bother us here in London again."

"It's the coincidence that I cannot forget, Ned," insisted William. "To see such willful destruction so soon after we left those three men dead in—"

"That's three Frenchmen, Will. *Three*." Edward's face hardened, the face of a war-seasoned veteran officer. "Balance that against all the Englishmen, aye, and Englishwomen and children, too, that your efforts might have saved. Then consider all the men, both English and French, who have already died in this war, and those still destined to fall before it's done, and, finally, Will, my own selfish desire to keep you alive. Balanced against all that, I would say your three dead Frenchmen come light as a feather, and not half so dear."

Grimly William scowled down at the charts on the table, as if he actually could concentrate on the depths of this channel or that inlet with so much unspoken churning inside him. Each time Edward spoke like this it reminded William of how much more his friend had seen of the world and done in it, of how Edward had been off bravely defending England and the Crown while William—well, William had not.

But was it such a marvelous thing that Edward could blithely tally bodies like shirts for the laundress? In the last battle Edward had fought, serving under Admiral Lord Nelson at Aboukir Bay in Egypt, he'd watched a thousand men die in a single fiery instant when the French flagship *L'Orient* had exploded. A thousand men, gruesomely blown to nothingness in less time than it took to tell. How could his three dead Frenchmen—one scarcely more than a boy—ever compare to that?

One man, one life, one soul: whether French or English or wild Hottentot, it did indeed matter to William. He knew he should be able to separate his enemy's souls away from those of his countrymen, the way Edward did. In wartime, a conscience was not only a wretched weakness, but a hindrance to true bravery and valor, and, too often, to survival. Yet the memory of those three still, dark shapes on the beach had continued to haunt his thoughts, unavoidable reminders of his own cowardly mortality, as well as that of one particular English orange-seller.

"It's Miss Treene's costume that the little rascal savaged," he said, as much to himself as to Edward. "That makes no sense, either, but I don't want her put in any more danger on my account."

"On your account, Will?" Edward straightened, regarding him with the open inquisition entitled to old friends. "Since when did you care whether Harriet Treene was in danger or not?"

"Since I asked her into this, that's when," answered William, belatedly on his guard. "Since she will be on board the *Fancy* with me, if she is in danger, it will follow that I shall be, too."

"It follows, aye," said Edward in a way that showed he believed a good deal more should be following, and soon. "Though the way I recall hearing it from you, Miss Treene's lack of either a past or a future was one of her strongest reccommendations for this role."

"Then you misheard." William's smile was carefully deliberate. He'd concede that Edward knew more about warfare, but where women were concerned his friend's knowledge and experience were hopelessly behind William's. "This girl is precisely as quick-witted and clever as I thought she'd be. *That* is what I said. She is worth a dozen Jenny Coltons, and her skill should make her worth the Admiralty's efforts to preserve."

"But not yours?"

"I didn't say that, either," said William, brushing an infinitesimal bit of lint from his sleeve. "You really must play closer heed, Ned, else I'll swear you've tumbled into your dotage. I like Miss Treene. I enjoy her company and her cleverness. We will work well together, because we already do. No more, Ned, and no less."

"Which is why you've kept away for these past two days?" asked Edward pointedly. "Why you bought half the exorbitant stock of Madame Deauville's shop, yet haven't come to see it displayed on Miss Treene's agreeable person?"

William felt his smile growing forced. He *had* kept away from Harborough House and from Harriet and from his own unsettled feelings these last two days, citing other business related to next week's journey, one more way that he was undoubtedly a coward.

"I never said Miss Treene's person was anything but agreeable," he said, still concentrating on his sleeve, "and I'm sure, for what she charges, Madame has fitted her out most splendidly, and so you may also tell your matchmaking wife. But no more than that, Ned, and no less."

"And you're being no more honest than a monkey's ass," said Edward as he began to roll the chart with quick snaps of his wrists. "Have you had her yet?"

William looked up sharply. "Whether I have or haven't is no affair of yours."

"And why the devil not?" demanded Edward. "Considering how every other time you can't wait to tell me every last lascivious detail. You care too much for this girl, Will, which, as you recall, you weren't supposed to. You care for her, and you're worrying about her, and that increases the danger to you tenfold. Even you can't deny that, can you?"

"What I do has always been dangerous," said Will, purposely not answering the question that Edward had asked. He'd follow his assignment, go to France with Harriet, and return when they were done. Beyond that he needn't explain anything else regarding Harriet, not even to Edward. "I hadn't realized it had changed."

"It hasn't, which you know damned well." Edward thrust the rolled chart back into its leather tube. "Take care, Will. That's all I'm asking."

"Asking," said William, his voice taut, "or telling?"

"Then I'll make it an order so there's no confusion," said Edward curtly, his patience finally at an end. "For your own damned good. Don't let your interest in this girl run away with your common sense, or make you start seeing plots around every corner. You've always been guilty of thinking with your cock, and until now it hasn't hurt you. But when you start following your heart instead, then you'll be of no use to anyone, and what's worse, you'll likely end up dead."

"What the hell are you really saying, Ned?" demanded William. "That I'm in love with this girl? That I can't be trusted with her, or myself? If you have so little faith in me that you'd—"

"Ah, *buon giorno,* my dear Bonnington!" exclaimed Francesca as she swept into the room past the footman holding the door. "You have made yourself such a stranger these last days that I am doubly—no, trebly!—delighted to find you here back among us now!"

But though William managed to murmur some sort of appropriate greeting as he kissed Francesca's offered hand, every other part of his being was focused on Harriet in the doorway behind the duchess.

No one would guess she'd been an orange-seller now. Her strawberry-gold curls were loosely gathered beneath a bandeau of seed pearls, and around her throat and wrists were bracelets of coral and gold beads. As William had predicted, Madame Deauville had done her absolute, most costly best: a deceptively simple chemise of white muslin printed all over with tiny pink carnations, the fabric so delicate and pleated so artfully into the high waist that the skirt seemed to drift about Harriet's hips and legs in a breeze of unceasing motion that brought out her own innate and unaffected grace.

Of course the chemise was cut dizzyingly low—at least it made William feel dizzy—in the French style, revealing Harriet's English breasts more than enough to rivet the attention of every man, English or French, with a breath left in his body. She'd tucked some sort of filmy pink scarf around her throat and down into the little valley between her breasts, less of an attempt at modesty than another emphatic way to draw attention to what didn't need one bit more attention attracted to it.

Or rather *them,* to be more precise. Jesus, how was he going to take her anywhere in London, let alone clear to France, looking as patently delicious as this?

Then she grinned and put her hands at her waist, ignoring how the fishwife's gesture bunched the elegant chemise over her hips, exactly the familiar Harriet he'd met in the park, the same one who could stop a man cold with her smile, then trip him up neat with her words.

Damnation, but he'd missed her.

And Edward, blast him, was right.

"Hey-ho, where have you been hiding yourself, Will?" she asked with a restive toss of her head. "Here I am in all me new finery, and no one to show it to."

He didn't miss the quick, startled exchange of glances between Edward and Francesca at Harriet's easy familiarity—exactly what she shouldn't have done when he'd been so busy denying his attraction to her.

"So that is what you think of me, eh, pet?" he said, not quite teasing. "As no one?"

"Any one and every one and only one and no one," she said, not quite teasing, either. "You're a clever cove, Will. You decide which you be."

"Yet no one is less than one," he countered. He could hear the challenge in her voice, an edginess that sounded like a match for his own. Well, so be it: in his present humor, nothing she said or did could make him feel one whit worse than Edward's blasted "orders" already had. "Unless, as the poets swear, Cupid can add one to one, and make not two, but one."

Ah, she did like to spar: her eyes were fierce as a fox, her chin raised as if ready to take whatever he'd try.

"Two from one, one from two?" she said. "Oh, aye, love can do that, until love makes a woman's belly great with a babe, and that one from two becomes three, then four, five, six, and more."

"*Santo ciélo,* enough of your ciphering!" exclaimed the duchess, wincing as she placed her palm to her forehead. "You make my poor head ache with such prattle! Have Bonnington take you out in his carriage if this is how you wish to pass the time, Harriet, for I cannot listen to any more of it now."

"Forgive me, Y'Grace," said Harriet quickly, but even as she dipped her curtsey she was seeking William's eye, her expression silently claiming victory—a victory that, in William's opinion, was most certainly his instead. "Will's carriage would be more agreeable for—for ciphering. Aye, ciphering."

"Infinitely so," said Francesca, suspiciously looking back and forth between William and Harriet as she drew a folded newsheet from under her arm. "The morning is surely pleasant enough for a drive in the park, though I will say, after reading *this,* that you two have already done a most excellent job of displaying yourselves to the world."

With a flourish she spread the paper on the table in place of Edward's sea-charts, and pointed to a column reporting the life among all the fashionable, titled, and simply rich people in London: the only people who *mattered.*

"There, Edward," she announced with satisfaction, not waiting until either man had had time to read the column. "It is exactly as I told you, *caro mio*. If one wishes to make one's pastimes known, all one must do is visit a first-rate milliner, goldsmith, or mantua-maker, and the whole kingdom shall read of it within three days' time."

The entire kingdom was precisely what William had wanted, and yet now, perversely, he'd rather wished he hadn't. With the same gloomy foreboding as if he'd been shown his own obituary, he dutifully stood beside Edward to read the newspaper.

> One of our most favorite dashing & handsome gentlemen, H.L. the EARL of BONNINGTON, was seen in the company of his newest nymph, the brave goddess CALLIOPE, at the establishment of Mme Deauville, clothing the lovely deity in the choicest Raiment of Fashion. Gentle Readers will recall our quest to discover the secret of this Fair One, whose beauty is celebrated by the divine brush of H.G. the DUCHESS of HARBOROUGH. But His Lordship has discovered the Goddess himself, adding another Bold Conquest of Beauty & Grace to his celebrated collection of trophy-hearts.

"There I be, plain Calliope again," said Harriet with a mournful sigh. "I should have made a special point of telling them ladies in the shop me own name. 'Miss Harriet Treene,' I should have said, as clear as that. It would have been mortal fine to see me name printed in the paper."

" 'Calliope' is quite enough," said William firmly as he thought again of the mutilated costume. "You don't want your own name made common."

Her eyes widened with indignation. "But I thought that's exactly what we be doing, Will! However else can them French folks know what we're about if they don't know me same as you?"

"These scandal sheets are all the same, Harriet," he answered with a contemptuous wave of his hand for the paper on the table. " 'Gentle Readers' have been feeding upon me for years, repeating every bit of breathless tattle they can find and linking me to more bad actresses than Shakespeare and Sheridan combined."

Her hands were at her hips again, her fingers this time curled into belligerent fists. "Was it all lies, then, that tattle?"

He shrugged impatiently, wondering what had become of that meek and malleable partner he'd envisioned. "The most base exaggerations."

"But there do be some truth in them stories," she persisted, "same as we wish it to be with me?"

"This has nothing to do with me, Harriet, and everything to do with you."

"Nay, Will, it does so have—"

"What do you wish me to say, Harriet?" he asked sharply. "That I am a disgraceful reprobate? A ne'er-do-well of the worst kind? A filthy whoremonger?"

She was, of course, not shocked. "I don't wish you to say anything, Will," she said heatedly. "Only mind that if you don't like what people say or write about you, then you'd best not go a-frolicking with low, poxy actresses and other whores."

"And you, dear Harriet, will cease telling me how to live my life." He took her by the arm, ignoring her squawk of protest as he jerked her to his side. "Pray excuse us, Francesca. Miss Treene and I regret that we have other obligations that must force us to bid you farewell."

Not waiting for either Francesca or Edward to answer, he turned swiftly, half dragging Harriet with him as he left the room.

"Let me go, Will!" she demanded, struggling to break free of his grasp as she stumbled across the polished floors beside him. "Here now, you let me *go!*"

She was strong, but he was stronger, and angrier, too. "I give the orders, Harriet, not you," he said as he marched her through the door held open by a blank-faced footman. "The sooner you can remember that simple fact, the easier this will be for us both. Now into the carriage with you."

"Why the devil should I?" she demanded breathlessly, pulling against him at the step of the carriage. "I don't have to obey you!"

"Oh, yes, you do," he said grimly. He was all too aware of the shocked but titillated faces of the passersby on the street, and as if to prove to them he wasn't kidnapping her, he released her arm. "Now climb into the carriage directly, or I shall strip every bit of that wickedly expensive clothing from your body and leave you standing here in the street naked as a bad bargain."

She gasped, scandalized, and clutched her hands protectively over her breasts. "You would not!"

"I would indeed," he said. "Test me if you dare."

She hesitated, stewing, clearly considering whether he'd do it or not.

"Don't think I wouldn't," he growled. "And if you're so hell-bent on getting your name in the papers, I can't conceive of a more effective way to do it."

"I wouldn't give you the satisfaction," she said, her nose higher in the air than any real titled lady would dare. She snatched up her skirts and clambered into the carriage, hiking her gown clear up above her garters to do it.

Not that he'd let himself be distracted by such a sight, not when he was in such a black mood, not even by the charming small freckle he'd glimpsed on the back of her knee.

Though he'd always been fond of that neat, vulnerable place on the back of a woman's leg, the slight crease above the swell of her calf, the skin smooth and devilishly ticklish, with that freckle like a tiny, tempting exclamation point . . .

Resolutely he followed her into the carriage. She'd braced herself in the corner of the seat, preparing for God only knew what. He didn't oblige her, instead sitting on the opposite seat with his arms crossed over his chest.

"No satisfaction, Will Bonnington," she said with a sniff. She'd mirrored him by folding her arms over her chest, or, more precisely, under her breasts, with a far different result. "No satisfaction at all, not from me, not for you."

" 'Bonnington' is my title," he said curtly, "not my family name. If you're going to insult me, then at least use the proper name."

Even in the shadows of the carriage he could see that she flushed. That had perhaps been a lower blow than he'd intended, for how would someone like her keep track of all his names and titles?

"Will-you, won't-you, Willy-nilly, Will-o'-the-wisp," she answered, though her heart didn't seem to be in the word-play this time. "There must be a score of others if Bonnington won't suit. Where do you be—where *are* you—taking me?"

"Back to Threadneedle Court, if I've any sense," he said, hearing how she'd corrected her grammar after he'd corrected her.

"Ah." She frowned unhappily down at her lap. "It's on account of me not knowing me—*my*—place, isn't it? On account of me speaking too free about them—*those*—whores and such?"

"It's more a matter of speaking too freely at the wrong times, and about the wrong subjects."

"I've always done it, Will," she confessed, though he noticed that she didn't apologize, or plead with him to change his mind. Even with her head bowed, there was something about her that would always keep her from looking like a true penitent. "It's my greatest sin."

"Oh, I doubt that," he said, thinking of a score of others he'd like to demonstrate. "But you'll have another chance. We are not going to your brother-in-law's house, but to mine."

"Yours?"

She looked up at him without lifting her chin, her eyes wary. He couldn't blame her, not if this conversation felt as charged to her as it did to him. Whenever they were alone together, the air between them seemed to simmer with wayward possibilities that he, at least, was finding it increasingly difficult to ignore.

"Mine." Why did the word sound so possessive when all he meant was his house?

She shifted restlessly on the dark leather cushions, the hem of her chemise fluttering around her legs. "I thought you said gentlemen didn't invite mistresses to their homes."

"But now I am, aren't I?"

"Then how do I know you won't change your mind about the rest?" she asked uneasily. "Being under your roof like that would make it powerful easy for you to—to take your way, and powerful hard for me to tell you nay."

"You must trust me, I suppose," he said. "Much as I am trusting you. It's past time you left the duchess's care. I want you close, Harriet, so I'll always know where you are, and that you are safe."

She swallowed, and flicked her tongue across her lips to moisten them. "And that is all?"

"That is all." He let that settle like a promise before he lowered his voice and finally continued. "I'm not holding you against your will, Harriet. You know that. I'm not forcing you to do anything you don't want as well. If you wish to leave now—"

"Nay." Skittishly she reached up to brush aside a curl that was teasing across her forehead, the sunlight glinting on the gold beads of her bracelet. "I don't quit, Will. If you want me gone, that's something else altogether, but you won't see me quit and go on me—*my*—own."

"No, Harriet," he said softly. "I don't wish you to leave."

"Then we agree," she said, "and I won't."

Harriet had expected him to smile in return, or at last she'd hoped he would. Instead all he did was watch her, study her, locking her gaze with his own until her chest felt oddly tight, as if she'd forgotten how to breathe. His eyes were half-closed, deceptively at ease, so shadowed that their sunny blue had turned dark and moody, and the way he'd carelessly thrown one arm over the back of the seat cushions made him seem as languidly relaxed as some great sleepy cat. But if he were the cat, then she was the poor little sparrow, so captivated by those seductively half-closed eyes and the latent, lazy power of his sprawling body that she couldn't move to save her own sorry self.

God in Heaven, what was she agreeing to?

He'd spoken of having no sense, when it seemed painfully clear that she was the one who was lacking. As soon as he'd told her they were going to his house, she should have asked—nay, *demanded*—to be set down right there. She should have stripped away the gold beads and pearls, shed the glazed kid slippers and fine clothes of soft, sinful, foreign fabrics and returned to her own honest English linen, just as she should have turned her back on the duchess and pretending to be a goddess and playing at spying on the French and even that foolish, selfish dream of a tea-shop. She should have run as fast as she could to Threadneedle Court, wed some plain-spoken, red-faced butcher or chandler, and never once looked back at the world of vanities where she did not belong.

But most of all, she should have undone the day

she'd fallen under the spell of the Earl of Bonnington, and forgotten how to say no.

"Here we are, Harriet," he said as the carriage rolled to a halt. "Neither so grand nor venerable as Harborough House, but it does for me."

Not so grand for a duke, perhaps, thought Harriet as he helped her to step down, but surely grand enough for most ordinary pashas. Bonnington House centered a terrace on the west side of Portman Square, with eight tall windows, each capped with a separate pediment, marching the length of the elegant façade. Up and up it rose, three imposing stories of polished stone above the street, enough to make Harriet lean back and marvel.

"I told you, sweetheart," said William, following her glance upward. "My humble family cannot hold a candle to the great Dukes of Harborough, and surely this house is all the testimony you need to see that for yourself. My grandmother was a West Indies heiress: sugar and rum, that's what built this house twenty-five years ago instead of mortar and stone. Now come, before your study of my vulgar roots in trade shames me more."

"There's nothing wrong with trade!" she said indignantly, still looking upward at the front of the house. "A man is no less a man for earning his living honestly and usefully, nor woman, neither. How many of you fine gentlemen can claim the same?"

"Take care, lass," he warned lightly. "You're sounding barbarously close to a Jacobin with sentiments like that."

"Not me," she declared. "But even His Majesty his own royal self needs something to spend his coin upon, and he could not do it without the wares that tradesmen have to offer him."

"Ah, yes," he said, his voice edged with world-weary bitterness. She was leery of this darkness in his mood today, and how she couldn't quite predict what he'd do or say next. "I quite forgot you had your beginnings in a kind of trade, too. Perhaps we should tumble my rum and sugar into your sweet oranges and make the devil of a spiced punch together, eh?"

That made her blush. There was no mistaking his meaning, or the wanton image that came far too swiftly to her own mind. After selling so many oranges to so many men, high and low, who fancied themselves great wits, she'd believe she'd heard every lewd remark that could be made involving oranges, and in all likelihood she'd already heard this one, too.

But not in William's voice, and not with the muscled band of his arm, slightly rough in its blue superfine sleeve, circling her waist to lead her into this grand house of his, built on sugar and rum, and filled with his own wicked charm.

And not that she'd turn meek and mousy and let him go free for saying such things to her, either.

"So spiced punch be your favorite, M'Lord?" she asked, unconsciously forgetting the effort it took to correct her speech. Deftly she slipped free of his arm to take three skipping steps down the pavement and away from him, where her thoughts would come more clear. "Hey-ho, what a pity for you that me oranges don't be for sale!"

"No?" He didn't follow, but he didn't take his gaze

from her, either. "And here I thought you were an orange-seller by trade."

"No longer, nay," she countered. "My oranges must be won, or given freely."

"And doubly rare for the trouble." He bowed slightly, and with a graceful wave of his hand. "Come inside, lass, and let me demonstrate how greatly I can value this treasure you hold dear."

Yet still she hesitated, rubbing the goosebumps from her bare arm even though the day was warm. This struck her as an odd sort of conversation to be having here in the street, with carriages and passersby glancing curiously their way, but if he didn't object, then she couldn't, either. "Mind you, Will, that be all. I won't be warming your bed, or your manly parts, neither. 'Tis all same as what you said before."

He nodded. "That is all, Harriet. You have my word."

"Ah, ah, but be that enough?" she asked, as much to her conscience as to him.

"For God's sake, Harriet, it's my word of *honor*," he said sharply. "Or have you come to doubt me and my abilities, too?"

She blinked, surprised by the vehemence of his reaction, and wondered who that other *too* was who had questioned him, and wounded him like this by doing so.

"I never have done that, Will," she said gently. " 'Tis only that I must look after me own self, for there's no one else who'll do it for me."

"Which is precisely what I am trying to say, sweetheart. That I intend to do the looking-after. Which I believe I am most capable of doing." He sighed with a heaviness that didn't seem to fit the conversation, and shook his head in frustration. "Blast it all, Harriet. Am I truly making such a bloody wretched mess of this as it seems?"

"Aye, Will, you are." Her smile felt wobbly on her face. "Not that I've done one whit better."

"Then perhaps if we try together, we can fashion one rational, reasonable argument between us. Our punch can wait for another time." He held his hand out to her. "Trust me, Harriet, as I shall trust you. Please. I cannot put it more simply than that."

"Aye," she said softly, taking his hand. "Though I shall be looking after you as well, you know. And I cannot answer more simply than *that*."

"I am glad," he said, and lifted her fingers briefly to his lips. "Now come, dear Harriet. If we are charged with one another's safety, then we've not a moment to lose."

He led her through the door and past the footman holding it open—Lord, would she ever grow as accustomed as the noble folk to living before so many expressionless witnesses in livery?—and into the cool of a circular entry hall. William was right: his house *was* different, very different, from Harborough House.

Despite the duchess's colorful intentions, the older house had been heavy, square, and solemn, mightily aware of its own awesome position, but Bonnington House was light and airy in the most modern style. Every reedy column stretched upward, every antique statue in its niche pointed toward the heavens and to the sunbeams shining through the skylight from three stories over their heads to the radiating pattern of the marble floor beneath their feet. Even the staircase seemed to float, splitting into wings that rose from the hall in twin sinuous curves that were emphasized by intricately carved balusters, the whole effect so beautiful that again Harriet craned her head back and gasped with delight.

But to William, familiarity had reduced the staircase to no more than a means to climb from one floor to the next, and as he began striding up the steps, Harriet had to gather up her skirts in one hand to keep pace.

"I—I like your house, Will," she said breathlessly. "It's most grand."

"That's what my grandmother wanted," he said, though his mind was clearly elsewhere, "and what she told Mr. Adams, the builder. 'Make me a house that will stop 'em all dead,' she said, and he obliged. Ah, Strode, here you are."

A short, freckled man with a chest as broad as a horse's had appeared on the landing before them, bowing once to William. Though Harriet guessed he must be another servant, he wore simple, well-cut clothes instead of livery, and the confident familiarity that mingled with his respect showed he was considerably more valued than any humble footman.

"This is Miss Treene, Strode," continued William, and the man now bowed to her. "Miss Treene will be our guest here for the foreseeable, and with luck, far-reaching future. Pray tell Mrs. Huchins to ready the Etruscan bedchamber for her. And tea. I'm sure you'd like tea, wouldn't you, sweetheart?"

"I told you nothing sinful, Will," she whispered urgently as Strode left them, "and here you go, up and ordering an Eee-truscan bedchamber for me, whatever *that* may be!"

Abruptly he stopped on the step ahead of her, so fast that she just stopped from crashing into him. "Ah, lass, what of my word, eh? Why must you insist on thinking only the very worst of me and my intentions?"

"Because—because of who you be," she said, wishing now for all the world that she could unsay her words.

He frowned imperiously. "What kind of bagnio amusements do you think I've arranged for you in there, pet? Outsize looking-glasses and knotted whips and satin cords to bind your limbs to the bedposts?"

She gulped, realizing she was straying far beyond the depths of her experience and knowledge. Worse, perhaps, was that he appeared completely at ease with the same ideas.

"How am I to know what fancies you be planning, Will?" she blustered weakly. "You're the one with all the scandalous, cunning practices, not me."

He held his silence for a long, awful moment, letting her stew. "The Etruscan bedchamber is a small, elegant lady's chamber, fitted out in white and gilt. Mr. Adams and my grandmother decided the style favored the ancient Etruscan people who were, I believe, second cousins or somesuch to the Greeks."

"Oh," said Harriet, all the comment she could muster.

"Indeed," said William dryly. "Bonnington House a fancy brothel. Ah, my dear grandmother would not care for that, Harriet."

Before she could answer, he swiftly turned, leaving Harriet to scurry after him up the last of the stairs and through a small antechamber. The next room was a long gallery that ran nearly the entire length of the front of the house, the same row of tall windows she'd first seen from the street now overlooking the square. From the number of sconces and chandeliers as well as the lavishly formal decorations, it was clear that the gallery had been intended for entertaining, and it was equally clear that a good long time had passed since those scores of candles had been lit to host an assembly or *ridotto*.

A long mahogany table now sat in the center of the room to serve as an oversize desk, with a soft Moorfield carpet beneath. Books, maps, and charts were everywhere, along with builders' miniature models for boats and ships and gleaming brass navigational instruments. It was not as cluttered as the duchess's studio, more organized, but this room did show the same testimony to one person's curiosity and interests, and with an intensity that Harriet would never have expected from William.

"Is all this yours?" she asked, gazing wide-eyed about the gallery. "All them tools and books and such?"

"Amazingly, yes." He shrugged out of his coat and tossed it onto the back of the leather-covered armchair before the table. "The darkest secret of the frivolous Earl of Bonnington, eh? Though my grandmother would no more care for her gallery turned into my office, observatory, library, and boathouse than she would her bedchambers into a brothel. Here, sweetheart. Have you ever seen a map of France to see where we're bound?"

He spread a map across the table, and cautiously she came to stand beside him. She had, in fact, never seen a map of France or anyplace else, but what intrigued her more now was the man beside her.

Strange how he'd seen her in little more than her shift, but she'd never before seen him pared down to only his shirt, waistcoat, and breeches. That billowing white linen sleeve beside her arm seemed a wondrously intimate thing, smelling faintly of starch and scorch and warm masculine skin. Only she would come close enough to know that scent, or see how the tiny careful pleats crumpled when he flicked the button at the wrist and shoved the sleeves up his forearms, dark curling hairs above his wrist and skin too sun-browned for most gentlemen. His hands were large and strong, his fingers expressive, as they traced the curving outlines of counties, rivers, countries, faraway places that now she'd see with him.

"This is London, here," he said, pointing. "I've moored the *Fancy* near Isleworth, where we'll—"

"You meant to fun me about your grandmother and such, didn't you?" she interrupted. "About them bagnio amusements? You wasn't—weren't—truly cross with me, was you?"

Still bent over the table, he looked at her sideways, one brow cocked, his dark hair falling across his forehead. She'd always loved the aristocratic line of his nose and mouth and chin—aye, his profile, that was it—so different from her own.

Fascinated, she shifted closer, her bare arm prickling where his sleeve brushed against her skin. Tiny beads of sweat glistened above his upper lip, and she found herself wondering ridiculously how they'd taste if she licked them clean. Now that upper lip twisted wryly, teasing, smiling, arching up to the single dimple in his well-shaven cheek.

"Trust, my dear Harriet," he said, his voice seductively low and rough. "Everything comes back to that, doesn't it?"

"Aye, Will," she whispered, daring to thread her fingers into the irresistible black silk of his hair. "I'll trust you, and you—you'll trust me."

And then, God help them both, she kissed him.

7

She'd never done this before.

She'd never dreamed she be so bold.

But then she'd already done so much else because of William that, at this precise moment, kissing him somehow seemed the most inevitable and perfect thing for her to do, and the one that she wished most to do as well. Swiftly, before she changed her mind, she slanted her head and leaned into him, just remembering at the last moment to close her eyes before she pressed her lips to his.

She kissed him gently, almost tenderly, relying on instinct because she'd so little experience to guide her. To her surprise—and her delight—William didn't move, instead letting her set the pace, and discover what pleased them both. His lips were warm and surprisingly soft, the way she remembered from that one other time, and she let her own explore his further, nibbling and teasing his lower lip with just the edges of her teeth. He groaned, or perhaps he chuckled, a sound of such pure male happiness that she knew what she was doing was pleasing him as much as her.

More boldly she licked her tongue across his lips to coax his apart, and tasted the saltiness that she'd glimpsed above his mouth, there on the beard-rough place that made her own lips tingle. When at last he opened his mouth to welcome her within, she took her time, cradling the back of his head with one hand as she lightly rested the other on his chest. Slowly she deepened the kiss and relished the taste and feel of him all over again, and the delicious dizziness that came with it.

Nay, she'd never done this before.

But when it was done, and she'd finally raised her mouth from his, she was quite, quite sure she'd want to do it again.

And so, she realized with a certain triumph, would he.

"Why, Miss Treene," he said mildly, that low chuckle rumbling from deep in his throat. "Whatever have you done to my maidenly virtue, eh?"

There was nothing maidenly about how he was looking at her now, and as for virtuous—ah, the wiliest wolf in the forest could muster ten times the virtue that William was showing. For a man who'd done next to nothing, he seemed extraordinarily pleased with himself.

Not, to be truthful, that Harriet cared, being rather pleased herself.

Hey-ho, Harriet, me girl, you be dished up proper now, don't you? Bamboozled and bitten, as proud as any Queen of Sheba, and for what? For what?

She raised her chin, composing herself as best she could. "You asked me to trust you, didn't you?"

"So I did, pet," he agreed, turning back to the map on the table before him, "and so, it rather appears, you have. Now, we'll join the *Fancy* here, and follow the Thames to the sea."

She blushed then, her face turning hot with shame and embarrassment—and anger, too. He knew how rare that kiss had been, he *knew*, blast him for a low, cunning rogue! She swallowed hard, struggling to control her emotions. He'd expect her to rail and rant, to jump to his teasing bait, for that was what he believed women did. But she'd show him a woman could play this wicked little game of his, and play to win. He'd learn soon enough that when she'd said she didn't quit, she also meant that she didn't *lose*.

"Our quarters on board will not be grand," he was saying, "and though you'll have to make do without a lady's maid to dress your hair, you shall find that Strode is remarkably agreeable to all manner of other requests, especially when—"

"How many guns are you carrying?" she demanded, rapping her knuckles impatiently upon the edge of the table. "I mean big guns, them cannons that the navy ships have."

"Cannons?" repeated William absently, without looking up from the map. "My, my, Harriet. I'd no idea you'd become so bloodthirsty."

"*I* don't be bloodthirsty," she said, trying hard not to lose her temper, "but I do worry about me own health and welfare. I heard plenty of talk at Harborough House about this war, enough to know that if you and me be sailing into French waters, we'll need more than your manly charms to make sure we can sail home again."

"That is why I'm bringing you, sweetheart," he said with maddening and deliberate evenness. "To add your feminine charms to my manly ones. We shall be away no more than a fortnight, I think, unless the weather—"

"Blast you, Will, *answer* me!"

At last he looked up from the map, straightening so he was pointedly looking *down* at her.

"The *Fancy* is a pleasure-boat, Harriet, a gentleman's plaything," he said. He scuffled through the papers on the table long enough to find a small engraving of a boat with a single raking mast and fluttering pennants, sailing on an improbable sea of triangular waves. "Even a landsman—or landswoman—can see that. She was built to be fast, and to be comfortable and amusing. She is most assuredly not a warship."

"No cannons?" said Harriet wistfully as she studied the drawing. When she'd imagined sailing to France, she'd hazily envisioned something larger and more substantial. She'd grant that this boat looked sleek and fast, a far more elegant craft than the scows and wherries she saw working the Thames. But even to her landswoman's eye, the *Fancy* also had the same overbred fragility as the rich men's racehorses she'd once seen bound for Newmarket, high-strung and overwrought and not entirely reliable. "No grand large guns to fright the Frogs?"

"No long guns, nor balls, nor powder, nor gun crews," said William. He wasn't jesting with her now. His voice was as deadly serious as the duke's, his face somehow harder, flinty, with all his famous teasing charm wiped clean away. "Any of that, and we become fair game for the French. We must be exactly what we appear to be, or suffer. No more, no less. And if you do not find that agreeable, Harriet, you should leave now."

She shook her head, tamping down her excitement and trying to be as solemn now as he was. This was part of the trust, having him tell her the details like this, and she meant to take it all every bit as seriously. "It's a danger you be willing to take?"

"Yes." He was watching her closely, waiting for her to falter or hesitate. "Though I try to anticipate as much of the risk as I can in advance. I learned at an early age that the line between bravery and stupidity is a remarkably fine one. I would vastly prefer to be a cautious but live coward than a bold, dead hero."

"You'd be a righteous fool to think otherwise," she said, determined to keep herself among the cautious, cowardly, and alive. "Have you—have you had to kill anyone else? To save yourself, I mean?"

Almost imperceptibly, his eyes shadowed, warning her away. "Yes," he said. "I have."

That was all, and yet enough to make her palms grow damp and her heart beat faster. Her arrangement for the tea-shop had seemed like a lighthearted lark when she'd agreed, with William himself the greatest danger. But the more he explained, the more she realized how much closer to the war she was going to be. Nay, not just close, but slap-bang in the middle of it, and instead of William being a charming peril to her virtue, he could well prove her only salvation at some time in the face of the French. What would a stolen kiss or two matter in the balance against life and death?

And there you be, Harriet, with the truth as sober-cold as an oak bucket full of January ice. . . .

"But we won't be alone against them French," she said, reassuring herself. "We'll have your crew, won't we?"

"Six of the finest men in Sussex," he said, and whether he wished it or not, the pride beamed from his face. "The best sailors, and better friends, men I've known since we were all lads together. You'll like them, Harriet. I've stood as godfather to their first sons, and every man knows if anything goes wrong, I'll keep their families from wanting. It's an excellent arrangement for all parties."

"It's more than that to you, Will, isn't it?" she said softly. "Like all these books and such. What them papers say about you, making you sound so rattle-pate and rakish with that rot about collecting trophy-hearts—they don't know the half of you, do they?"

He shrugged elaborately, chafing beneath the weight of her words. "They write what they will, Harriet."

"But they don't see the truth, do they?" She smiled, and impulsively rested her hand on his arm. "You be a better man than that, Will Bonnington."

"Will Manderville," he corrected, his smile lopsided with bitterness. "Don't start envisioning fancies and follies in the clouds, my fair Calliope, or composing line after line of your epic poesy to hail my bravery."

"But isn't that why you were so cross-tempered with the duke and duchess?" she said, suddenly understanding. "They're your friends, true enough, but when your friends believe the false tales and forget the good ones, it's all the more hurtful, isn't it?"

"I told you, Harriet, I want no fictions told of me,"

he said sharply. "I'm not a gallant hero like Edward, eager to slay every last one of England's foes. I'll never have a single medal pinned to my breast, or have the horses unhitched from my carriage so people can pull me through the streets in worshipful gratitude. The little errands I run to France for the Admiralty are no more grand than a country wife's journey to market-day. I'm only the amusing Earl of Bonnington, with my 'celebrated collection of trophy-hearts.' "

"Oh, aye, and I'm a three-headed salamander with wings to match," she scoffed with disbelief. "I should peal your ears for you, Will, speaking such as that about your own fine gentlemanly self, and I—"

"No more, Harriet," he said gruffly, removing her hand from his sleeve. "Your loyalty is most touching, however little actual foundation there may be for your belief. You leave me little choice now but to earn it fairly, yes?"

Before she could answer, he went across the room to open the door of a tall cabinet, returning with a mahogany box that he set in the middle of the table.

"There," he said, snapping the box open. "We may have no long guns on board the *Fancy,* but we've plenty of smaller tricks in our arsenal."

Nestled in shaped green flannel lay a pair of gentlemen's pistols, the long barrels gleaming dully around the polished flintlocks. Harriet had never seen such guns, not close like this—city-dwelling piemen like her father and brother-in-law had no reason to keep guns about their homes or shops— and she studied the pair now with wary curiosity.

"We're all of us armed," he explained, "though we

don't make a show of it. Pistols, muskets, and cut-lasses are part of our stock, and I imagine most of the crew keep sailors' long knives as well tucked into their belts or inside their jackets. This pair is new from my gunsmith this week—two more ways to help my luck along the proper course, you see."

She nodded eagerly. "I'm good with a knife, Will. All of us orange-sellers are, on account of working alone like we do in the park. I'd show you, excepting that the duchess took my blade away with me old clothes. She said no proper lady nor goddess should carry one, especially not in her house."

That, at last, made him smile. "Francesca said that to you? Most likely she is right about her house, but if you wish to defend yourself, I'll see you have a new knife before we sail."

Longingly she looked back at the pistols in their box, at once both beautiful and dangerous. "Would you show me how to fire a pistol, Will?"

"You?" He shook his head, and frowned. "Ah, lass, there's no point in that, is there?"

"Aye," she said stubbornly, folding her arms across her chest. "How am I to look after you and keep you safe, like I promised, without knowing my way with a gun?"

"Costardmonger's logic," he grumbled, but he took only a moment more to consider before he lifted one of the guns from the case and placed the grip in Harriet's hand. "Here. Feel the weight of it in your hand first, how it balances."

Harriet frowned, concentrating. The pistol was heavier than she'd expected, and the long barrel wobbled unsteadily in her hand.

"Clap on both hands like this," said William, coming to stand directly behind her. He reached around to place her second hand over the first, adding his own for good measure. "It's not elegant, I know, but you'll never have a decent aim unless you can stand perfectly still."

But standing perfectly still meant being perfectly aware of him behind her, his chest pressed to her back and his arms circling her. Her gown was of such insubstantial linen that she could feel the heat of his body warm against hers, even the worked buttons of his waistcoat against her spine. But positioned like this also made her almost painfully aware of how well-matched they were in size, how comfortably they fit together as a man and woman should, and exactly as she and William shouldn't.

"Choose your target, pet," he was saying, drawing her attention back to where it should be. "Say that old armchair there, the one covered in blue damask with the extra cushions. Pretend that's some villain of a Frenchman with a blunderbuss aimed straight for your heart."

"Or yours," she suggested. "Mind I'm learning this to be able to protect *you*."

"Very well, then," he said, easing a fraction closer. "It's my poor fragile heart that's in peril, and only you can save me. Make sure your aim is a good one, for I'm depending upon you."

But gentlemen like him didn't have hearts, did they? Or had he meant something else entirely, something she didn't want to understand?

"Close one eye first," he continued. "Now line up that little notch at the very end—that's the sight—

then stand as steady as you can. Set your lock, release it, squeeze the trigger, and ha! Your Frenchman is as dead as yesterday's mullet. Go on, try for yourself."

Sight, release, squeeze. She could remember that, and she did, the lock clicking forward as soon as her finger pulled on the trigger.

"Splendidly done," he said, taking the gun away from her. "Your rogue is now quite dispensed to the devil, and I am eternally in your debt for saving my miserable life. Are you ready to try it with gunpowder and a ball?"

"In *here?*" she asked, stunned. "In your grandmother's gallery?"

He shrugged and grinned wickedly. "Gunshots at midday in Portman Square! Merciful heavens! Won't we give the old tabbies something right royal to gossip about today?"

"Oh, aye," she said, unconvinced. "They'll say you're daft and stark witless, and with good reason, too."

"Perhaps I *am* mad," he mused. "Though if I am, then most likely you are, too, you know, both of us destined for the choicest cells in Bedlam."

"Speak for your own self," she sniffed, and he chuckled.

And what danger that merry, knowing chuckle spells for you, me girl!

It wasn't just their bodies that matched so well together; their wits did, too, or, considering this conversation, their half-wits. Harriet could at once anticipate what he'd say, and yet be surprised and delighted by it when he did. It didn't seem to matter that there could be no lasting future to share between them. The perplexing sense of *completion* seemed to grow stronger with every exchange, and no guard that Harriet raised was proving strong enough to stop it.

Daft, daft is what you be, Harriet, if you let yourself believe the fine Earl of Bonnington cares a green fig for the likes of you!

She watched as he deftly cleaned and loaded the pistol, ramming home the cloth-wrapped lead ball that, to her, looked more like a large blackened pea than something that could kill with such lethal ease.

"You will teach me how to do that, too?" she asked. She'd been raised to be capable, to look after herself, without any ladylike fears or misgivings. "It don't look that hard."

"It's not," he agreed, "else our armies would be in a sorry state, given the limited intellectual capacities of most English soldiers. But I shall show you later, if you judge it might be useful."

"If it keeps me from dying, then useful it shall be," she said, and he nodded. She realized that this was simply one more way in which he was daring her, testing her, the same as she'd done to him, and while a kiss wasn't the same as a loaded gun, she wasn't about to back down now any more than he had.

"Come along," he said finally, holding the pistol pointing safely downward as he waited for her to step back in the same place before him. "Don't lose your courage now."

"I'm not certain it's courage that's gone missing here," she said, "shooting off guns in a house like it be Guy Fawkes."

But still she came to stand before him again, her back to his chest, and held her hand out to take the pistol. He slipped his arms around her with the same practiced ease with which he'd loaded the gun that he now settled firmly into her fingers.

"There, now, my brave Calliope," he whispered into her ear, his breath warm, his voice low and rough as a cat's tongue. "I've set the lock to full-cock for you. That damask-covered Frenchman is waiting to pounce upon us still."

She swallowed, longing for a sure way to control both the roaring thump of her own heart in her ears and the trembling of her hands that held the gun. Firing a gun, even in such peculiar circumstances, would itself not make her this nervous, but combined with the headiness of William's proximity—ah, that she'd been carved from stone, so he wouldn't see the effect he had on her! Surely he must hear her heartbeat, the way it was drumming so loudly in his own ears, and surely, too, he would feel the dampness of her hands beneath his own fingers.

"I'm unsettling you, pet, aren't I?" he asked, a foolishly obvious question if ever there was one. "Then here. I'll set you free."

He lifted his hands away from hers, holding them out in the air in a way that made the full sleeves of his shirt seem like wings on either side of her. White wings, aye, but not belonging to any angel from heaven. William must have come from a darker place, for when he finally drew his hands back, it was only to rest them squarely on her hips, his fingers spreading to cover more of the soft, rounded curves and to make her gasp with startled pleasure.

Yet she didn't pull away, and except for the first little gasp, she didn't cry out or protest. Instead she lifted her head and squared her shoulders back against his chest, and closed one eye the way he'd told her to as she steadied the little wedge of the sight against the blue damask armchair. She hooked her finger tight against the hairspring trigger, and fired.

The gun jerked back in her hand like a living thing, a dragon that barked and spouted acrid yellow-white smoke that stung her eyes and nose. Yet still she held steady, controlling herself along with the gun, and as the smoke faded from the muzzle, she could see the jagged hole she'd shot into the first cushion, and the languid snowfall of feathers drifting downward to the floor.

She closed her eyes, and as she slowly lowered the pistol, she felt the tension draining from her body. William was drawing her closer, supporting her against his body, and she let her head drop back against his shoulder.

"Damnation, but you're brave for a woman, brave as blazes," he whispered with open admiration. "You're everything I guessed you'd be, Harriet Treene, everything and more."

She shivered, feeling his words against her throat as much as hearing them. His hands had shifted from her waist to glide along her ribs, holding her halfway between a caress and an embrace, a wondrous in-between that made her move restlessly against him. She'd seen enough of life to know that the thick, hard shaft that was pressing against her bottom could be far more dangerous than the pistol in her hand had been, and that wriggling against it was begging for disaster.

But her body refused to be still, not with the way

William was touching her now, and when his fingers found her breasts, she groaned and arched her body into his hands as if to beg for her own ruin. With practiced ease he tugged the deep neckline of her bodice lower still, cupping and caressing the heavy flesh of her now-free breasts in his palms. Gently he rubbed and teased at her nipples until they grew taut and hard against his palms and the rest of her body melted with sensation.

Who would have known so simple an act would bring so much pleasure? Wicked as it was, wrong as it was, glorious as it was, leading her deeper and deeper into this magical sensual world of his making!

"My own brave Harriet," he whispered roughly, nipping at her throat. "I knew from the minute I saw the painting of you that you were meant to be with me, and when—"

"My Lord?" called Strode from the doorway. "My Lord, are you well?"

With an embarrassed little yelp, Harriet scuttled away, pulling her bodice back into place and leaving William to swear a stream of the blackest curses at lost chances, inopportune interruptions, and the general unfairness of life.

Why the devil had Strode chosen *this* exact instant to appear? And, more confusingly, why in blazes hadn't he come five minutes sooner, before matters with Harriet had gone so far beyond reason?

But Strode had heard similar tirades before, and worse. Unperturbed, he stood patiently in the doorway with a tea tray in his hands, waiting for a pause from William before he spoke.

"I am sorry, My Lord," he said mildly when, at

last, the break came. "I heard the shot, and when you did not answer my call, I thought it best to investigate."

"Damnation, man, I am perfectly fine," growled William, still struggling with both the hideous reality of where all that prime passion had nearly tumbled him and with the physical discomfort of the interruption. If Strode had come five minutes earlier, his little amusement with Harriet and the pistol would still have been a game and no more. Five minutes later instead, and William would have had her on this table with her skirts around her waist and her ankles even higher, bringing them both to a bliss they'd never forget.

But instead, he and Harriet had crossed into an in-between place where they were not quite lovers, but not exactly the impartial partners he'd envisioned, either. Already he knew it wasn't a comfortable place to be, and one he should leave as soon as was possible. The most honorable path out would be to find another woman—a plain, unimaginative, uninspiring, un-Harriet woman—to take with him to France, so he could offer to set Harriet up properly as his mistress, with all the frills and finery and none of this balls-wrenching frustration. She'd be safe, he'd stop worrying, they'd share a most fulfilling and lascivious summer, and she'd still get her tea-shop in the end. The only difference would be in how she earned it.

But that, unfortunately, would not be the way that Harriet would see it. He knew her well enough by now to realize she'd never agree to such a scheme, for no matter how honorable it was for him, it didn't do nearly the same for her.

Hell. Since when had he begun considering the niceties of honor and the virtue of some low-bred orange-seller?

Since he'd let himself become beguiled with Harriet Treene, that's when. ...

"We are both well enough, Strode, thank'ee," said Harriet. She smiled sweetly, showing him the pistol still in her hand as if that were explanation enough for everything. "I was practicing my marksmanship, that's all."

She certainly had put herself back together swiftly enough, a rare and admirable quality in a woman, with only a lingering flush to betray what they'd been doing. No, her nipples were still hard. He could see them, round as ripe berries, thrusting through the soft linen of her bodice, and small comfort to his own aching cockstand.

As if reading his thoughts, she glanced at him quickly, for only an instant, but sufficient for him to see the unfulfilled desire still in her eyes, a promise, an invitation, and a secret between them, and much, much more than sufficient to make him nearly groan aloud.

Hell, hell, *hell.* He *had* to compose himself. She'd turned him wrong side out when she'd kissed him earlier, and he still hadn't recovered. He was supposed to be the man with all the experience, wasn't he, the jaded gentleman of the world?

"Yes, Miss Treene," replied Strode, and to William's horror he saw that his manservant was actually *blushing* beneath his freckles. "I've brought you your tea, exactly as you wished."

Wonderful. Strode with a tea-tray in his hands besotted by Harriet with a pistol in hers.

"For God's sake, Strode," he said. "What are you doing with that blasted tea-tray? Why didn't you leave that for one of the girls from the kitchen?"

"The gunshot, My Lord." Strode centered the silver tray precisely on the table before Harriet. "Until I knew its origin, I thought it best not to endanger one of the lasses."

More wonderfulness. Strode was behaving like a Drury Lane gallant, practically dropping on his belly on the floor for Harriet to walk upon his back. Not that William could blame poor Strode. Harriet had that effect on men. Look at what she'd done to *him*.

She glanced at him again, wickedly gleeful, and he felt his insides lurch. God help him, it wasn't just that he craved her body. It was her wit and charm and cleverness, too, damn near everything else about her. He wanted her with him on board the *Fancy* when he went to France because he couldn't bear the thought of leaving her behind and missing something unforgettably entertaining that she'd say or do. The two days he'd kept away from her had dragged as if they'd been a month; a fortnight without her would stretch like eternity.

"How righteous thoughtful of you, Strode!" she marveled as she traded the pistol for a teacup, and Strode beamed. "I'll wager you have more sweethearts than you've fingers for counting, don't you?"

"You're too kind, Miss Treene, too kind by half," murmured Strode, clearing his throat self-consciously before he looked back at William. "My Lord. A word in private, if you please."

"Can't it wait, Strode?" He had to talk to Harriet *now,* at least to try to make sense of what was happening between them.

"I fear not, My Lord," said the servant delicately. "I fear it concerns your, ah, plans for next week."

"Oh, lah, if it's about sailing to France, Strode, then you may spit it out before me," said Harriet blithely, pouring tea into her cup. "If William doesn't mind, then it's all the same to me."

In doleful silence, Strode appealed to William, an appeal that William was in no mood to humor.

"Go ahead, Strode," said William testily. "You're the gallant with the ladies. Just spit it out before Miss Treene, as she asked."

"Very well, My Lord." Strode nodded with resignation, and pulled a lumpy bundle wrapped in greasy calico from the pocket of his coat, placing it on the table beside the box with the pistols.

"Cook found this at the back door beside the milk cans this morning, My Lord," he said as he gingerly unfolded the dirty cloth. "I wouldn't have given it much more than a thought until Miss Treene became your, ah, guest this morning. Now it seems more than mischief, My Lord."

More than mischief, indeed, thought William grimly. Inside the calico lay a torn copy of the same scandal column that Francesca had shown him, the one that had described how he'd taken Harriet to Madame Deauville's shop. Every mention of Harriet as Calliope had been jaggedly underlined in dark red, so it wouldn't be missed. With a sickening jolt,

William realized the red wasn't ink, but dried blood, and he could only pray it had come from a bird or animal.

But what was wrapped inside the paper was more ominous still. There lay a small wooden ha'penny doll with its head savagely snapped off and missing, its clothes and crudely carved limbs daubed with the same dark red blood to make the connection with the scandal column all the more unmistakable.

"Oh, Will," said Harriet in a horrified whisper, the color draining from her cheeks. "Who'd do such a foul thing?"

"I'm sorry, sweetheart," he said, slipping his arm around her shoulder to comfort her, and to turn her eyes away from the mangled doll. "Strode, take this away at once. Try if you can, Harriet, to forget you've seen it."

"But I—I cannot," she said, her voice faltering as she watched Strode swiftly gather up the doll and its wrappings, and leave. "And it be better that I can't, Will. If someone hates me that much, I would wish to know it. Though why that French boy from Madame Deauville would want to—"

"That boy didn't do this, Harriet," said William. "The way the doll is dressed to mimic one of the costumes you wore to pose for the duchess, the one that's been copied the most in the common prints—surely that much detail must be another woman's handiwork. Do you have any enemies, Harriet? Anyone who might begrudge you your current fortunes?"

"What, with you, Will?" She tried to smile. "Nay, none that I can think, leastways not to do this."

"I'll still speak to Madame Deauville," said

William firmly. He'd also, of course, show the damned doll to Edward, and call down all the help that the Admiralty could give him to catch whoever had sent it. With all his heart he wished he hadn't insisted that Strode unwrap it in the first place, but then, where Harriet was concerned, he wished for a great many things that didn't seem fated to come true.

"Even if this wasn't done by the boy Madame blamed," he continued, "she might know someone else in her shop who could have dressed the doll in such a way."

"Or she might not know anything," said Harriet with a tremulous sigh. "You're guessing it's someone French, while it could be someone else altogether, someone who doesn't approve of me dressing up like them pagan ancients."

"Possibly," said William, not wishing to frighten her any more. Though he wouldn't admit it to Harriet now, he was certain there was a connection between the doll and the slashed costume at the mantua-maker's shop, a connection he was determined to discover before anything else like this happened again. At least she'd be under his roof now, where he'd know where she was day and night. "It may be no more than the unfortunate price of having one's affairs reported in the papers."

She sighed again, easing away from William to go stand beside one of the tall windows. "So next you'll be telling me that I must stay locked away inside," she said, gazing forlornly out at the square below, the sunlight finding all the rose-gold in her hair. "No theater, nor Vauxhall."

"I didn't say that, pet." He joined her at the window, reaching out to take her hand. Living at Harborough House had made her fingers softer, more like a lady's, but he didn't doubt the strength that remained in them, and in the rest of her as well. "I refuse to be driven into hiding by some wretched bully. With a few precautions, you should be safe enough."

Her smile had more confidence; he wished he shared it. "More hiding in plain sight, like you said before. Then might we still go to the Gardens?"

"I didn't say that, either, not exactly." He wasn't sure exactly *what* he was saying, not really, but he plunged ahead anyway. "After this morning, Harriet, it would seem that our original partnership may have changed too much for us to continue as—"

"I'm not quitting, Will," she said fiercely, pulling her hand free of his. "I told you that before, didn't I?"

"We also agreed that there'd be no physical dalliance between us," he said, inwardly wincing at how primly he'd phrased that. "Yet I do recall you kissing me earlier, and later that I—"

"I know what you did," she said hastily. "Nay, I know what *we* did."

He raised a single eyebrow, unable to resist teasing her, even now.

"Nay, don't," she chided gently. "I know the risk we take, same as you do. But you asked for my trust, and I gave it, didn't I? And there's the truth of us. Everything's even and fair, with neither taking advantage of the other. If that don't make for good partners, then I don't know what does."

Trust and truth, even and fair: had he ever used such words with a woman before?

And had he ever believed them like he did now, with Harriet?

"The Earl of Bonnington as a good partner," he said softly, more touched than he'd ever admit, especially not to her. "You're a brave woman, Harriet Treene, a brave woman indeed. And I'd not wish you any other way."

Robitaille looked down at the papers stacked high on his desk, not bothering to hide his impatience with the frail young woman sitting on the bench before him. This was the fourth time in his brief conversation with the woman that the coughing had overwhelmed her, forcing her to hunch over the filthy, bloodstained handkerchief that she clutched with both hands to her mouth.

"If you cannot continue, citizeness," he said tartly, raising his voice over her cough, "then I must conclude that this interview is done."

"No, I—I beg you, listen!" she gasped, her feverish eyes filled with dread. "I—I will tell you more!"

"More?" Robitaille did not believe her. He had always found consumptives disagreeable and overly dramatic, and this miserable chit was no exception. Besides, once her looks had begun to fade, she'd lost much of her usefulness to him. Only the fact that she spoke English had made him keep her in his pay as long as he had.

Now he flicked his hand toward the English newspapers that the woman had brought with her from London as her wretched proof. "What more could there be, citizeness? You were sent to learn all you could of the English lord's family, and instead what you gave me is only this: the name of his newest concubine."

"But he has no wife, no children!" cried the woman, her voice rising higher with her desperation. "He is known to be a selfish, idle nobleman, living for his own pleasure and indulgences! Except for now, except for this woman, this newest mistress, a celebrated beauty whose picture is in every shop. The Londoners speak of little else, saying she is the first to have captured his heart."

"Sentimental claptrap," sneered Robitaille. "All a man gives to a whore is his gold and his lust. I want his own flesh and blood, the one that is a part of his soul, the one he would trade his life to protect."

The way that my son had been to me. He himself had been the one to send Jacques with the other two to patrol the beach for smugglers, but still he could not bring his boy back from the grave. No matter how many times he tried to bargain with both heaven and hell, no matter how many tears he wept or oaths he swore, the finality of his loss would never change. All he could do was to offer this vengeance to his son's memory, and make certain that Bonnington's suffering would be as painful as it was just.

"But they say the lord's mistress is—"

" 'They say, they say.'!" Disdainfully Robitaille jabbed his forefinger at the frivolous foreign newspapers. "Words like these are empty as air, as worthless and unreliable as your deeds. A gown slashed by an overeager hireling, a broken dolly daubed with pigeon's blood, a handful of newsprint scraps! Can you wonder that I have already sent another in your place, one I trust will do more than your insipid little threats? For the sake of my reputation and for the good of the country, citizeness, our association is at an end."

"No, please, no!" The woman lurched forward from the bench to lean on Robitaille's own desk. "I told you, sir, I have more information, true, all true! Within a fortnight, Bonnington himself will return once again in his pleasure-boat, here to Abbeville!"

"Why?" asked Robitaille, careful to contain his own excitement at such news. "Why would he risk himself in such a way?"

"For amusement, sir," said the woman eagerly, "to impress his mistress. He delights in such peril, sir, for he is easily bored."

"Is he." He did not believe that, either. Though the rich of every country ignored the war and continued to travel for pleasure, using their money to blanket themselves from every unpleasantness, it was still remarkable that this English lord would choose to return so soon to Abbeville. That would be four times in the last six months, and though Robitaille had investigated thoroughly, he could not discover Bonnington's reason. The puzzle had nagged at him, eating at the edges of his revenge, for if he learned the English lord's secret, then Robitaille was certain he'd find the key to contriving the most exquisitely painful ruin for him. To have him here with his whore, in this town, was a most auspicious beginning.

He tossed a drawstring purse across the desk to the woman, not wishing any closer contact. "We are done, citizeness. France thanks you for your service."

With unsteady fingers the woman opened the purse and counted the coins, gasping unhappily at the disappointing tally. "Please, sir, please! This—this is less, much less, than we agreed!"

"It is sufficient for your service, citizeness." He rose, wanting her gone. She was no longer his concern; likely she would be dead before summer's end, the streets rid of another hapless, diseased woman.

No, not his concern in the least. But finally justice, real justice, seemed to be smiling his way, and as Robitaille walked slowly from his office, he was seen by others to almost—almost—be smiling himself.

8

"*T*here's no reason at all that you couldn't have come to these gardens on your own before this," said William, fondly patting the gilly-flower nosegay that Harriet had just tucked into the top buttonhole of his coat. While the sun had not yet completely set, he was dressed for evening in elegantly somber black and white, and though the bright flowers were the only touch of color on him, they seemed more of a match for his mood on this warm June night. "That has always been one of Vauxhall's greatest delights. High or low, anyone with a shilling for the door can gain admission, and rub elbows or whatever other parts they please with one another. You and your sister could have taken a wherry from the Westminster stairs, put on your half-masks, and found yourselves a duke apiece for sweethearts among the shrubbery and fairy-lights."

"Go *on*," scoffed Harriet, deliciously scandalized by even imagining such an unlikely event. She reached up to smooth back her hair from her cheek, the gold and coral bracelets clinking gently together as they slithered down her forearm. "Tom'd never let us do something like that. He said Vauxhall was naught but a haven for whores and tricksters and other low folk with no morals nor honor."

"But you always wanted to go, didn't you?" asked William in a low, confidential voice, as he leaned closer to her in the narrow boat. He was a charming, blue-blooded, black-clad devil of seduction and ruin, exactly defining everything that Tom Fidd scorned and dreaded most about Vauxhall. "Despite Mr. Fidd's wise concern and fraternal counsel, you still wished to go to these sinful gardens, didn't you?"

Harriet wrinkled her nose and laughed. "Aye, 'course I did. I *do*. They say the lights and the music and the pictures be wonderful fine, like a magic place. Which makes me no better than all them other low, immoral folk."

"Nor am I," declared William. "Which makes *me* all the more delighted to have you here at my side instead of Mr. Fidd."

"Mr. Fidd would likewise agree, I am sure." She laughed again, settling more comfortably against the plump pillows that cushioned the wooden bench. Of course William wouldn't rely upon the common wherries for hire when traveling the river to Vauxhall; he'd had his own boat waiting at the steps near Whitehall, painted as gaily as any Venetian gondola and complete with a pair of burly-armed boatmen in his livery and a wicker basket with little cakes and wine to sustain them on the brief journey gliding upstream.

"Mr. Fidd's loss is my inestimable gain," said

William, lifting her hand, turning her fingers to kiss her palm, sending a small thrill of pleasurable sensation purring through her body. "You'll make me proud tonight, pet. You'll be the fairest lady at Vauxhall, forcing me to be the most possessive gentleman."

She laughed softly, languidly, for his kisses always did that to her, no matter where on her person he placed them. If she was the fairest lady in Vauxhall tonight, it would be because he'd made her feel that way. True, her plum-colored gown dotted with gold spangles would twinkle like a thousand tiny stars beneath Vauxhall's celebrated lantern-lights, just as the tall, curled plumes and feathers in her headdress made her look as regal as any queen.

But the real magic had come from William. He had been the one who'd looked behind her basket of oranges to discover something finer and better, and he'd been the first man to treasure her for what she was, and not scorn her for what she wasn't. He'd made her his partner, accepted her as his friend, and, though they both knew the danger, he'd desired her as his lover as well.

William *was* the magic in her life now, turning everything as bright and shining as the gold bracelets he'd placed around her wrists. Yet like all magic, she understood how insubstantial, how temporary, it was, and must be. She would always be a base-born orange-seller, and he a high-born earl, and no conjurer's tricks could ever make the distance between their stations vanish. As much as she savored his kisses and enjoyed this game together, for the sake of her heart, she must never confuse the magic with love, and she must never forget it would not, could not, last.

"You are prepared for this, Harriet?" he asked, more seriously. "Vauxhall is not a place for the faint-hearted or shy."

Her smile was guarded. "I never thought I was either, Will."

"Not tonight, anyway," he said, linking his fingers into hers. "Everyone goes to see and be seen, sweetheart, and you are going to be the center of considerable attention. Not just because of your beauty, or because you'll be with me, but because you'll be recognized from the duchess's paintings."

"I thought that's what we wanted," she said uneasily, tugging her shawl over her bare shoulders against the breeze from the river. "Making folk wonder who I am."

"Well, they're wondering, all right," he said, his brows coming sternly together. "I'll wager that we'll scarcely be inside the gates before some jackass begins braying out about fair Calliope. Mark my words now, Harriet. Within five minutes."

"Ah, Will, don't be daft," she said, squeezing his hand to reassure him. If she did not know him better, she'd make a wager of her own: that he was already jealous of that fearsome, shouting idiot. "Any woman who goes a-walking rigged out like this expects idiots to whistle and shout after her."

His frown deepened. "Ladies don't."

"But I'm not a lady," she said gently. "I don't even pretend to be. I'm as common as oak and twice as strong. And we can always leave after a bit, Will, if this don't feel right to you. We don't have to stay."

He didn't answer, leaving her to smile wistfully. "But I'd like to see fireworks, Will, just for once."

He sighed. "You can see all the fireworks you please, sweetheart," he said, "as long as you're not responsible for causing any of your own."

He winked, and she relaxed. She'd no business looking for trouble where there wasn't any. Not even William could be lighthearted every minute of the day, and besides, when she remembered the decapitated doll, she was grateful for his caution.

"Mind that you stay close to me, sweetheart," he warned, as if reading her thoughts. "On an evening as fair as this one, the gardens are bound to be crowded, and I don't want you lost on your own."

"No, My Lord," she answered obediently. She would have felt safer if she could have had her old knife back, tucked neatly beneath her petticoats, but the airy muslin of this fashionable gown left no place for hiding anything, nor were there any pocket-slits cut into the slim skirts. Though she carried a tiny beaded reticule shaped like a pineapple on a chain from her wrist, it could barely hold more than her handkerchief, a tortoiseshell comb, and a few coins. It seemed the only weapon a lady was permitted would be the ivory blades of her fan, a sorry defense at best, and with a sigh she resolved to stay as firmly attached to William's side as he'd requested.

Aided by the well-placed oars and oaths of the two boatmen, their boat nosed its way through the crowd of waiting wherries and skiffs. At the narrow landing-stage, Harriet clambered from the boat herself, in her excitement—and from independent habit—forgetting to wait for William to assist her.

"No bolting, now," said William as he came up behind her, tucking her hand firmly into the crook of his arm. "Stay close, for both our sakes. I've no wish to lose you before we're even properly inside."

They fell into step with the others walking up the lane to the gates. It was, as William had warned her, a remarkably diverse crowd: old and young, breathtakingly beautiful and outlandishly ugly, women who were undeniably aristocrats walking not ten feet away from chambermaids preening in their mistress's castoffs, fine gentlemen and military officers beside barbers' apprentices and dissipated blades.

Yet even in so much laughing, chattering company, she was instantly aware of how she and William seemed set apart. Some of the other revelers tried to be coy or discreet, stealing glances at them over their shoulders or behind their fans, but others gawked outright, pointing and commenting loudly to their friends. William was bound to be recognized. He was young, handsome, titled, and notably rich; he traveled in the fast, fashionable set of the Prince of Wales, and he'd lived most of his adult life in London and in an ostentatiously public way.

But had the duchess's paintings really had so much influence that her own face was known as well? Certainly people appeared to be looking at her every bit as closely as they were regarding William, and self-consciously Harriet touched the largest plume in her headdress, wondering if it had been blown a-kilter while they had ridden in the boat.

"Five minutes at most, from the time we enter," whispered William, giving her hand an extra pat of reassurance. "The jackass *will* bray. I'll wager you a guinea that I am right."

"Hey-ho, Will, what kind of addlepate cove do you take me to be?" she whispered in return. "I say five minutes is three too many. Two minutes, says I, and done it be."

But Harriet forgot wagers and minutes and everything else as soon as they walked through the façade, designed like a grand country manor, and past the gates into the gardens themselves. Dusk was just giving way to darkness, and there, spread before her in the twilight, lay an unimaginably exotic playground of arched pavilions and domed towers, statues on pedestals and paintings on screens, an orchestra on a stage, and everywhere crowds of people in their best summer finery.

Yet what made Harriet gasp aloud with delight and awe were the lights, hundreds and hundreds of tiny lanterns, glimmering and winking in every tree and bush as far into the distance as she could see. Though the tears in her eyes blurred the lights, still she looked, hungrily striving to remember every last detail for always.

More magic, more magic that for all its beauty would never last beyond the summer....

"Ah, Bonnington, here you are at last!" called a gentleman with a hawkish nose and a progression of elaborate curls arranged across his ruddy forehead. "Finally returned to the world of the living, eh? And look what a little prize you have brought with you! Lady Calliope, isn't it?"

He chuckled as he circled around Harriet, inspecting

her greedily from all sides before he came to stand next to her, entirely too close for polite comfort.

Wicked old bird, thought Harriet with disgust. Rich or poor, she'd seen more than enough like him in her time, and deftly she glided away from him and closer to William.

"Aye, I'm the grandest prize in these gardens, sir," she said, snapping her fan open to flutter it before her face. " 'Tis not often that a true goddess like me comes to frolic here among you low mortals."

"She has you there, Snellgrove," drawled William, slipping a possessively reassuring arm around Harriet's waist. "She should make you kneel before her in the dust and kiss her slippers."

Snellgrove's eyes gleamed. "Ha, ha, Bonnington! I'll kiss her slippers, then lift her skirts to worship at her very altar, ha, ha!"

"There's only one worshiper admitted at a time to my temple," answered Harriet, swaying back against William, "and Lord Bonnington is the one who's keeping my Sabbaths now."

" 'Sabbaths,' ha, ha!" Snellgrove licked his lips with unpleasant and unwarranted anticipation. "Where in blazes did you find such a prime little hussy, Bonnington?"

"The Duchess of Harborough deserves the finder's fee," said William in the same slightly bored tone. Idly he pulled aside Harriet's shawl and ran his hand up and down her bare arm, calling the other man's attention to what was *his*. "I spied her in one of Her Grace's paintings, and swept her away before some bastard like you could spoil her."

The duchess's paintings: suddenly Harriet realized

she'd met this vile man's wife, there in Her Grace's studio, and her disgust mushroomed. Oh, she knew that rich gentlemen could blatantly disregard their wives at home, but having Lord Snellgrove drool over her like this was enough to turn a decent woman's stomach.

Not, of course, that she was supposed to be either decent, or entitled to such revulsion. How wretchedly women could be treated in this fine, privileged world, wives and mistresses alike!

"Oh, I'd spoil the little trollop well enough, given the chance." Snellgrove leaned closer, pointedly studying her breasts. "Do you like diamonds, Lady Calliope? Or rubies?"

"She's not taking either from you, Snellgrove," said William, the territorial warning unmistakable in his voice. "We've hardly begun to explore one another, the goddess and I. Besides, I wonder at your desire to wallow in my leavings once again. Or have you found dear Emily so well trained that you'd wish to bid upon another filly that I've ridden first?"

Unconsciously Harriet tensed. Of course William would have other women in his past, beautiful, willing women by the score, by the hundreds. This was how gentlemen spoke of women, carelessly and callously, and why she must be so careful to guard her own heart and feelings with William. Instead of letting herself feel such unreasonable regret, she should be remembering instead poor castoff Emily, doomed now to sell her favors to this hideous Lord Snellgrove. Even more importantly, she must remember that her presence here was all for show, anyway, and all for her tea-shop and her independent future.

"Emily's well enough in her way," said Snellgrove, too fascinated by Harriet to react to William's insults. "You know what a clever little bitch she can be, and tight as a velvet glove, ha, ha! But she's not a goddess like this one, not at all. I say, Bonnington, when you're finished with her—"

"But I'm not," said William easily, "nor do I intend to be for a good long time. Pray excuse us now, Snellgrove, so I can see that the goddess receives her supper as promised. Her appetites, you know, are not to be denied."

"Pay up, Will," whispered Harriet as soon as William steered her away. "You be owing me a guinea."

William nodded at another couple before he looked down at her. "A guinea? For not kicking Snellgrove in the balls like he deserved?"

"Nay, though he did," she said, following his lead to smile at another nodding pair, even though the gentleman was ogling her through his quizzing glass. "Our wager, mind? The jackass brayed in less than two minutes. Less than one, truth to tell, and what a choice one he was, too."

"He is the Marquis of Snellgrove, and his family owns most of Northumberland. He could pepper you with diamonds and rubies, if you wished it."

"Do you think that carries water with me?" she asked indignantly. "A jackass is a jackass, no matter who his dam or sire be."

William laughed. "And you were magnificent with him, pet, making him nibble the carrot direct from your fingers," he said. "But if you've had enough and wish to leave now—"

"Nay, Will, I've only started," she said with a determined nod, "and I do be expecting me supper, and them fireworks, too. But mind you, if you've any more friends such as that one, I'll not promise I'll behave one whit better."

"Don't," he said, shaking his head solemnly. "Because some of them are a great deal worse. Ah, here's our supper box. I hope you find it agreeable, yes?"

How could she not? The box was more like a small stage, framed by a pointed arch that was painted with bright Gothic designs and golden flowers. Along the back of the box hung a large painting on a screen with a life-size scene of some long-ago king and queen sitting grandly on their thrones. The pavilion with the orchestra was close enough for the music to be heard, but not so near that the songs would overwhelm polite conversation, making this one of the choicest boxes in the entire garden. The dining table and chairs faced out toward the trees and walks, offering an unobstructed view of the strollers who would, in turn, have an equally open view of the diners at their meal. Everyone would be on display, exactly as everyone wished—though, of course, in the most genteel and tasteful fashion possible.

"This is rather like sitting in a shop window, isn't it?" asked Harriet as she let one attendant seat her while another filled her glass with sherry. "Fancy being mistook for barley-sugar and ginger nuts, or new ladies' goods for spring, eh?"

"In a way, you rather are," said William, shifting his chair close enough beside hers so he could curl his arm fondly over her shoulders, "exactly as I predicted. I only hope that before the night is done, I'll not have to issue any challenges to protect your honor."

She grinned happily, wondering if he realized the pleasure she took in having him touch her this way, as if he couldn't quite bear to be separated from her for even a moment. Sometimes, though she knew she shouldn't, she even dared to wish it were so.

"You wouldn't risk a duel of honor, no matter what I do," she teased, smoothing the heavy linen napkin across her lap. "I'm only your mistress, mind?"

But to her surprise, he didn't smile in return. "For you, Harriet, I just might," he said, his expression completely serious as he reached for his glass and raised it toward her. "For your sake, I might be tempted to risk far more than I should. To you, dearest pet, and to our success together."

"To success," echoed Harriet softly, and sipped the sweet wine as she searched his eyes for the truth.

It all be play-acting on this tiny stage, me girl, nonsense and stuff and worth no more, empty words to give life to your ruse for the French. He be the righteous fine Earl of Bonnington, not your sweetheart Will, and nothing—nothing—you do or say will ever make him yours. . . .

Not that she'd ever let him know, not even a hint, and when another attendant set her plate on the tablecloth before her, she seized on the supper as a way to forget her confusion.

"What is this, Will?" she asked as she studied the thinnest slice of ham she'd ever encountered, suspending it delicately on the tines of her fork. "Surely it cannot be for eating, not for any mortal hunger?"

"But you are not mortal, dear Calliope," said

William, immediately joining into her game. "I know that nectar and ambrosia are your chosen sustenance there on Mount Olympus, but neither, alas, are offered here in London. Instead I have ordered for you something equally insubstantial yet costly: Vauxhall ham. Isn't that so, Laurence? Hitchborn, you agree, don't you?"

Wide-eyed with feigned wonder, Harriet saw that two other gentlemen with a lady on their arms between them had come to stand at the table. She did know how to play to an audience, though this time with the ham as her subject instead of a basketful of oranges.

"You would treasure this, M'Lord?" Gingerly she held the slice aloft, as if it truly were a rare marvel. She peeked at William beneath it, and was rewarded by the first chuckle from the gathering crowd. "This very Vauxhall ham, M'Lord? So pink, so pale, so whisper-thin, a right royal zephyr among hams?"

"The same," said William, raising his voice and grandly spreading his arms like some practiced Drury Lane favorite. "My fair Calliope, you offer divine inspiration to countless poets. You above all others must be able to see the glory that is Vauxhall ham!"

"Aye, I believe I do." Ah, but she did adore foolish nonsense like this! She rose to her feet, hoisting the dangling ham on the fork before her like a valiant soldier's sword as she raised her voice:

> *Fine gentlemen, attend my cry,*
> *Such splendid ham for you!*
> *So fine it passes needle's eye,*
> *And nigh transparent, too!*

The applause was instant, mingled with good-natured laughter, and with a gracious bow Harriet sank back into her chair, her cheeks pink with excitement.

But while William had led the applause, he wasn't done himself. Gallantly he raised his glass toward Harriet, his other hand over his heart.

> *Prized by this earl,*
> *From Olympus above,*
> *A rapturous pearl,*
> *To be my love.*

This time the applause was tempered with appreciative sighs from the ladies and grunts of envy from the gentlemen as William cradled Harriet's face in his fingers and kissed her, a full, lasting, true lovers' kiss that made her breath quicken and her heart thump with the unfairness of it, and thoroughly banished any further poetry from her head.

"Ah, Will, why'd you go do that?" she whispered afterward, almost sadly. "Weren't the ham enough?"

He didn't answer, and not even his blue eyes revealed the truth she so wished to hear. But his face still hovered close to hers for another endless half-minute, as if they were the only two left alone together in the entire world.

Which, being in the middle of Vauxhall Gardens in June, they most certainly were not.

"Bonnington, that was deuced fine," declared the thin young gentleman in green whom William had called Hitchborn. "Who'd have thought you'd play the poet for us like that, eh? And you, sweet goddess! Such wit combined with such beauty, to be able to mimic some wretched street peddler's cry so perfectly! I cannot tell you how I laughed to hear it!"

But Harriet only smiled politely, and wondered what he'd say if she'd explained why she was so very good at those wretched street peddler's cries.

An attendant appeared with extra chairs and Hitchborn claimed one, pulling it forward to lean his elbows on the table as if he'd been invited, and so, too, did his friend Laurence. The girl didn't wait for a chair, but simply perched on Hitchborn's knee.

"So where did you find such a jewel, Bonnington?" he asked as he beckoned for more port to be brought to the table. "She is the most original creature to be unearthed this season. Don't glare at me so, Poppy; you were unearthed last year, and thus do not count in this reckoning."

William sighed wearily, so wearily that Harriet suspected that much, at least, wasn't for show.

"My Calliope rose full-fledged from the waves on a scallop-shell," he said as he emptied his glass, "just like Venus herself. All I had to do was gather her up from the sands at Brighton. Even a damned dullard like you could have done it, Hitchborn."

The girl clicked her tongue and leaned across the table to Harriet, who'd seen enough of real ladies at Harborough House to realize that this girl wasn't one, no matter how costly her gown and jewels appeared to be. She was as pertly pretty as a porcelain shepherdess, but the rosiness had been painted on her round cheeks and full lips, her gown was cut so low that her breasts threatened to spill free, and the breezy unconcern with which she perched on Hitchborn's knee, swinging her foot in a striped silk slipper against his leg, all betrayed a cheerfully dissolute and precarious existence.

Ah, Harriet, there you be, putting on airs and judging the lass to be common, as if you weren't no better your own self!

"*I* know the truth about you, Calliope," the girl was saying proudly. "*I* know that Lord Bonnington found you having your portrait taken, not on any miserable beach. Oh, and I am Poppy. Suffice to say that I've another name, too, but Poppy will do for me just as Calliope does for you."

"I am most happy to make your acquaintance, Poppy," she replied carefully, for once remembering to fix her speech. Clearly Poppy was the genuine article, Hitchborn's mistress, and Harriet figured if she could convince *her,* then she'd be ready for whatever the French could dish her way. "Do your acquaintance be—oh, blast, that is, I mean is your acquaintance with Mr. Hitchborn of long standing?"

"Lord Hitchborn, you mean," said Poppy as she reached across the table to pluck a strawberry from the top of a custard and drop it into her mouth. "Though he's only a viscount, kept to a pittance by his old bitch of a mama. I haven't the luck you've had, Calliope, finding a lovely man like the earl, who has pots and *pots* of lovely gold, and if you—"

"Sweetheart, listen to me," said William, keeping his voice low so the others couldn't hear. "I must go for a moment. There's a man I must see in regard to our, ah, business."

As explanation, or maybe apology, he showed her a crumpled, cryptic note, half-hidden by the edge of the tablecloth, that one of the attendants had passed to him.

"I will not be long, I promise," he said, pushing back his chair, "and you'll be safe as long as you stay here with the others. Only a few minutes, I promise you, and then I'll return."

"Take care, Will," she said, and he kissed her lightly on the forehead while the others waited expectantly for an explanation.

"As you were, friends," he said with a grin, easing his way around the tangle of chair legs crowded into the supper box. "I'll only be a moment or two. I find I've an urgent meeting with an old friend."

The men guffawed raucously, thumping their palms on the table as if this were the greatest witticism they'd ever heard.

"Have you ever heard such a great pack of fools?" said Poppy with disgust, reaching across the table for another strawberry. "As if none of *them* has ever needs gone to the privy!"

Yet as Harriet craned her neck to watch William go, moving easily through the crowd, she couldn't quite tamp down her anxiety. A great many mishaps could occur in those few moments of his, and as she thought again uneasily of the bloodstained note, she murmured a fervent little prayer for his safe return.

"So *you* are Calliope, are you?" demanded the woman behind her. "And here I'd heard you were such a celebrated beauty."

Harriet turned back toward the table, instantly on her guard. To her regret, Lord Snellgrove had found his way to their supper box, and now stood on the walk before their table with a woman clinging to his arm. The woman was exotically attractive, her complexion burnished gold and her hair glossy black, and her movements had the easy fluidity of a lioness. Like a lioness, too, she was clearly out for blood, even if she hadn't greeted Harriet with that first, swift insult.

"Ha, ha, Lady Calliope!" called Snellgrove as if they were after foxes in the field instead of five feet away. "When Miss Poynton here learned you were in the Gardens, she insisted I fetch her over to you, so she could make your acquaintance. Emily, my honey, might I present Miss Calliope. Miss Calliope, Miss Emily Poynton."

"Miss Poynton," said Harriet with the slightest and frostiest of nods. To think that she'd actually *pitied* this same woman earlier in the evening! "I am honored, ma'am."

"There's a chair, Emily, directly beside Miss Calliope," said Snellgrove, ushering the woman toward William's empty place. "Surely you two lovelies will have much to discuss, yes, ha, ha."

He stepped back as Emily arranged her skirts in the chair, practically licking his lips with anticipation. Obviously he was expecting an out-and-out brawl between the two women, a screeching, bodice-ripping, hair-pulling entertainment. Harriet herself knew plenty of men who loved this sort of show, and she'd heard of brothels where women fought while men wagered, like rat-baiting and cock-fights.

What a pity for Lord Snellgrove that she'd no intention of obliging him.

"So," began Emily, her perfunctory smile not reaching her eyes. "You have not been long with Bonnington, Miss Calliope, have you?"

"We still be—*are*—learning about one another, aye," answered Harriet cautiously. If Emily Poynton wished to act the lioness, then she'd be the wiliest of alley-born tabbies. "There is so much to know about a gentleman as fine as Lord Bonnington."

"Oh, my, yes!" Emily puffed out her cheeks with a small, humorless laugh. "He is *such* a vastly particular gentleman, wishing everything exactly to *his* tastes, regardless of your own."

"Truly?" asked Harriet with a disingenuous smile. "I've always found that my dearest Will—ah, Lord Bonnington—has always put my pleasures first above his."

"Indeed?" Emily's laugh became markedly unpleasant, and Harriet knew she'd drawn blood herself. "You surprise me, Miss Calliope. I know Bonnington has always held the highest reputation for pleasing his ladies, but I myself found him most selfish, except when it came to sharing my favors with his friends."

"Sharing?" repeated Harriet with a gulp, unable to keep from glancing around the table at the other gentlemen.

"Bonnington does love an audience, and to be praised for whatever he does, however paltry those . . . *efforts* may be," said Emily archly, taking a glass of hock from an attendant. "One must suppose it comes of him having been raised as the only boy in a family full of fawning women."

"One does, aye," echoed Harriet faintly, still pondering that sharing and praising. She'd absolutely no reason to believe anything that Emily said, yet the unsettling possibilities—and the images—that she'd planted were difficult to ignore. Harriet knew that William had shared his past with other women, and that she'd no more right to be jealous of them than he would to have challenged former sweethearts of hers—if, of course, there had been any, which there weren't. But to have to sit next to Emily Poynton and imagine her doing unspeakable things with William was nearly beyond bearing.

Oh, she was such a miserable green noddy!

"Such early spoiling does make for a selfish man," continued Emily, glancing at Harriet's wrists as she made sure to catch the light in the rubies of her own bracelets and rings. "I see he is no more generous with you than he was with me. Coral beads strung with gold, la! How *tawdry*! As if he were trading for favors among the American savages! Praise heaven that Lord Snellgrove knows the *value* of what he is receiving, and makes his rewards accordingly."

Protectively Harriet covered the coral beads on her wrist with her hand. William himself had chosen them, saying the color of the beads reminded him of her rosy-gold coloring, and she wouldn't trade the bracelets for a king's ransom of rubies.

And where in blazes was William, anyways?

"Perhaps 'tis not that he is selfish," she said warmly. Her future tea-shop was hovering there on the slippery edge of her conscience, but then she was earning that honestly, not expecting it as a gift owed to her. "Perhaps it is more that I'm not greedy, not like some at this table. Perhaps I am with William for himself, instead of what I can steal away from his pocket."

"Then what you are, Miss Calliope, is a fool," said Emily scornfully as she polished the face of the largest ruby in her ring across her sleeve. "A fool who'll likely die penniless in the gutter for not profiting from her situation."

"I should scarce call Calliope a fool, Emily," ventured Poppy, unexpectedly joining the conversation before Harriet could defend herself. "She's only come among us this spring, and yet everyone in town knows her face on account of the Duchess of Harborough's paintings. Haven't you seen how every man who's walked by has stopped to ogle her? Why, she's nigh as famous as the queen herself, and *that* doesn't come from being a fool."

Emily's mouth pressed into a tight, hard line. "Fah, what good will that bring her, I ask you?"

"She's received at Harborough House," answered Hitchborn with unabashed glee, "and through the front door, too. Which is more than *you* shall ever be, darling Emmy. More than most of us will, for that matter."

Beside him Laurence moaned, clasping his hands together in quavering, beseeching parody. "Oh, to be welcomed into the daring duchess's own sacred studio! To be shown the infamous *Oculus Amorandi*—heaven in this life, Hitchborn, purest heaven!"

The others all laughed, including Harriet, even though she didn't entirely understand his jest, or what the duchess's *Oculus Amorandi* might be, either.

But Emily wasn't laughing, her lovely face mottled with anger as fiery as her rubies. "And where exactly will such an invitation get her, Hitchborn? Through the door and into the duke's bed, then once again into the streets with a fresh dose of the Italian pox?"

Raised eyebrows and nervous titters circled around the table. The Duke of Harborough was a gentleman of impeccable honor and so famously faithful to his wife that none who knew him and his power would have dared speak such a slander, even in jest.

"I say, Emily," warned Snellgrove uneasily. "That's putting it a bit strong."

"Is it?" demanded Emily shrilly. She flung her hand out behind her, pointing toward the large painting on the screen behind them. "That's King Henry and Anne Boleyn, three hundred years ago, and *that's* the last time any titled gentleman wed his whore and raised her to his station, and for what? So that he could chop off her head like a sparrow's when he tired of her?"

Chop off her head: that was what had happened to the bloody doll left on William's doorstep. Here they'd been thinking the warning had meant a French guillotine, and instead it could have been sent by an envious Englishwoman.

Oh, where was *William, so I could tell him, and ease his worries?*

"It's not been three hundred years since the last time it happened," mused Poppy as she nibbled on the tip of another strawberry. "More like two. And recall what become of Emma Hart, that posed for Mr. Romney's pictures."

"Darling Emma," said Hitchborn fondly. "Such a pretty peach, that one! Packed away to Naples as Charles Greville's castoff, and came back as Lady Hamilton, the ambassador's wife. There's nothing so impetuous as a man in rut. Who can guess how high

Bonnington will take our fair Calliope, eh, as besotted as he is?"

But Harriet was too focused on the angry woman beside her to make such idle speculation.

"Are you truly so jealous of me, Miss Poynton?" she asked, more curious than perhaps was wise. "If you wanted Lord Bonnington so badly, then whyever did you let him go?"

An ominous, wordless growl rose up from Emily's throat, and before anyone could stop her, she threw the rest of her hock over the front of Harriet's gown.

And Harriet, jumping to her feet in surprise as the hock shimmered and dripped from the spangles on her gown, had all the answer she wanted.

"Here now, none of that," ordered Hitchborn, seizing Emily by the arm to keep her from lunging at Harriet. "Mind your temper, Emmy, or the guards will come and toss you out of the Gardens altogether. Calliope, pray, don't leave the rest of us because of Emily!"

But Harriet was already wriggling around the chairs and past the others, determined to find William and tell him what she'd learned.

"Let her go, Hitch," advised Poppy sagely. "Most likely she and Bonnington have already arranged to meet, and not about some 'old friend' at the privies, either. What better reason is there to come to Vauxhall, I ask you?"

What better reason, indeed, thought Harriet as she hurried down the path in the direction that William had gone. Yet it seemed that for every reason there must be a score of revelers who shared it, for the Gardens were far more crowded now than when she and William had first arrived. She didn't so much walk as she was swept along in the tide of people, carried forward with them along the walks that led deeper into the Gardens and farther away from the supper boxes.

Dusk had settled into night, and despite the lights in the branches overhead, the shadows had grown darker, deeper around the trees and bushes. The celebrated nightingales had begun to sing, valiantly striving to overrule the orchestra and the off-key bellowing of those patrons well-fortified with sherry, port, or hock.

Vainly Harriet searched for William, craning her neck for a glimpse of his black coat, but the farther she walked, the more confused she became by the twisting, shadowy paths. The crowds had thinned here, too, and from the giggles and sighs and murmurs she realized she'd wandered in among the deepest recesses and mazes meant for lovers.

"Harriet!" came a faint call from the shadows. "Harriet, here!"

"Will?" she called warily. No one else in these gardens seemed to know her proper name, but she wasn't going to take more risks than she had to. Sounds echoed oddly in the maze of bushes, and she couldn't tell from which direction the call had come. "Is that you, Will?"

"Harriet?"

From habit she reached for the knife that she used to carry at the back of her waist, and found nothing but the soft muslin of her gown. Trust, then, was all she'd have.

"Damnation, Harriet, where are you?"

Now that did sound like her Will, and confidently she turned toward the voice.

Until the man's one gloved hand closed over her mouth while the other jerked her backward, off her feet, into the bushes, into the darkness, and away, God help her, far away from William.

9

Where the devil had Harriet gone?

William stopped and swore softly, his gaze sweeping across the paths. Ever since he'd returned to the supper box and discovered she'd gone, he'd been following her at a distance, seeing the plumes in her headdress bobbing in the distance ahead of him as he'd tried to make his way through the crowds to reach her. Several times he'd thought to his despair that he'd lost her, yet she'd reappeared, and when he'd finally come close enough to call her name, she'd vanished again and now—now he hadn't the faintest notion of where she had gone.

Not that he could fathom why she'd left the box in the first place. His friends claimed she'd gone after him, which made no sense, not after he'd told her so specifically to wait and that he'd be returning.

Didn't she realize the danger she could be in? Or had that bitch Emily Poynton been filling her head with such ridiculous tales that she'd decided to flee while she could?

"Harriet?" he called again. "Harriet, where in blazes *are* you?"

"If she was here, mate," growled a man's drunken voice from the shadows, followed by a tipsy female giggle, "then she wouldn't be wanting t'see *you*, would she?"

Oh, yes, that was all he needed now, thought William grimly, to be reminded of his place by some Vauxhall seducer. He heard more scuffling in the bushes to his left, a man's deep grunt as he, at least, reached some sort of animal satisfaction. Shaking his head, Will turned to head back from this path where he most certainly did not belong.

"Damnation, Harriet," he muttered, "if this is what you wanted—"

"Will!"

Swiftly he swung around just as she crashed through the bushes, scattering twigs and leaves and spangles and broken feathers as she threw herself into his arms, nearly knocking him backward.

"Harriet, lass," he began as he hugged her, relief washing over him at an astonishing rate. "Are you unhurt? Are you well? Ah, sweetheart, you cannot know—"

"Not now, Will," she ordered, pushing away from him as she frantically shook her head, wisps of un-done hair waving before her face. "We must go away from this place, now, before he wakes, and comes!"

"Who, Harriet?" he asked, his uneasiness building. "What has happened?"

"I had to do it, Will," she said, her voice wavering, though she bravely did not cry. "I went looking for you, and lost me way, and then I—I had to do the rest, to save me own self. That man—he was asking for it, Will, pawing at me that way, trying to stop my breath, and if I hadn't found that bottle there beneath them bushes, why, I—I—"

The blur of movement caught Will's eye and automatically he turned toward it, just as the man lurched through the bushes, the knife in his hand glinting in the light from the distant lanterns. William twisted sharply, jerking Harriet from the man's path, then swinging his arm up to lift the knife harmlessly to one side. The man grunted, trying to swing around, and deftly William stepped around him and caught the man squarely beneath his chin with his fist. The man's head snapped back with a gasp of pained surprise, and then the rest of him fell backward, too, crashing through the brush before he lay still with his legs and arms sprawled out in the dirt.

"Will, Will, I told you we had to leave!" cried Harriet as she rushed to his side, hugging him tightly around the ribs. "Oh, I am so sorry, causing such mischief as this!"

"You weren't the mischief-maker here, lass." Breathing hard, William knelt beside the unconscious man, and touched his fingers to the side of the man's grizzled throat, fortunately finding the rhythm of his still-beating heart. He was large-boned but thin, his worn, patched clothes falling around his frame loosely to show he'd not always been this way. Everything about him spoke of hard times, and William had no doubt that someone else had paid his shilling admission to the Gardens.

"Is he—is he dead, Will?" asked Harriet fearfully, coming to crouch beside him. The knife the man hadn't been able to use still lay in his uncurled fingers.

"Not this time, no," said William. "Not that the bastard didn't deserve it."

"If only I'd had me own knife, Will—"

"And it's just as well you didn't," he said firmly, flipping open the man's coat to search through his grimy waistcoat pockets. "His was enough. I'd hate to think what could have happened if he'd been able to use it against you. Ah, here we are."

He held out the small coins he'd found in his palm for her to see. "Those are French coins, sweetheart, francs. I wonder how many he earned for following us?"

"Us, Will?" she whispered unhappily, hugging her knees.

"Sweetheart, there aren't many secrets in our comings and goings. Ah, what's this—"

He broke off at the sound of excited voices on the path, hurriedly stuffing the last scrap of paper he'd found unread into his own pocket before a lantern's golden light washed through the branches, catching him still bending over the unconscious man.

"Halloo, there!" called a bear-shouldered guard with the lantern. "Leave that poor fellow be now, and come out so's I can see you. Lively now, lively, and speak your name up proper!"

Slowly William stepped into the light, letting the guard focus all his attention on him and shielding Harriet as best he could behind him. She'd already been through enough without having to be interrogated by some bully with a lantern.

"William Manderville, Earl of Bonnington," he

said, confident that no one in the growing crowd of
curious onlookers would challenge him. This was
more display than he'd bargained for, even for a
night at Vauxhall, and wearily he realized he'd need
to show a bit more bluster and brass to get Harriet
free. "I am glad you are here, guard. You and Mr.
Tyers very nearly had a most grievous tragedy to account for."

"We did, My Lord?" asked the guard, his overbearing authority dwindling before both William's
title and the name of Mr. Tyers, Vauxhall's owner. "A
tragedy?"

"Most certainly," said William firmly. "What a
sorry night it is when ladies can no longer enjoy the
innocent pleasures of these Gardens without fearing
for their safety and virtue! I had always believed that
Mr. Tyers permitted admission only to a genteel custom, and not base-born villains such as this one."

Dramatically he stepped aside, letting the lantern
light shine on the unconscious man, who chose that
moment to groan. As long as that was all he did: the
last thing William wished now was for him to wake
and begin babbling in French, or worse, to start
weaving English slanders about Harriet. The less
William actually had to volunteer about what had
happened and the more the guard assumed, the better, and the sooner they could leave.

Unfortunately, however, he hadn't counted on
Harriet.

"Oh, sir, what that bully-ruffian tried to do to
me!" she exclaimed, stepping forward into the
lantern's light herself. "Dragging me off the path and
into the dark, wanting to have his way with me!"

Once again the bystanders gasped, for Harriet's fragile gown had been just enough torn over her pale skin for titillated outrage. A handsome earl, a groaning body, and now a beautiful woman in torn clothing: what stage in all London could offer more of a show?

"Did he cause you harm, miss?" asked the guard, unable to take his gaze away from Harriet's torn bodice.

"Not—not the worst harm, nay," she said with a brave warble. "But the shock of it was something terrible to me, sir, wicked terrible."

She'd pitched her voice higher, making herself sound even younger, more vulnerable, the only sure indication William had that she, too, was acting for their audience, for Harriet was not by nature vulnerable or fragile, and her strength was one of the things he liked best about her. She simply *had* to be acting now, hadn't she? Inventing the peddler's cry had been quick thinking, he'd grant her that, but this was a rarer gift altogether.

William slipped his arm around her shoulders to comfort her, but also wanting the guard to understand that she was under his protection. Hell, right now she had every man within hearing ready to defend her—at least the ones who weren't panting to rip off the rest of her clothing themselves—when she'd been the one who'd thumped the attacker in the first place.

With a bow, the guard came to stand beside the unconscious man, prodding his ribs with the toe of his boot. "He don't look like a proper guest for the Gardens, not at all. Mayhap he climbed over the walls, or slipped in the back. We try to stop them, My Lord, but it's just like rats with a ship: the cunning ones will always find a way."

"How vastly troublesome for you," said William, inwardly wincing as the man on the ground groaned again. *Don't wake,* he pleaded silently, *don't wake, not yet, don't wake.*

But the guard only shook his head, not offering the man any more assistance than another poke from his boot. "We'll truss him up and send him to the gaol, no mistake. You did us a righteous favor, My Lord, knocking him silly like this before he hurt the lady."

William nodded, graciously accepting credit and thanks, and squeezed Harriet's fingers to warn her not to speak up with the truth.

"We shall leave him to your care now, guard," he said, already beginning to guide Harriet forward. "I see no need in making this poor lady suffer any further. If you or the magistrate wants more information, you may find me at Bonnington House, in Portman Square."

The guard bowed, bobbing up and down like a rooster. "Very good, My Lord, and I thank you again for being so obliging. But one more favor, My Lord: Mr. Tyers will be wanting the lady's name and house, too, to send his own regrets and apologies."

"How vastly kind, sir," said Harriet, her smile radiantly grateful, and William's appreciation of her gifts for such guile rose yet again. "I am Miss Calliope, sir, and since I am such a special friend of Lord Bonnington, I am staying at Bonnington House, too."

Good lass, thought William proudly. She couldn't

have handled that any better if she'd had a month to practice.

"Now, sir," she was continuing, "if you please, sir, I should like to repair to His Lordship's boat where I might ... where I might ..."

Her eyes fluttered shut as she swayed back into William's arms. He prayed she was still play-acting, for she was doing a damned worrisome fine job of swooning against him.

"You will excuse us," he said, his voice clipped with such lordly finality that no questions could possibly be asked of either of them.

Instead, a cordial was fetched to restore the lady, and a bench brought for her to rest upon, and, finally, two stocky attendants came trotting up with a sedan chair to carry her safely to the river and back to the waiting boat. With growing genuine concern, William stayed at her side, and did not leave it even when his friends invited him to return to the supper box for a final round of toasts to the evening.

Yet when he looked at Harriet, curled limply in the sedan chair in her tattered gown, he never gave staying to drink and carouse with his friends another thought. Hitchborn and Laurence and the others weren't merely disappointed. They were out-and-out stunned.

Their Bonnington, composing doggerel poetry in honor of his latest lady-bird? Brawling in the shrubbery to defend her honor? Choosing to play her nursemaid and meekly returning home—and before ten o'clock, too, when the night was still unspeakably young—instead of having one final dram with his friends?

William had brought Harriet to Vauxhall to make

sure the two of them would be linked together in the town's gossip. He could not have invented a more certain—or more intriguing—way to do it.

And the most preposterous part was that he hadn't even meant it. Gingerly he climbed into the boat beside Harriet, not wanting to rock it any more than was necessary. She lay wanly against the pillows, a soft wool coverlet pulled up against the chill from the water, and when he reached for her hand, she didn't return the gentle caress he gave her fingers.

"Harriet, sweetheart," he asked as the boatmen shoved away from shore and the boat glided out into the river's currents. "We've only a little longer to go before we're home."

She sighed, rattling in her chest. "We are on our way at last?"

"At last, pet," he said, tucking the coverlet more closely around her. "There's only the two of us here now, aside from the boatmen."

"Ah." Slowly she opened one eye, followed by the second, cautiously peering about to see for herself. Then, satisfied, she pushed herself up higher on the cushions, linked her fingers behind her head, and grinned. "Hey, ho, Will, didn't I tell you we'd be powerfully fine as partners?"

He stared at her suspiciously. "That was all for show? You are not really wounded or ill?"

"Nay," she scoffed, kicking aside the end of the coverlet to prop her crossed ankles against the side of the boat. "I'm a bit shabby and tattered, aye, but I still be me, Will, and I'm not going to be bettered by that rascal in the bushes."

She could say what she pleased, but a shadow

seemed to remain in her eyes, even by the light of the boat's lantern, that he wasn't as ready to dismiss, or deny.

"You are quite well, pet?"

" 'Course I'm well," she insisted. "I'm no shrinking lady-violet, you know. That's why you asked me to work with you, mind? Because I'm strong and able, aye? But once I saw how things were passing with that guard, how you were being all grand and gallant about that cove what—what was so rough with me, why, I saw what I had to do."

She nodded for emphasis, as if to demonstrate her determination all over again. " 'Tis powerful hard, Will, to talk around and over a cove what's mostly dead and lying still at your feet. I had to *act* weak and pitiful, or that guard would've kept worrying at us like a bitch with a bone."

The fact that she was likely right wasn't convincing him, either. "I'm still of half a mind to send for a physician once we are home."

She wrinkled her nose with disdain. "Better to toss your coin into the river here than give it to some fat Dr. Wigsby on my account. Now come, tell me. I saw you with my own eyes. What was writ on the paper you found in that cove's weskit pocket?"

"Oh, blast." He'd forgotten completely about the paper—that was what came of worrying over another, wasn't it?—and now to his embarrassment he had to search his own pockets to find it, finally holding it up to the lantern to read. The paper had been folded and unfolded so many times that the creases were soft and the words blurred, but if he tried, he could still make them out.

"Well?" she asked, leaning forward with eagerness. "What does it say?"

"My name," he said slowly. "My house, on Portman Square. Another street I do not recognize, Pulhawley Lane."

"I know where it is," she said, "and a wretched sort of street it be, too, near the docks, and full of foreigners and such."

"That would make sense, then," he continued, frowning as he deciphered the smudged words, "for everything's writ in French."

"Everything? Like them French coins, the francs?"

"Everything," he said heavily. "Damnation, Harriet, your name's here, too, or at least Calliope's is."

"The French again. Oh, Will, I am such a fool!" She bowed her head over her lap with shame and disappointment, her disheveled hair falling forward around her cheeks. "And here I'd thought I'd figured it all for me own self, thinking it was no more than Emily Poynton wishing me ill, not the—not the *French*."

He covered her hand with his own, wishing he'd something more comforting to tell her than the truth. "It's better we know than not. I'll send word to Edward as soon as we return home, and he'll have someone go ask a few words of that Frenchman in the gaol as soon as he wakes, as well as to that address in Pulhawley Lane. I doubt we'll learn much—underlings seldom know anything of value—but we might be able to learn a few clues that will help."

"Leastways we know they're linking us together, Will," she said solemnly, "though I don't see why them French would wish us so much harm."

"Because we're wishing *them* harm, lass, by what we're doing," he said dryly. "That's rather part of war, isn't it, and if—what the devil was *that?*"

"Fireworks," she whispered with awe, staring past him back toward Vauxhall as the next set of rockets screamed into the night sky. "Oh, Will, look, *look!*"

Though they had nearly reached the Whitehall Steps, William ordered the boatmen to rest on their oars so he and Harriet could look back and watch the display upstream. With everything else that had befallen them this night, he'd forgotten how much she'd wanted to see the fireworks, how the bright explosions of gunpowder and dye were the first thing she'd mentioned about Vauxhall.

As fireworks went, these shooting up behind the last row of pavilions were perfunctory at best, nothing to compare to the grand displays staged by true fireworks aficionados like the Duke of Richmond, and besides, at this distance, the colored flashes and banshee shrieks of the rockets hadn't nearly the same giddy effect as when viewed from inside Vauxhall's gates. Yet being able to see them reflected in Harriet's shining eyes made the whole gaudy business new again, as if she'd given him back a piece of his own long-lost innocence to match her own.

"Oh, Will, have you ever seen anything so beautiful?" she whispered after one particularly brilliant cascade of pink and white. "Like stars, or raindrops caught in the light, or—or diamonds! Like diamonds tossed on black velvet, Will, exactly like that!"

He opened his mouth to tease her about that—precisely how many diamonds on black velvet had she seen in her life for comparison, anyway?—when he realized she was crying, the tears shining wet and unchecked down her cheeks, reflecting yet again the bright flashes of the fireworks.

"Oh, pet," he said softly. "The fireworks really are quite a beautiful sight, aren't they?"

She snuffled and nodded, and dashed at her tears with the heels of her hands, the way a child would. "It's not just that, Will. It's—it's everything, isn't it?"

"Everything?" he asked cautiously, mystified. "Everything how?"

"Oh, you, and me, and this, and—and *everything!*" She flung her arms out to either side, managing to encompass most of London as well as the two of them in the little boat. "When that villain of a Frenchman snatched me from the path, I was scared worse than I've ever been, Will, ever. It wasn't that he tried to rape me, not like I told them in the Gardens, because he didn't. He didn't bother with hoisting me petticoats or such, nor touch me where he shouldn't, I swear, not at all."

"Then what—"

"I think he wanted to—to kill me, Will," she said with a shuddering sob. "He pulled me back and covered me mouth so I couldn't scream, and then he put his other arm across me throat. He didn't say nothing, just pulled that arm tighter and tighter while I kicked and fought as hard as I could, fighting to keep me own breath and stop being so scared so I could stay alive."

He hated hearing this, imagining her terror when that bastard had dragged her from the path, hated that she'd suffered on his account. He longed to put his arms around her now, to hold her and at least make her feel safe now, but in the narrow boat, the awkward best he could do was take her hands and twine his fingers into hers, and nod to the boatmen to take them the rest of the way to the Steps.

"Ah, Harriet, I am sorry," he said, feeling the woeful inadequacy of words. "I should never have involved you in any of this."

"But I wanted to be there, Will," she said, almost pleading. "I still do, if you'll have use for a noddy like me."

"Of course I've use for you," he said, more sharply than he realized. "Don't you realize how well we work together?"

She sniffed again, her voice breaking as fresh tears streamed down her face. "But that's how it was with me, too. I didn't want to die, not like that, and you were the reason. Aye, Will, *you*. You'd trusted me more'n anyone else ever has, and you made me your partner and your friend, and then here I was, going to get me own self killed and ruin everything, and oh, Will, oh, Will, look at me now, a blubbering, blowsy mess!"

"No, you're not, sweetheart," he said softly. "You're beautiful."

"Oh, aye, with twigs in me hair and holes in me gown, and enough buffle-headed stupidity in me head for an ox," she said forlornly, slipping back into the comforting familarity of her old speech. "How can I believe that from you? It don't be your fault, Will, not really. But you know more grand, beautiful women in London than there's stars in the sky, with every last one of them fair begging to be yours."

"Do you think I care about them, Harriet?" he

said, appalled that this was the best she could think of him. "Especially when I'm here with you?"

She pulled her hands free of his and hugged herself, rocking slightly back and forth in solitary misery.

"All I had to make me different, to stand apart from them other ladies, was that I be clever," she said. "But now, after blundering about and nigh getting me own self killed, I don't even have that."

"Yes, you do," he said firmly. "You're clever and beautiful besides. And as for all those others you seem to be spying around every corner—I don't give a damn about them, lass, and I don't think I ever did. All I want is you, Harriet. All I want is you."

The boat bumped into the landing, and the nearest boatman hooked them close to the Steps.

"Whitehall Steps, My Lord," he announced dutifully, hopping ashore to hold the boat steady for them to follow. "The carriage is waiting for you at the top."

But neither William nor Harriet moved. How could they, with William's words hanging in the air between them?

What devil had made him say such a thing, and to say it now, when Harriet was so unsure of herself?

All he wanted: all he'd ever wanted before this was amusement and variety, another pretty face and a willing body to help pass his nights and days. He'd always made it a rule to be honest with women, never dangling empty pillow-promises for a shared future that he'd never had any intention of keeping.

But Harriet—Harriet was different. And she proved it, too, in the very next moment.

"Please, Will," she said softly, leaning forward so

close that he saw she was crying again as she placed her fingertips across his lips. "You wanted me to trust you, and I have. Don't spoil it now by telling me lies like that one. From you, if you can, I'd wish nothing but the truth."

She clambered from the boat and ran up the stone steps with the coverlet flapping around her shoulders like a cloak, forcing him to trail after her like the low, squirming toad that she'd made him feel to be.

She reached the carriage before him, too, and by the time he joined her, she'd already pressed herself as far into the corner of the seat as she could with her feet tucked beneath her and the coverlet tightly wrapped around her, determinedly staring out the window into the dark street and away from him.

With a sigh of frustration, he settled into the carriage himself, wondering how an evening that had begun pleasantly enough could have disintegrated so woefully, and in such a short time. The unyielding line of her back, the unpinned hair trailing unevenly down over one shoulder, told the entire story. He recognized that unfocused-gaze-out-the-window for the evasion it was, because he frequently employed it himself.

She'd good reason for using it, too. That much William did understand. For no matter how much the Frenchman had hurt her in the Gardens, he himself had wounded her more grievously with a handful of clumsy words, words he'd have given anything to have unsaid, even if, deep down, he wondered if they'd been true.

But how in blazes was he supposed to set things back to rights? Because Harriet *was* different from other women, his usual tactics wouldn't work. She'd shrugged away his first apology as if she hadn't heard it. Coaxing her with compliments was bound to fail, considering that it had been a kind of compliment that had landed him in this pit to begin with. Promising her a new gown or jewel would only offend her more, and as for masterfully taking her into his arms and kissing her until she fair melted into swooning submission—well, no.

And so, since she behaved like no other woman he knew, he took the only logical step left. He'd talk to her as if she were a man.

"I've good news from Edward," he began offhandedly. "That was where I went from the supper box, you know. Edward does like to make matters more complicated than they need be."

She didn't turn, but he could tell she was listening.

"It's the Navy that's made Edward turn everything into a grand spectacle," he continued, "sending that courier to me whilst I'd rather sip my brandy and ogle the doxies, but I suppose his message was worth the trouble."

"What message would that be?" she asked finally, curiosity making her twist about to face him. "And did you mean trouble for him, or for us?"

"Trouble for none of us, I trust." He reached into his coat to find the thick cream card of the duchess's invitation and held it out to Harriet. "Here, read for yourself. It's two notices, really. The first is requesting our attendance at a *ridotto* at Harborough House, later this week."

"A *ridotto?*" Harriet tipped the card to read it by the faint light coming in through the carriage windows; he could see, too, that she'd stopped crying. "What kind of flummery is that?"

He smiled at the skepticism in her voice. "It's a kind of assembly, pet, a gathering with music, food, and drink. You shall be entertained, I assure you. Francesca does these things better than any other lady in London."

"Then we'll go." She traced her finger across the tiny ducal crest embossed into the surface of the card. "Where is the second message?"

"Turn the card over," he said. "That dashing, blotchy hand belongs to Edward himself. You see where he says he'll lay five guineas on me and the *Fancy* for a race on Thursday? That's our sailing day, Harriet, the one the Admiralty's picked for us. We'll make our show at Francesca's event, clear off to where the *Fancy*'s moored downstream the morning after that, and then we're bound for France."

"For France," she echoed, with a hint of the same wonder that she'd shown with the fireworks. "What is this here at the end? 'Be sure'? Does His Grace think we'll turn coward and run before we've fair begun?"

"Hardly," said William. "He's asking me to be sure of you."

Her expression didn't change. "And are you, Will? Even after tonight?"

"Yes," he said, and he was. "You reacted quickly, played your part with great aplomb, jousted with Emily Poynton, and defended yourself when you had to. Your only real error was to leave the others when I'd warned you not to, an error that, I am sure, you shall never repeat again."

"Oh, Will," she said softly, covering her throat with her hand as if to protect herself from the memory as well. "I'll never take that risk again."

But it wasn't until they stood beneath the night-lantern in the entry hall at his house that William could see how the bruises had bloomed on the white skin of her throat, and another, as purple and bulging as a plum, above her left eye.

"Damnation, Harriet, you *are* hurt," he said, appalled. "I'm sending for the physician directly. Strode, have one of the men fetch Dr. Pool."

"And I say 'tis nothing, Will." Skittishly she moved from the light and farther up the curving staircase toward the waiting maid, pulling the coverlet higher to try to mask the bruises. "I'll be well enough in the morning, and without some surgeon poking and bleeding me dry."

William took one step after her, then stopped. This was the moment in their day that he never wanted to come, when she'd go to her bedchamber and he to his own apartments, each of them to sleep chastely alone. Or maybe *she* would sleep. Ever since she'd come to stay beneath his roof, he doubted he'd slept more than a single hour altogether, and after he'd come so close to losing her forever, the parting was even less bearable.

If it had been desire, lust, simply the fascination with a new woman, he would have understood. He'd been coping with trials like that since he'd left boyhood. But this was Harriet, and, like her, this was different.

Far, far different. And all his famous worldly experience regarding the gentler sex didn't seem to be worth a brass farthing.

"You will send your maid to me if you feel in the least unwell?" he said. "You will not be brave and suffer without reason, understand?"

"I won't," she said, stepping up another riser. "Suffer, I mean."

But she was trying too hard to be noble now, that was clear enough to him, her smile wobbling all over the place. It would take next to nothing to make her weep again.

"Well, don't," he said carefully. "You'll be safe here. And I promise the world shall be a more agreeable place with the dawn."

"Aye." She swallowed, so hard he could see the movement along her bruised throat. "Thank'ee, Will, and—and good night."

"Good night, lass, and the sweetest of dreams," he said, though she'd already disappeared from the landing. He doubted she'd come back—why should she?—yet still he lingered, still he waited, letting himself remember exactly how she'd looked half-turned upon the stair.

"I would hazard that this was not the evening you had planned, My Lord?" asked Strode, waiting beside him.

"Indeed," said William, his expression hardening as his thoughts shifted to more urgent matters. "Trouble has found us, Strode. I've a letter to write for His Grace, and it cannot wait a moment longer."

10

I'll be well enough come morning....

That was what Harriet had told William, and what she wanted desperately to believe herself. Yet by the time she'd been washed by her maid and dressed in her night dress, and sat at the dressing table to have her hair brushed dry, Harriet felt as brittle as the twigs that she'd pulled from her clothes, and as ready to snap, too. Through sheer will alone she managed to keep her composure until the maid was done and had gathered up the tray with the untouched tea and buttered bread.

When the other woman had finally closed the bedchamber door after her, Harriet was sitting on the edge of the bed with her hands clasped so tightly in her lap that her knuckles were white. Now that there was no one to watch, she gave herself permission to cry, but the tears, bottled up too deeply inside her, wouldn't come. With a dry sob, she bent her head, and stared at the flame of the candlestick beside her bed.

Flicker and dance, bob and bright, until the measure of the wick was burned to its end, or a quick breath of air cut the flame short—exactly the same way as her life had nearly been snuffed short not six hours before.

If she hadn't turned her head away from the man's arm, if she hadn't kept her windpipe free from being crushed, if she hadn't fought so hard that he'd lost his balance and toppled backward to the ground, if some long-past reveler hadn't tossed his empty bottle into these bushes for her to find . . .

If she'd died without seeing William's smile again, or hearing his laugh one more time, or kissing him, aye, kissing him to feel so gloriously, wickedly alive . . .

If, if, if . . .

She could not sit here alone and watch that flame flicker into darkness. Swiftly, before it happened, she snatched her dressing gown from the bench at the end of her bed, threw open the door, and ran down the hall, away from her chambers and the dying flame and toward Edward's apartments, and to life.

"Are you there, Will?" she called frantically, thumping on the door. "Will? *Will?*"

Desperation made her impatient, unable to wait for a reply, and when she found the latch unlocked, she shoved the door open herself.

"Harriet, lass, what is wrong?" Clearly he had risen from his writing table as soon as he'd heard her at the door, the chair pushed back and the pen lying across the paper where he'd left them, and he'd come striding across the room to meet her, his long blue silk dressing gown billowing out around him. "Harriet, are you all right?"

"Aye," she lied, her hand still gripping the door-knob, then shook her head. "Nay. Oh, Will, I do not *know!*"

"It must be one or the other, pet," he reasoned, his smile engagingly lopsided. "You've only the choice of two."

He held his arms out to her, the sleeves sliding back over his forearms as he waited for her to come and claim the solace and comfort he was offering. He hadn't bothered to tie the dressing gown closed, and beneath it all he wore was his breeches, the brilliant blue silk framing the symmetrical pattern of dark, curling hair on his chest tapering down to his low-slung waistband. She had guessed he'd be leanly muscled, but to see so boldly for herself made her feel, well, *odd:* not shy, not exactly, but with a definite sense that if she ventured too closely to that blue silk and tanned male skin, she'd be playing with hot coals, and bound to be burned.

"I—I could not sleep," she stammered, forcing herself to look back to his face. "I am not accustomed to being alone, Will, nor to having that great large chamber all to my own self, especially tonight."

He swept his arm toward his bed, the silk sleeve fluttering to emphasize the gesture like a pantomime conjurer's. "Then sleep here, and I shall give you all the companionship you need."

She stole a quick glance at the bed, and flushed. It was the largest bedstead she'd ever seen, too large to fit into most ordinary parlors: tall and heavy and extravagantly old-fashioned, with carved mahogany posts and headboard, swoops of plush burgundy curtains, dark blue swags with bullion fringes and tassels. If the bed in her room was genteelly virginal, painted white and delicate gold, then his here was overwhelmingly male, and a showy, confident male at that. The coverlet had been turned back by a servant, but the sheets and pillows were still smooth, untouched. Yet no nightshirt had been laid out for him, and the possibility that perhaps he didn't bother with one flitted sinfully through her imagination.

"I cannot sleep here, Will," she said, both tempted and scandalized. "*We* cannot."

"Of course you can," he said easily. "Consider and heed my exquisite choice of words, Harriet. I asked you to *sleep* here, no more. I offer you not my person, but my bed, and my conversation, which will, I am told, most assuredly send you to deepest slumbers."

He retreated to the desk, poured her a tumbler full of brandy from a bottle there, and brought it to her along with the one he'd been drinking from.

"Brandy," he said as he handed the glass to her. "Smuggled, of course. Perhaps we'll bring more back with us, yes? Drink up, now. It will help you sleep as well as fortify you most wonderfully."

"I don't want to ask what I'll need fortifying *for,*" she said, sipping the rich liquor, feeling it slide down her throat and settle in her stomach with a radiating warmth. "Or you, Will. Do you be requiring fortifying, too?"

"Always, sweetheart," he said, raising his tumbler toward her in salute before he finished the contents in a single long swallow. "On general principle."

His smile faded, and he reached out to brush the backs of his fingers over her cheek. "Tonight, Harriet, you should choose whatever gives you peace. I would give the world to undo what happened to you earlier, but since I cannot, I'll be your Cerberus instead, and keep the demons and the shadows at bay. I owe you that much, Miss Treene."

Oh, that was nearly enough to make those stubborn tears flow again, and swiftly she looked down, away from him, blinking fast to make them go away. She could trust him, or she could choose the inconstant comfort of that single, lonely candle and her own crushing fears.

Trust, and William, and no real choice at all for her to make this night.

She drank the rest of brandy in a swift, burning swallow, and thrust the empty tumbler back into his fingers without meeting his gaze. Without pausing to reconsider, she flung back the sheet and climbed quickly into the big bed, as if moving swiftly would somehow make it less improper.

The featherbed sighed and gave beneath her, soft as swansdown as she settled against the pillow-biers and pulled the coverlet high beneath her arms. The linens carried his scent, wrapping around her like an invisible, intangible embrace from him, making her feel peculiarly secure. Not long ago, that much closeness would have made her wary and uneasy, but now she realized she welcomed it. Already she could feel the brandy's effect, the tension and fear beginning to slip from her muscles, and with a small sigh of gathering well-being she finally looked back at William.

"I shared a bedstead with my sister until she wed," she said, almost apologetically. "I've never been accustomed to sleeping alone since."

"Which is why, I suppose, that you cling to that

side as if it were a veritable cliff," he said, coming to sit on the far—very far from her—side of the bed, the rope springs creaking beneath his weight. "You miss her, sweetheart, don't you?"

"Aye." She stared up at the pleated canopy of the great bed, remembering when she and Bett had been little girls together, giggling and sharing secrets in the dark. Those had been the happy times she wished to remember, not the sharp-tempered parting that she couldn't forget. "We've never been apart this long, Bett and me, not since I was born. Though likely she's happier now with just Tom and the baby, without me bumbling about making trouble in the middle."

"I'd wager you bumbled about most cunningly," he said softly.

"With a butcher knife in one hand and a rolling pin in the other, and my clothes all covered with flour and grease: most cunning, aye." She smiled, remembering herself exactly that way in the pie-shop's kitchen. "But what Bett would say to see me here! When I left, I was bound to pose for Her Grace's pictures and nothing more, and look at me now: wearing fine gowns from Madame Deauville, sitting in a supper box at Vauxhall, and invited to a ridotto at Harborough House!"

"And lying snug in the bed of the evil old Earl of Bonnington," he said idly, swinging his bare feet up onto the bed as he looked at her. "What would she say to that?"

"*I* would say that you best keep outside the bedclothes," she warned, "where you belong."

"Ah, Harriet," he sighed dramatically, "I'd thought, as friends, we trusted each other more than that."

"As partners, aye, but lying here like this puts me in a very doubtful place for trust." She sighed, still too troubled for their usual bantering. "Bett wouldn't understand any of this, nor would I fault her. I don't understand it entirely myself."

He smiled wryly. "Nor do I, pet. Which is, I suppose, the reason why we get on so vastly well together."

"Don't be saying such, Will," she said wistfully. "I know I shouldn't have called you a liar before, but it was hurtful, hearing you say things you don't mean as truth."

"But what if I do?" he asked, his expression unexpectedly moody. "What if I—"

"Don't," she pleaded. "Please, Will. I cannot bear it tonight. Speak of something else. Anything."

"Anything." How the devil was he supposed to speak to her of anything when she refused to believe everything he said? It wasn't as if he knew exactly what was happening here between them, either, because he didn't—he wasn't trying to play the lord and master, not with Harriet—but they'd never sort it out if she wouldn't listen, especially not when they were in a situation that seemed tailor-made for such conversation.

He looked at her now, lying there on his pillows with her hair tumbled charmingly around her shoulders and over the pale yellow ruffles of her dressing gown. Though she'd described his bed as a very doubtful place for her to be, to him it seemed absolutely and most comfortably right. The only part that struck him as inappropriate was that he wasn't there under the covers beside her to comfort her in the best possible way he knew how, which would have been very good indeed for them both.

But here they were instead, he thought glumly: he who was almost never at a loss for words, beside the one woman he'd discovered who was his match in wit and loquacity, and both of them struck dumb as posts.

"Anything?" he said again, as if that word among all others could magically unlock the silence that had closed down around them.

"Anything, Will," she said softly, shifting to her side with her head propped on her elbow, too, unconsciously mirroring him. "You decide. And if you don't, I'll need to ask you about certain things Emily Poynton told me about you."

"Emily spoke to you of me?" he repeated, blatantly stalling while he adjusted to such a hideous fact. Emily telling tales about him to Harriet: ah, what a churning snaky-black stew of treachery *this* could prove to be! "I didn't think I'd left you alone long enough for you to become such, ah, confidants."

"She wasn't interested in confiding in me so much as painting you as dark as she could," she said. "Not that I believed it."

"Loyal lass," he said, and he meant it with all his heart. Why in blazes hadn't he begun speaking of roses, or turtle-doves, or even slate tiles for roofing, when he'd had the chance, and spared himself from this?

"Mayhap." She shrugged with a carelessness that was not reassuring. "She said you was selfish, for one, which I know is wrong, and said you liked to—to do certain practices with her that were not quite nice, not for a gentleman."

He gulped. Jesus, what *had* Emily said? In the early days with Emily, in the first hot flush of lust, they'd exhibited their attraction with a louche lack of discretion that hadn't exactly done either of them proud. In particular there had been one long, drunken fortnight last summer at Hitchborn's house in Devon, when a party of his friends and their women had performed acts, with each other and in diverse combinations, that Harriet would decidedly judge as "not quite nice," and, sober now, he'd have to agree with her.

"When gentlemen amuse themselves," he said cautiously, feeling as if he were treading barefoot on shards of glass, "they will, on occasion, behave in ways that may not, ah, appear to the world in the most honorable light."

"Oh, aye, isn't *that* the truth!" she said, wrinkling her nose. "If we common folk behaved as wickedly as you nobles, why, we'd be locked away in gaol, or at least tossed from our parishes. The talk I heard in the studio at Harborough House, when those grand ladies treated me as deaf and mute, and spoke so free before me—lah, such tales I heard fair singed my ears!"

"I can well imagine," he murmured, and of course, from first-hand practice and experience, he could. "My poor sweet innocent!"

" 'Tis a rare thing to be any sort of innocent for long at Harborough House, to be sure." Self-consciously she frowned down at the coverlet, poking little valleys into the plush with her finger. "But there was some things Emily said, Will, that I've never heard from you myself. Some things I wished to know—nay, that I *should* know, being your friend, like you say—if you'd but tell me."

For the first time in his life since he'd come to London, William wished heartily that he'd led only the bland, blameless past of a country curate. No sins, no lurid secrets, no parade of past mistresses and peccadilloes to confess now.

But he'd be honest, no matter what it cost him. He wouldn't lie, not to Harriet.

"What sorts of things, pet?" he asked, as lightly as he could. "What state secrets do you wish me to divulge?"

She smiled shyly. "Not state secrets, Will. Manderville ones. Emily spoke of your family, your sisters and your mother, and made me realize you'd said next to nothing of them to me. You know all of me and Bett and the pie-shop. If I am your friend, then I wish to know such of you, too. Who your sisters are, and if you had a dog when you were a lad, and what special mischiefs you did to grieve your mama. Those kinds of little things, Will, the secrets that friends share to bind them tighter together."

"Ah, *those* kinds of things!" He laughed with relief, and flopped down on his back on the bed, linking his fingers together on his chest. "No one is interested in *those* kinds of things about a gentleman, sweetheart. Certainly Emily never was, despite what she might have told you."

"Don't laugh at me, Will!" she said indignantly, now jabbing her finger at his arm instead of the coverlet. "I, for one, am powerfully interested!"

"Then you truly do wish me to keep my promise to talk you to sleep?" he said, still laughing as he put his other hand over his arm to shield it from her. "Is that it? For surely there will be no better way than to hear a recitation of my favorite nursery puddings."

"Go on, you great giddy cove, tell me!" she demanded, though now she was laughing along with him. "Tell me all!"

He loved to look up and see her laughing over him like this, her cheeks flushing and her eyes gleefully bright as her hair fell about them like a curtain to tickle his chest. For a fleeting second, he considered reaching up to pull her face down to his and kiss her on her merry, laughing mouth.

Then she curled her hair behind her ear, pushing it back and away from her face, and as she did the candlelight found the ugly bruises on her forehead and around her throat, and his laughter died as he remembered how close he'd come to losing her forever.

"Go *on*, Will," she said, unaware of his thoughts. "Tell me everything."

"Oh, lass, there's not so much that's worth the telling," he said more quietly, though his smile lingered. "My boyhood was tediously ordinary."

"Hey, ho, how tediously ordinary and vastly humdrum," she teased, neatly imitating his accent. "For a poor boy-earl to suffer so!"

"I wasn't the earl when I was a boy," he said. "Father was. I was Viscount Carew, because I was the only son. I didn't become the Earl of Bonnington until Father died, when I was thirteen, and I inherited his title then."

"I was sixteen when my own Fa died," she said. "He fell down the back stairs and broke his leg, and when it turned putrid, the poison in his blood killed him. What killed yours?"

"Apoplexy," said William evenly. "I was at school when it happened. Bluff and hearty he was at Michaelmas, taking me sailing on the bay same as always, then next I see of him he's cold and very dead in his coffin in the drawing room, where they'd kept him until I came home. It was the stench I recall the most, and everyone trying so bloody hard to be noble and ignore it. I couldn't. I vomited, there on the drawing room floor before the fireplace, and humiliated myself so thoroughly I was convinced I was meant to die, too."

"Poor young Will," she said softly, crawling closer to him on the bed to curl her fingers into his. "How dreadful hard for you! Everyone expecting you to be behaving solemn and grave like a full-grown proper earl should be, and you only a grieving little lad, missing his own father wicked fierce. How could you want to take his place like that?"

"Yes," he said, the single word coming out wooden and hollow, even to his own ears. "Yes."

He'd never told anyone else that part about the smell of his father's body making him ill, not even his mother. He'd let everyone believe it had been the meal he'd eaten at the coaching-inn that morning that had caused him to retch.

"How sad, how wicked sad," she murmured, turning her fingers more closely into his, warm and soft. "Though my own fa suffered terrible at the end, at least we'd all the time to make proper good-byes before he died, and have him forgive us all our little sins. But not you, still a young lad, when such matters even more. Oh, dear, sweet Will, it wasn't your fault, you know. Your father would have understood, I am sure of it, just as I am sure he must have loved you as his only son."

William didn't answer, though he knew he should. He couldn't. Here he'd been the one who should be comforting her, yet she'd somehow turned everything which way around, making him cling to her hand like a drowning man.

How had she known, he wondered, how had his dear humble orange-seller guessed what none of his noble aunts and uncles and sisters and even his own mother ever had? Though the shame had not been so very shameful, not compared to the later ones that crowded into William's life, it had loomed enormously in his conscience as the first time he'd disappointed his father without hope of being forgiven.

Until Harriet had done it for him.

"But there must have been happy times, too, Will, aye?" she asked, sensing how much her last question had unsettled him. "Living in the country like you did?"

"As I still do, when I'm not in London." He sighed, determinedly turning his thoughts to safer topics. "Charlesfield—that's the name of my family's house—lies not far from Hastings, with our land running along the Sussex coast. It's not an elegant place, not like this house."

"None of your grandmam's sugar-money, then?" she teased.

"Not at all," he said, smiling. "I fear that Charlesfield's shabbiness is what drove her to have this house built, a sort of compensation. Charlesfield's old and rambling, with each new earl patching on a new porch or parlor, but never quite figuring out a way to make the roof stop from leaking in the front hall when the wind blows hard from the east. But when it did rain, the house was a splendid place for playing hide-and-seek with my sisters, with so many rabbity little cupboards and stairways."

Harriet settled back cozily onto the pillows, smiling with contented anticipation. "How many sisters do you have? What are their names?"

"Five," he said, amused that she'd find any of this interesting, but also oddly pleased that she did. "Three older—Perditia, Lavinia, and Diana—and two younger—Georgianna and Allegra. You can see why I was the only young cockerel in a house full of hens. All but Allegra are married now, giving me vast crowds of nieces and nephews to dote upon. Allegra is still the baby, only nineteen, but old enough that Mother frets that she's grown far too wild living at Charlesfield to ever find a husband here in London. You would like Allegra the best, I think."

Now what devil had made him say that? Allegra and Harriet would never meet, let alone like one another, because he could never introduce his youngest sister, Lady Allegra Manderville, to his common-bred mistress. Mother would have his head if he even suggested such a scandalous notion.

Yet when he looked at Harriet there beside him, drowsy and tousled and becoming more dear to him with each day, he found himself imagining her at Charlesfield, walking along the chalky pale cliffs with him, or fishing for eels in a skiff in the marshes, or climbing up into the octagonal tower over the chapel to watch the stars slide in and out of the mists. And if they were wed, the way that Edward had wed the thoroughly unsuitable Francesca, then not even his mother could object. . . .

Damnation, what was he thinking?

"The duchess told me you and the duke were a pair of wild young pups in those days," Harriet was saying, fortunately innocent of his thoughts. "She said no one would've guessed you were lordlings, not from what the duke's told her."

"Oh, we *were* wild, and always filthy," he agreed, "covered with sand and leaves and burrs and who knows whatever else we'd blundered into. The Ramsdens lived at Winterworth, directly beside Charlesfield, though Winterworth was far the grander of the two."

"On account of them being dukes," she said, clearly as enthralled as if he'd begun with "once upon a time." "And you being earls. They would have the grander house, Will."

"But Ned preferred Charlesfield, no question," he said. "He almost lived with us. We would skip out from our tutors to build forts in trees and hide in the marsh-reeds and sail in the river and the bay. You couldn't find two happier boys in all England, at least as long as it lasted."

"Because your father died?"

"That was part of it for me," he said, his smile fading, "but later. First, on Ned's tenth birthday, his father shipped him off to the Navy, and he never did come back to Sussex. Ned was the fourth son, you know, and of no conceivable use to his evil old bastard of a father."

"His own father did that?" asked Harriet, indignantly. "A duke treating his own son like he was some low, drunken sweep? How wicked cruel!"

William nodded. "That it was. Though it's all turned out well enough for Ned, hasn't it? He outlived his brothers, inherited the title, and married Francesca. He became a great war hero with a chest covered with medals and ribbons for his valor, next only to Admiral Lord Nelson himself. And as for me—I'm collecting all those trophy-hearts, remember?"

He sighed ruefully as he stared up at the canopy. It wasn't that he was envious of Edward's life—Ned's motherless boyhood had been a horror, ruled by a cruel father and bullying older brothers, and all those medals he wore had come at the cost of a great deal of pain, anguish, and close brushes with gory death—but still William couldn't help but wonder how differently his own existence might have turned out if he'd faced the same tests, too.

Hell, raking over these ancient coals for Harriet was making him doubt himself all over again, and for what? Father had been the only one who'd challenged him to better things. But once he had died, William had stopped trying at school, for there hadn't seemed to be much point. He was already rich and titled, and Mother and the girls would worship him regardless. He was witty and charming, with more friends than he could recall, and pretty girls and women adored him. He had everything life could offer—except, he'd finally discovered, a good reason for living it.

That was why he'd begun the voyages to France for the Admiralty, following distantly in Edward's exalted footsteps, but hoping that he'd find some of Edward's purpose and satisfaction as well. He had, too, or at least he had until he'd brought Harriet into his game. No, those bruises on her throat were reminder enough that it wasn't really a game, but the same kind of sudden, ruthless danger that had left those three Frenchmen dead in the sand in Abbeville.

Even knowing that it had been all Jenny Colton's fault didn't ease his conscience, not a bit. She'd been his responsibilty, too, hadn't she? But when he'd rebuffed Jenny's advances in the *Fancy*'s cabin, he'd no idea that out of spite she'd turn to a French soldier she'd found in some Abbeville tavern, or that she'd babble enough of William's plans to her new lover to make herself feel important. No wonder William, Jenny, and the men from the *Fancy*'s boat had nearly been captured. The real marvel was that they'd managed to escape the three soldiers waiting to ambush them there on the north beach outside of town, let alone not been killed themselves.

Responsibility, hell. If William had any sense of honor now, he'd insist that Harriet remain here in England while he sailed on to Finisterre himself. But since he didn't—and since she was too stubborn to behave like an honorable woman, anyway—he'd take her with him as they'd planned, and be prepared to risk his own life to save hers.

Which was, now that he thought of it, perhaps even more uncharacteristically noble than insisting she stay behind.

She was nearly asleep now, soft and relaxed as a kitten nestled on the bed beside him, her eyes so heavy-lidded he wondered that she could keep them open at all. He smiled at her fondly, curling a strand of her hair around his finger. To his surprise, she dragged herself back to wakefulness long enough to smile sleepily in return.

"I warned you, pet," he said softly. "Didn't I say I'd turn morose and tedious, and send you straightaway to sleep?"

"You're far too hard upon yourself, Will Manderville," she said. "If you don't stop, I'll tell everyone that I fell asleep in your bed from boredom."

He laughed. "No one would believe you, lass."

Actually, what no one would believe was that a woman as enticingly lovely as Harriet was lying here in his bed, wearing only a filmy ruffled night dress and that he, that infamous old seducer the Earl of Bonnington, was by choice planning to sleep alone in his dressing room and leave her here in his bed.

And all because she trusted him, and for this once in his life, he didn't want to ruin it.

"Likely they wouldn't." She reached out and traced her finger along his jaw. "What they should believe, Will, is that you are a far better man than any of them knows. Not a fine gentleman, mind, though you're that, too, but a good *man*."

"Am I?" he asked, trying desperately to slip back into their old familiar teasing. No woman had ever told him that. Good, yes, in many ways and in many positions, but never simply at being a man. A good man: how could such humble words make him feel as if he were glowing from inside?

"Aye," she said, her yawn extravagant as her eyes inexorably slipped closed. "Else I'd never have taken you for a partner. Good night, me own Will."

"Good night," he whispered, though he doubted she heard, "my own dear Harriet."

His own dear Harriet, far different from any other woman he'd called either *his* or *dear*. In such a short span of time, she'd challenged and changed his perception of what that woman should be.

No, she was changing more than that, and he shook his head as he drew the coverlet higher over her shoulder.

She was changing him.

The news for Robitaille was not good.

Word had come from Paris this morning of more changes in the government, another Director forced out by the restlessness of the newly elected Councils, another fresh set of names and histories for Robitaille to learn and more pockets to fill with bribes if he wished to keep his own position. Defeat after defeat was rolling over the army on every front, making the skittish citizens in Abbeville even more uneasy than usual. Farmers complained the spring rains had been too brief for their crops, and the inflated prices in the market had grown higher still.

But the worst news of all had arrived in the packet of English newspapers brought to Robitaille's offices this morning. Ah, Mother of Jesus, how he'd come to hate those English papers, as much for their tiny cramped type and tortuous words as for the unwelcome messages they brought. Impatiently he had flipped past the descriptions of battles that the English had won, ignoring the shrill tales of exaggerated heroics in the name of the mad English king, to the pages dedicated to the activities and amusements of the people of fashion.

At once his eyes had picked out Lord Bonnington's name, there in the middle of a description of a frivolous evening with his mistress and friends at a London pleasure-garden. But even as Robitaille hissed with contempt at such vain and useless pursuits, the bile of disappointment rose in his throat.

The mistress had been attacked, her doubtful virtue in peril and barely saved by the efforts of Bonnington himself. The wounded villain was taken to gaol to await trial where, alas, he was attacked and beaten by other prisoners as a presumed French spy, and died of his wounds. No clues to the dead man's family or friends, nay, even to his name, were found upon his person, and while he could not be proven to be a spy, he most assuredly was an indigent Jacobin, a disturber of the London peace, and a threat to the decency of all Englishwomen.

While Bonnington and his whore lived, and laughed, and danced merrily upon the grave of another loyal citizen of France.

Furiously Robitaille swore, smacking his open palm against the paper in disgust and frustration. Germain had been one of his best men, efficient and without sentiment when it came to women, and yet he had failed with Bonnington's whore. Robitaille's only solace was that Germain had paid for that failure with his own life, and that he'd been wise enough not to carry any papers to link him inconveniently to Abbeville, or to Robitaille himself.

But he could not afford to send anyone else to

England. Already there were questions being asked
and notice taken; the Directory was not so forgiving
in such matters as the *ancien régime* had been. While
he knew that to avenge his son's death would be a
triumph for France as well, others in the Council
would not agree.

No. The one hope that Robitaille clung to now
was that Bonnington would return to Abbeville, and
bring the whore with him. He had come before, and
if justice and vengeance were to be served in his
son's name, the English lord *must* come to him.

And this time, Robitaille would rely only on himself.

11

"*Harriet, cara mia,* you have come!" cried the duchess, clapping her hands with delight as she greeted them in the antechamber at the top of Harborough House's stairway. She was dressed in dark red silk embroidered with gold and silver thread fit for a sultan's favorite wife, with a yellow striped turban on her head, green slippers with curled-up toes on her feet, and the famous Ramsden family pearls wrapped around her throat and wrists. "Oh, I was so vastly afraid that you and Bonnington would not!"

" 'Course we came, Your Grace," said Harriet as she rose from her perfectly executed curtsey, her white muslin skirts drifting around her legs and the white plume in her hair nodding gracefully. William had helped her improve her sweep and balance so she'd curtsey like a lady, not plump down like a clumsy goose of a costardmonger, and she was justly proud of the results. She and William had worked on a great many improving lessons these last days together, though most of them involved pistols, knives, and gunpowder, as well as a few more dangerous ones that centered upon kissing—none of which she could reasonably display here tonight at the Duchess of Harborough's *ridotto*. "We'd never miss an invitation from you, Your Grace."

"Wouldn't you?" The duchess smiled knowingly as she held both of Harriet's hands in her own. "Ever since you took flight to Bonnington's house, the world has seen precious little of you both. At White's I hear there was speculation that Bonnington had expired completely. For him to be in so little evidence, they judged him at least to be at death's very door. The change you have wrought in him has been *meraviglioso miràcolo*—a most marvelous miracle, yes?"

"Nay, I do not believe it so," said Harriet, uneasy with being credited with any such saintly miracles. True, she had treasured these last few days she'd spent in William's company, time when they'd laughed and teased and sung silly songs together as well as practiced loading and firing pistols, but she'd never forgotten how fleeting—and bittersweet—this time together must be.

And though they kissed, they didn't do anything further. It wasn't because they didn't *want* to—Lord knows they both did, in spades—but because they wanted to stay partners, as they were. Didn't the duchess realize that as well? "Will's still Will. I cannot change that, nor him either."

"When our Bonnington has become your Will, then things have changed, *cara*, and much for the better for you both. Isn't that so, Bonnington?" The duchess laughed fondly, and held her hand out to William as he joined Harriet in the line of arriving guests. "Aren't you the better for knowing our darling Harriet?"

"Vastly improved, Francesca," he declared, gallantly kissing the back of her hand. "In every conceivable fashion, I would say. Why, I was a virtual baboon before I met Miss Calliope, a constant shame to my family on account of how I dragged my knuckles upon the floor before me when I attended the belles inside the ropes at Almack's."

"Go *on!*" scoffed Harriet, narrowing her eyes at him as she placed her hand upon his chest and gave him a shove for good measure. "It wasn't Almack's at all. It was at Newmarket, there at Rowley Mile for all the world to see, when *you* went hopping by like some great ape upon your hands, to scatter the ponies and terrify the ladies. Oh, Will, it was a most fearsome sight!"

William sighed mightily, and shook his head with resignation, as if every other guest within hearing wasn't standing with their mouths open in wide-eyed astonishment, clinging to every outrageous word.

"You see how it is, Francesca," he said. "My Calliope has saved me. Saved me, quite."

"*Bène*," said the duchess merrily, tipping her head to one side. "Indeed, I do see how it is. Along with you now, Bonnington. If you decide to turn your nose up at Signor Ricadelleo's singing, then you may follow the other Philistines to the card and faro tables in the Red Room. And pray, Bonnington, do look for my husband, for he wishes a word with you. Now, Harriet, *per favore*."

With William dispensed, the duchess warmly embraced Harriet, forcing the others in line behind her on the stairs to wait another moment longer to be greeted and pass into the next rooms, and the rest of the gathering.

"We must speak further, you and I," whispered Her Grace, her hoop earring bobbing against Harriet's cheek. "I've something most important to tell you. I must play the hostess for now, but I shall find you when I have a moment, and we'll slip away for a *tête-à-tête*, yes?"

"If you wish, Your Grace," murmured Harriet uncertainly. She liked the duchess, and had missed their conversations in the studio once she'd left Harborough House, but there were also plenty of times when she didn't entirely understand what the other woman was saying or doing on account of her being foreign, and this was one of them. "Whenever you please."

"Then be forewarned that I shall hunt you down." Swiftly she kissed Harriet on the cheek before they stepped apart. "I'm sure you saw how I'd placed the first picture I made of you back downstairs, in your honor, for it's still one of my favorites. But if you can find your way upstairs to the studio later, look for the one of Calliope that I've just finished, still upon my easel."

Harriet nodded, and moved aside, and the duchess turned her attention and smile to greet the next guests in line.

"Do you understand what has just occurred, pet?" asked William, his blue eyes crinkling with amusement as he tucked her hand into the crook of his elbow to lead her along. "I do not believe you do, else you would have fallen at my feet in an awestruck swoon."

"Then I must not," she said, holding onto his arm

more tightly for reassurance. He was leading her through the drawing room toward the music room, already crowded with beautifully dressed ladies and elegant, confident gentlemen, and yet she couldn't help wondering which among them might be French, or wish to do her harm the way the man at Vauxhall had. Her heart was racing and her hands inside her long gloves were so damp that she wondered she hadn't soaked the white kid through from nervousness. "Oh, Will, I do not belong here!"

"Yes, you do," he said firmly, covering her hand with his. "And that is exactly what I meant. What Francesca just did for you is paramount to being dipped in gold, or struck by lightning, or made visible to those who were blind, or otherwise anointed by some all-important deity."

She glanced at him sideways, skeptical. "You're daft, Will."

"No more so than the rest of this infernally foolish society," he said cheerfully. "By inviting you to come here with me, Francesca acknowledged your existence, a rare feat that Emily Poynton and her ilk will never achieve. Then Francesca hung your portrait in a place of honor, embraced you as a dear friend at the top of the stairs where no one could miss it, and kissed you on the cheek like she would a sister. You have been blessed, dearest Harriet, whether you wished it or not, and you will now be received with me at any house in Britain short of the palace."

Harriet remembered how envious Hitchborn and Poppy and the others had been of her connection to the duchess, and how it had, at the time, struck her as odd. It still did.

"But I do not understand, Will," she asked, frowning and perplexed. "Why should Her Grace grant me such favor, when all I did was sit for her to paint?"

He hesitated for a moment, his cheerfulness losing some of its sparkle as he considered.

"Because you were your own sweet, clever self when you did it," he said finally, just late enough that Harriet was convinced it wasn't the first reason, or the one that mattered. "Just like Francesca herself, you have never pretended to be other than what you are, and she admires you enormously for it. As, my pet, do I."

But before she could reply, a plump older lady in puce-colored satin that Harriet recognized as Lady Swithin swooped down upon them to prove the truth of what William had explained about Francesca's "anointing."

"Lord Bonnington, Miss Calliope, good evening! My dear, you have come *precisely* in time to save us!" she exclaimed, vigorously fanning herself as if Harriet's salvation had come only in the nick of time. "Whilst we wait for Signor Ricadelleo to grace us with his glorious gifts of song, we have asked all the young ladies present to perform for us."

"Perform, My Lady?" repeated Harriet doubtfully, thinking again of how few of the skills she'd been practicing with William would qualify.

"Yes, yes, *yes!*" cried Lady Swithin enthusiastically as she herded them into the music room. "A brief piece to display your talents and to amuse us, that is all we ask. If you play, Her Grace has supplied both a pianoforte and a harp, and if you sing, we can arrange for someone to accompany you."

.Harriet saw the young lady who had just finished, a sad-faced stick of a girl with wilting flowers in her hair. The girl still stood beside the pianoforte though her piece was done, waiting for more than her doting mother and her friends to applaud her efforts. But the rest of the crowd in the music room was clearly there only to make sure they'd have a prime seat for Signor Ricadelleo, and they all continued to chat and laugh and flirt, pointedly oblivious to the poor young lady waiting at the front of the room, as rude and ill-mannered a lot as Harriet had ever seen.

"Surely you can persuade her, Lord Bonnington?" begged Lady Swithin, simpering at William over the edge of her fan. "Surely a muse like Miss Calliope will grace us with her song?"

"Ah, I cannot answer for her, Lady Swithin," said William with a frown that managed to be both doleful and charming. "This is only lowly Harborough House, not Mount Olympus, and muses don't often sully their gifts by squandering them on mortals like—"

"I'd be honored, My Lady," declared Harriet. The sad-faced girl had finally retreated, unnoticed and unappreciated, to sit by her mother, and the forlorn droop of her shoulders is what convinced Harriet. She couldn't play a pianoforte or harp or sing in the airy, high-pitched way that a true lady would, but hey, ho, she'd make these coves pay attention.

"You are sure, my dear?" asked William with a wicked spark of anticipation in his eye, as much a dare as anything he'd ever say. "You have not, ah, prepared anything, have you?"

"Oh, I am prepared, Will, sure enough," she said resolutely. "You watch me, eh?"

Swiftly she made her way past the rows of little gold chairs to the front of the room, pausing only to pluck five oranges from a silver bowl on a sideboard. The oranges had probably been placed there for decoration more than as refreshments, but in Harriet's hands they'd serve a new purpose altogether, and she smiled to herself with gleeful anticipation.

The smooth, slightly dimpled fruit had a familiar feel in her hands, old friends from her past, and with four cradled in her arm and the fifth in one hand, she stood beside a most uneasy Lady Swithin. Heads turned toward them and conversations dwindled to a stop, and not entirely from curiosity, either. Though Harriet might be dressed like all the other ladies, her face glowing with the celebrated beauty that had been made famous by the duchess's paintings, it was the silent challenge in how she held her head so high and lightly tossed the orange in her fingers that, within seconds, had captured the attention of every person in the room.

"You would sing, Miss Calliope?" asked Lady Swithin, her fan now fluttering with the anxious speed of a hummingbird's wings. "Have you music for the accompanist?"

"Nay, I'll sing my own self," said Harriet, searching the crowd for William. " 'Before the Barn Door,' by Master John Gay."

"Very well." Nervously Lady Swithin cleared her throat. " 'Before the Barn Door,' by Master John Gay, sung *a cappella* by Miss, ah, Miss Calliope."

There was William, lounging against the wall with his arms crossed over his chest. He didn't know what she'd planned, but he knew her well enough to believe it would be a dandy little show, and the slow wink he gave her over the rows of plumes and diamonds held all the favor of a true conspirator.

Harriet grinned, and with practiced aplomb tossed the first orange high into the air. Before it began to fall, she'd thrown the second after it, then the next and the next two after that, until she had all five dancing through her hands in a flying circle, the way she'd learned to do in the park whenever sales had flagged.

The audience gasped with wonder, and wryly Harriet wondered where they'd lived all their tedious, high-bred lives, that they hadn't seen such a common juggler's trick before. But she wasn't done, and in the same lilting but loud voice she'd used to cry her wares, she launched into the song she had purposefully chosen from *The Beggar's Opera*, the one that the highwayman MacHeath sings to his covey of lovers.

> *Before the barn-door crowing,*
> *The cock by hens attending,*
> *His eyes around him throwing,*
> *Stands for a while suspended,*
> *Then one he chooses from the crew,*
> *And cheers the happy hen,*
> *With a how d'ye do, and a how d'ye do,*
> *And a how d'ye do again!*

Not waiting to let this settle upon her audience, she rapidly began to catch each orange out of the rotation with a flourish of her wrist, and tuck it back into the crook of her arm, calling each orange as if it were a hen back to the roost:

Hey, henny-hen, back to your cock!

When she came to the last orange—and the last henny-hen—she didn't hide it into her arm, but threw it across the room, a bright ball barely skimming beneath the crystal drops of the chandelier, directly to William.

Of course he caught it, easily, and with one hand. He grinned, and bowed to her, holding her gaze so long that she felt as if they were the only two left in the room. When they'd met, she'd given him an orange to remember her by, but this one was to make him remember the promise of this evening as well. Without looking away from Harriet, he dug his thumb into the orange and skinned back the peel, sliding his fingers inside and spreading the plump segments to ease one free. Slowly he lifted it to his mouth and bit into it, licking the juice from his lips and his fingers while Harriet blushed, and smiled triumphantly just for him.

Twisting around on the narrow gilt chairs to watch, the others in the room gasped, and laughed, and swore, and applauded, and cheered, and not one of them could wait to tell of what they'd witnessed to the poor unfortunates who hadn't been there to see for themselves.

"*Thank* you, Miss Calliope," said Lady Swithin, her face nearly purple with discomfort that even her fan was unable to relieve. "That was, ah, an unusual offering."

"Unusual?" repeated William, coming up to draw Harriet into his arms. "It was sheer perfection, Lady Swithin, and I defy old Signor Ricadelleo to come anywhere close to rivaling it. Such a cunning lass you are, my dearest, always ready to surprise me!"

He tipped her back against his arm and kissed her then, quickly, for the next hapless young lady was fussing about with the harp. But still he kissed her for all to see, and with such ardent, unabashed passion and possession that Harriet nearly let the rest of the oranges fall forgotten from her hands to the floor. The duchess might have graced her with respectability, but that kiss of William's marked her forever as his.

"Very well, Bonnington," said the duke mildly, suddenly there beside them when, at last, Harriet could find the strength to open her eyes. "Now that you have congratulated this lady and robbed my wife's entertainment of any scrap of respectability, could I steal a word with you alone?"

"Forgive me, Your Grace," she said hastily, realizing now that while what she—and William—had done had, for the most part, delighted the other guests nearly as much as it had themselves, such a performance was more appropriate for the supper boxes at Vauxhall than the duchess's music room.

But William wasn't inclined to relinquish his hold on Harriet, not yet, and he left his arm where it was and where it belonged, snug around her waist.

He knew he should go with Edward, and that as delicious as this scene had been with Harriet, it was past time for it to end. He was also displaying wretchedly bad manners by letting it continue, and neither Ned nor Francesca deserved that.

But nothing seemed to matter as much as holding Harriet just a moment longer, relishing that magic he'd felt singing between them across the room. No, *she* was the magic, and the more time he spent in her company, the more bewitched he'd become. Conjurers' tricks and ribald songs about cocks and hens, a body like a goddess, a voice like an angel, and a wit that would win her the first seat in most London coffeehouses: sweet Jesus, no wonder he could think of nothing and no one else beyond her!

One more moment, that was all he asked. Slowly, slowly, with teasing, sensuous care, he broke free another segment of the orange and slipped it into her mouth, rubbing his fingertip over the sensitive cushion of her lower lip, sliding the sweet juice over her skin, and felt the tremor of desire vibrate through them both.

"William," said Edward, a single rumbling word of warning. There was gossip, and there was scandal, and then there was social outrage, and from the expressions of other guests that William glimpsed around them, he was veering dangerously close to the last.

"Are you going to have us flogged, Ned?" asked William, still unable to resist. "Is that the next order of entertainment for your guests?"

"*He* won't," said Francesca sweetly as she joined Edward, the edge of warning sounding much more sharply in her voice than in her husband's. "But *I* will, Bonnington. Perhaps I shall hold the cat-o'-nine-tails in my own little hand. True, it's something I've never tried, *caro mio,* but that does not mean I shouldn't like to try. Life is meant to be experienced, isn't it?"

"Which, darling Francesca, is all I am trying to

do." He released Harriet, who went to Francesca with a reluctant sigh of her own. She licked the last of the orange's juice from her lip and gave him one final, fleeting glance of such longing that William nearly risked that promised flogging to kiss her again.

But then, with Harriet, there always seemed to be a certain amount of risk involved, didn't there?

"At least I have an excellent notion of how you have been occupying yourself these last days, Will," said Edward as the footman closed the door to the library behind them, shutting out the music and voices from the party. Edward was wearing his full dress uniform, an impressive show of dark blue and impeccable white glittering with gold lace and honors, and centered by the last, his gold medal from the victory at the Nile. He poured himself brandy, pointedly not offering any to William.

Well, well, so be it, thought William. *He thinks I'm already drunk as an emperor, the only excuse he can conceive of for that last bit of extravagant behavior with Harriet.*

Ah, dear, sweet, slightly-off-key Harriet...

"I trust," said Edward, interrupting William's thoughts, "that you have spared a few moments from your amusements to read through the packet I had delivered to you?"

"I did," said William, dropping into the nearest armchair and stretching his legs out before him as he popped the last of the orange into his mouth. "Everything seemed clear enough."

"Did it now," said Edward, sitting in the opposite chair. "Because it sure as hell did not seem—"

"I still haven't made love to her, Ned." The orange was sweet, full of juice, reminding him again of Harriet.

" 'Made love?' " repeated Edward incredulously. "For God's sake, William, since when have you described what you do with a woman like that?"

"If any other bastard had said that, Ned, I would have had to ask you whether you preferred pistols or swords," said William, determined not to lose his temper with Edward. "Each night she sleeps serenely in her own bed, and the only time she has passed the night in mine, I slept in the cot in my dressing room. If you don't believe me, you can ask Strode. He can't quite fathom it, either."

"Damnation, Will, do you think I care?"

"Yes, Ned," said William softly. When they'd been boys together, they'd sworn to always be friends, mates forever. "I rather thought you did."

But Edward only sighed impatiently, in no humor to be sentimental. "Whether you have bedded Miss Treene or not, you cannot deny that there seems to exist a certain intimate attachment between you two."

"Nor shall I deny it, despite your clumsy phrasing regarding amatory matters," said William, falling back upon the languid, drawling wit that had become his most familiar defense against Edward as Captain Lord Ramsden, hero of the Nile and savior of England and the devil only knew what else. "It's a good thing you prospered as a sailor, Ned, for you shall never make your name as a poet."

"Then I shall try being blunt instead," said Edward curtly. "Francesca believes you are in love with this woman. Not just physical desire, but real love, and for the first time in your life. And I agree."

William chuckled. "Which is why, obviously, dear Francesca has gone out of her way to make Harriet so *acceptable*. The invitation here tonight, the painting hanging in the entry, the sisterly embraces on the stairs for all the world to witness and remark. The only one who did not smoke it was Harriet herself, bless her dear innocent head."

But what reason had he given her to think otherwise, innocent or not? He'd never promised her anything, never sworn his devotion, or asked for hers in return. He'd acted from long practice, of course, the reflex of self-preservation in a world where too many women were far too quick to see attractions and commitments where none were intended.

But then Harriet wasn't like those other women. She wasn't like anyone else he'd ever known, was she? He couldn't remember what his life had been without her in it, and he couldn't imagine how it would be when they returned from France, and she left him for her tea-shop.

When she *left* . . .

But damnation, what if he didn't want her to go? What if she really were the one in the world that was meant to be his, the one the poets promised to every man, the one he'd always been too jaded and skeptical to believe existed for him outside of Francesca's first painting? What if Harriet really were the one, and through a lifelong surfeit of easy glibness, he'd lost the ability to explain how he felt?

What if she were the one he was meant to love, and yet through some terrible irony, he never found a way to tell her before she disappeared from his life?

Edward was drumming his fingers on the arm of the chair. "You're begging the question, Will."

"Because *you* are being indelicate without even having asked it," answered William languidly, making a small, careless tent of his fingers, as if his heart weren't throbbing and his stomach churning beneath his waistcoat. "You and I may be the oldest friends in the world, but I still fear that my intentions—even my inclinations—regarding Harriet Treene are none of your affair, nor your loving little wife's, either."

"Then I shall speak of one that is." Angrily Edward rose from his chair and began pacing, his hands clasped tightly behind his back. "You read the report in that packet. You know that the situation in France has worsened, and that we need the information you will bring to us from Abbeville more than ever before. Yet if you insist on taking Miss Treene with you, I do not believe I can trust you to make the correct decisions for the success of your mission."

"You do not trust me, Ned?" asked William, slowly standing to face Edward. Trust, trust: why the devil was everything coming down to that one blasted word?

"No, Will, I do not." Grimly Edward shook his head. "You think like a lovesick civilian. If you had to choose between your country's welfare and Miss Treene's safety, then I—"

"Miss Treene is my partner in this, Edward," interrupted William, "and though you do not trust me, she does, as I do her. We'll join the *Fancy* the day after tomorrow, and follow your orders from there."

"For God's sake, Will, listen to me, I—"

"I thank you for the concern, Ned, on all counts," said William, bowing before he left. "But no matter what you choose to believe, you have my word that I will not fail you."

Nor Harriet, he added silently to himself. *I won't fail you, either, lass. . . .*

The only question left was how to do it.

"I did not mean to be spoiling your party, Your Grace," began Harriet contritely as soon as the duchess had closed the door to the little study upstairs and away from the others. "I shouldn't have gone and sung that song, I know, and—"

"Oh, *perdizione,* your little song was nothing," scoffed the duchess, settling herself on a small bench. Clearly the room served as her office for managing such a grand house, with bookshelves and ledgers and a long writing table, painted boxes for bills and an impressive ring of keys on a hook near the door, and, because it belonged to this particular duchess, an enormous Chinese vase of flowers from the country.

"Poor Signor Ricadelleo was the greatest voice at the Teatro dell'Òpera before Napoleon chased him from Rome," she continued, "yet all anyone here tonight will recall tomorrow will be you and your cocks and hens. No matter. What I wish for my guests is amusement, entertainment, whether it comes from you or the Signor."

"Thank you, Your Grace," said Harriet, not quite certain how else to respond.

"Though I do not believe it shall be quite all my

guests will speak of tomorrow." The duchess smiled, more shyly than Harriet would have thought possible. "Later this evening, you see, Edward and I will announce that I am with child, and that we hope to be blessed as parents by the new year, God willing."

"Oh, Your Grace, that is most grand news!" cried Harriet, her excitement genuine. She'd seen what joy a baby had brought to her sister, the special miracle a tiny new child was for women. For a duchess, of course, there'd be the additional satisfaction of bearing an heir, but for now, and for this duchess, Harriet was sure the babe itself would be her first concern and delight. "You and His Grace must be most wonderfully proud."

"We are," she said simply, resting her hand protectively over the slight swell of her belly. "And I thank you for sharing our joy. But you see, *cara,* I tell you this before the others for a reason. Everything with me has a reason, *naturalmente,* yes? Because Bonnington and Edward are such old, dear friends, we hoped that you, too, would have an announcement to make to the world this evening."

"An announcement, Your Grace?" asked Harriet warily.

"It is no secret to any of us, Harriet," said the duchess, leaning closer. "Bonnington loves you as he has loved no other woman. To watch the two of you together, the little glances and sighs and smiles that only true lovers share—that was the real show for us earlier, and not you juggling the oranges. Surely a marriage cannot be far away?"

Troubled, Harriet stared down into her lap. The duchess was putting into words what she herself didn't dare even think: dangerous words, words that had neither truth nor future, but could hurt her, oh, so much.

"I do not believe so, Your Grace," she said carefully, thinking of how proud William was of his family and his grand houses. "Not between a noble-born gentleman like the earl and an orange-seller like me."

"Look at me and say that, dear Harriet," said the duchess gently, reaching for Harriet's hand. "My father was an artist, and my mother a Neapolitan woman who was his model but never his wife. In London, I am regarded as dark and dangerously foreign, and I still speak Italian more easily than I do English. The duke could not be a more perfect English nobleman of an ancient family, a gentleman of impeccable honor and courage. Yet we fell in love, and though all you English gasped in shock and horror, we wed, and are most happy. As, *davvero,* you and Bonnington should be, too."

"But Will—Bonnington—he isn't like the duke," said Harriet miserably. "Oh, he is most generous kind to me, and we do laugh, and find joy in each other's company, and toss words about like those oranges, but that's only his nature. We are partners, Your Grace, pure and simple, for the sake of our arrangement, and nothing more."

She'd known what he was from the first word they'd exchanged, there in the park. A flash gentleman, a charming rascal, a rogue with the power to make any woman he met sigh with pleasure. He'd never speak of love, and why should he?

She'd *known,* and she'd told herself never to expect more from him than was in him to give. Yet here she was now, practically disintegrating into little heartbroken shards upon the duchess's carpet.

"And thus Bonnington's nature doesn't permit him to fall in love?" asked the duchess. "Especially not with a woman as perfectly suited to him as you are?"

But again Harriet shook her head. "Will's emotions are more . . . *practiced* than the duke's would ever be. Will guards his heart too close to ever be in love."

"But not you, Harriet?" The duchess smiled sadly. "All you wish for in life is your little tea-shop? You don't wish to laugh and toss words for the rest of your life with a man who adores you?"

But Harriet did wish it, and want it, more than she'd ever find words to say, because she did love him, fool, fool, fool, that she was and always would be!

"What of the passion of love, *cara*," continued the duchess, her softly accented voice giving life to one forbidden dream after another. "You've no need for that, either? You see, I have been very good and not asked you if the rumors about Bonnington's famous skills are true—though from your smile after he kisses you, I'm quite certain that they are."

She was right about that, too. If kissing William could bring such extraordinary bliss and havoc to her senses, then what must it be like to be his lover in every possible sense, freely and openly?

But the duchess wasn't finished, having saved the keenest weapon she had for last. "Tell me, Harriet," she said gently. "Have you no woman's wish to be cherished, to become wife to the man you love and to bear his children?"

Automatically Harriet's gaze again lowered to the duchess's belly, at the familiar hand perpetually stained with paint from her studio, and she thought, too, of her sister Bett and the second child she was carrying.

What beautiful children she'd have with Will, clever, quick, beautiful children with his laughing blue eyes and dark curling hair. How much she'd like to share the love and joy of a baby with him, husband and wife, and how wretchedly impossible it would ever be!

"You must tell him how you feel, *cara mia*," urged the duchess as she spread her fingers gently across her unborn child, cradling it with her love as much as her hand. "With this journey to France, you must not wait. Though your reasons are the best and most noble, Harriet, you're putting yourselves in the path of great danger, you and Bonnington both. Imagine your grief if one of you were killed before you—"

"If you please, Your Grace, I—I must go." This conversation, the heavy scent of the flowers in the small room, the deceptive lulling of the duchess's voice as she spoke of the finality of death, all were smothering her, pressing down like a weight of stones that she had to throw off. "You—you are most wise in your advice, Your Grace, but I must excuse myself now."

Unable to listen any longer, she bolted from the little room, gasping or sobbing or maybe both as she ducked into a dark little alcove framing a window. Struggling to control her emotions, she placed her palms and back flat against the cool plaster wall and her eyes squeezed shut. Everything the duchess had

said had been right: if she cared enough about
William to love him, then she must tell him so now,
before they sailed, even if it meant breaking their
pact, and the risk that he might cast her off altogether.

How would she find the words? She'd never be
able to look at him with the same eyes, not after this
conversation with the duchess. She felt painfully conscious of what had been said, and what she'd admitted to herself as much as to Her Grace. Surely
everything would be written all over her face, bold as
polished brass, there for Will to see for himself
whether she spoke or not.

*Ah, Harriet me girl, you be right roasted and turn-
ing on the spit now, don't you? First you treat the
duchess's music room like some bawdy circus, then,
when she tells you things you should know about your
own foolish heart, showing you more kindness than a
saucy jade like you deserves, you run clear away, as if
you've no bloody manners and the sense of a goose!*

No manners and no sense, she thought with growing despair, and a heart as heavy as lead.

12

*W*illiam found Harriet upstairs, away from the others, standing alone in an alcove beside a window. Clearly she was lost in her own thoughts, her expression turned so inward that he almost hesitated to interrupt her.

"Harriet?" he asked softly. "Harriet, pet, why in blazes are you hiding yourself away here? Is anything wrong?"

Her startled gaze flew toward him, almost as if she'd wakened, and though she seemed glad to see him, he could have sworn there were tears hovering in her eyes, too.

"I was only talking with Her Grace for a bit," she said, her smile unsteady, "and she gave me much to think upon. I am meaning to go back belowstairs directly."

"Please don't," he said, screwing up his face in a fair approximation of excruciating pain, hoping he could make her smile less forced. They had to talk—he'd known that even before he'd left Edward—and he had come looking for her with that specific purpose, but having her on the verge of tears would not make for an auspicious beginning. "Francesca's Italian fellow is singing."

Echoing up the stairs from the music room, the Signor's famous voice was loud enough to be heard by dogs clear across Green Park, and perhaps enough to make them howl, too. But it did make Harriet's smile genuine, and for that William was grateful.

"Would you like to see Calliope instead?" she asked, taking his hand. "Her Grace said the painting is finally done and waiting on her easel, if we want to go view it. I know how to reach the studio by the back stairs."

"Then lead the way, sweetheart," he said, "and spare my suffering ears. Besides, I wish to speak to you alone, and the studio will do as well as any place."

She took a candlestick from one of the hall tables and headed confidently up the back stairs to the landing which, she felt sure, must lead to the duchess's studio. But somewhere among the turnings of the large, rambling house, she became confused, and instead of opening the door to the studio, she found an empty hallway lined with a series of small paintings on panels, and lit only by the moonlight filtering in through a row of clerestory windows.

"This isn't right," she said sheepishly. "Mayhap if we'd gone left at the landing instead?"

But William wasn't listening, instead walking farther down the hallway to peer at one of the paintings.

"Pray hand me the candlestick, pet," he said excitedly, beckoning to her. "Hah, Harriet, Harriet! Do you know what you've discovered? Speak of lost treasures!"

"What treasures?" she asked curiously, coming to stand beside him with the candlestick raised to shine upon the picture. "What—oh, *Will!*"

Doubtless the painting was unlike anything she'd ever seen, though "treasure" was likely not the first word she'd use to describe it. The scene showed two pink, laughing young women with grape leaves woven into their hair and not a stitch upon their plump persons, lolling about beside a stream. With them was a half-man with a goat's nether-quarters below the waist, a prodigiously endowed satyr, lasciviously disporting with the two women in a most uninhibited fashion.

"Oh, Will, that is the most wicked lewd picture I've ever seen!" she sputtered, shocked. "Who would think fine, noble people like the duke and duchess would keep such—such *rubbish* in their home?"

But Will only laughed. "Then you won't care for the other pictures, either," he said, moving the candle to shine on the next paintings.

Again Harriet gasped, stunned speechless. Despite the genteel gold frames, every one of the pictures—and there must have been two dozen, all the same size and by the same artist—showed the same sort of outrageously sinful pleasures of ancient nymphs and gods, satyrs and goddesses, warriors and queens, even a zealously enthusiastic Leda engaged with an enormous swan.

"You know what we've stumbled upon, Harriet?" he asked, more entertained by her outrage than by the pictures themselves. "These are the infamous *Oculus Amorandi*—the Eye of Love, as in a Peeping Tom— that the duchess's father painted years and years ago. He'd invented some nonsense about their educational values, and for a shilling or two, he'd show them to young gentlemen visiting Naples on their Tour."

"Her own *father?*" asked Harriet as she stared, aghast. "She had these pictures in her home as a little girl?"

"I suppose she must have," said William. "And mind this was Naples, where such matters are seen in a far different light. She carried on the family trade after her father died, you know, showing them herself to much panting admiration before Edward met and married her, and made her leave such work to the bawdy-houses. But to think all this time Ned had the old *Oculus* hidden away here at Harborough House, ready for his own amusement!"

"Naples *must* be different, if this is what the Neapolitans consider amusement," she said primly, but he could see how she was studying the nearest painting with more than a moralist's interest.

It wasn't one of the more outlandish couplings, with only an ordinary god and goddess frolicking to- gether on a farfetched cloud. Each was, respectively, handsome and beautiful, at least to the extent of the artist's limited talents, with the naked goddess writhing demonstrably atop the naked god and a few tiny winged *putti* scattered about around them as ogling witnesses.

To William, it wasn't the subjects that were mak- ing these paintings so intensely erotic. It was how they'd been hidden away up here like a wicked secret by Edward and Francesca, a secret that he now was sharing by candlelight with an innocent like Harriet.

Or, more accurately, not-quite-as-innocent-as-she-once-had-been Harriet, studying the painting as if it contained every truth in the universe. Which, as William considered the possibilities, in many ways it did.

God help him, he hadn't planned for things to fall this way. He'd sternly promised himself that he'd declare his feelings to Harriet, to tell her how much he truly regarded her, to give her the chance to accept and return his noble affections, or to toss them back in his face as she had the orange in the music room. He *had* to do it. He couldn't wait until they were on their way to Abbeville, when everything would be so much more complicated. Most of all, he had to be as honest and straightforward as Edward himself must have been when he'd first addressed Francesca, the way Harriet deserved. He'd speak without any flirting or teasing, so that she would know exactly what he was about.

If, that is, he could first determine that for himself. Standing in the dark with Harriet and dozens of copulating ancients wasn't helping square his thoughts, either. Old habits—especially pleasurable old habits—were the hardest to break.

"So this is your favorite, pet?" he asked, slipping one arm familiarly around her waist as he leaned over her shoulder to admire the picture with her. "This is the one you find most titillating?"

"I never told you anything of the sort," she said quickly, but he noticed that she didn't look away from the picture, either. "To make such a picture—what could Her Grace's old Fa be thinking?"

"Likely he was thinking precisely the same things that you're thinking now," he said, close enough to her that he could lower his voice to a confidential whisper. "All those times you dressed as some goddess or another for the duchess, wearing those loose, open gowns that drifted over your breasts and thighs and hips without any stays or whalebone to interfere, lolling languidly on the Roman bench in that patch of warm sun on her model's stand—didn't you wish that a handsome god would come to you like this?"

"I *never*," she denied vehemently. "Not like that."

"Then how, pet?" He prised the candlestick from her fingers—ah, so her hands were moist with agitation!—and gently moved it back and forth above the picture, the flame flickering. "Look. It's only a trick, I know, but see how the light makes the figures seem to move on their own, how much that comely little goddess is enjoying herself with her god! She's free to move upon him like that, riding him with her legs spread wide so he can come deeply inside her and give her the pleasure that's making her smile so."

He set the candlestick on the sideboard below the painting and gently drew Harriet against his chest. He liked holding her this way, her back to his front, his hands sliding up and down along her ribs, teasing the full curves of her breasts with his fingertips, the same as he'd done the day he taught her to fire the pistol, except now there wasn't any risk of being shot. Singed, yes, scorched and burned, but not shot. He was careful to make sure she could still see the painting and let her imagination simmer and bubble with the image and the words he was using to spice the mix.

"How long do you think the goddess will last at her play, pet?" he whispered. "How long before her greedy body will demand surcease, before she'll toss back her head and arch her back and let her god drive her hard and straight to paradise?"

Her breath was coming in short, shallow bursts as she moved restlessly against him, her skin hot through the light fabric of her gown, and even before he reached up to cup her breasts in his palms, he wondered if she could in turn feel how he was pressing against her bottom, hard as a bar of iron for her.

"My sister Bett says that way is best of all," she gasped. "Riding randy-pole, she called it, and—and said you feel it deep and sure and blissful."

He felt himself jolt longer, harder still at that. What man wouldn't, not when she was wriggling herself against him, fair begging for it every way a woman could. Riding randy-pole, indeed. Even here, like this, Harriet knew what to say to him, better than any other woman alive.

But damnation, they should stop this game *now*. He needed to talk to her, to show her the respect he felt for her, not just this unbelievably intense lust that was robbing them both of any sane thought beyond one.

He must stop. But then she moaned his name, *his* name, and not that unknown god's, and leaned forward to brace her hands on the edge of the table and rock her bottom up against him, and every sensible thought flew from his mind and conscience.

"You'd like to be that goddess, wouldn't you, Harriet?" he rasped, urgency reducing his voice to a gruff growl as he caressed her breasts, letting the soft flesh fill his hands, tugging gently, insistently at her nipples until they hardened tight against his palms. All he'd have to do now was pull her skirts over her hips and unbutton the fall of his breeches, and she'd be his.

"You'd like to ride your god like that, wouldn't you, wanton and hard and open to take him deep," he said, burying his face in the scent of her hair, "with your thighs snug at his waist, riding randy-pole to find bliss like Bett said?"

"Bett said—Bett said it is best," she stammered, whimpering as she pushed against him, "for pleasure and for putting the man's seed deep for—for making a babe."

He stopped abruptly, stunned by the words he'd no wish to hear. "What—what did you say, pet?"

"I said, I said—oh, Will, what I did say!" she sobbed. She twisted and broke free of him, reeling away from him with her hands pressed, shaking, to her cheeks. "My conscience must have spoken, to remind my wicked flesh. Those pictures and what we were saying and what we almost did—ah, it would be wicked wrong for us, Will, for us being what we are!"

Being phenomenally frustrated was what he, personally, was, and he didn't think she was any better, not jabbering nonsense like this.

"Harriet," he said, and took a deep, rational breath to steady his voice and his balls. "Harriet, sweetheart, we must talk. I came to find you with that in mind, you know, before we became, ah, distracted."

She sobbed again, dry, wracking sobs with anger and no tears, and shook her head.

"You won't be talking me into more of that, Will

Manderville!" she cried, blindly tugging and smoothing her disheveled clothes back into place with quick jerks of her hands. "I came precious close to the cliff with you, but I'll not tumble over it just yet."

"Sweetheart, please, listen—"

"Nay, Will, don't," she begged. "*Don't*. What I said is right, and if you don't know it, too, then you are a worse rascal than ever I judged."

If only he'd said what he'd had to earlier, before they'd found the paintings and before it had become impossible to use words like *devotion, respect,* and yes, even *love*. "Hell, Harriet, all I wished to do was talk!"

"And you already did, talking plenty," she said, taking another step away from him, "same as I listened, and look where it almost took us! Doing such acts is blissful fine for married folk like Tom and Bett and—and the duchess and the duke, those who wish for babes to bless their lives. But not for us, Will, not for how we are."

He smiled, desperate to appease her and shift away from this disturbing talk of ill-gotten babies. "If that is all that troubles you, pet, why, then I know of other ways we can pleasure each other without any risk of getting you with child."

Instantly her face closed against him, and his heart plummeted as he realized he'd said the absolute wrong thing, and his wanton goddess was gone, perhaps forever.

"I want to leave now, Will," she said, taking up the candlestick and heading with it toward the door and the stairs, and pointedly leaving him behind, alone, in the dark.

He swore to himself, furiously raking his fingers back through his hair as if that could somehow help. He'd damned near ruined it all, hadn't he? Anything he ventured to say now would sound like an afterthought, a haphazard patch that wouldn't begin to mend the rift he'd made, and wouldn't fool a half-wit, let alone his dear, clever Harriet.

No, she wasn't his, not now, not after this, and likely not ever, either.

"Are you leaving with me, then?" he called after her, disappointment and bitterness making him hostile. "Or have you found some other poor simpleton to trick and trip?"

"Aye, I'll go with you, M'Lord, for I've no other choice," she said, ignoring the rest. "God may take me for a fool for saying so, aye, but with you."

And for the first time since they'd met in the park over her basket of oranges, he and Harriet sat in complete silence in the carriage back to Bonnington House, with not one word to say.

The next morning Harriet was awake early, before the sun was even a glow across the city's rooftops, and though early rising was a lifetime's habit for her, this night she'd slept so little it scarcely had seemed like waking at all. The rest of the evening with the *ridotto* had begun with such promise, such anticipation, yet all she could remember now was the bitter, hateful way it had ended with William.

She tried to tell herself that it had been better that such a scene had happened when it had, and not later, after she'd given him her heart the way she'd planned to do, and that it was better, too, to have discovered this side of him when she had. But still her heart ached with what she'd lost, just as her unfulfilled body foolishly yearned for what it now could never have.

And worst of all, she loved William still. That hadn't changed, not in the least, and though she resolved otherwise, this morning when the pain was so raw, she wondered if it ever could.

Everyone else in Bonnington House was still abed, for from the lowest kitchen maid upward, all the servants took their cue from their master's fashionable hours. Quickly Harriet dressed herself in her simplest gown for day and made a halfhearted breakfast of the remains she'd kept from last night's supper tray. With dismay she studied her collection of ladies' slippers of glazed and stenciled kid. She would much prefer to walk to her destination, the way she used to, but her sturdy leather shoes had long since vanished, and these slippers, though lovely, were made for drawing rooms and not the city's dirty streets.

With a few coins from her own savings tucked into her reticule and the slippers in her hand, she hurried down the stairs to the front door, unbolted the heavy box-lock, and slipped outside. Portman Square was deserted save for the pigeons and a drowsy boy sweeping the pavements who, for a ha'penny, trotted to the next street and found her a hackney. She gave the driver the address for Threadneedle Court, and as she climbed inside, she tried not to think of everything—*everything*—she was leaving behind.

The streets grew more crowded as soon as the hired carriage left the neighborhoods of the West

End and crossed the Westminster Bridge. Here people had already begun their day's work, and nosily, too, with drivers of creaking drays and wagons shouting at one another, peddlers calling their wares and tradesmen shouting their skills, apprentices jostling and challenging each other while pretending to do their masters' bidding, women gossiping and quarreling, and children shouting and crying, the din of the streets reminding Harriet happily of home.

Eagerly she sat close to the window as the hackney approached her old neighborhood. But how was it, she wondered, that in the few weeks she'd been away Threadneedle Court and the other lanes around it seemed magically shrunk, every building dwindled and more humble than she remembered? Even her father's shop seemed somehow sadly diminished, the familiar swinging sign of a huge meat pie overhead looking in need of a fresh coat of paint to its crust.

"Should I wait, M'Lady?" asked the driver as he helped her down, taking extra care to see that she could place her slippered foot on a dry place in the street. Of course he'd be solicitous; from Harriet's clothes and her address on Portman Square, he'd obviously guessed her to be a sizable fare with garnish to match. "Beggin' pardon, but this don't look like much of a place for an unattached lady."

"But it is, sir," she said, smiling as she fished in her reticule for the fare. "It's the house where I was born."

And as soon as she stepped inside the shop, it was as if she'd never left. Though the benches were empty of customers this early in the morning, the greasy gleam of the trestle tables was exactly as she'd remembered it. There, too, were the ceiling beams blackened from years of smoke from diners' pipes and the fireplace in the corner, the stacks of dog-eared newspapers, the hammering and sawing from the joiner's shop next store, and, most evocative of all, the scent of the fresh pies baking from the brick ovens in the back kitchen. Standing in the middle of the shop, she closed her eyes to better savor the rich, familiar smell.

"*Harriet?*" shrieked her sister, and instantly Harriet's eyes flew open. "Harriet, do that truly be you?"

"Bett!" Harriet rushed across the room and threw her arms about her sister's shoulders, weeping with joy. Here was the one person who might understand what she was suffering over William, the one person who knew her well enough to advise her. "Ah, Bett, how I've missed you! Here, here, let me look at you proper!"

Laughing a little at her own tears, Harriet stepped back, still holding Bett's hands. "Hey, ho, but your belly's enormous! This one will be a boy, no mistake, eh?"

"So the midwife says, too." Bett flushed happily, as close to a glow as her always weary face would ever have. "Tom, he'd like nothing better, so's each night I pray it be a boy, for him."

"You should be praying first for the babe to be born strong and healthy," chided Harriet gently, "and for your own safe delivery."

Bett's happiness faded. "I pray for many things," she said softly. "For you, Harriet, for one."

"For *me?*"

"Aye, for you," replied Bett, slipping her red-knuckled hands free of Harriet's, her troubled face looking downward. "You say to look at me, Harriet, but look at your own self first. Look at them gold bracelets on your wrists and the necklace around your throat, and at them fine lady's clothes, lace and muslin and a plume and silk ribbons on your bonnet. Look at them, Harriet, and tell me how you earned such with honest work, the way you'd told me you would when you left."

"But I have, Bett, I swear to you I have!" cried Harriet defensively, even as she realized she couldn't explain more. William had made it most clear that she could tell no one about the purpose of their voyage to France, not even her sister, and she'd only to remember the dangers that had already nearly claimed her to understand the risk. "I cannot tell you exactly what I do, save that it's most honorable, and honest."

"Oh, aye, *most* honorable," repeated Bett, obviously not believing a word. "Do you think I be daft, Harriet? Don't you think we be hearing all about you and your noble gentleman what keeps you? The papers be full of it, though Tom tears them stories out to burn soon as he sees them, to keep tales of your sins from sullying me own eyes, and to keep your shame from our shop."

"But those are no more than *stories*, Bett," insisted Harriet. "And Will—Will's a most wonderful gentleman, and most generous and kind to me. You know he's promised to set me up with my own tea-shop when we're done, like I always wished to have?"

"So you be calling an earl by his Christian name, do you?" Bett sniffed with distaste. "No man, high or low, gives a woman jewelry and clothes and a *tea*-shop unless she's giving him something righteous fine in return."

Now Harriet was the one who flushed, remembering what had happened—and what had almost happened—with William last night. "But it isn't like that between Will and me."

"Then how do it be, Harriet?" asked Bett. "Has he asked you to wed him, and take that noble name of his for all the world to see? Has he asked you to bear his children, and not just his bastards?"

"Nay," said Harriet, barely above a whisper. "Nay. But I do love him, Bett, and I do believe he loves me, too."

Bett sighed, and sat heavily on a bench. "If you only be believing it, then I expect he hasn't told you his own self. What did he say when you said it to him?"

"I—I haven't, not yet," confessed Harriet. "There hasn't seemed to be a right time."

"You're living day and night beneath the man's roof," said Bett incredulously, "likely under *him* as well—yet you cannot find the time to tell him you love him? Since when have you been such a ninny, Harriet Treene?"

"Since I met him," said Harriet softly. "Since I fell in love with him."

"You're true pickled then, for sure," said Bett, shaking her head. " 'Course you should leave him directly, sensible-like, but I don't expect you'll do that. Nay, you won't, not and be me own sister."

She took Harriet's hand again, patting it gently. "But mayhap your gentleman will show me wrong, Harriet. Mayhap if he loves you enough, he'll forget who you be and where you be from, and he'll wed you proper, as he should. But first you must tell him you love him, so's he can tell you back. Men can be peculiar that way. Tom will only say them words when it be just the two of us, in the dark. Love makes men daft, too, only in different ways."

"Aye, it certainly does." Harriet tried to smile, fresh tears stinging in her eyes as she squeezed her sister's hand. She wasn't sure if her advice would work with Will, but it was certainly worth trying. "Thank you, Bett, thank you. I'll do what you say, and come back as soon as I do. And to see this new babe of yours, too."

She rested her hand upon the hard mound of her sister's belly, and felt such a strong, answering kick from inside that they both laughed.

"That's a boy, for sure," she declared, thinking of the duchess's baby, and how though the circumstance of the two births could not be more different, the love that the two mothers would give to their new children would be boundless. "But where's little Nan? I'll wager she's grown, too, the sweet little angel."

"Nan's sleeping in her cot, or should be, anyways." Awkwardly Bett stood, her expression full of sadness as she patted Harriet's arm. "Some other time you can see her. But best now you be on your way, Harriet, before Tom comes home and finds you here. He'd be wicked angry if he did."

Harriet nodded unhappily, understanding all too

well what Tom's rages could be like, and understanding, too, that as long as things remained as they were with William, she wouldn't be welcomed in this house.

"God be with you, Bett," she said, hugging her sister one last time. "You take care now, mind, of your own self and the babe and little Nan, too."

She stepped out into the patch of sunshine slanting down between the other houses and shops, gazing up at the same familiar patch of sky that she'd seen so many times before as a girl. How hard it was to believe that the same sky covered all London, Threadneedle Court, and Bonnington House and even Vauxhall alike!

"Hah, if it don't be the great whore o' Babylon herself!" jeered a man in the street before her. "Come back to hoist your petticoats for the rest of us now, are you, Harriet Treene?"

She gulped, but squared her shoulders defiantly, her head high.

"That's enough from you, Bob Wren!" she called back at the man, recognizing him as the butcher's assistant from the shop down the court, a large, bullying man who'd once tried to court her. "You shut your mouth, before any more of your foul-smelling rubbish and lies drip from it!"

"Wouldn't I'd like to see you try to make me, Harriet Treene!" Behind Wren were several other leering men, bolstering his confidence as he lurched toward her. "Give me your own whoring mouth to kiss, hussy, or mayhap I'll drop my breeches and give you something tastier to suck upon, and stop your words!"

She was shaking, both with anger and fear, for while the street was crowded with people, people she'd known all her life, none were coming to her defense. Instead they were lingering to watch, even to cheer, their hostile judgment of her clear enough on their faces. It had taken her longer, but she'd finally come to the same conclusion as the hack driver had: she no longer belonged in Threadneedle Court, and the sooner she left, the better.

A rotten turnip, soft and foully slushy, arched through the air and thumped at her feet, splattering over the toes of her slippers. Cruel laughter rumbled ominously behind her, and swiftly, her head still high, she turned and began walking as fast as she could away from the shop.

"Don't turn your back to me, Harriet!" Wren's voice was close behind her now, though she didn't dare turn. "Unless you like it the way the beasts do, on your knees with your arse in the air, beasts and whores both!"

She felt his fat fingers dig into her arm and tried to jerk free, wheeling around to face him in furious desperation.

"You leave me be, Wren!" she howled. "You leave me be *now!*"

But Wren was no longer there, and instead of holding her arm, he was lying flat on the cobbles at her feet, his dazed eyes staring up at the sky and his mouth working wordlessly.

And beside her, his hand still curled into a fist, stood Will, her own dear wonderful Will.

"If no one else has anything useful to venture," he said to the others gaping in a ring around Wren, and though his manner was genteelly mild, none of them now doubted the vehemence behind it, "then I believe Miss Treene and I shall wish you good people good day."

With the same nonchalance as if they'd been walking in Green Park, Will tucked Harriet's hand into the crook of his arm and led her, unchallenged, around the corner to where his carriage—too large for the narrow court—was waiting.

Being Will, he didn't look back. Being the Earl of Bonnington, he didn't have to.

And when Harriet climbed into the carriage with him, she didn't sit across from him, the way she had last night, but as close to him as she dared. She needed the comfort of him there more than he'd ever know. Her heart was still pounding with fear, her legs trembling with the desperate urge to run that, thanks to him, she hadn't needed to do, and when she wove her fingers into his, she didn't care that he'd feel how nervousness had made her gloves damp.

"Thank you, Will," she whispered as the carriage lurched forward. "Thank you."

He didn't answer, or even look down at her, his proud profile staring steadfastly ahead, but his fingers worked around hers with a tenderness that made her want to weep yet again.

"You're not my whore," he said finally. "I never want you to think that, no matter what swine like that say. You must not think it, not even for a moment."

"I don't," she said softly, surprised by his vehemence. "I never have."

He nodded solemnly, still not looking her way. "You're my friend, Harriet, my partner, my accomplice, my amusement, my goddess, my muse, and, yes, my orange-seller, but never my whore. I care too much for you for it to be otherwise."

"Oh, Will," she said, smiling wistfully. He hadn't included "wife" in that list, but there'd been so much else to amaze her that she didn't care. "That's most wondrous fine, and a great deal more than I ever thought of being."

"Truly?" At last he turned to look at her, his expression unabashedly bewildered. "Because it's not enough, not by half. Not for you, sweetheart, being what you are. Being so—so perfectly right for me, and being yourself, too, without compromise. Oh, Jesus, Harriet, I'm making another wretched mess of this again, aren't I?"

"Nay, you're not, not at all." Her smile was so tight that her cheeks hurt. "If you mean last night, Will, then part of that was my own fault, too. You didn't do anything to me that I didn't wish you to do, double and double that. I wanted to be that goddess in the picture, Will, exactly as you said, and I wanted you to be my own god on that cloud with me."

"Did you indeed." He let his breath out in a long, slow whistle, puffing his cheeks out as he did, and she noticed now that he, too, had little drops of sweat on his forehead and upon his upper lip.

"I did, indeed." She swallowed, striving not to think of how salty those little drops would be to kiss away from his face. "I'd no right to be so wickedly shrewish afterward, but I was—I was feeling out of sorts, and all jumbly and wrong inside."

"Ah," he said, clearing his throat. "That likely sums up my feelings at the time as well."

"And I shouldn't have spoken to you about babies that way," she continued, "and I wouldn't have, if the duchess hadn't put it into my mind. Mind you, I do want children, but not quite yet."

"I suppose I do, too," he said slowly. "I have to, or the title and Charlesfield and the rest will all go to some damned old cousin in Scotland. But I thought you'd left me, lass. When Strode said you'd gone, I thought you'd left."

"But I did leave," she said. "I wanted to see my sister before we sailed, like a soldier, in case I didn't come back from France. I wanted to make things right between us, you know. But I wasn't about to wait for all you slug-a-beds to rise before I went, either."

"I meant leave *me*," he said. "As in 'to Hades with you, Will Manderville.' As in 'I've gone away forever and I'm not coming back.' That kind of leaving."

"Oh, Will." She twisted around on the seat so she could cradle his face in her hands and *make* him listen. "I'd not do that, not to you. Most likely I should, but I couldn't. I can't."

"And I couldn't let you go, either." He frowned sternly, and beneath her fingers she felt the muscles in the side of his face turning down. "I love you, Harriet. There, I finally said it, and for the first time in my life. I love you, lass, and no other."

"Ohhhhh." She kissed him, sweetly, and then giggled with foolish relief and joy as he pulled her more firmly onto his lap. He hadn't asked her to marry him, the way Bett would have wished, but he had said he loved her, and suddenly that, for now, seemed more than enough. "And I love you, Will."

"Fine words all around." His frown relaxed, curving upward into a smile that was infinitely more agreeable, as was the way he was sliding his hands up and down her hips as she sat on his lap. "But only words, lass, and I have always believed that words need actions to fortify them."

"Fortifications, aye." She licked his bottom lip, and laughed again. "As in the kind used for randy-pole riding?"

"How vastly clever you are, Calliope," he said. "But the first time I make love to you, I wish to do it with the greatest pleasure and aplomb possible, and that means my bed. We'll save the carriage for another time, such as tonight."

She laughed again, and wondered if she could ever be any more happy. "Then to your own bed, Will. The fortifying can't wait, and neither can I."

13

Though William was still a youngish man, he'd passed through the beds of more women than most of his counterparts ever would in a lifetime of dreaming. Women of varying ages and stations, complexions and nationalities, and he didn't believe he was flattering himself too grandly to claim that they'd enjoyed themselves as much as he had. Growing up in a household with so many females had made him highly attuned to what pleased them as a gender, and what didn't, and it had also given him an uncharacteristic respect for feminine wishes and whims.

If the notion of respect didn't seem to mesh with his friends' envious assertion that Bonnington could have anything in skirts, it was only because he'd early on learned the first and truest secret of seduction: be nice to her, and she'll be nice to you. The rest, he'd say with a self-deprecating wink, was all tinsel and flash.

So simple, so obvious.

And right now, on this early afternoon in June, in

his bedchamber at last with Harriet Treene, so deuced *challenging* that he couldn't imagine one thing more difficult in all the world.

"Hey, ho, Will, here we be," she said, spinning a half-turn on her toes as she untied the ribbons on her hat. She lifted the hat from her head, holding it raised there for a second, and grinned. At this time of day, when the sun came in the strongest across Portman Square, the blinds had been drawn over the tall windows to protect the furnishings against fading. Only the thinnest rays of sunlight could push their way through into the shadowed room, bright, straight stripes that slipped over the curves of Harriet's body. "Here we *are*."

"Indeed," said William, self-consciously clearing his throat. Damnation, he was supposed to be the one who knew what to say and do next, which was not to stand here gulping air with his heart hammering in his chest.

But then, he'd never actually made *love* to a woman, because he'd never loved any other woman the way he loved Harriet. There, that was the real challenge, directly in the proverbial nutshell. They would both remember this afternoon for the rest of their mortal days, and he wanted to make certain it was worth remembering. He wanted everything to be perfect, as perfect as she was, as perfect as she deserved.

All in all, it was a staggering responsibility, and he hadn't much experience with responsibilities, either.

"Most folk would think us wicked sinful for no more than standing in a bedchamber in the middle of the day, with the sun still a-beaming outside," she said as she lowered her hands and tossed her hat onto a chair nearby.

"Fortunately," he said, "we are not most folk."

"Indeed, we are not," she declared, but more quietly this time, her grin melting into something warmer, more satisfying. "Strode's not going to come a-blundering in again, will he?"

"Not unless he wishes this day to be his last."

"Good," she said sweetly, letting her shawl slip from her arms to the floor in a slide of soft blue wool. "Because I have always liked Mr. Strode, and I would not like to have to cosh him for his actions."

"You would have to wait your turn, lass," he said, watching her draw off her gloves, tugging the pale kid from each finger in turn, slowly, slowly. "As his master, I would have first rights, you know."

"Ah," she said, dropping the gloves on top of the discarded shawl and flexing her now-freed fingers. "But as the mistress of the master, wouldn't I have my rights, too?"

He hadn't noticed before now that the gown she was wearing unfastened to one side of the bodice with a row of small round buttons. He was noticing now because she wanted him to, drawing his attention to the buttons as she absently touched them with her fingertips.

Absently, hell. She wasn't moving so much as an eyelash without a purpose, the wicked little creature, and for the first time since Strode had closed the door after them, William smiled. If he didn't seduce her, then by God she intended to do just that to him.

Harriet, Harriet: *this* was the woman he loved, with all the daunting connotations of that, but this was also his own dear, delicious Harriet, his best friend, his goddess, and all those other splendid titles he'd granted her.

She blushed, and gave her shoulders a wriggling little shrug. He reached out and touched her face, just the lightest touch, and she caught her breath.

Perhaps he was in familiar territory after all.

"Here," he said, reaching higher. "Let me take your hair down for you."

Only her eyes shifted, the rest of her remaining motionless as her gaze followed his hand. One by one he took the pins from her hair, not jerking them out hurriedly, the way a woman would do herself, but carefully sliding every pin free so that each curled lock would slowly tumble down around her shoulders and back. When he'd done, he spread his fingers apart and combed them back, cradling her head and relishing the silky weight of her copper-gold hair over his wrists. She stretched against his hands like a cat, and practically purred her contentment like one, too.

"If it were for me to decide," he said, "you'd never pin your hair up again, but always leave it down like this for me."

"Ha," she said, her voice enticingly low and husky. "Make me look like a slattern, would you?"

"I'd make you look like a goddess," he said, lifting her hair only to let it fall and spill over his hands again. "*My* goddess."

Without thinking, she sighed her happiness, then turned the sigh into a self-conscious giggle and looked away from him and down at her feet. He understood; the air was so charged with the heat and tension, anticipation and attraction swirling between them that he could hardly fault her if she wished to let it simmer a bit.

"Oh, Will, look at my shoes," she said sadly. "Turnip-mash and other filth, fit to ruin them, and all the work of that Bob Wren and those others."

"The shops are full of other shoes," he said gently. He'd hated seeing what had happened to her earlier, and he'd never forgive himself for not figuring out where she'd gone ten minutes sooner, and arriving in time to have been able to spare her the fear and humiliation she had suffered. "Don't worry yourself over this pair, and try as well to forget what happened to you today."

She shook her head, still looking down at the soiled shoes. "I was born above that shop, Will, and I lived there all my life. It was my home, always. But they don't want me coming back, not even Bett, not really."

He could have told her that. He'd had a passing glimpse of her sister standing in the doorway of the pie-shop—a woman faded and worn before her time, her belly swelling beneath her apron with another brat—not the fate he'd wish at all for his vibrant, clever Harriet. But far more damning was how her sister had simply stood there and watched as their neighbors had attacked Harriet, and how she hadn't said one word in Harriet's defense or taken her side.

"The court was always my home," she was saying, "but I don't belong there any longer."

"That's because you belong here, pet." The bullies in Threadneedle Court were nothing to him. He'd

take on all London to defend her if she needed or
wished it.

But again she shook her head. "Nay, not here. Not
exactly."

"No?" he asked lightly, unable to accept that she
might refuse him. "You find Portman Square and my
grandmother's house lacking?"

"Nay, Will Manderville, you great sap-headed
cove," she said, looking up to him at last. "What I
meant is that wherever you are, wherever you go,
where I belong is with you."

His smile twisted crooked. "Because I love you,"
he said, the new words still a marvel to him. "My own
Harriet."

"Then show me, Will," she said, the marvel in her
eyes, too, plus another dare he couldn't resist. "Show
me how much you love me."

William kissed her then, the way Harriet had
silently been praying he would ever since they'd
come into his bedchamber, and she couldn't help a
small sigh of bliss when their lips finally met. But this
kiss was different from the others they'd shared,
more blatantly seductive even to her, who'd never
been seduced.

Until now. He held her face in his hands, his fingers still tangled in her hair, kissing her slowly, almost lazily, his tongue flicking and twining against
hers, coaxing the heat in her body to build at her
own pace. When she reached for his shoulders to
draw him into her arms, he held her gently back to
make her wait while he kissed not just her mouth,
but her forehead, her cheeks, the feathery tips of her
lashes and her eyelids besides, and that exquisitely

sensitive place she hadn't suspected lay below her ear.

But then, being seduced appeared to involve him knowing all sorts of things about her that she didn't expect, or even know herself. For example, he seemed as familiar with the intricacies of a lady's dress as she was herself—perhaps even more so, really, since most times she'd needed a maid for guidance—and he knew exactly what to unhook and unbutton and untie to be able to whisk her gown from her body. He managed to make even that a way to build the heat growing in her body, the soft cloth gliding over her skin, turning into a subtle caress of its own.

It didn't seem fair that she wasn't as adept with his clothes, nor as patient, and the distracted, clumsy uncertainty of her hands didn't help. Untying his neckcloth was as easy as undoing her own bonnet ribbons, but she struggled mightily to shove his coat from his shoulders and down his arms, and blindly her fingers fumbled with the double row of buttons on his waistcoat.

"Blast this wretched waistcoat of yours, Will," she muttered, breaking free of his kissing to scowl down at the perplexing buttons. "Who'd think a great grown man like you would need so many swaddling clothes?"

He laughed, guiding her fingers to the right paths.

"It's only practice, sweetheart," he said as, finally, he shrugged off the waistcoat. In a sweep of white linen, he tugged his shirt free of his breeches and pulled it over his head, grinning before her, fine as a lord.

Which, of course, was only right, considering that was what he *was*.

"Hey, ho, Will," she whispered with awe. "What a comely man you are!"

He was, too, his chest lean yet muscled, and he'd none of the softness so many gentlemen acquired from idleness and excess. His shoulders were broad and his waist and hips narrow, and he didn't need a tailor's tricks to make them that way. His skin was darker than she'd expected, browned and burnished by the sun in a fashion that earls weren't supposed to follow, with the dark hair across his chest narrowing to an enticing V that dipped into the waistband of his breeches.

And then there was what lay inside those breeches, that mysterious maleness behind the buttoned fall, the telltale bulge that inexorably drew her gaze, blushing as she did.

Oh, she'd thought she knew about what men hid there, didn't she? There had been precious little modesty in Threadneedle Court, particularly on a Saturday night when certain men had staggered home from drinking in the taverns, roaring and pissing in the street and shoving equally drunk women up against the alley walls. No modesty, and no romance, either, and if Harriet had had any questions left, Bett had answered those, sharing every detail in the exhilarated flush of her marriage to Tom Fidd.

Nay, though Harriet was a virgin, she wasn't ignorant or sheltered, and she certainly wasn't a fool. But none of Bett's tales could have prepared her for the very male reality of William, and especially not for that thick, shadowy shape thrusting insistently against the front of his breeches.

Clearly William's form of seduction had been as arousing to him as it had been to her.

She hadn't felt shy about standing before him in only her shift, for he'd seen her like that already. But having him here before her now, the two of them alone in his bedchamber with that enormous bed not six feet away—*that* was something else altogether, and though she hadn't intended it to, her apprehension must have shown on her face.

"Second thoughts, lass?" asked William. "If you don't want this, tell me now, and we'll stop. God knows this wasn't part of our bargain, was it? But the farther we go on, the more difficult that stopping will be for both of us."

She nodded, understanding, even as she weighed her wariness against the heady excitement he'd stirred in her body. She longed for him, ached for him, enough that she realized how difficult it would in fact be to stop, and how very much she wanted this with him.

Yet there'd been a moment earlier, when they'd first come upstairs, that she'd wondered if he'd had misgivings himself. She'd sensed then that he'd been guarded somehow, uncharacteristically reserved, holding back from her for reasons she couldn't guess while he measured his own doubts and fears. Even noble gentlemen with rakish reputations, she supposed, must suffer from those once in a while.

But when she searched William's face now, all she saw were passion and desire and love, the kind of love no one else had ever shown her.

"Nay, no second thoughts," she whispered, coming nearer to rest her hands upon his bare chest, and this time he let her. "I love you too much for that, Will. I've trusted you this far, and I'll not turn back now. We're partners, aren't we?"

"We are, lass," he said, gathering her up in his arms. "We are indeed."

He kissed her again, with such intensity that she would have gasped if he'd let her. His hands roamed so freely over her body now that she'd swear he'd figured a way to touch her everywhere at once. He peeled the narrow straps of her shift over her shoulder, then down her arms until they were freed, until her breasts were bare and her nipples could tighten against the hair on his chest, until the light linen slithered around her waist and over her hips into a puddle around her feet. All she'd left now were her stockings and her pink striped garters and her hair loose down her back, and none of it of any defense against the onslaught of sensation he was building within her now.

When he guided her backward into the center of the vast bedstead, the featherbed gave way beneath her with a soft *whoosh,* and she swallowed, her heart racing with excitement simply to be in his bed, in his sheets with his scent, her head on his pillows.

Behind the drawn blinds, in the drowsy afternoon twilight, the air in the tall curtained bed seemed to shimmer and swelter, her skin so warm that she lay on the sheets as flagrantly naked as a pasha's odalisque in pink garters, without a thought for pulling the coverlet over her. Why should she, when her pasha-lover was the Earl of Bonnington, stripping off his breeches to climb onto the bed with her?

She longed for more light to be able to look at

him and see for herself all the mysteries she'd only guessed at, but he was already leaning over her, making her hold her breath with anticipation and desperate desire.

"You'll trust me, pet," he said, more an order than a question or even a request. His mouth was so close to hers she could feel the force of his words upon her lips, his eyes so dark she'd never know they were blue. "No matter what I do."

"Aye," she breathed, not hesitating for even a moment as she slid her hands along his upper arms to his shoulders, across the bridge he'd made of his body arching over hers. "I'll trust you, Will."

He leaned down to kiss her, a quick, rough swipe of his mouth over hers. "Know I'll never hurt you, Harriet, and though, if you wish, I'll pleasure you senseless, I'll always keep you from harm. You have my word, always."

She nodded, not quite sure what that could mean, but before she could wonder aloud he'd rocked back on his heels just far enough to be able to shift his hands to her waist, slowly sliding them upward along her ribs to cover her breasts.

She gasped with surprise and delight, and as his hands teased her breasts until they felt heavy and full and her nipples taut and hard and aching for more, he kissed her mouth and her chin and the little hollow at the base of her throat before, at last, at last, his lips found first one breast, then the other. Her gasp threaded out into a shuddering cry as his tongue moved across the sensitive crest, drawing it back into his mouth and grazing it with the edges of his teeth.

Yet he knew the exact instant when she could

bear no more, holding her hips as he kissed the softness of her belly, rubbing the slight roughness of his bearded cheek across her skin in another kind of touch. Gently he bent her knee, untying the ribbon of her garter to hold it taut between his hands and teasing the silk along the same path his lips had just taken over her body.

"You—you are *wicked,* Will," she murmured, her voice echoing the shudders racing through her body.

"But not so much that you'd wish me to stop, would you?" he asked, his smile proof that he knew her answer before she shook her head weakly against the pillows. "That's what a lover is for, pet."

Her *lover,* she thought, the single word meaning so much more now to her overwrought senses. She wasn't his mistress, or he her master or keeper. They were lovers, equals, like the friends and partners they already were, now bound together by their hearts and souls and flesh, and she longed to tell him how infinitely much he meant to her.

But instead he eased her legs farther apart, smoothing his palms along the insides of her thighs, higher and higher until he'd reached the special place in between. She was already swollen with wanting, and when his fingers parted her to slip inside, she cried out, straining against him for whatever was hovering there, tantalizingly unknown and just out of her reach. Wantonly she let him lead her there, stroking her sleek, wet flesh as she twisted and whimpered and wordlessly begged.

He'd said he'd pleasure her senseless, and on the fraying edges of her consciousness, she would happily concede that he'd done so. But then he bent his head lower so his dark, damp hair fell over his forehead, and put his tongue where his fingers had been, and every coherent word flew apart from her head as the pleasure he'd promised rocked through her body.

"Ah, my own sweet Harriet," he murmured as he moved higher over her again. "We've only begun, pet, haven't we?"

And while the shudders were still rippling through her and her breath was still ragged in her chest, she welcomed his weight full upon her, greedily slipping her arms around him to keep him there. She wanted to be *his* lover as well and return the pleasure he'd just given her. When he nudged her legs farther apart, she shifted to help him settle there, and leaned up to kiss him for extra reassurance.

He groaned, reaching down between their bodies, and then suddenly he was pushing into her with something far larger than his fingers had been, blunt, hard, and hot. Startled, she fluttered against him, but he didn't stop, forcing his way deeper into her body. He butted against the tender resistance of her maidenhead, paused, and swore, then with one last thrust he was there, buried in her as far as he could go, and dear God in heaven, so was she.

"Harriet," he began, his voice raw, labored. "Damnation, Harriet, I'm sorry, but—"

"Don't!" she cried frantically, struggling not to let him know how strange it was to have him within her, how much she felt stretched and torn, all the magic gone. "Do not say it, Will, I beg you!"

He'd already given her so much that she couldn't bear to have him go, not yet, and instinctively she curled her legs over his hips, cradling him there. He groaned again, pressing deeper, but this way the hurt seemed to lessen, and when she rocked against him, taking him deeper still, she felt the first tiny ripple of pleasure return.

Cautiously he moved within her, drawing nearly out only to slide back in, and she gasped, not with pain, but startled delight. His shoulders and back were slick with sweat, his face knotted with concentration. He kissed her, sliding his hands beneath her hips to lift her into his thrusts, and she moved in response, learning the pattern of his rhythm and his desire. She felt the tension return, building within her, giving her movements the same fierce urgency that his had.

Over and over, her cries matched his groans as he drove into her, harder and faster, until she felt the same arching release seize her and let her go, spinning away from herself. An instant later she felt his body tense, too, and with a final roar, he thrust into her one last time, pulled out, and collapsed upon her, his seed spilling hot and sticky across her belly.

"Oh, Will," she cried forlornly. "Whatever have you done?"

He groaned, still breathing hard as he raised his face from her shoulder. "I—I promised I'd not harm you, lass, and I didn't."

She flushed as she realized what he meant, that by coming outside her body, he'd spared her the risk of conceiving his child. She realized, too, that she should be appreciative of his thoughtfulness and even more of his restraint and control, to put her pleasure before his own. That he'd done so showed his experience even more than the way he'd loved her.

But instead of gratitude, she felt empty and bereft, hollow where she'd been full. "You didn't tell me you'd—you'd do such, Will."

"Nor did you tell me, lass, that you were a virgin." With a sigh he rolled off her, reaching into the drawer of the table by the bed for a handkerchief that he used to wipe her clean. "You should have, you know. I would have been less . . . forceful. More considerate. Next time I promise it will be better for you."

She watched him briskly blot away the sordid reminders, her blood mingled with his spendings, and she blinked back the tears that burned in her eyes. She'd given him her innocence, freely and joyfully, a gift she could only give to one man, and only once.

Yet though he'd considerately meant to spare her any consequences, he'd also broken the bond of their union. No matter how lost in passion he'd seemed, he'd managed to keep his wits enough to remember to withdraw from her, and save his precious Manderville self from breeding with her unworthy, low-born person.

"You're quiet," he said, touching the tears on her cheeks, "and sad. Did I hurt you after all?"

She shook head, unable to find words for her jumble of emotions, and he sighed, a low, grumbling, ominous sigh.

"Damnation, Harriet," he said grimly, "if all you were to me was an evening's tumble and toss, then believe me, I would have stayed exactly where I was, and the devil with you."

Still she didn't answer, biting on her lower lip as she stared up at the canopy overhead.

"For God's sake, Harriet, listen to me," he said, leaning over her so she'd have no choice but to look at him. "What I said earlier in the carriage about you not being my whore—I meant that, Harriet, and meant it again here. If you'd been like Emily Poynton or any number of others, then prevention would have been your responsibility, not mine, though if you'd had to come to me later, I would have made the honorable provisions. I do believe in paying the piper."

"Then why didn't you just treat me like that?" she asked bitterly. "Why am I so special?"

"Because, damn it, you *are*," he said urgently. "Why can't you accept that? Why can't you accept *this*? It's special between us, Harriet, and I'm trying my hardest to keep it that way. This is the first time in my entire life that I've been in love, and so help me, I don't want to ruin it."

"Oh, Will," she said, reaching up to rest her hand on his cheek. She understood exactly what he was saying now, though if he kept talking like this, saying things that no rakish London noblemen were ever supposed to, she most certainly *would* cry, and it would be entirely, entirely his fault. "You know I love you, too, don't you?"

"I do." He kissed her again, with tenderness instead of passion. "What I feel for you, sweetheart, is likely too deuced fine for an old wastrel like me, and I don't dare blink from fear you'll vanish clear away. Where it shall lead, I cannot say, for everything's far too new for me, and likely for you as well. And neither of us, pet, needs a child to muddy the waters further. Not now, not as we are."

She looped her hands around his neck and tried to

smile. This, then, must be her choice, and what he was offering to her was, in its way, wonderfully fine. She'd have his love and his lovemaking, his company and his devotion. Day by day, she could have his love, and most likely the tea-shop as well, if she still wished it, when that last day inevitably came. What she wouldn't have was either his name, or his children.

She didn't see the fine distinction he was making about her not being merely his mistress. That seemed exactly what she was, now in fact what before she'd only been pretending to be. But this much at least she did understand, painfully clear and without any doubt: she could have this much of him, and stay, or leave and have nothing but loneliness left in her life.

And how her pride wished it weren't such an easy decision to make!

"I love you, too, Will," she said. "Truly, mind? And the rest, what you made me feel—that was righteous fine, you know."

"Well, I'd rather hoped it was for you," he said gruffly, "for it was more than fine as far as I was concerned. You're so much my match, pet, that it almost frightens me."

He kissed her, a good thing, not only for the kissing, but because that way he wouldn't see in her eyes the sorrow as well as the joy that her decision had brought her.

"I love you, Will," she said again, sure of that if nothing else. "I love you, and I do believe I always will."

They left London the following morning, traveling by boat along the river to Twickenham, where the

Fancy was moored. Strode had gone ahead with their dunnage last night, so now they only had one small trunk between them, and a hamper with food and drink. The Thames still served as London's busiest roadway, and William had insisted on starting before dawn, trying to avoid as much of the river's day-traffic of boats, wherries, and barges as possible, particularly between Blackfriars and London Bridge.

He was also anticipating showing Harriet the sights along the river's bank. Being city born and bred, she'd little concept of life beyond London's boundaries, with Green Park being the largest swath of grass and trees she'd ever seen. Summer along the Thames could be a beautiful sight indeed, from the handsome palace and hospital at Greenwich to the patchwork fields of rising crops and Kent's small villages clustered around church towers and spires, honeysuckle nodding in fragrant bloom, the herring gulls against the blue skies and old willows drifting their leaves languidly into the water.

But when William had been imagining such a romantic idyll, he'd overlooked the other side of an English June: chilly, gray, and damp, which was precisely what they found to greet them on this particular morning. Instead of sunshine and warm breezes, he and Harriet sat bundled in heavy wool wraps beneath a low roof of lashed sailcloth. In place of the flowery straw hat he'd bought her to shield her face from the sun, she wore a thick hooded cloak, and her nose turned red anyway from the cold. The fog was drifting thick enough over the water's surface that only the very banks were visible, and none of the sights beyond, and by evening the mist had turned to drizzle and the drizzle to out-and-out rain, the drops driving hard into the river.

He also hadn't predicted how much the gray, wet day would reflect Harriet's mood. Last night, after they'd made love, she'd been so quiet and thoughtful as to be almost melancholy, enough to raise his concern. It was understandable, of course, considering the step she'd taken with him, and he'd done his best to comfort her.

Yet it was the river, and not his understanding, that finally seemed to rouse her from her sadness. As the morning passed, her familiar cheerfulness returned, and her excitement grew. To her this journey was all a grand adventure, a lark, regardless of the weather, and she cared not a farthing for that ruddy-red nose of hers, nor how frizzled her hair became.

She boldly shared William's brandy, giggling as she swigged it from the bottle. She tossed scraps of bread to the bedraggled gulls, sang along with the boatmen's songs, and snuggled close to William beneath the coverlets, seeing how far and familiarly their hands could roam without the boatmen noticing. It was all enough to win his heart afresh, and if he hadn't already been in love with her, he would most definitely have declared himself so by Greenwich.

Though originally he'd planned to board the *Fancy* that night, because of the weather he decided instead to spend one more night ashore. They stopped at a favorite inn of his near Isleworth, where they dried their shoes and stockings before the fireplace and ate venison at a table in the common parlor, the foul weather having kept away most other guests. Yet he and Harriet talked and laughed and fed one another strawberries as if they hadn't been together the entire long day.

Or, as William marveled yet again, as if they were head-over-heels in love, and which, to his boundless joy, they certainly seemed to be.

"You've found a rare one in that lady, My Lord," said the innkeeper with approval to William. Across the room, Harriet was demonstrating her juggling prowess to the man's amazed young daughter, using strawberries instead of oranges and a considerable amount of laughter to cover her mistakes. "She's not like the others you've had traipsing with you in here before. Bright and quick as a new penny, this lady, without putting on airs with others. But then I expect you know that for yourself, My Lord, don't you?"

"What was that, Smythe?" said William absently, so enchanted with watching Harriet with the little girl that he hadn't really been listening to the innkeeper. Harriet was good with children. She didn't treat them as precious little beings or as unspeakable underlings, but with the same good-natured respect she showed adults, and clearly the innkeeper's daughter was ready to worship her for it. No wonder Harriet wished for children one day; she'd be an excellent mother to the children fortunate enough to be so blessed.

As would the man who would be their father, and her husband....

"That is, forgive me, Smythe," he said quickly, shoving aside that wayward possibility as he turned back toward the innkeeper. "I have to admit I was too lost in my own thoughts to pay heed."

"Too lost in *her*, My Lord, you should say," said Smythe with a sage nod, wiping his hands on the front of his green apron. "Begging pardon for speaking honest, My Lord, but I cannot recall the last time I saw a gentleman and lady so much in love."

"Miss Calliope and I enjoy one another's company, yes," said William uneasily, hoping he sounded more like his usual lighthearted self than he felt. Damnation, he'd thought being in love was a private condition, not one visible to the entire world. It was one thing for an old friend like Edward to challenge him about his feelings for Harriet, but quite another to hear it spoken as fact from the innkeeper of the Red Ivy. "And as you know, Smythe, this being our first visit together to your establishment, that in the first flower of a new sweetheart, everything smells doubly sweet."

But Smythe, blast him, was undeterred. "First flower, aye, My Lord, but I'll wager a bottle of my best port that this lady will be with you long past the first frost as well."

"Ah, Smythe, would that I had your gifts to see into the future!" William leaned back in his chair with a studiously idle nonchalance. If he could not fool a convivial English innkeeper like this one, he'd never succeed among the suspicious French. "I can myself only see as far as this week, when I have promised to run Miss Calliope beneath the guns for a day or two in Abbeville. Poor lass, she's never been to France."

"You would take this girl to Abbeville?" asked Smythe, shocked. "You'd run beneath the guns of both fleets for a bit of fun?"

"Why not?" William shrugged, and flashed his most world-weary smile. "You know I like to pace the *Fancy* against the best, and the danger does add a measure of piquancy to an *affaire de coeur*."

It should have been easy, pretending like this. Not long ago, it hadn't been acting at all. William remembered how, when he'd first met Harriet, she'd seemed so perfect as his partner because her entire person had seemed worth so shamelessly little. Now he could think only of how impossibly dear and precious she was, because he'd committed the greatest sin possible for a man in his position. He'd fallen in love with his partner, a woman whose life the Admiralty considered expendable.

But Smythe, unaware of any of this, could only shake his head. "Then I take back my wager, My Lord, and my bottle of port," he said gravely. "No gentleman would take a lady he cared for into danger like that, not for sport. It must be as you say, My Lord, between you and this girl, first flower and nothing more."

"Exactly so, Smythe," said William softly, his conscience mercilessly wringing his heart as he watched Harriet laugh. "First flower, and nothing more."

14

$\mathcal{W}$ith a restless sigh, Harriet looked up from her work and across the *Fancy*'s cabin to where William stood, leaning over the long table with charts of the waters around Abbeville and Brest spread before him. She knew what he was doing was important and necessary, but not so much that he couldn't have spoken at least one word to her in the last half hour.

Ever since they'd come aboard the *Fancy* two days earlier, William had been fussing and making apologies to her about their quarters: how the *Fancy* had been built for speed rather than luxury, how the furnishings were intended only for rough old bachelors like himself, not ladies like her, how nothing, really, about the cabin was worthy.

But Harriet had loved the cabin from the first. It ran across the entire stern of the sloop, with a long sweep of windows that looked out over the water. The walls, or bulkheads, as William called them, followed the shape of the hull, curving inward toward the deck overhead. Brass lanterns hung from the beams, polished to gleam like gold. As much of the furniture as possible—bookcases, benches, cupboards, even the bed, or bunk—had been built into the bulkheads to keep them from flying about in a high sea, and the few pieces that weren't—the long table that served for dining and as William's desk, and the chairs—had been made of heavy mahogany that would not be easily shifted or smashed.

She liked the brightness of the cabin, the light that reflected up from the water even in the rain, and she delighted in the seaman's ingenuity that could make such clever use of the space. But what made the cabin so special to her was how quickly it had become *theirs,* the place that she and William shared together, awake and asleep. After all the grand show of servants and ornate rooms at Bonnington House, the *Fancy*'s cabin was small and intimate, and when they sat together as they did now, Harriet almost felt like an ordinary wedded couple, content and snug in their cottage at the end of the day.

But the truth was that neither she nor William was ordinary, any more than they were wedded or even content, and instead of a snug night before their own fire, they would soon be climbing into the *Fancy*'s gig to row to shore and dine with an admiral.

With a long sigh, she put aside the stone she'd been using to sharpen her new sailor's knife, and slid the blade back into its sheath. She imagined the knife wasn't particularly ordinary for a lady to carry, either, but she'd feel much safer having it with her once they reached France.

She glanced out the stern windows, where more ships than she could count were moored in the anchorage of the Nore, here in the Thames estuary near the mouth of the River Medway. Most were navy warships, either newly returned from duty or waiting to put to sea, and once again Harriet felt a quick rush of excitement to think that she and Edward, in their small way, were going to be part of something so grand and noble.

"Are you ready then, pet?" asked William, reaching for his boat-cloak. "I can hear Strode scolding on deck, which means the gig must be waiting alongside for us."

"Aye, aye, M'Lord Captain," she tried to tease as he helped her with her own cloak. "Or Captain M'Lord?"

But though he smiled, he also shook his head to discourage her. "You talk like that before these officers, Harriet, and we'll both be clapped in irons. They take their ranks more seriously than any peer in the House of Lords. I am a mere cowardly nothing in their eyes, and they shall not take kindly to hearing you call me 'captain,' even in jest."

"You're no cowardly nothing, Will!" she said, loyally indignant on his account as he ushered her up the short companionway to the deck. "The *Fancy*'s yours, and what you're doing, risking your own life and property for them, should be worth a share of something!"

"In their eyes, lass, I am no more than the owner of a pleasure-boat," he said, trying so hard to be flippant that she immediately knew how much it bothered him. "Which makes me nearly the lowliest creature in their high-minded naval world. To them I'm scarcely a sailor, let alone a great exalted captain."

"That's neither true, nor fair," she insisted, giving his hand an extra squeeze of conviction. "I've heard the duke say that you could outsail him any day and in any wind. I've seen it, too, how you can read the currents and such as if it were written in words. You've chosen the best men for your crew, and you give them the orders. *That* is why you win all those races, not just because you own the *Fancy*."

But William only shook his head. "What these men do isn't sport, Harriet, especially not to them. Though I suppose if my life was as filled with bad food, bad pay, danger, death, and discomfort as theirs, then I wager I'd show little charity toward someone like me as well. Here now, mind your skirts when you climb down."

She clutched her skirts to one side as he'd ordered, climbing slowly over the side and down the half-dozen steps into the waiting boat. William hovered above her and two men in the boat held their hands up to catch her if she slipped, all of them making her feel rather like a baby bird with too many mothers trying to guide her into the nest. Not that she objected; far better to have them fussing over her than to tumble into the bottomless, dark water of the sea.

Yet as she made her way to the bench to wait for William to join her, she gloomily wondered if perhaps falling into the sea would be such a bad fate for her. The way things were going between her and William, drowning might indeed seem an improvement.

The first day they'd spent together on the Thames and at the Red Ivy had been the last time he'd seemed truly happy, and with each day since he'd become more and more preoccupied and lost in thoughts that didn't include her. The closer they'd come to the Channel, the less he'd laughed, or even smiled, and by the time the *Fancy* had moored here among the English fleet, he might have been another man entirely from the one who'd sung doggerel verse to her at Vauxhall.

The only time they still felt like lovers was when they lay together in the cabin's bunk. Then there were no difficult words or stilted silences, with their bodies and hearts free to express what by day they'd each somehow become too tongue-tied to say. Then Harriet could forget the walls she'd put up around herself in defense. She could remember what William had said about her being so much his match that it almost frightened him, and she could believe it, too. What they found and shared in the bunk was passion, true, but it was also love, pure and tender and filled with wordless understanding, and it was what sustained them both through the rest.

Except, of course, for that last part of himself that he always held back from her, the abrupt withdrawal that each time seemed to put another crack in her heart.

Finally William joined her on the bench, pushing his hat down lower on his head to make sure it wouldn't blow away. He nodded to the pair of sailors at the oars, who pushed away from the sloop and began to pull toward shore. The *Fancy* sailed with a crew of only six, strong-backed Sussex men who seldom spoke in Harriet's hearing, but two of them bending over the oars now could make the little boat fly over the choppy water.

"Not exactly the sort of night you'd wish for going calling," said William, hunching his shoulders against the blowing spray. "You'd think an admiral would order more agreeable weather."

So this was how it was going to be tonight, all talk of the weather, at least while they were in the boat and in the hearing of the two crewmen. Harriet pulled her cloak more tightly around her, and not entirely from the chill of the wind off the water, either.

"How am I to behave with Admiral Murray, Will?" she asked, choosing this as a safe enough topic, and useful besides. "Should I be Calliope again, or plain Harriet?"

"Never plain, sweetheart." He glanced at her, his smile lopsided with wistfulness. "Not my own dear love of a Harriet."

Quickly she looked down at her lap, not sure what to say in return. This was what made all of this so confusing between them, not knowing when he'd be distant and all brusque business with her, or woo her like this with such heartbreaking charm.

At least this time he didn't wait for her to answer, but continued. "Admiral Murray is an old friend of Edward's, which is the sole reason that I can fathom for us to have been invited to dine, and the only one I have for accepting. I imagine he knows our true reasons for being here in the Nore, but I intend to let him speak first, to make certain. What worries me more is him preferring to play the host at an inn ashore instead of aboard his own flagship. How sorrowfully unskilled must his cook be, I ask you?"

She smiled at him. Cooks, like the weather, were always safe for conversation. "Mayhap instead it is that the cook at the inn is that much better."

William snorted. "In the kitchen of an inn at Sheerness? Clearly, lass, you have never visited Sheerness, a tiny blot of a town, hardly the place to find brilliant cookery. There are some who maintain that Sheerness only exists in its woeful state to make going to war seem like the better alternative for His Majesty's sailors."

"So that is your hope, too, Will?" she asked with a shy half-grin of her own, pushing a blowing wisp of her hair away from her mouth. "That if this admiral's meal is so wicked awful, then I shall be fair begging to jump beneath the French guns when we sail tomorrow?"

Instantly his face closed against her, and just as instantly she realized she'd somehow blundered into saying the worst thing possible.

"No, Harriet," he said, each word clipped taut. "That is not my 'hope' for you, nor will it ever be so."

"Nay, Will, please, I did not mean—"

"Here is the landing place now, Connor," he said to one of the crewman, his voice still sharp, leaving no space for her to make headway or peace, even as he now was acting as if she hadn't spoken at all. "We shall be at the Capstan, around that corner opposite, as guests of Admiral Murray. Pray wait for us here, by this jetty, for I do not believe we shall be above two hours or so."

He jumped from the boat even before it bumped into the stone landing, and turned to offer his hand imperiously to Harriet.

"Mayhap I won't be coming after all, Will," she said rebelliously, making no move to leave the boat. "Mayhap you can give your blessed admiral my regrets, and frolic without me to hinder you."

"Enough, Harriet," he said sharply, reaching for her hand to lift her from the boat. "You will come ashore with me directly."

"Nay, I won't," she said, tucking her hands stubbornly beneath her arms inside the cloak. "Better I should sit here all the night on this beach than go with you where I'll only be a burden."

"Damnation, Harriet, you *will* come," he growled. "I have no intention of leaving you here in sight of God knows how many thousand men. Despite what you may believe, I care greatly what becomes of you, and—"

"*That* is what troubles you?" she asked, incredulous. "That when I jested about me and the French guns, you believed I meant it as gospel? Oh, Will!"

He raised his chin defensively, as much as admitting that that was exactly what he'd believed, or at least admitting it to her, because she knew him that well.

"Admirals expect promptness from their guests, Harriet," he said almost primly, as if he'd ever been prompt himself for anything in all his life, "and we are already keeping Admiral Murray waiting."

"*I* am not keeping him waiting," she said, scrambling from the boat without taking his hand. "*You* are, you great heaving dunderhead. How can you be so daft as that, believing such a low thing of me, Will, of *me?*"

"We're both bloody well daft," muttered William,

flipping back the edge of her cloak to find her hand. "Now come, this way."

He hated that they were quarreling like this, and over something this foolish, too. He could feel her slipping away from him, and yet he seemed incapable of stopping it. He'd imagined that once they were together on the *Fancy,* they'd continue as blissfully as they'd begun, or even grow closer, without the distractions of London around them. But instead the river and the boat and now the Nore with all its navy warships, even this invitation tonight, had all only served to remind him of the danger that he was so blithely leading her into, risks that she had no way of knowing. Because she loved him and trusted him, she'd follow him anywhere, and he knew it—shallow, irresponsible bastard that he was—and hated himself for knowing it as well.

Every time he let her smile at him made him less worthy of her. She deserved a true hero like Edward, a glittering paragon who in turn would deserve the boundless love she was wasting on him. Frustration had silenced him around her, the constant fear that he'd say or do something that would suddenly make her understand, and leave for good. Yet the fatalistic certainty that it *would* happen made him churlish and sharp when they did speak, as if he wished to force the inevitable and be done with it, like a rotting tooth that needed to be pulled to stop the pain.

The only time he still could feel that old closeness between them was when he made love to her in the *Fancy*'s bunk. There he was confident, endlessly understanding, assured, able to make her body sing with joy and her heart with it. It *was* making love, too, passionate and tender and emotional, with every ounce of pleasure he gave her returned to him a hundredfold. Experience might have taught him how to please her, but that same experience also told him how utterly unique their love was.

And damnation, *he did not want to lose her.*

Now he could feel the chill of her hand inside her glove, her fingers loose and noncommittal in his hand as he led her between the wagons and stacked barrels on the wharf, across the lane to the inn. He could not blame her for being wary, not after he'd just barked orders like some overbearing ass. He could say they were both daft, but more likely he'd be the one in leg-irons in the dirty straw of Bedlam Hospital, while she'd be one of the visitors come to pity him.

He squeezed her fingers anyway, trying to apologize in even that ridiculous fashion, and took a deep breath to compose himself before they joined the others in the inn.

At least he hadn't been exaggerating when he'd described the meanness of Sheerness to her. All the official necessities of the fleet—the dry docks, rope yards, sail-lofts, and smiths needed for fitting out and supplying vessels for voyages, and even the tawdry pawnshops, taverns, cheap lodgings, and brothels that catered to sailors—were attended to at Chatham, farther inland on the River Medway, and most ships remained in the Nore only long enough to receive final sailing orders or to meet other vessels for a convoy or fleet action. Few seamen and fewer officers ever ventured from the ships, and from lack of their interest Sheerness consisted of only a handful of faded cottages, shops, and warehouses, and, of course, the Capstan.

In the combined thickening of dusk and fog, the inn seemed respectable if unimpressive, three stories of plain hewn stone squared solidly toward the sea, and an ancient capstan salvaged from some long-wrecked vessel hung over the door to serve as its signboard. The innkeeper was likewise squared and solid, an old seaman with an oak post for a leg that thumped unevenly as he ushered Harriet and William back to a private dining parlor.

"My Lord Bonnington, Miss Calliope, I am honored!" boomed the admiral as soon as they entered the room. "A fine, fine good evening to you both!"

Murray charged forward to greet them as if they were a fresh prize to be seized, vigorously shaking William's hand and making a great show of kissing the air over Harriet's hand. He was a smallish, intense man with twin thatches of sandy-colored brows bristling over his eyes and a face as browned and lined as a walnut, the candlelight glinting off the brass buttons and gold lace on his uniform like sparks from an unruly fire.

Gold lace for faithful service and medals for bravery: no wonder Harriet was smiling so at the admiral. What stouthearted Englishwoman wouldn't?

"The honor, Admiral, is entirely ours," said William, guarding his own feelings with a disinterested wave of his hand as he dropped into the armchair nearest the fireplace. Besides, until he knew how much Murray had been told, it was far safer for him to remain in his established character as an overbred, indolent nobleman. "Oh, entirely so."

But Harriet glared at him, not understanding.

"We are most honored, Admiral Murray," she said with the warmest smile she could muster, bless her, determined to show that at least one of them knew enough not to be rude. "Having us here to this inn to dine and such."

The admiral nodded, his brows bristling with fierce intent to show he'd rather talk to her anyway.

"Oh, the Capstan's not the Clarendon, I'll grant you that in a whelk's shell, Miss Treene, but the keep is an old gun-captain of mine who used his prize money to open this place. Handsomely, too." With approval he glanced at the waiting table, set for only the three of them. "I always patronize him whenever I must tarry in the Nore, for his oysters in particular are a wonder."

"Oysters, sir?" asked Harriet politely. "I do love a nice oyster, sir."

Oysters, thought William glumly. The last thing either of them needed tonight was oysters, and their deliciously amorous effects.

But the admiral didn't seem to be listening, at least not to be able to answer. Instead he was leaning closer to her, peering at her mouth as if she were a horse at the fair whose teeth needed checking.

"You, Miss Treene," he said finally. "You are from London, and not from the West End, either."

"Nay, sir," she said warily. "From London, aye, but not the West End. I was born in—"

"No, no, Miss Treene, permit me to hazard a guess!" boomed Murray again. "It's a conceit of mine, you see, begun long ago as a lieutenant striving to sort out the diverse speech of my men. Now which is it in London: Cornhill, or Cannon Street?"

"Neither, sir," she said, "but precious close, in the same crook of the river. Threadneedle Court, sir."

"Threadneedle!" exclaimed the admiral, rocking away from her. "Hah! I should have smoked it!"

"Bravo, bravo," said William, clapping his hands with a show of weary, blatant sarcasm. "For your next trick, Admiral, perhaps you can guess the lady's age as well."

"Will!" gasped Harriet, shocked. "That is most wicked rude of you!"

"Not at all, Miss Treene, not at all," said the admiral quickly with a self-conscious laugh. "His Lordship is not required to be entertained by my little accomplishments. After all, we are here to celebrate and give thanks for His Lordship's talents instead, are we not?"

Hurriedly he plucked the open bottle of wine from the table and poured it into the three waiting glasses, striving to cover the awkward moment with business. William took the offered glass, slowly rising to his feet, as if he could scarcely be bothered to stand for a toast that was, after all, in his honor.

He smiled faintly at Harriet, hoping she'd understand. But unless she'd become an even better actress than he'd first suspected, he guessed from her expression that her main wish now was to dump the rest of the wine from the bottle into his lap.

Ah, lass, have we really fallen so dangerously far out of step? There was a time when we'd play like this, when your unhappiness with me wasn't blinding you. Once we were so close we were nearly one, weren't we? But I still love you, sweetheart, I love you still, and more. . . .

The admiral cleared his throat as he composed his speech, determined not to spoil the moment he'd planned regardless of what was happening between William and Harriet.

"You have noticed, My Lord," he began, "that I have invited no other guests tonight. That is because I wished to speak as freely as my heart and my men would wish, without fear of being overheard. Captain His Grace the Duke of Harborough has told me of your work, My Lord. He has told me how you have most bravely and selflessly devoted your energies and risked your life to bring the freshest advice and information from France through the port at Abbeville."

Oh, hell, Ned, why? Didn't you realize I'd never want this, especially not before Harriet?

"You overwhelm me, sir," he said, wondering if either Harriet or the admiral noticed how he was holding the wineglass so tightly he prayed the crystal wouldn't shatter in his fingers. "The risk was not so very great."

"Do not be modest, My Lord!" exclaimed the admiral. "The danger was real enough. We've locked the French in tight enough at Brest, but we've neither the men nor ships to close off every port. What we've learned from your source in Abbeville has told us where to go next, what harbor or inlet the French will try to use to break the blockade. You've saved many lives, My Lord, by risking your own, and I know it even if you won't admit to it. For a noble gentleman to venture so much for his country is rare, most rare. To you now, My Lord, to you and your heroic crew!"

But William could not make himself drink. "I tell you, Admiral," he insisted, "any dull-witted man could do what I have done, playing errand-boy and go-between."

"Only a dull-witted man with nerves of steel and courage to match," declared the admiral. "And your task is only growing more dangerous now with the Directory in such disarray, and the French ripping into one another like the jackals they are. Take care, My Lord, take extra care, for you shall need it."

Damnation, he did not need to hear this again, not now! Hadn't he read the reports that Edward had sent him from the Admiralty to know himself the fresh dangers he'd face with Harriet? Didn't he understand the chance that one or both of them could make this journey and not return, left behind in a French prison or shot by soldiers or executed as a spy on the guillotine in the Abbeville square?

"And you, Miss Treene!" The admiral turned toward her, glass in hand. "For a lady to be so gallant and brave, to risk not only her life but her honor for the sake of her country, is most—"

"She's not going," said William, setting his untouched glass down on the table. "Miss Treene will be remaining here in England."

"Will!" she cried. "What is this, then? What do you mean by saying such?"

He forced himself to look at her levelly, forced himself finally to be accountable and responsible for the woman he loved more than his own life, and see the shock and anger and hurt that now filled her lovely eyes. "I mean that you shall not be sailing with me in the *Fancy* to Abbeville, Harriet. I mean that I have changed my mind, and I intend to continue alone."

She was shaking her head back and forth, fighting her tears as she refused to believe him. "But Will, you cannot mean to do this now, not after—after everything else!"

"I do indeed mean it, sweetheart," he said evenly, determined not to waver, even though the effort of wounding her like this was nigh killing him. For her sake, for her love, what choice did he have? "If I am to be responsible, Harriet—"

"Oh, to hell with your damned responsibility!" she cried, shoving him hard with both hands. "Nay, Will Manderville, to hell with *you!*"

She turned and fled before he could stop her, slamming the door as she ran down the hallway, through the common room and the parlor full of tobacco smoke and startled faces and into the street and fog outside. She kept running past the corner of the inn, around the corner and alone and out of sight of the door, before she came to a staggering, gasping stop. With a groan, she leaned against the damp stone wall and closed her eyes, her head bowed and her arms clasped tight around her heaving sides.

She knew it would come, that he'd leave her. She'd known from the beginning. It had been her own sorry fault to fall in love with him, not his. But she'd never expected him to end it like *this,* coldly, deliberately, as mercilessly as an empty-hearted man could. She hurt too much to cry, instead sliding down along the wall until she was crouching at the bottom, her breath coming in painful, wracking dry sobs.

So lost in her misery was she that she didn't feel

the first gentle shake of her shoulder, or even the second. But still the shaker persisted until she lifted her face from her hands to turn toward him.

Not William, no, not that she'd expected him, but a boy, ten, perhaps eleven, years old. He was dressed like any other boy his age in a port, rough wool and linen homespun stitched by his mother into shirt and breeches and coat, a knitted cap that, belatedly, he remembered to pull from his head from respect. He looked well-fed, but hungry now, his wide blue eyes cautious, his wavy black hair flopping loose from the strip of leather holding back his queue, his jaw strong and determined for a boy his age, and all of him, every last mended sleeve of him, so much like William that, speechless, she wondered if she had gone daft, mad, the way he'd said.

"Forgive me, mistress," said the boy, even the cadence of his still-reedy voice like a ghostly version of William's. "But you're the lady that came with Lord Bonnington, aren't you?"

She nodded slowly, too shocked to say more.

"Then I did right," he answered, nodding his head with satisfaction. "I must see His Lordship, mistress, must see him tonight, before he sails. My name is Ezekial West, mistress, and I am His Lordship's son."

15

*W*illiam stood at the table in his cabin, with the boy waiting before him and Harriet sitting off to one side, letting him sort this out for himself. He'd asked the boy to sit with him, to show that he could be companionable, even under these circumstances, but the boy had refused. Not sullenly, but firmly, believing in keeping his place, whatever that was.

The boy. William had better begin thinking of him in some other way than that. One look at the two of them side by side, and there wasn't even the remotest chance that the boy wasn't his.

The *boy:* blast, he'd done it again.

"So your name is Ezekial," he said, repeating himself like a doddering old fool, which was surely how the boy was seeing him anyway. "Zeke. What the devil kind of name is that, anyway?"

Something flickered across the boy's face—contempt? amusement? pity? fear?—though he was quick enough to recompose his features before William could decipher them.

"It's taken from one of the Hebrew prophets, My Lord," he said, "writ at the time of the fall of Jerusalem. My mam was precious fond of her testament, My Lord, especially after she'd known you."

"Was she now?" asked William, drumming his fingers on the edge of the table. The headache that had begun when Harriet had reappeared with the boy and everything had changed was growing sharper by the moment. "Your, ah, mother did?"

"Yes, My Lord." The boy smiled slightly, and blinked, so eerily like himself that William felt the hair prickling on the back of his neck. "You knew my mam when she was Sarah Greenow. She said if that weren't enough for remembrance, to remind you of the Unicorn Tavern, when you were having the *Dasher* built on the ways in Plymouth."

He did remember now. She had been a plump, fair girl with slightly bucked teeth and a ripple of a laugh, who'd worked the Unicorn's tables bringing ale to the men from the shipyards. The *Dasher* had been the first boat he'd had built for himself, and he'd spent one wonderfully occupied summer fitting her out and testing her in the waters off Plymouth by day, and dallying with Sarah Greenow by night. Swiftly he did the reckoning in his head: he was thirty-one now—just—and he'd launched the *Dasher* when he was nineteen, making Ezekial roughly ten.

Jesus. He had a ten-year-old *son*.

"Why didn't your mother come to me before now?" he asked. He didn't want to consider how a boy this young would have made his way alone from Plymouth to Sheerness, or what disasters could have been waiting for him every step of his journey. "I would have been happy to offer her whatever assistance she needed, as your father."

"But you aren't my father, My Lord," said Ezekial, likely more warmly than he realized. "My da was Samuel West, who married Mam before I was born and made me Ezekial West, from the purest goodness of his heart, though he's dead now, too. I'm your son, but you're not my father, not how it matters. You were only the Old Weakness. That's what Mam always called you, when she called you anything. The Old Weakness."

So that was how he'd been remembered, thought William grimly, as the Old Weakness? What kind of disreputable legacy was that for a man, anyway, let alone a father?

He'd always remembered his own tenth summer as the last of his boyhood, the one before Ned was sent away, but how much worse it had been for Zeke. He looked at the boy now, seeing himself, and wondered if he, too, somewhere, had once had a fort in a tree, too, and a rowboat, and dogs—though if he had, they'd all come from the man he'd called his father, not the Old Weakness.

He sighed, struggling to sort all this out with himself. He was coming into his son's life barbarously late, and he didn't deserve much of anything in return. But he could try to change things with the boy standing before him, couldn't he?

"You are blessed to have had Mr. West in your life, Zeke," Harriet was saying, deftly smoothing over the rough waters. "Mind you don't forget that. When did your mam finally tell you about His Lordship?"

"Not until she was dying," said the boy, determinedly keeping his emotions to himself. "Last month, when the consumption got so bad, she knew her time was coming."

Harriet's face softened. "Sad, sad," she said quietly, sharing his grief in a way that William found he could not, though touched deeply all the same. "I am sorry for her, Zeke, and for you, too."

"Thank you, mistress," he said softly, his fingers twisting in the ribbing of the cap his mother had doubtless knitted for him. "But now she's free of her suffering, and I must keep mindful of that."

"Yes, Zeke," said William, reaching out to lay his hand upon his son's shoulder. Now that the first shock was fading, he was surprising himself by how honestly—if a bit awkwardly—such a gesture came. "Now that she is gone, you must tell me what I can do for you."

But the boy's jaw shot up like a bolt. "I don't want nothing from you, My Lord, nothing, hear?" he said fiercely. "Mam said to come to you for work, My Lord, not charity, and to take not a farthing that wasn't earned, nor shall I."

"Nor would I expect you to," said William quickly, understanding how pride was likely all Zeke had left. "But I am in need of a strong, reliable boy aboard this sloop. The *Fancy*'s built for speed, and I only hire on the kind of sailors who can make her fly."

"Aye, aye, My Lord," said Zeke eagerly. "I saw at once she was a crack vessel."

"She is," said William solemnly. "You'd be expected to obey all orders, with no special favors shown to you, nor will you receive a penny more than you earn. We sail tomorrow, Ezekial West. Are you with us?"

Wide-eyed, Zeke nodded vigorously. "Aye, aye, sir. That is, yes, My Lord. Will your wife be sailing with us, too?"

"My wife?" repeated William with a frown, the words drifting for a moment too long before Harriet seized them.

"If you mean me, Zeke," she said as quietly as she'd spoken of his mother, "then nay, I'm not Lady Bonnington, nor am I sailing in the *Fancy* tomorrow."

The boy nodded, accepting, yet still his glance darted about the cabin, noting Harriet's comb on the shelf before the looking-glass, a shawl folded on the bunk, her garters draped across the back of a chair, as graphically as if he'd pointed to them outright, and as impossible to ignore.

"I am most fond of Miss Treene, Zeke," began William uncomfortably, all too aware of how he and Harriet had parted earlier in the evening over this exact same issue. "But I have decided, for her own safety and welfare, to leave her behind."

Ezekial nodded again, his expression suddenly wooden. "Like you did with Mam, My Lord," he said softly. "Just like."

"No, it's not like that, not at all!" exclaimed William without thinking. Automatically he turned toward Harriet, and though he was speaking to the boy, he could not make himself look away from her. "That is, your mother and I were young and, ah, liked each other fine for a summer, but what I have with Miss Treene—I love her, Zeke, love her with all my heart."

But Harriet gasped, clearly shocked. "How can you say that, Will, after—after you sent me away this very night, when we were with the admiral?"

"I can say it because it's true," he answered, determined to keep his temper with Zeke standing between them. "I do love you. And damnation, Harriet, I didn't send you away. I'm leaving you here where I know you'll be safe. I'm going to France, and then I'll come back to you. There's no 'sending' anywhere in that."

"You leave me behind like that," she said, her chin lowered defensively, "and I'll not promise to be here waiting when you come back."

That wouldn't be an empty threat, not from her. "It's not a punishment, Harriet. It's for your own good."

"All settled so neat and tidy, oh, aye, indeed, that is *good*. But you are forgetting that I'm a wicked untidy woman, Will, and I'm not going to let you pack me away in cotton-wool like one of those little china shepherdesses."

"I love you, Harriet," he said again, returning to the one thing he knew was certain, the only one that might persuade her to stay, "and I'm only trying to—"

"Then try to let me finish, Will," she begged. "Just try to *listen,* instead of talk. We are lovers, aye, but we are also friends, and partners, and all the other fine things. *That's* why our loving's so strong, Will. It's all the rest that makes it that way, or leastways it did, once."

"Hell, Harriet, it still does!"

She gulped, and managed only half a smile. "Then you should understand, Will. Once we promised to trust one another, remember? To look after each other, and keep the other safe and happy, best we could. How can I do that for you staying here?"

He shook his head, and suddenly saw Zeke again, standing silent and forgotten, his eyes enormous.

"Go find Strode, Zeke," he said, "and tell him you're sailing with us. He'll find you supper and a place to sling a hammock. Go, now. No need for you to have to listen to our quarrel."

"Aye, aye, My Lord," said the boy, pulling his hat back onto his head. "Not that you should mind me and the quarreling, My Lord. Mam always said quarreling was a kind of loving. If you didn't care enough to fight, she said, then you didn't care enough to love, either. Good night, mistress, My Lord."

He scurried away before William or Harriet answered, and after he'd left, they didn't speak, either, for what seemed to William to be at least an eternity. She was still wearing her gown for the evening, pale pink silk that glistened softly in the murky cabin's light, and he thought of how he couldn't imagine not having her here like this, with him.

Outside the tide in the Nore had turned with a rush of waves that helped fill the silence between them, and the *Fancy* was tugging at her moorings as she felt the pull of the flow, making the cabin's lantern swing back and forth. The dancing shadows played over Harriet's face, making her mood harder for him to read.

But how in blazes could she have believed, even for a moment, that he wished to end with her?

"A wise boy, that," he said finally. "Clever, too. His mother did well with him, God rest her soul."

"He should be," she said, and to his surprise she wasn't jesting, either. "He has a clever, wise man for his father."

William grunted. "No, he doesn't. He has a damned pompous braying jackass. And for you to have to be confronted with one of my by-blows like that—"

"He's not a 'by-blow,' Will," she said sharply. "He is your son, and so much like you it steals my breath away. How could I feel wrong about him?"

"You can't," he said, "because you're too good a woman for that. You didn't really believe I was casting you off, did you?"

She ducked her head, as much as telling him yes. "I didn't know, Will," she confessed. "When I think of who I am, where I'm from, and then you, an earl and all. And then your voice, there with the admiral at the inn, your manner—"

"Forever," he said firmly. "That's how long I mean to love you, Harriet. Forever."

She smiled wistfully, clearly wanting so much to believe him that it tore at his heart. "Then these last days when things haven't been—haven't been as they should between us—"

"Those days are done," he said, holding out his hands to her. "That's about the best I can say, and how vastly sorry I am to have caused you grief."

"And I'm sorry, too, Will," she said, taking his fingers and letting him draw her closer, until they were standing directly before one another, almost as if beginning a dance. "But when you did not talk to me, what else was I to think, I ask you?"

He sighed mightily, the old trouble returning. "It's

only when I see all these navy ships, lass, and think of all the men like Edward who've gone and done something important with their lives—"

"Hush," she scolded, putting her fingers over his mouth. "Just you hush, Will Manderville! You heard Admiral Murray, didn't you? Saying how brave you were, how the work you did is so precious important?"

"I heard him, yes," he said through the screen of her fingers, "but I didn't—"

"No buts," she said, clapping her hand more securely over his mouth, "and no more braying, either, My Lord Jackass. You *are* a hero, bless your long furry ears, and if you decide that this voyage is your last, then you'll still have done far, far more for your country than most Englishmen ever dream of."

He pulled aside her hand from his mouth. "It's doing both, together," he said heavily. "It's doing what I have to for the good of my mission in Abbeville, putting my honor and duty to England first and all, and then loving you at the same time. Not even Edward believes that I can do both, that if I were tested, truly tested, then I'd choose to protect you instead."

"Oh," said Harriet, wrinkling her nose. "What a gloomy quandary *that* is!"

"I'm not teasing now, Harriet," he said. "I'm as serious as I can be. I never told you this, but last time, we had to leave Abbeville rather, ah, abruptly, from the beach rather than the docks. As we did, soldiers from their militia tried to stop us, and though we got clear away, we left three of them dead or dying on the beach."

Her face had turned very serious now, as serious as his. "Meaning if you left them dead, you and your men killed them?"

"Meaning the pistols and guns aren't just for show, Harriet," he said evenly, wanting everything finally to be as clear as possible, no matter that speaking of those three dead men had brought back the memory of their dying with horrifying clarity. "Though my contact there swears no one has linked their deaths to me or the *Fancy,* I can't help but think somehow someone has, especially after all that has happened to you once we became partners."

"The torn costume at the mantua-makers, and the bloody doll," she said slowly, "and the Frenchman at Vauxhall. You think those are connected to this?"

"If I knew, it wouldn't be a mystery, would it?" He tried to smile, brushing his fingers across her cheek. "Perhaps I'm simply being overcautious, pet, seeing tartars in the kitchen garden, and we'll dance in and out of Abbeville as easy as you please. But there's also a possibility—no, a reasonable chance, this being France—that there shall be some sort of unpleasant welcome waiting for us."

She frowned, absently toying with the gold beads around her wrist as she sifted through all that he'd told her, which, even for a clever woman like Harriet, was a deuced great amount.

"Hey, ho," she said finally. "You might have told me before now, Will."

"I know," he said unhappily. "But knowing it all now, what danger you'll likely be in—you're not as determined to sail with me tomorrow now, are you?"

She didn't hesitate, not even a second. "Of course

I am!" she said, adding an indignant gasp for good measure. "You shouldn't even have to ask me that, Will. We are partners, in easy times and bad, and besides, how else can I show you I love you?"

He turned her hand and lightly kissed the palm. "Most women I know would, oh, send a nosegay of flowers to demonstrate their affections, or perhaps knit a pair of fancy stockings. You're the only one who'd rather offer to lay her neck upon a French chopping-block."

"But that's why I'm going, Will," she said firmly, refusing to be distracted by his lips on her palm. "To make sure it isn't your neck there, either."

"And so around and around that same old maypole we go again, don't we?" He sighed wearily, looking down at her hand in his. "I've never had to think much at all about anyone other than myself, Harriet. You're the first, you know, and now Ezekial shows up on my doorstep, too. Hell, I've no business hauling him off to Abbeville, either, the poor little rogue."

"You'll do fine with him, Will," she said gently. "Just as you've done with me."

"Oh, righteous fine." His smile was bittersweet, unable to share her endless optimism. "You make me shudder, lass, you do. My ineptitude in such matters must be more glaring than the sun in the sky."

"What shows is that you love me after all," she said softly, "nearly as much as I love you. With the two of us together, those Frenchmen haven't a crooked leg to stand upon. Together, mind? Love me, and trust me, just as I shall you, and the rest—ah, the rest, Will, shall take care of its own self."

But what took care of its own self now was how rapidly they progressed from the deck to the bunk, shedding their clothes along the way in an untidy trail. He made love to her with an urgency, a fever, that he'd never felt before. He pulled her astride him, the way she liked best, the way that reminded them both of the licentious secret paintings at Harborough House. His fingers held tightly to the soft, swelling flesh of her hips to guide her rocking movements and to tip her breasts forward, heavy and full, to graze against the rough hair of his chest. He loved it this way, too, with her spread wide and open for him to touch and stroke, so that he was able to slide even deeper inside her, past her coppery curls already soaked with their juices.

Over and over he brought her to the very edge of her release, and then held her there, bringing her whimpering and trembling back only to push her relentlessly again. He wanted to lose himself in her and to make her feel the same way, to be able to forget everything else except their love, and this moment. He drove into her with an animal passion that was dangerous to his self-control, that she matched with cries of her own as she writhed over him, until with the last shred of his awareness he knew he'd have to stop.

Yet as tight as her own body was, twisting against him, she felt him begin to slip away, and held him fast.

"Stay," she gasped. "Don't—don't leave me, love, not tonight!"

She was his love and never would belong to any other man, his love forever. And with a final cry torn from his soul and his heart, at last he let himself join her in a hot rush of love and release.

She was his. . . .

Though the sky remained gray, the winds favored the *Fancy,* and with the sloop's speed, their crossing was quick and easy. Once, far in the distance, one of the crewmen glimpsed the crosstrees of a frigate, but the sloop darted away before they ever learned if the ship was English or French, and the next mark spied was the irregular coast of France itself.

"Mr. Strode says we're bound for France," said Zeke, standing at the taffrail beside William as they both studied the horizon.

"That we are," said William, handing the spyglass to Zeke. He didn't want the boy to know too many of the details of their journey, but by now their destination seemed safe enough. "We're bound for Abbeville, a snug little harbor in what used to be known as Brittany, but now, thanks to Robespierre and the rest, is called Finisterre, for Land's End."

Zeke peered through the spyglass a thoughtful, silent minute before returning it to William. He enjoyed Zeke's company, especially these times when there were just the two of them together like this, man-to-man, as it were. They hadn't quite maneuvered through the lordship business, and there were many long-term questions to be settled about schooling and such, but for now William was enjoying Zeke much as he did his nieces and nephews, only more. With Harriet there besides, it was strangely as if he'd found a family ready-made for himself, and a damned fine one at that.

"Mr. Strode says we'll be in there no more than a day or two," said Zeke. "He says you've been there before, and that's all you ever stay."

William nodded, wondering how much other useful information he was gleaning from his conversations with Strode. "This time it may not even be that long. France is a sad and sorry place these days. There's little use to lingering there longer than we must."

"Aye, aye," said Zeke, twisting his face into sage agreement, partly from working his tongue into the place where he'd just lost a baby tooth. "Will you be marrying Miss Treene when we return to England?"

"Impudent monkey." William raised one brow with surprise. "That's a damned personal question for one gentleman to ask another, Zeke. Or did you hear that from Mr. Strode, too?"

"No, My Lord," he said, tugging that misshapen knitted cap of his down lower over his brows. "I reckoned it for myself. You love Miss Treene, and she loves you, and you've already set to housekeeping, all familiar. What's left for you but to wed her?"

William smiled, for the question was one that had been on his own mind constantly. It was a strange phenomenon. Once he'd let the idea of making Harriet his countess into his head, he could think of nothing else, and no real objections.

True, as an earl, he was supposed to be looking after the welfare of his family, the title, and his estates, and it could be argued that bringing an orange-girl into the fold was hardly improving the Manderville stock. But anyone who argued like that had never met Harriet, his dear, clever, brave, passionate, beautiful,

and thoroughly-perfect-for-him Harriet. Already she
could be carrying the tiny seed of his heir in her belly,
and his smile widened with secret happiness.

All that really mattered was that she loved him,
and he loved her. The only question remaining now
was when, and how, to ask her.

Not, of course, that he'd share any of this with
Zeke.

"You're a pip, Zeke," he said mildly instead. "But
I do believe impending marriages are for your elders
to decide, not you."

"Aye, aye, My Lord," said Zeke, not in the least
perturbed. "But Miss Treene—she's not one you
want to let go free, My Lord."

"Oh, I've no intention of that, Zeke," said Will as
he smiled, and looked out to sea, and imagined how
utterly beside herself Harriet would be when he proposed. "None in the least."

Robitaille labored slowly across the empty beach,
his shoes already heavy with the soft sand and his
walking stick doing little to help ease his progress.
Mother of God, it was like dragging his feet through
the snows of winter, and he pressed his hand to his
heart to try to stop its uneven racing. A man his age
belonged beside his fire, not on this beach, where the
sea blew into his face as if to taunt him all the more.

Yet each day he came, each day he found time to
walk this bleak forsaken scrap of nothingness in
honor of his son. Here, near this dune, had been the
footsteps to mark where Jacques and the others had
chased the English toward their boat. Here had been
the deep rut in the sand where the boat had been

pulled ashore to wait, the swath from the woman's petticoats and the deeper footsteps of the sailors as they'd hurried to push the boat free. There was where the first man had fallen, twisting in his final agony, and there, behind him, had been the second, his loaded musket still clutched in the unyielding fingers of death.

And here, near these three stones, was where his Jacques had fallen, here where the water had come hissing forward to kiss his icy lips, here where the sand had sucked his blood from the wound from the English gun, here where his hat had slipped from his head to let his hair toss one last time in the ruffling of a spring breeze.

They'd said it was English, yes, the same smugglers who had plagued this coast as long as anyone could remember, Englishmen with no regard for life or law. An old woman had seen their vessel in the moonlight, a raking single mast that was so much the mark of the smugglers' cutters that no one in Abbeville had questioned it. A pity that the three young soldiers had died for such a shallow cause as old brandy destined for some duke's table. Better they had been less zealous in their patrol, and saved their lives for General Buonaparte's grand army. A tragedy, a loss, but in these times, what house did not have such losses among its sons?

Only Robitaille knew the truth. The English Lord Bonnington who brought his whores to Abbeville for amusement had sailed in a pleasure-yacht with the same raking mast, and had cleared the harbor the same night that the three young men had been killed while patrolling the coast. The whore had been unfaithful to Bonnington; she had made assignations on this very beach with a dragoon captain on leave in the town. That much Robitaille had learned. The rest he'd been left to guess.

None of it had brought back his son.

Sacred Robe of Our Mother, but the wind was sharp today! For the last time he raised the worn old spyglass to his eye, scanning the horizon as he did each day in the name of his son, the name of his vengeance.

And today, praise God, he was rewarded. He rubbed his eyes, afraid he'd imagined what he wanted so badly to see, but there it was again, sharp and clean against the sky: the raking mast, the English flag, the long, trailing pennant of Lord Bonnington's sloop, bound for Abbeville, and for his destiny.

16

"*B*elieve me, pet," said William, sitting beside Harriet in the shabby hired carriage, "twenty years ago, even fifteen, and Abbeville must have been another place entirely, though I'll grant you it's hard to imagine it that way now."

It was indeed difficult for Harriet to look at the town around them now and envision it as the fashionable summer retreat for the nobility that William was describing from his father's time, a charming spot by the sea filled with taverns specializing in oysters and local wines, shops with the latest bonnets and gowns from Paris, and inns that did not question wayward lovers.

There was, alas, little of that glory to be found in Abbeville these days. Most of the buildings were in shabby disrepair, the most elegant shops and inns long closed and shuttered. The ostentatious frivolity that had once made the town so popular was now a dangerous sentiment in Revolutionary France, and many, many of the noblemen and women who had made Abbeville prosper had been killed in the Terror.

But while only the spirits of those ladies and gentlemen remained, Abbeville was far from a ghost town. Now, with the major military port of Brest so firmly blockaded by the English, Abbeville had become a favorite spot for officers on leave from the wars. The brothels flourished, the taverns were full, gambling was everywhere, and by night the streets seethed with all manner of bawdy revelry.

Harriet had seen at once that it was not a place for respectable people. But for the jaded, wealthy Englishman that William was supposed to be, in pursuit of illicit and dangerous amusement with his latest mistress, it would be unadulterated heaven.

"We leave tomorrow, Will," she whispered, ignoring the two hussars beside their carriage who were determined to catch her eye even as they ogled the rest of her person. "You said three days would be enough, and mind me, it shall, or I'll be leaving without you."

"Smile, sweetheart," advised William pleasantly as he leaned back against the seat in the open carriage. "It's a splendid idea to make them envious, as long as you keep from forcing me to duel on behalf of your honor."

"Bother my honor, Will," she said uneasily, smiling but also tugging her shawl up higher over her breasts to the disappointment of the hussars. "This is worse than Covent Garden on a Saturday night."

"You have no argument from me," answered William softly. "As long as you find something that pleases you at the shop, then we shall sail with the tide in the morning, and be done with this place forever. Ah, but here we are at Girard's, sweetheart, and time for your finest performance yet."

With a rush of excitement, Harriet turned toward the jeweler's shop as the carriage slowed. This was the reason they'd come all this way, the place where they were to receive the charts and messages the Admiralty so desperately sought. To succeed, she and William must continue to appear exactly as they had been these past two days, with William infatuated but a trifle bored, and Harriet charming, shallow, and selfish.

And if they didn't—if anyone doubted or questioned them, or saw exactly what Girard was passing to them—why, then, the small prison that faced the weedy town square was waiting to accommodate them, as well as the courts and guillotine still in quite active use nearby in Brest.

"Come, my dear," said William, purposefully raising his voice a bit as he helped her down from the carriage. "Monsieur Girard does know what baubles delight you ladies the most. All I ask is that you do not beg for everything in his shop, yes?"

But Harriet only cocked her head to one side and laughed merrily, making no such promises. Today she'd purposefully worn an extravagant hat, bright green silk with silver tassels dangling from the brim and down the back of her neck and green gloves to match, her gown a fluttering confection of pink muslin. She'd already discovered that if she were to play a gaudy bird, it helped to have the proper plumage as well, and this morning she'd even worn her auburn-gold hair loose, curling over her shoulders with a showiness she hadn't dared in public since she'd been a child.

With her head high as a queen's, she swept into the little shop, leaving William to follow a step behind. She smiled at the small, wiry Frenchman who hurried forward to greet her. Two other customers, a gentleman and a lady, were being helped by an assistant, and though they glanced up only briefly when William and Harriet entered, Harriet couldn't help wondering anxiously if the couple were waiting to pounce.

"Good day to you, Miss Calliope," said Girard, his bow an obsequious reminder of the *ancien régime*. The worst fervor of the Terror had faded by now, and titles were gradually coming back into use, especially for foreigners who'd never abandoned them in the first place. But though Girard had pinned a tricolor ribbon to the front of his waistcoat as a defensive nod to current politics, William had said that it was his loyalty to the old ways and lost friends that had made him so willing to pass secrets to the English. "How you honor me with your custom! How much I have anticipated your visit!"

"As well you should, Girard," said William with indulgent resignation as he guided Harriet to the small stool beside the counter. "She will be like a veritable child among the sweets once she sees your wares."

Girard clasped and unclasped his hands with anticipation as he slipped behind the counter to begin showing them his choicest pieces. He was the last jeweler of any repute left in Abbeville, though even he had had to begin stocking pinchbeck and marcasite, inexpensive pieces that the soldiers would buy for their sweethearts.

But for the earl, Girard would show only his best, and with a flutter of his full-sleeved shirt, he unlocked the first cabinet.

"Miss Calliope is not entirely unknown to me, My Lord," he said, pulling out a velvet-covered tray. "As you can see, her beauty has already inspired other artists beside the Duchess of Harborough. There has been much interest in this miniature, My Lord, nearly matching the anticipation of viewing the original."

He held out a minature on ivory that had been copied after one of Her Grace's paintings of Harriet as Athena, framed in gold and seed pearls and hung on a chain. Harriet gasped with genuine delight, then recalled her instructions: she was to ask William to buy her only the ruby necklace, for packed within its case would be the papers.

"Nay, Mr. Girard, I think not," she said, adding an imperious sniff. "The likeness doesn't favor me at all."

"No, pet?" asked William idly as he held the miniature swinging in his fingers. "I believe it's rather like. Put it aside for me, Girard. I might wish it as a memento, to carry with me if ever we be apart."

"Truly?" She glanced at him, surprised, unable to tell if this were part of their plan or spoken from his heart.

"Truly." Gallantly he lifted her hand to his lips, and she felt herself smile, her face soften, the way it always did when he looked at her like this. "Not, of course, that I wish ever to part with you, dearest. But show us other pieces, Girard, some things more pleasing to the lady's tastes."

The jeweler nodded, and in the next hour pro-
duced a bracelet of sapphires, a diadem centered with
Neapolitan cameos, rings and ear-bobs and necklaces
of every kind for Harriet to consider. As lovely—and
costly—as each piece was, however, she dutifully
managed to find some flaw in each to make it unworthy and destined only to be scorned and sent back.

It felt like the same sort of game she'd always
played when she'd sold oranges, half acting, half flirting. The only difference was that now William was
her partner, and that if she erred or went too far, it
wasn't just the sale of an orange or two she was risking, but both their lives. Yet her fickleness drew the
attention of the other couple in the shop, and two officers who'd come later, each of whom were undoubtedly eager to spread the story of the greedy
young Englishwoman who refused to be satisfied
with any of her lover's offerings.

Which was, of course, exactly what they wished.
Who would ever suspect them of being spies when
they'd openly draw this kind of attention to themselves?

Yet with each piece that Harriet rejected, each
murmur of surprise that whispered through the others, she felt her heart beat a little faster, her voice rise
a bit higher from knowing how much was at stake,
and what the price would be if they failed.

"Girard," said William finally, "have you anything
in fine rubies? A necklace, say, to demonstrate the
passion I feel for my Calliope?"

Ah, the rubies at last, she thought, the rubies: she
must not let herself be distracted.

"Aye," she said, all haughtiness as she drew her

hand away from William and curled it artfully over her breasts. "But only *fine* rubies, sir. Pray don't shame His Lordship or me by showing us ill-gotten ones."

The jeweler bowed, disappeared into a back room briefly, and returned with a large, shaped leather case.

"I purchased these only last week, miss," explained Girard as he unhooked the case and turned it toward her. "They are the finest rubies I have seen in years."

Slowly he opened the case. Harriet gasped, as did all the bystanders, and who wouldn't? Six carmine-red rubies the size of almonds, each surrounded by a fan of diamonds, had been fashioned into a spectacular necklace with long, dangling earrings to match, a king's ransom in jewels, certainly, or at least for someone of high rank.

"Here, Miss Calliope, try them," urged the jeweler as William draped the necklace around her throat to the appreciative sighs of the others. "See how handsome they will be with your hair, your skin."

But handsomeness was not what Harriet thought when William clicked the clasp closed. The stones were cold, laying hard against her skin, and their weight made Harriet think of what lady had worn them before, and what sorry fate she must have met to have given up her necklace now. The longer Harriet studied her reflection in the looking-glass the jeweler held for her, the more the pear-shaped stones seemed like drops of blood around her throat, a dreadful premonition that made her long to tear the jewels from her neck.

"Beautiful, Girard," declared William. "As always you have saved your very best for last. You are pleased, my dear?"

"Aye," whispered Harriet. She must put aside her own feelings about the necklace, and remember that the real treasure was not the rubies, but the papers that lined their case. "They are most beautiful."

"But not so beautiful as you are, pet," said William fondly. "Yet as taken as you are with your new toy, Harriet, I do not believe you should wear such stones publicly here in Abbeville. It would not be wise, yes?"

She pouted, barely remembering her role. "But I wish to wear them!"

William shook his head, reaching out to unfasten the clasp. "Better we save them for London, my dear, where people are still free to enjoy such amusements," he said as he handed the necklace back to the jeweler. "I would hate to have you come to some misfortune for the sake of mere decoration. But I do believe I have something that will make you forget your disappointment. Girard?"

What was he doing *now?* Everything else had gone exactly as it was supposed to; there was no reason to go adding anything else now. The rubies were supposed to be the end, and if she and William had followed their plan, they were now to leave the shop, dine one last time upon the famous oysters at an inn nearby, then retreat to the *Fancy* and prepare to sail. There'd been no mention of anything to soothe her disappointment, and she wondered uneasily if she were meant to accept it, or refuse, as she had everything else.

But unlike the other pieces, Girard did not show her this last one himself, but handed the small leather box to William instead. Even more peculiar was how William frowned down at the box in his hand, almost as if he were at a loss for words—which William almost never was, especially not here—before he finally took Harriet's hand and, to her considerable amazement, the Earl of Bonnington knelt on the floor before her.

"My own dearest lass," he said softly. "My Calliope, my orange-seller, my friend, and my lover. Will you do me the inestimable honor of becoming my wife and my countess as well?"

Surprised, shocked, stunned beyond reason, she caught her breath and gripped the edge of the counter to keep from sliding from her stool to the floor beside him, the shop spinning around and around with William's face at its center. Desperately she told herself that this wasn't real, that it wasn't happening the way it seemed, that it must only be another scene from their little Abbeville show, some part he hadn't remembered to tell her about, a handful of words that meant nothing to him and would only break her heart forever.

"Oh, Will, Will," she whispered miserably. "How can you be so wicked cruel?"

He smiled crookedly, the way he always did when he wasn't sure of himself but wanted the world to think he was. "I'm not cruel, sweetheart. I'm in love."

"Ah, Will," she said, tears in her eyes, clogging her throat to make her croak. "So am I."

"Then I shall take that as your acceptance." He opened the box, fumbling with the latch in a charmingly uncharacteristic way. He took a ring from the satin nest inside, and slid it onto her finger before she could say anything else.

She stared down at the ring, her eyes swimming so much that she could scarcely see it. One large diamond with others around it, a white flower of sparkle nestling on her finger as if it had always been there, and always would be in the future. Most miraculously, it fit.

So, she realized, did they.

And laughing with pure, giddy joy, she flung her arms around William and nearly knocked him over before he caught her around the waist and danced her in a small circle. Everyone else in the shop cheered and clapped, delighted to have witnessed an even more wonderful scene than the two protagonists had ever intended.

"Ahoy, My Lord!" called Zeke excitedly, squeezing through the adults like a determined puppy. "Did you do it, then, My Lord? Did you ask her?"

"Yes, Zeke, I did," said William, holding out Harriet's hand for the boy to see the ring on her finger, "and more importantly, she accepted. But what in blazes are you doing here, Zeke? Why aren't you on the boat with Strode, where you belong?"

"I *was* with him, My Lord," said Zeke defensively, "but he wanted to buy something or another here in town, and he said I could come, and then when we passed here and saw you inside, he said I could come here with you while he went to the other shop."

"Oh, very well," said William, pulling the boy next to him and ruffling his hair. He was so damned happy at this point that nothing was going to upset him. He didn't know why he'd been so worried that Harriet would refuse him. He knew she loved him, that she'd loved him for a good long time now, nearly as long as he'd loved her. Perhaps his dread was simply natural for men asking women to marry them. He'd have to ask Edward if it had been so with him and Francesca. Now, however, Harriet was his only concern, and he grinned at her again like the ecstatically happy idiot he felt himself to be.

She'd been brilliant with the necklace, absolutely perfect in how she'd played to the others, and when they would return to Girard's after supper for the necklace, no one was going to question the two sailors he'd bring with him as guards. Still, he was considering sailing tonight, and not waiting until the morning. He couldn't say exactly why—a certain unfathomable uneasiness, a sense that they shouldn't linger if they didn't have to—or perhaps it was simply because he was eager to be home and making wedding plans, and done forever with Abbeville. That thought alone was sufficient reason for him to kiss Harriet again, quickly, but enough to make her giggle and blush in her thoroughly enchanting way.

"Lord Bonnington," said a Frenchman behind him, and William turned, ready to accept more congratulations. But while this man was smiling, too, his smile did not include his chilly, pale eyes, and there was nothing about him that seemed inclined to celebrate happiness. Though he was older, his shoulders seemed bent more from furtive habit than age, and the sorry state of his clothes—the linen of his shirt was gray and spotted with ancient grime, the tattered hem of an old-fashioned coat hanging around his

knees, flecks of tobacco dusted across his waistcoat—
told both of preoccupation with other matters, and
the absence of a wife or other woman to look after
him.

Yet clearly the man was no ordinary old bachelor-
scarecrow. As soon as he'd entered the shop, the
laughter and excited chatter among the other customers had stopped, and one by one they'd left themselves, hurrying away.

"Lord Bonnington," said the man again. "When I
heard that the famous English beauty Calliope was
in Girard's shop, refusing every gift her lover tried to
offer, I confess that I came like the rest, to steal a
glimpse of such a rare creature. But then to be privileged to witness the rest of your joyful scene—ah, I
had to add my own felicitations, Lord Bonnington, to
you and your new lady!"

"I thank you, sir, as does my fair Calliope."
William smiled, but remained on his guard, sure that
somehow the man was not the simple old fellow he
wished them to believe. There remained too much
craftiness in his rheumy eyes, too much art in the way
he held his hands like some quivering mendicant.
Harriet felt it, too, saying nothing but edging closer
to William, a mark of her uneasiness. "We're delighted to be able to share our joy."

"Joy and beauty, beauty and joy. How long it has
been that I've had any measure of either!" The man
laughed, a rattling, humorless cackle, dry with disuse.
"But you, Lord Bonnington, you shall have both,
yes?"

"I am fortunate, sir, with—what is it, Zeke?"
asked William as the boy jostled into his side.

"Ah, Lord Bonnington, your *son!*" cried the old man, his expression growing abruptly more agitated, even distraught, as he stared at Zeke. "I'd not heard you'd been blessed with a son and heir, My Lord, such a perfect replica of yourself!"

"The boy is not my heir, no," said William carefully, truthfully, venturing nothing else. "He is my cabin-boy, learning a sailor's trade."

"Ah, ah, but he *is* your son!" cried the old man again, his gaze greedily focused on Zeke. "The blood, the bond, you share is unmistakable!"

William could feel how Zeke shrank against him, and with good reason, too. He no more wished Zeke embroiled with this mad old man than he wanted to be himself, and he gave the boy a little pat on his shoulder to urge him on. "Go find Strode now, Zeke. We'll be along in a minute or two, after I've settled my accounts with Master Girard."

Instantly the boy ran through the door, thankful for the excuse to escape. But to William's surprise— and relief—the old man understood as well.

"Forgive me, Lord Bonnington, forgive me for claiming so much of your time," he said, already shuffling toward the door. "Ah, ah, farewell, and much joy, much joy!"

"Hey, ho, Will," said Harriet uneasily when the door swung shut behind him. "*That* was blessed peculiar, aye?"

Girard rushed forward, wringing his hands with mortified dismay. "I am so sorry, Miss Calliope!" he cried. "I would not have let such a man in my shop, not for—"

"No matter, Girard, no matter at all," said William

heartily, a bit too heartily, really, trying to lighten the unsettling mood that the man had left behind. "The old rogue is gone, and no harm done. Now come, Girard, let us make our arrangements so that my dear bride and I can celebrate. I'll be back in a moment or two, pet."

He followed the still-apologizing jeweler into the accounting room, leaving Harriet with only the assistant. She smiled at him, rubbing her arms as if to rub away the chill that still lingered in the shop.

"You should not let old Robitaille bother you, miss," said the assistant, briskly dusting the top of the counter. "Once all Abbeville feared him, you know, but his power has faded with the new government, and there are some who whisper that soon he, too, will be called to the judges in Brest to account for his sins."

"Is he some sort of constable, or beadle?" asked Harriet curiously. The old man had had that kind of interfering inquisitiveness, for all his protestations of good will.

"Robitaille's the superintendent of the port, miss," explained the assistant, "not that *that* means as much as it once did. Once he could meddle with every sailor and merchant ship that entered the town by water, and 'twas said he had spies who answered only to him. He may still. You see how people avoid him even now."

She nodded thoughtfully. "He does seem an old ragamuffin, doesn't he?"

"Some say he is mad." The assistant shrugged. "He had one son, a boy of much promise. Robitaille refused to let him serve in the grand army, fearing he'd lose him to war, and arranged to have the boy serve with the local patrols instead. But what good did that bring? The boy was shot dead on the beach with two others by brandy smugglers, not three months past, and so much for Robitaille's interference. Fate will always claim her due, won't she?"

But Harriet wasn't thinking of fate. "Three men killed?" she asked, her fear racing as fast as her heart. "This very spring, after His Lordship's last visit?"

The assistant paused, striving to remember. "Why, I suppose it was," he said carelessly. "But there are so many little mishaps like these in France these days that one soon forgets."

But half-mad Robitaille would not have forgotten, neither his son's death nor the Englishman who had caused it. No wonder he had been so fascinated by poor innocent Zeke, the obvious son of the man who in turn had murdered his.

"Where did Robitaille's son die?" she demanded. "Here in Abbeville?"

"On the north beach, miss, beyond the wharves," said the assistant, obviously mystified by her interest. "Likely you passed them yourself from where His Lordship's boat is moored."

Swiftly Harriet glanced at the closed door to the office where William was with Girard. There wasn't time to wait and explain, not now, and she felt for the small flintlock pistol she had carried in her reticule throughout this journey. It wasn't much of a weapon, but it could be enough to save Zeke. It *had* to be.

"Tell His Lordship that I'll be back as soon as I

can," she called to the startled assistant as she raced to the door. "Tell him I'll explain everything then."

"You have made the wisest decision, Lord Bonnington," Girard was saying as he ushered William back into the shop. "I regret having to part with your company so soon, but you are right to sail as soon as you can. You would not wish any harm to come to those rubies, would you?"

William smiled. "Ah, Girard, if you could but see how fast my *Fancy* sails, then you'd know you'd no reason at all for worrying that we'd be caught," he said, then stopped as he glanced around the now-empty shop. "Damnation, where has my bride vanished to?"

Nervously the shop's assistant stepped forward. "She—she left, My Lord. Ran off down the street, toward the water."

"Toward the *water?*" repeated William, dumbfounded. That made no sense, not even for Harriet. "Why the devil for?"

"I—ah—I was telling her of old Robitaille," explained the assistant. "The old man who was here."

"Yes, yes, I know," said William impatiently. Girard had told him of the man's position in the town, too, reassuring him that, with Robitaille's diminished power, he'd become no more than an unsettling nuisance. "But why should that have made her run to the water?"

"I cannot say, My Lord," said the assistant miserably. "I'd just told her about how Robitaille's only son had been killed by smugglers this spring, how some said that explains his madness, and then off she ran, wanting to see the very spot on the beach where the three men were shot. She said she'd be back directly, and that she'd explain to you then."

But William didn't need to wait for Harriet's explanations, because to his growing horror, he'd already figured it out for himself.

The three men who'd surprised them on the beach, the three who'd been killed in the scuffle as they'd fled, the one who'd come closest not more than a boy, Robitaille's son . . .

He thought of how he'd sent Zeke out into the street on his own, not waiting for Strode, and, heartsick, he thought of how eagerly Robitaille had followed after him.

Robitaille's son, and Zeke. And now, God help them all, Harriet, too.

An eye for an eye, a tooth for a tooth, a son for a son, and vengeance is mine, mine. . . .

His, his, thought Robitaille, yet it hadn't been easy, had it?

He'd caught the boy, that had been simple enough, telling him his father had wanted him back. But the little demon had fought him, biting and clawing until Robitaille had to tie his own coarse neckerchief around the boy's throat, jerking it just enough to make him gasp and go pale and nearly limp, the way to tame any wild animal.

He'd come quietly enough after that, even if Robitaille had had to do much of the work, half dragging the boy when he'd stumbled from weakness, taking care neither to break his neck nor crush his windpipe. A fine line, that, but Robitaille knew the difference. Twice they'd been stopped by meddlers, concerning themselves with the little wretch, but when Robitaille had told them the boy had been caught picking pockets, they'd stepped aside, letting justice be served.

Justice, ah, sweet, sweet justice . . .

If he'd only had Bonnington's whore, he would have tortured her, and made him suffer through her to even his score. But because Fate had given him the boy instead, Bonnington's own son, Robitaille would show mercy toward the child. He would kill him quickly, a single shot to his forehead, so he would not feel the pain.

Yes, yes, merciful justice, right and good, the only joy he'd left . . .

He shoved the boy forward one last time, to the place near the same three stones where his son had fallen, where he'd died. The boy fell forward, barely conscious on the sand, and with almost tender care, Robitaille arranged him in the same position as his Jacques had been, one arm thrown forward, his head turned, just so, just so. Then, with the same care, he pulled his pistol from his belt, and aimed it at the boy's forehead.

"Damn you, Robitaille, look at me!" roared William from the top of the dune, his heart pounding in his breast and his clothes soaked with sweat from running, the pistol in his hand pointed at the old man who had now, slowly, turned to face him.

In Girard's shop, Robitaille had seemed weak, unsteady, a caricature of a ruined old man, but there was nothing weak about the hatred that burned in his eyes now, and nothing unsteady about how he held the pistol to Zeke's innocent head.

"An eye for an eye, Bonnington!" the old man shouted back. "You killed my son, and now I shall kill yours. Even if you shoot me now, my gun will fire first, and take your precious son to hell with me!"

Damnation, he was right: he was *right,* yet still William's aim did not falter. When he'd met Strode in the street, he'd sent him to the *Fancy*'s boat, waiting for them near the docks, to have the men row around here, to the north beach, as fast as they possibly could. But there was no guarantee that Strode would be able to find all the men in time, or that their fastest rowing would be fast enough. All William could do now was pray the old man would shift, that he'd drop the gun, and then William would fire.

How could he find his son only to lose him like this? Oh, Zeke, forgive me, you little monkey, to let you get snarled in this!

"You've no proof I killed your boy," he shouted back, desperately hoping to distract Robitaille. "They said it was the smugglers, didn't they?"

"You and I know better, Bonnington!" Robitaille's voice broke with emotion, but his hand with the pistol stayed steady. "You killed him, you and your men and the last whore you had with you! And if you kill me now, what will the scandal be, eh? You won't be able to run away to your precious England this time, will you? You will be held for my murder, and searched, and questioned. There will be scandal, Bonnington, even if you are not executed for my death. I *will* have my justice, Bonnington, even from my own grave, an eye for an eye!"

William swore, long and hard, for again the old man was right. Where the devil was Strode with the boat? If he didn't come soon, William could be searched, held, perhaps tried; not even in France could he hope to escape after shooting a French official in broad daylight. The papers he carried with him now would be found. Their information would never reach the Admiralty, the English ships would never benefit, and he and Harriet would be convicted as spies.

And Zeke would still be dead.

Or he could turn his back and walk away and sail back to England with Harriet and all his papers and secrets. This old madman would still murder the boy, but what was the life of one small, illegitimate child worth balanced against the English cause against the French, the other countless lives of greater value and significance?

It was exactly as Edward had predicted, wasn't it? He wasn't brave enough for this, wasn't man enough to make the hard choices that war, that England, required of its greatest heroes....

And damnation, he didn't want to be like that. He wanted love and happiness with Harriet, and with Zeke, too.

Ah, Harriet, I'm sorry I dragged you into this, my dear, sweet, trusting Harriet. ...

"Robitaille!" shouted Harriet from the reeds on the far side of the dune, her voice shocking him, shocking Robitaille. She stood there with the silver tassels on her hat tossing gently in the wind, the small pistol in her hand held exactly the way he'd taught her. "Robitaille, you bloody old coward, let the boy go free!"

But that half-second that Robitaille turned toward Harriet was enough for William. For in that half-second, without thinking, he squeezed the trigger, and became a hero.

The old man cried out, the force of the gunshot striking his body tossing him to one side just as his own pistol discharged, the ball landing in the water with a harmless, hissing splash. He fell on his back, twisting once, then lay still in the same sand where he'd lost his son.

And it was done. *Done.* Somehow William reached Zeke, pulling the dirty cloth from around his neck, cradling him, holding him tight. Somehow Harriet was there, too, her arms around him and her kisses on his face as the tears of relief and joy streamed down her cheeks. And there, too, at last, at last, was Strode, with the *Fancy*'s men pulling as hard as they could on the oars to meet them, and carry them back to the sloop and England.

"Oh, Will, I told you, didn't I?" Harriet gasped, laughing and crying at the same time. "You love me and I love you, and the rest takes care of its own self, mind?"

He held her close, burying his face in her hair. "Forever, my love," he said. "Forever, mind?"

And forever, for them, it was.

Epilogue

~❧~

London

$\mathcal{T}$he wedding at Harborough House was small, the precious few invitations in such demand that the fashionable throngs who claimed to have attended was at least ten times the actual number of guests standing in the duchess's flower-filled drawing room. Whether they were there in reality or not, everyone agreed that the bride was far more beautiful than she appeared in Her Grace's paintings, and her groom as handsome and properly besotted as any reformed rake should be. There was, of course, much else for the guests to whisper about, from the bride's unusual origins—*can you fancy it, an orange-seller in the park!*—to the groom's illegitimate young son—*the image, the very image of the earl himself, the bold rogue!*——who'd been scandalously included in the wedding party, but not even the most jaded and cynical among them could claim that the Earl and Countess of Bonnington had wed for any other reason than purest love.

"Hey, ho, I feel not one whit different," announced

Harriet as she perched on the wall in the garden where she and William had retreated to escape their guests, if only for a few minutes. "The same old Harriet, like her or not."

"I like her just fine," said William, chuckling as he leaned forward to kiss her. "In fact, as you may recall, I swore to love her, too, not an hour past."

"And powerfully well you did it," she said happily, looping her hands around his shoulders. "You spoke up loud and declared yourself, clear as a watchman calling the hour."

"Because, pet," he said, unable to keep from kissing her again, "that's how I wish things to always be between us."

"You wish things to be loud?" she asked, teasing, "or punctual?"

"Loud, and punctual, and clear as the Westminster bells," he said. "I love you, Harriet, and I don't ever want any confusion about that. Understand?"

"Oh, aye, I understand," she said, her expression softening, "because that is how I love you, too, Will."

Gently he brushed his fingers across her forehead, smoothing back a wisp of hair that had slipped free of the wreath of white roses she wore like a crown. "Like it or not, sweetheart, in the eyes of the great world, you *are* different. You're the Countess of Bonnington now, with all the pomp and foolishness that that entails."

She smiled wistfully. "As long as we don't have to go back to France, Will, leastways not for a bit."

"Not ever, as far as I'm concerned." His smile faded, the memory of the disaster they'd only narrowly escaped at Abbeville still too fresh not to treat seriously. Though the information they'd smuggled back with the ruby necklace had proved invaluable to the navy ships stationed off Brest, William had been firm when he'd told Edward that this had been his last journey. Even heroes could tempt fate and luck, and for the sake of the love he'd found with Harriet, he knew it was time to quit the game while fortune still smiled his way.

"Besides," he said, striving to smile again and lighten the mood, "I've another mission here that's far, far more important, and that's to secure my title by dutifully producing an heir."

Her eyes lit, and she grinned wickedly. "Oh, aye, you *do*," she said, sliding off the wall and into his embrace. "*We* do. For the good of the country, mind."

"For England," he said, bending down to kiss her. "For you, my dearest love."

"Ah, me own Will," she sighed happily. "I wouldn't have it any other way."

Breathtaking romance from

MIRANDA JARRETT

The Captain's Bride

Cranberry Point

Moonlight

Star Bright

Starlight

Sunrise

The Very Daring Duchess

Wishing

Sonnet Books
Published by Pocket Books

**Visit the Simon & Schuster
romance Web site:**

www.SimonSaysLove.com

**and sign up for our
romance e-mail updates!**

Keep up on the latest
new romance releases,
author appearances, news, chats,
special offers, and more!
We'll deliver the information
right to your inbox—if it's new,
you'll know about it.

POCKET BOOKS

2800.02